D1482779

Legacy

DISCARDED

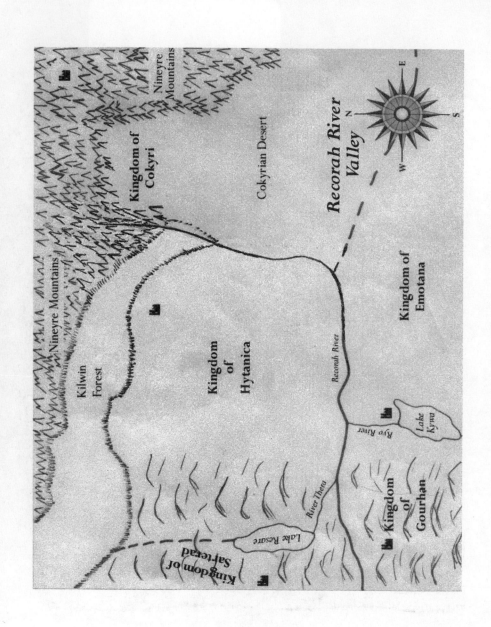

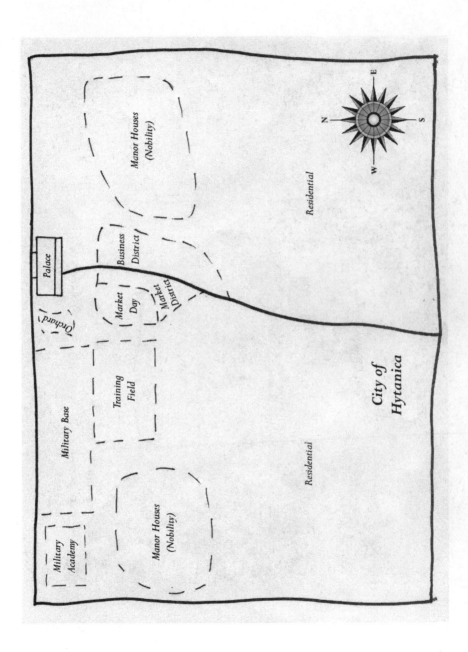

City of
Hytanica

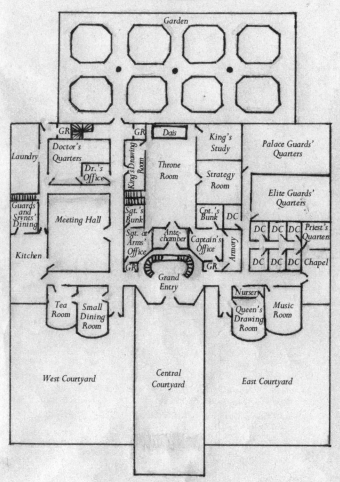

Hytanican Palace
First Floor

Garden

Laundry

GR Doctor's Quarters

Dr.'s Office

Guards and Srvnts' Dining

Kitchen

Meeting Hall

GR King's Drawing Room

Dais

Throne Room

King's Study

Strategy Room

Palace Guards' Quarters

Elite Guards' Quarters

Sgt.'s Bunk

Cpt.'s Bunk

DC

DC DC DC Priest's Quarters

Sgt. at Arms' Office

Ante-chamber

Captain's Office

Armory

DC DC DC Chapel

GR

Grand Entry

GR

Tea Room

Small Dining Room

Nursery

Queen's Drawing Room

Music Room

West Courtyard

Central Courtyard

East Courtyard

DC = Deputy Captain's Quarters
GR = Guard Room

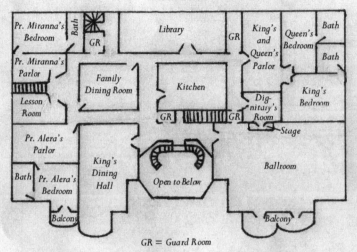

Hytanican Palace
Second Floor

GR = Guard Room

Legacy

*"At some point, the choice you will face
is whether to carry out your duties
or live your life."*

By

Cayla Kluver

Forsooth Publishing

The characters and events portrayed in this book are fictitious. Any similarity to real persons, living or dead, is coincidental and not intended by the author.

Text copyright © 2008
by Cayla Kluver and Kimberly Kluver.
All rights reserved.
Printed in the United States of America by Eau Claire Printing Co., Inc.
415 Galloway, Eau Claire, WI 54703

No part of this book may be reproduced, or stored in a retrieval system, or transmitted in any form or by any means, electronic, mechanical, photocopying, recording, or otherwise, without express written permission of the publisher.

Published by Forsooth Publishing
PO Box 1105
Eau Claire, WI 54702-1105

www.forsoothpublishing.com

The Night Feather Logo is a trademark of Forsooth Publishing.

Library of Congress Control Number: 2007942714

ISBN-13: 978-0-9802089-7-9
ISBN-10: 0-9802089-7-1

Edited by Kimberly Kluver
Front cover photography © Photographer: Freesurf69/Agency: Dreamstime.com
Title page photography © Photographer: Yulia Rud/Agency: Dreamstime.com
Back cover grunge frame © Konstantin Kalishko/Agency: fotolia.com
Compass on maps © ELEN/Agency: fotolia.com

Table of Contents

Prologue

The first boy disappeared on the day of his birth, on a night when the pale yellow moon of the nighttime sky turned red and bathed the heavens in the ghastly color of blood, the same night the Kingdom of Cokyri abruptly ceased its merciless attack.

Across the land of Hytanica, in the villages, infant boys continued to vanish. The King turned a blind eye somewhat foolishly, seeking no explanation. Instead, he concentrated on refortifying his Kingdom for fear that Cokyri would resume its brutal onslaught. It was when children inside the city's walls began to disappear that he was forced to take notice. A count was made of the number missing, but the royal advisors could not determine what action should be taken. Then, as suddenly as they had begun, the disappearances stopped. The last Hytanican child to vanish was the newborn son of a wealthy Baron and Baroness.

Within the week, as the bleeding moon waned, the decomposing bodies of the infants were found outside the gates of the city, a final word from the greatest enemy Hytanica had ever known. Grieving parents collected the rotting bodies of their sons, but there was one mystery that would for many years remain unsolved. There were forty-nine babies taken, but only forty-eight bodies returned.

No one knew why the Cokyrians withdrew from the land, or why the enemy had not been able to destroy Hytanica and her people. The Cokyrians were superior to the Hytanicans as fighters and strategists, but still Hytanica had not fallen. And no one knew what force of evil had led Cokyri to steal and murder infant boys. But after a century of war, the citizens of Hytanica did not seek answers to these questions.

I was born shortly before the end of the war, a Princess of Hytanica, my parents' first heir. As my Kingdom settled into a long-awaited time of peace, I was brought before my people and grew to be a young woman, living in freedom such as the war-torn generations before me had never known. All such things must come to an end, however, and that is where my story begins.

Chapter One
The Obvious Choice

"I think I'm going to vomit."

I fretfully paced in front of the cold stone fireplace that spanned most of one wall in my parlor, clasping and unclasping my hands in front of me. My younger sister, Princess Miranna, had retired to her quarters after giving me a quick hug and assuring me I would have a lovely evening. Fair and rosy-cheeked at the age of fifteen, with strawberry-blonde hair that flipped in waves and curls all the way down her back, she was much more enamored with the man I would be meeting for dinner tonight than was I. In fact, it had undoubtedly been notions of romance that had motivated her to dismiss my personal maid so that she could attend to me herself. The flowing, long-sleeved, shimmering gray gown that now adorned my slender figure had been of her choosing, as had been the delicate silver locket that graced my neck. Although my dark brown hair usually fell about my shoulders, she had stylishly gathered it into a loose bun, with wispy strands framing my nearly black eyes and softening my angular features. Now it was only London, my bodyguard and a member of the King's Elite Guard, waiting with me in the richly furnished room.

"You're not going to vomit. Just try to relax," London calmly advised, although one eyebrow was raised in bemusement. He moved toward the parlor's burgundy velvet sofa and picked up one of my books from the oak side table that stood beside it, then began to leaf through it absentmindedly.

"How can anyone expect me to eat?" I asked, my voice shrill even to my own ears. "I don't think I can go through with this."

"It's going to be fine. He's just another suitor, and like all the rest of them, he has to impress you, not the other way around. Besides, as far as I can tell, you have no real interest in him, so I don't know why you're working yourself into such a state."

"You don't understand," I said frantically. "If something goes wrong tonight, Father is going to be so disappointed...."

"Well, unless you've made plans that I don't know about to marry Steldor, you're going to disappoint your father in the long run no matter what."

I stopped and faced London, who had dropped the book back onto the table and was now leaning nonchalantly against the tapestried wall by the door into the corridor, arms crossed over his muscular frame. Unruly silver bangs fell across his forehead, contrasting sharply with his deep-set indigo eyes, which were fixed upon me as he waited for a response.

"But I can't stand him! How can I possibly spend the entire evening with him?"

"It's just one evening. You can survive one evening. Although I hope you're up for a little after-dinner romance — the weather is ideal for a moonlit stroll in the garden."

London's words filled me anew with dread, despite the tease in his voice.

"He won't demand that of me, will he, London?"

"If he does, tell him you're feeling ill and that you must return to your quarters at once. He can't argue with that."

His tone was now serious, as he tried to allay the new worry that he had inadvertently created for me.

I sank into one of the elaborately carved armchairs near the hearth, buried my head in my hands, and moaned. My father, King Adrik, had arranged for this dinner between Lord Steldor and me, as Steldor was the young man he favored to be my husband. He trusted Steldor and felt he was better suited to be King than anyone else in the Kingdom. As the heir to the Throne, I was to marry on that basis alone, for it was my husband, and not I, who would come to rule Hytanica.

Even I had to admit that Steldor was the obvious choice. Three-and-a-half years older than me, he was the son of Cannan, the Captain of the Guard, and had one year ago become a military Field Commander at the age of nineteen. He was charming, intelligent and strong, with stunning good looks, but I had disliked him from the first moment we had met.

A sharp rap on the door interrupted my ruminations, and I reluctantly rose as London stepped into the corridor to speak with the servant who had been sent to summon me.

"We'd better be going," my bodyguard said upon reentering. "Steldor has arrived and is waiting for you in the Grand Entry."

London opened the door for me and we left my parlor to walk through the wide second floor corridors of the Royal Residence toward the Royal Family's private staircase at the rear of the Palace. In addition to my quarters and those of my sister and parents, the Residence included a library with an extensive book collection, a family dining room, a large kitchen, and a lesson room that doubled as a parlor. The expansive Royal Ballroom and the cherry-paneled King's Dining Hall accounted for the rest of the space on the second floor.

We descended the tightly-spiraling stairs, and then turned to our right, London offering me his arm to escort me down the long, lantern-lit corridor toward the Palace's main entrance. As we walked, I hardly glanced at the multi-colored stone floor, or the intricate tapestries that adorned the walls, for my attention was drawn to Steldor, who nonchalantly awaited me at the end of the hall. Casually supporting himself with his left hand on the stone wall, he was expertly flipping a dagger over and over in his right, having perfectly positioned himself for maximum visual effect.

"Have fun," London said glibly as we stopped mid-way down the passage, Steldor having noticed my approach.

"You're not going far, are you?" I asked, a bit shakily.

"No, I would wager you'll need more protection tonight than on most occasions. Besides, I'd be a pretty poor chaperone if I did, although I will try to give you two lovebirds some privacy."

I exhaled grumpily, annoyed by London's irreverent tone.

"Just go right ahead and enjoy yourself at my expense, won't you?" I complained, eyes riveted on Steldor, who had returned his dagger to its sheath in one of his highly polished knee-high black boots, and was striding toward me.

"If you want to know the truth," London said, leaning conspiratorially closer, "I'm staying back so I don't murder him in your stead."

The abrupt change in my bodyguard's mood caught me by surprise, but I had no time to respond, for my handsome dinner companion was drawing nigh. Although Steldor was dressed somewhat informally this night in an open-necked white shirt topped by an unusual vest, dark gray in color, but with red across the shoulders, his deportment made any clothing appear elegant. He was tall, broad-shouldered, and well-muscled, with dark brown hair that edged on black and fell in a perfectly careless manner to just below his prominent cheek bones. His eyes, rimmed with long, ebony lashes, were a dark and smoldering brown, guaranteed to make most girls swoon, and his smile was irresistible, given his straight and even white teeth. My skin prickled as I realized that our attire, as well as our dark features, made us a matched pair.

"My Lady."

Steldor greeted me silkily as he stopped before me. His eyes approvingly swept my form, then he bowed and kissed my hand romantically.

"Allow me to escort you to the dining room."

With an uncomfortable glance at my bodyguard, Steldor deftly drew me from him, and I was certain London had given warning that he intended to take his duties seriously tonight. As Steldor led me into the dining room and to our table, London lagging behind, the savory smells emanating from the kitchen aroused my appetite, and I ruefully thought that I would at least be getting a delicious meal out of the evening's ordeal.

The small, first floor dining room was designed to accommodate intimate gatherings. There were double marble fireplaces, one on each side of the room, with an oblong oak table that could seat forty-five centered in between. Three multi-tiered, candlelit chandeliers were suspended above the table, and fragrant, oil-burning lanterns were attached at equal intervals along the walls. A smaller, round table draped with white linen had been prepared for Steldor and me at the far end of the room in front of the large bay window that afforded a view of the west courtyard of the Palace. Two flickering candles upon the table provided subtle illumination, aided feebly by the last residue of the day's sun as it filtered through the pane. I sat across from Steldor and he offered me a glass of white wine, which I accepted with some trepidation, having no more liking for wine than I did for the man extending the goblet.

"I must say," Steldor amorously observed, "you are exceptionally beautiful tonight, Alera."

He paused as if permitting me an opportunity to extend a similar compliment. When none was forthcoming, an impertinent smile played upon his lips.

"I am used to my dates dressing well when they accompany me, but few take the extraordinary step of coordinating their clothing with mine."

I paled at his brazen implication, but he continued before I could formulate an appropriately caustic remark.

"You seem a little overwhelmed... perchance from hunger, although I do tend to have that affect on women. Some food may restore you." He indicated to a servant with a flick of his hand that we were ready to receive our meal. "Perhaps some sustenance will enable you to find your voice as well."

I stared blankly at the man my father desired me to wed, feeling ill-equipped to deal with his flirtatious, and slightly disrespectful, attitude.

The arrival of the servants with vegetable-laden platters, a variety of warm breads, and a full roasted chicken saved me from further embarrassment. Steldor nodded curtly to dismiss those who were waiting upon us, then sliced the sizzling capon, adding a piece to each of our plates. We ate in silence for a few minutes, although I found it difficult to do more than nibble, for his eyes continued to shamelessly peruse me and my stomach continued to churn.

"I hope we shall come to spend considerable time together," Steldor finally said, voice a practiced blend of honey and conceit, velvety smooth but with an undertone of boredom that not even he could conceal, "although I should caution you that the military demands much of me. Of course, I am well suited for such a life. When I attended the Military Academy, my combat instructors always said I was the best in my year, maybe in the history of the school, and I proved that many times. I was not the most substantial person in my class, but I was by far the most skilled. Everyone was astounded by my progress, and I was allowed to graduate from the Academy a year early."

He pushed his plate forward a few inches so that he could stylistically rest his left forearm on the edge of the table.

"After fifteen months as a foot soldier, I went into officer training and became the youngest Field Commander in Hytanican history. But in spite of the demands of my position, I find time to help train the students at the Academy in hand-to-hand fighting. The instructors at the military school continue to hold me in high esteem and readily welcome my assistance."

As he spoke, I became aware that I was paying greater attention to his gestures than to his words, for his movements were so fluid they seemed almost rehearsed. He comfortably settled back in his chair, holding his goblet of wine aloft, and I couldn't help but notice that he always looked perfectly posed.

"It's not as though I did anything special to win such

admiration," Steldor went on. "I was simply born with enviable talents. It was only natural that I would become the favored one.

"You can understand that, can't you Alera? It's much the same with you," he added with an air of condescension.

"And how is that like me at all?" I challenged, his arrogance at last goading me to reply.

"She speaks," he gently mocked, then matter-of-factly elaborated. "Well, you didn't ask to be born into the Royal Family, did you? I likewise didn't ask to be the most admired man in the Kingdom."

"More admired than my father? Well, then, I suppose I should feel honored just to be here with you."

"Most girls do feel honored, but as you are the Crown Princess, I would say feeling appreciative would be good enough."

The on-going churning in my stomach could no longer be attributed to nervousness. Steldor had achieved a new feat. His company was making me physically ill.

When I did not converse further, Steldor glanced to the other side of the room where London was sitting in a chair, booted feet resting on the oblong table.

"It's too bad your bodyguard has to be here, isn't it?"

"Maybe from your point of view," I crisply retorted.

"Don't take offense, Princess," Steldor said with a self-satisfied chuckle. "I only meant that, perhaps if we were alone, we could make things a bit more... intimate."

He leaned forward to reach for my hand, dark eyes lazily scanning me as if I were a gift that he was about to unwrap.

"That would be a bit improper, would it not?" I scolded, hastily picking up my napkin to prevent him from achieving his purpose, and he slowly sat back, wearing an insufferably indulgent expression.

"And have you never done anything improper, Princess?" he drawled. He stood when my only response was a deep blush. "As you don't seem to be particularly hungry," he continued, gazing expectantly at me, "I suggest we forego dessert in favor of a stroll in the moonlight."

I tried to think of an excuse not to go, but my brain had stopped working. In combination with my inexplicably dry mouth and limp tongue, I found myself truly speechless.

"I'll take that as a 'yes,'" he said, with a confident smile. He slipped a hand under my elbow, directing me to my feet. "To the garden, shall we?"

Steldor's arm snaked its way around my waist, and he began to escort me from the dining room. As we approached the oblong table, London made to accompany us.

"No need to keep such close watch," Steldor muttered to my bodyguard. "She's in good hands."

"That's an interesting assertion, considering your reputation," London coolly replied, and I knew he would follow us, regardless of Steldor's desires.

We walked down the corridor London and I had earlier traversed, toward the back of the Palace and the double oak doors that led into the enclosed garden. The garden extended from the rear of the Palace to the northern section of the walled city. Beyond the forty-foot-high stone wall of the city stretched the forest that climbed into the foothills of the rugged Niñeyre Mountains.

Steldor acknowledged the Palace Guards who were stationed at the rear entrance, then held one of the doors open for me, but I vacillated, reluctant to go into the dark grounds with him, as I did not trust him at all.

"I'm not sure this is a good idea," I fussed, still struggling for words, uncomfortably aware that my periodic lapses in speech were probably coming across as girlish excitement, when in reality all I wanted was for the evening to be over.

"Whatever do you mean?"

"I am a bit cold, and I did not bring a wrap," I somewhat lamely asserted. It was still comfortably warm, but as it was the beginning of May, a chill would advance as night settled over the land.

"Just stay near to me, Princess," Steldor said, somewhat amused. "I assure you I'll be able to keep you warm."

I nodded unenthusiastically, and he again draped his arm about my waist to guide me forward as one of the Palace Guards loudly announced my presence, informing the others who patrolled the area that I had entered the grounds.

The garden was divided into four sections by wide stone footpaths. A double-tiered white marble fountain with a ten-foot diameter base was centrally located on the path between each section, and granite benches were adjacent to every fountain so one could sit and enjoy the beauty of the flowers and trees.

Stars were beginning to glimmer in the clear nighttime sky as we strolled along, assisting the moon in its efforts to illuminate the pathway, for although the torches around the perimeter of the garden were burning, their flickering light did not penetrate the garden's depths. I was certain Steldor viewed our surroundings as spectacularly romantic, but my emotion would have more accurately been described as dread.

After we had walked for a time, Steldor stopped beside a bench and sat down, pulling me along with him. Taking my hands in his, he gazed deep into my eyes, silently telling me that he had claimed me as his own long before I had been aware of his pursuit, and my heart began to hammer in apprehension of what he might do.

"You enchant me, Alera," he whispered, leaning in close to me, and my senses reeled as I inhaled his rich and provocative scent. It was deep and musky, but with the warmth of nutmeg and cinnamon, woven with a hint of violet. As the fragrance washed over me, he played with a wisp of my hair, then smoothly slid his hand to the base of my neck and pressed his lips against mine in a firm and entirely unwelcome kiss.

I pulled forcefully away, eyes widening, appalled that he would make such a presumptuous move on me. For an instant, he seemed annoyed, but then he dropped his hand with a wicked grin.

"I didn't know that would be your first kiss," he chided, and my cheeks began to burn. "Not that I mind," he continued, his manner cavalier. "It's just that you are more naïve than I anticipated."

He reached out to touch my necklace, letting his fingertips delicately trace across my collarbone.

"Of course, this does mean many other firsts will follow," he caddishly claimed.

I glared at him in outrage as I floundered for words. Just as it looked as though he might try to kiss me again, a voice cut through my humiliation, disbelief and dislike, abruptly arresting his movement.

"Princess!" London called briskly, striding into sight. "I'm afraid there's an emergency in the Palace and I must return you to your quarters. You'll have to come with me now."

I sprang from the bench and almost ran to my guard, warm relief spreading through me. Steldor came to his feet with a scowl, intending to accompany me, but London held up a hand.

"You'll have to go," he said adamantly. "You're not needed."

Steldor glowered at London in an attempt to intimidate him, but London met his stare steadily, without a trace of indecision. Other than the fact that my bodyguard was a bit shorter than my date, the two men were a physical match. They even had the same youthful appearance, although, in truth, London had been alive for almost double Steldor's lifetime, just one of the things that made the man in whose protective shadow I had lived for sixteen years a mystery to me.

Realizing that London was not about to yield, and knowing that, as a Deputy Captain, the Elite Guard held rank, Steldor backed down. I didn't look behind as London and I hastily left the garden, but imagined my jilted dinner companion reentering the Palace shortly after us and stalking belligerently down the corridor.

"You were right about the level of protection I would need tonight," I gloomily admitted as London and I climbed the Royal Family's spiral staircase.

"Indeed."

My bodyguard had evidently lost his good humor about the evening, as he seemed to be inwardly fuming, although whether at himself or at Steldor, I couldn't tell.

"And your father expects you to *marry* that pig?" he irritably muttered.

"Apparently."

I was surprised by London's forwardness in expressing his opinion of Steldor. While I knew he did not think highly of my father's top choice of a husband for me, and was grateful that I had someone with whom I could share my feelings, I had only ever known him to listen to my complaints and not articulate his own.

As my thoughts returned to Steldor's kiss, I began wiping at my mouth in disgust. London raised a sardonic eyebrow as he took note of what I was doing.

"I don't suppose that was the way you envisioned your first kiss," he mused.

"Why does everyone assume that was my first kiss?" I demanded, annoyed that my life was so transparent.

"Don't forget you're talking to me," he replied, with a knowing smirk.

I briefly averted my eyes, willing myself not to blush.

"Well, in any case," I rejoined, "I'm glad you stepped in. Who knows what he might have tried next."

"What happened to telling him that you felt ill if you wanted to make a hasty exit?"

"When we were sitting on the bench, I couldn't think. He has this amazing… " I trailed away as I lost the battle to stem the color rushing into my face.

"Amazing what?" London impatiently prompted.

"Scent, amazing scent," I said defensively, cheeks now aflame.

"He smells good?" London teased, breaking into a laugh. "As if he needs another way to attract women. On top of everything else, he *smells* better than the rest of us!"

Returning to my quarters, I murmured goodnight to London,

and he shut the door behind him. I knew he would be headed for the east wing, to the first floor rooms where most of the unmarried guards chose to live. As my primary bodyguard, he was on duty from the time I awoke until the time I retired. At night, Palace Guards regularly patrolled the corridors to provide security.

I walked unseeingly through my parlor toward my bedroom, my limbs heavy with weariness due to the stress of spending time with Steldor. Upon entering the room that had been my refuge for as long as I could remember, I sank into the chair that stood before my dressing table and pulled the pins from my hair. With a shake of my head, my thick locks tumbled about my shoulders, and I stood, letting my eyes wander over the familiar furnishings that made this space so comforting.

Across from me stood a generously sized canopy bed with a feather mattress, topped by a cream-colored spread and deliciously soft, overstuffed feather pillows. Placed against the same wall was a large wardrobe that nonetheless had difficulty containing my vast array of gowns. Along the near wall, a pair of deeply padded, rose velvet lounging chairs beckoned from in front of the double-sided fireplace that was shared with the parlor. A doll house and a few other toys from my childhood, including a top and a skipping rope, stood in the corner, while colorful woolen tapestries decorated the walls, and rugs added luxury to the floor.

With a sigh, I crossed the room, walking past my overflowing bookcase, and pulled open one of the two large wooden doors that led onto my balcony. Though I shivered as a cool night breeze brushed my skin, I stepped outside to await the arrival of Sahdienne, the golden haired, round-faced young woman who served as my personal maid. From my balcony during daylight hours, I could see the rolling terrain that spread toward the lake that marked the western border of our Kingdom. As it was, I could only see what the moonlight permitted — the looming shapes of the shadowy buildings in the city.

Hearing the creak of my bedroom door, I retreated inside as

Sahdienne entered. She unlaced the back of my gown, and then drew the rose velvet drapes across the window to the right of the balcony while I donned my nightdress. I slipped under the covers that topped my bed, nestling my head amongst the pillows, and fell asleep before she had completed the tidying of the room.

Chapter Two
An Unwelcome Encounter

It was dusk, my favorite time of day. I cherished the moments when I could stand on the expansive balcony off the Ballroom and gaze beyond the courtyard gates of our Palace into the walled city, watching for the points of light that would appear as the inhabitants lit lanterns to ward off the darkness. Beyond the city, farm fields sloped gradually toward the river that bordered our Kingdom on two sides. Though I could not see the Recorah from where I stood, I knew that the untamed river flowed south out of the forest, eventually curving west to become our southern boundary.

It was the occasion of my seventeenth birthday, and the upper society of my Kingdom and other nearby Kingdoms had gathered to honor me on this tenth of May in the Royal Ballroom of the Hytanican Palace. There was an added air of excitement in this celebration, as it was customary for a female heir to marry the man who would become the next King upon her eighteenth birthday, and I was therefore expected to choose a husband within the year. I had retreated to the balcony when the whispers and speculations as to who was in my favor had at last gotten the best of me, hopeful that the fresh air would provide relief from the stuffiness of the room as well as the conversation.

Though I myself should have been allowed to rule, tradition steered my father's and the Kingdom's views on leadership, dictating that their trust and preference fall into the hands of a man and not a woman. As my father had no male heir, I would be crowned Queen, but not ruler, and as such would play no part in the actual governing of the Kingdom. The function of the Queen was to supervise the household, plan and execute the social events, and raise the children. While the line of descent would continue to flow through my blood, the man I married would reign in my stead.

Hearing footsteps from behind, I turned, assuming that one of the many young men who sought my attention had seen me leave the Ballroom. Instead, I saw Miranna gliding gracefully to the railing to stand beside me, absolutely radiant in a sky blue dress. With her porcelain skin and delicately sculpted features, she was destined to break the hearts of many a would-be suitor.

"Are the celebrations too much for you, sister?" she asked, her curly hair bouncing as she moved her head and her blue eyes sparkling playfully, for she knew I rarely embraced festivities that cast me in a starring role.

"I find myself struggling for breath in that Ballroom." I smiled wanly, and we stood in silence while I pulled the refreshing air deeply into my lungs. Then Miranna lightly touched my hand.

"Tell me, has anyone managed to draw your interest this evening?" she inquired.

"No one who would meet Father's approval," I said with a touch of bitterness. "And I cannot marry without his approval."

"True, but there are so many intriguing possibilities!" My sister's face shone with enthusiasm, for she had, of late, developed quite an interest in the male population. "And Father is not unreasonable in his assessments, although he can be a bit demanding. He has many times proven himself to be a good judge of character."

"I am not as convinced of his reasonableness as you," I responded with a resigned sigh, indicating that, unlike her, I saw no pleasure in the task that lay before me. "Let me review a few of the candidates. Lord Thane is kind and witty, but he has chosen to study medicine, which disqualifies him, as Father insists a military background is necessary for a King. Then there is Lord Mauston, who is in the cavalry, but his family has fallen on financial hard times, so he wouldn't bring enough wealth to the marriage. Baron Galen is a Field Commander who inherited his father's title, lands and holdings, which ought to make him acceptable, but he is Lord Steldor's best friend so is relegated to second choice at best. And Father wants me to marry someone who is at least a few years older than me, someone with the maturity to ascend to the Throne immediately, which eliminates all the noblemen of my age as well." With forced pleasantness, I finished, "So, you see, the problem is not a lack of interest on my part, but Father's rather extensive list of qualifications."

"And what of Lord Steldor? I don't know if you've spoken with him tonight, but he is looking very fine indeed," Miranna ventured.

She was heedful of my father's preference for the Captain of the Guard's son, and, of course, had helped me prepare for the dinner he and I had shared a few evenings ago.

"I have never seen an occasion when he did not look fine," I replied cynically. "As he has attracted *your* notice, have no misgivings on my account about pursuing him, Mira."

"What is it about him that you dislike so?" Miranna pressed.

"If you must know, it's his ego," I emphatically declared. "Steldor doesn't walk; he struts. He doesn't converse with someone; he blesses them with his presence. He doesn't even laugh; it's a haughty and degrading sound that twists my insides until I feel sick. On top of that, he is the most possessive and hot-tempered person I have ever known, and that frightens me more than I can say."

Miranna distractedly twirled a strand of hair around the fingers of her left hand, and I knew she had understood my point.

"Still, he has many exceptional qualities," she finally countered. "And though the issues you've raised may make him less appealing to you as a husband, they hardly detract from his promise as a ruler. Besides, he will have both our father and his to guide him. He will make a good King, Alera. Everyone sees it. Why can't you?"

"We should return to the festivities," I said dismissively. "Father and Mother will be making their entrance soon, and will be expecting me to join them."

I turned from her and reentered the Ballroom, sweeping my long, glossy hair over my shoulders and putting on my most genial expression. As I walked, the ball gown that had been created for me especially for this occasion floated airily around my ankles. It was made of white silk chiffon that followed the curves of my body, and its lace-accented bell sleeves almost touched the floor. Upon my head I wore an intricately designed silver tiara, its delicate diamond flowers offset by tiny leaves forming three gentle arches that crested in the middle. Miranna walked at my side, probably with a mind toward resuming our discussion, but I made a point of greeting everyone we passed so that no such opportunity would arise.

A voice rang out from the front of the room, a voice I recognized as belonging to Lanek, the Palace herald and my father's personal secretary. Although Lanek had incredible lung capacity, he was rather short and stocky, and bore a marked resemblance to an over-fed and contented cat.

"All hail the King, King Adrik of Hytanica, and his Queen, the Lady Elissia!"

Everyone bowed or curtsied before my parents, including Miranna and me, as they entered the Ballroom from the Dignitary's Room onto a raised stage-like platform. The Dignitary's Room was adjacent to my parents' quarters, and served as a waiting area for the King and Queen, and occasionally special guests, prior to making their formal appearances.

My parents were accompanied by the Captain of the Guard, Cannan, a tall and imposing military leader with dark hair and eyes who rarely smiled. Two years older than my father, Cannan was a member of the nobility as well as the Commander of the Hytanican Military, having assumed that position during the Cokyrian War shortly before my father had become King. In the years since then, he had earned both my father's respect and friendship, and often accompanied the King as an advisor and bodyguard.

My parents were dressed in similar colors this evening, as was their habit on formal occasions, according to my mother's wishes. My mother wore a gown of gold with intricate red stitching on the bodice, and her skirt was split to reveal a deep red underskirt. A crown of gold and rubies adorned her up-swept honey-blonde hair. My father, whose hair and eye color matched my own, was likewise clothed and crowned in gold, and he shouldered a floor-length deep red robe decorated with thick gold cording on the sleeves and at the neckline. While my mother was demure and dignified, my father was very jovial in nature, with laugh lines around his brown eyes and a little extra weight around his girth.

"Welcome!" my father proclaimed, inclining his head slightly toward the crowd. "This celebration is not to honor me or my Queen, but in honor of our daughter, Princess Alera. By the end of her next year she will marry, and the man who becomes her husband will ascend to the Throne. I trust that you will show the new King the same loyalty and respect you have shown me throughout my reign. Until then, long live Princess Alera!"

My father motioned to me with his hand, beaming broadly, and our guests repeated his petition, shifting as one to gaze upon me. As I curtsied receptively, I saw my father look directly at Steldor, who had conveniently located himself close to the platform upon which my parents were standing. Steldor's counterpart, Galen, a young nobleman one year his senior, was with him, and a few steps away from the two of them stood the rest of Steldor's following — two burly soldiers of aristocratic birth called Barid and Devant.

A little shorter and less handsome than Steldor, Galen had wavy ash brown hair, warm brown eyes, and a build that was quite impressive, though not as remarkable as that of my would-be husband. His father had died in the war when Galen was but three years old, and Cannan had been as much a father to him as he had been to Steldor. Galen and Steldor had both become Field Commanders upon graduation from the Military Academy, and were practically inseparable, though Galen was noticeably less cocky and more level-headed than his comrade. I sometimes wondered if it was solely Steldor's influence that brought out the reckless side of Galen's personality.

Barid and Devant made up the rest of Steldor's cadre, having become tag-a-longs during military school. They struck me as being much less intelligent than their leaders, though they had to add value to Steldor in some way or he would never have allowed them to be counted among his friends.

I had not had many encounters with Steldor and his associates as a group, but their rowdy reputation preceded them. They relished in making life as unpleasant as possible for the people they viewed as beneath them, which, for Steldor, was just about everyone, though he and his following concentrated primarily on terrorizing the young cadets at the Military Academy. They never did anything truly harmful, but I was sure the students were tired of having their horses untethered, their boots filled with mud or rocks, and their water salted so it was undrinkable. I had also heard that it was fairly common for the cadets to end up swimming in water troughs.

Steldor and company also had a reputation for making the rounds of all the taverns in Hytanica in a single night, growing a little louder with each drink, and pulling some fairly outrageous stunts, the details of which were rather fuzzy in the memories of everyone involved.

It was both amusing and irritating to me that regardless of how fast the rumors about Steldor's behavior circulated, as long as he acted the perfect gentleman around my parents, they remained blind to his faults.

My father and mother stepped down from the stage and approached me, accompanied by Cannan, with the King's personal guards falling in behind. As the assembled guests went back to their bantering, I saw Galen good-naturedly shoving his best friend in my direction, although I doubted he needed any encouragement. An arrogant smirk was upon Steldor's face as he began to move in my direction. He was clothed this night in black, with silver trim on his form-fitting dress coat, and he moved with a natural grace that subtly gave notice of his physical abilities.

"Alera," my father said cheerily, as he and my mother arrived before me. "How do you like the decor? Do you find it tasteful for this occasion?"

I scanned the vast torch-lit hall, with its planked wooden floor and tapestry-covered stone walls, noting the large and glorious flower arrangements evenly spaced around its perimeter, and the white chiffon and lace that draped the edges of the refreshment tables just as it draped my body.

"Yes, the decorations are splendid, Your Majesty," I replied.

"Now, now," my father chortled. "You know I don't stand on formalities."

"But how can I help myself when you look so magnificent?" I teased.

My father reached out a hand and brushed my cheek affectionately.

"You are just as deserving of that title as I am, my dear," he asserted, his tone momentarily serious. "I would like to speak to you later this evening about the selection of a husband for you. I know you understand the importance of this decision, but all the same..." He trailed off as Steldor, with impeccable timing, came to stand beside me.

"Your Majesty, My Lady," Steldor said with a bow, addressing first the King and Queen as was proper. Then he turned to face me. "Princess Alera."

A self-assured grin replaced his arrogant smirk as he gallantly kissed my hand, and my father, looking immensely happy, gave me a wink.

"Lord Steldor." I acknowledged him coolly, refusing to return in any measure his romantic overture.

Steldor's gaze hardened almost imperceptibly and he crossed his arms, a shadow of a pout gracing his features. I furtively glanced at

Cannan, who stood as impassively as always. His job was to protect the Royal Family, not to become emotionally involved with its dealings, but I thought I could detect the faintest urge within him to roll his eyes at his son's behavior.

Conversation resumed, with surprisingly little input from Steldor, for he was watching me as though developing a plan of action. Displeasure at his manner flared briefly within me, and I moved further away from him as Miranna, clasping the hand of her good friend Semari, fluttered into our midst.

Semari was the fourteen-year-old daughter of a wealthy land owner, the Baron Koranis, and his wife, the Baroness Alantonya. Semari's parents were among those who had suffered the loss of a child toward the end of the Cokyrian War. Their lives had always been overshadowed by a hint of tragedy and mystery, for their first-born had been taken in the night from his cradle a week after his birth, and had never been recovered. His body had not been among those returned by the Cokyri. The family had moved on as best they could, and two years later, Semari had been born, followed over the next five years by two more daughters and a son, Koranis bent on having a male heir.

With my effervescent sister and Semari now capturing everyone's interest, I took the opportunity to steal away and exit the Ballroom inconspicuously. With a nod to the Palace Guards in the corridor, I stepped onto the landing of the open double staircase that was just to the west of the Ballroom, and peered over the railing to the floor twenty-five feet below. Seeing no signs of movement other than those of the guards stationed by the double doors that granted entry to the Palace, I rapidly descended the set of stairs to my left and stepped out into the Grand Entry Hall. From the Entry Hall, one could pass under the Grand Staircase and into the Throne Room, or proceed into either the west or east wings of the Palace.

The west wing contained a large meeting hall, the King's Drawing Room, the small dining room that had been the scene of my date with Steldor, a smaller tea room, the office of the Royal Physician, and the service areas of the Palace. The east wing led to the Queen's Drawing Room, the Music Room, our Chapel, and the living quarters for both the Palace Guards and the Elite Guards. My father's study, the Captain of the Guard's office, the Sergeant at Arm's office, and a strategy room all opened off the Throne Room.

I chose this night to stroll through the spacious corridors of the west wing, listening as I walked to the scuffing of my leather-soled slippers against the cold stone beneath my feet. These floors had not been kind to me in my youth. Running up and down the halls barefooted had made my feet sore, and tripping had been disastrous — skinned knees and bloodied noses aplenty. My parents had often been too busy to tend to me when I was hurt, as my sister had been very sick as a child and had needed special care. They had, of course, also been trying to put the Kingdom back together in the aftermath of the war. As a result, my personal bodyguard had acted as more of a parental figure to me during my early years than had either of my parents.

I glanced around. London was nowhere to be seen. A small smile crept across my face as I realized that he might not have seen me leave the Ballroom, for he had been moving among the crowd, alert for signs of trouble.

Reveling in my unexpected freedom, I turned to walk past the meeting hall and toward the rear of the Palace, intent on seeking sanctuary in the garden. As I reached the back entry, the Palace Guards drew open the heavy oak doors and I stepped outside. As was procedure, one of the guards then made known my arrival to his peers who patrolled the area's perimeter.

My father had often told my sister and me not to enter these grounds without a bodyguard. He feared that the garden was an ideal target for enemy infiltration, as access to the Palace estate could be gained by scaling only one barrier, the wall that the garden had in common with the northernmost wall of the city. His concern was counterbalanced, in part, by the wildness of the forested and mountainous terrain that lay to the north of the city, and in part by the fact that this portion of the city's barrier rose ten feet higher than the rest. In any event, I had never believed there could be danger amidst such beauty.

It was now fully dark, and only the moon and the torches anchored to the exterior of the Palace and the stone walls of the garden provided light. I took a deep breath of the scented air, and then walked forward into the beckoning dimness, glad for the opportunity to savor the quietude of the evening on my own.

"Don't think I didn't see you leave the Ballroom."

I jumped and spun around to find London leaning against the Palace doors, one eyebrow cocked tauntingly. He was dressed, as always, in a fitted dark brown leather jerkin layered over a long-sleeved white shirt. Leather bracers covered his wrists and forearms, and a silver ring shone on the first finger of his right hand. He wore tall brown leather boots folded down below the knee, and I could see the handle of a dagger extending from one of them. Twin long-knives hung from the belt at his waist.

"I was — I was just going for a walk," I stammered. "I didn't want to bother you with something as trivial as that."

London smiled in genuine amusement.

"Nice try. It's my job to protect you and make sure you don't go off and do something foolish — like this. I'd like to see you try that excuse on your father."

"Oh, London, you're not going to tell him, are you?" I asked, feeling a rush of panic.

Years of war had left my father extremely paranoid, as evidenced by the fact that Miranna and I were almost constantly accompanied by our bodyguards. I knew only too well how displeased he would be if he ever learned that I'd deliberately slipped away from the man charged with my protection, for I had been bruised by his righteous anger in the past.

"No, I won't tell him," London responded with a short laugh. "I just said that because I knew you'd lose your nerve if I did."

I fixed him with my most withering glare and turned to stalk off down one of the pathways.

"Well, I suppose you'll have to come with me, then," I tossed over my shoulder. "Just drop back as far as you're permitted and don't say a word."

"Right. Whatever you say, Princess."

I heard the hint of mockery in his tone, and felt the need to clarify myself.

"I *mean* it, London."

"Of course. I can appreciate your desire for some peace." This time there was sincerity, and a trace of an apology, in his voice.

"Good."

I walked serenely along the paths, soothed by the rustle of the plants and the trees in the soft breeze. Crickets chirped around me, and I found myself enjoying the sounds of the night as much as I did the garden's fragrance. London was true to his promise and was completely silent — I would not have known he was with me had he not earlier disclosed his presence.

I turned a corner and gasped, barely stifling a full scream. Eyes. A pair of luminescent green eyes stared at me from the darkness. As I struggled to focus my gaze, fear now coursing through my veins, I could discern the shadowy figure of a man, clad all in black. He stepped toward me, and a glint of metal told me there was a sword in his right hand.

"Princess," he said slyly, the pitch of his voice suggesting that he was young.

I backed away, but before I could turn to run, London seemingly fell from the sky and landed between the intruder and me, twin double-edged blades drawn and ready. He swiftly engaged in combat with the young man, who had been so startled by my bodyguard that he had loosened his grip on his sword, making it that much easier for London to disarm him. I stood rooted to the spot as I saw the trespasser's weapon fly through the air and land a few feet away. Dropping his left blade, London twisted one of the intruder's arms behind his back, pressing his other knife against the man's throat.

"Tell me, *Cokyri*," he spat, as if the name were a bad taste in his mouth. "How many of you are there?"

The Cokyrian made no reply, and I took a small step forward, wanting to get a better look at the assailant, even though my body still tingled with fright. As I did, my mouth fell open in surprise.

"You're... a woman?"

The intruder made no response except to snort in disdain at my stupidity for thinking she could be anything *but* a woman.

"Stay back, Alera!" London snapped, and I halted, having been unaware that I was putting myself in danger. "Call for the guard!"

I had a moment of short-lived hesitation, for the only guard I'd ever had to call was the one right in front of me, but London sharply reminded me of the urgency of the situation.

"Now!"

"Guard!" I shouted, hurrying back toward the Palace, repeating the call several times as I proceeded.

By the time I reached the pathway that formed the perimeter of the garden, three of the men on patrol duty were hurrying my way.

"London needs assistance," I quickly informed them, pointing down the path from which I had emerged. "There is an intruder."

I followed as they swiftly moved to my bodyguard's aid.

"Take her to the dungeon," London barked when the guards reached him. As the ranking officer, he issued the necessary orders before releasing the Cokyrian into their custody. "I will alert Cannan and the King."

London grabbed my wrist and hurried me back into the Palace. I stumbled along behind him, trying to keep up with his fast pace, as we climbed to the second floor using the spiral staircase that was reserved for my family's private use.

"Where are you taking me?" I demanded, vainly trying to plant my feet in an effort to prevent him from dragging me any further.

"To your father. I must tell him what has happened."

"And what exactly did happen?" I asked in frustration, hoping I didn't sound completely idiotic.

London swiveled around to face me so suddenly that I almost crashed into him.

"Do you not know who intruded upon your precious garden?"

"N-N-No, I—"

"Well, perhaps you have heard of her people — the Cokyrians."

"I have, but what does this mean?"

London did not answer, but merely tightened his hold on my wrist and continued down the corridor toward the landing of the Grand Staircase. I did not fight him, but insisted once more that he explain.

"Tell me, London!"

"This may come as a shock to you, but it is imperative that you refrain from asking brainless questions! I need to think!"

I hated the tears that suddenly welled as a result of London's abrupt and rather rude denunciation. He had never before snubbed me so, and on the inside it hurt as much as if I had been slapped. Wiping the excess moisture from my eyes, I sped up so as not to hinder him any more than I could help. He stopped outside the door to the Ballroom and turned to me.

"I'm not going to haul you in there. It's better if we don't make a scene. Just follow behind and go straight to the King."

As his manner invited no response, I simply nodded. We entered the Ballroom in an outwardly composed fashion, although London wove swiftly through the celebrating guests. He advanced on my father, who stood beside my mother in a group that included the Baron Koranis and his wife, Baroness Alantonya, as well as Cannan and his wife, Baroness Faramay, I but a step behind.

London spoke before anyone had a chance to acknowledge him. He ignored Cannan, his commanding officer, to whom he should have been reporting, choosing to address my father directly.

"Your Highness, there's been a disturbance. I would advise that your guards escort you and your family to your quarters at once."

My father smiled good-naturedly at London, as though my bodyguard had launched into a humorous tale.

"This is a little unorthodox, don't you think?" he asked with an unconcerned chuckle.

"Your Majesty, I believe you to be a man of some intelligence; therefore, I expect you are wise enough to follow my suggestion. Please, I implore you, do as I say."

London then directed his attention to Cannan, and rather brashly issued an order.

"Come with me. We must secure the Palace."

Cannan's brows drew together in a scowl at London's blatant, but not uncharacteristic, disregard for chain of command, but he said nothing, given the urgency in the Elite Guard's voice. Instead, he glanced around for Kade, the Sergeant at Arms in charge of the Palace Guard, who was "slightly less" than Cannan in every way: slightly younger, slightly shorter, slightly lighter in coloring, and slightly less serious. Kade was already moving quickly our way, apparently having noted London's hasty approach to the King. Cannan spoke briefly to the Sergeant as he joined us, giving him his orders, and then strode off with London.

As soon as Cannan and London had departed, Kade and my father had a surreptitious exchange, and then my father put a hand around my mother's waist, guiding her toward my sister, who stood nearby with Semari, Steldor, and Galen (who had predictably rejoined Steldor). After speaking quietly to Miranna, my father motioned to Kade, who assisted the King's personal guards in ushering my family onto the platform and through the door that led to the Dignitary's Room. Steldor made an attempt to follow us, but was pushed aside by the Sergeant at Arms, and I glanced back with some satisfaction to see my would-be suitor's face redden in anger.

Chapter Three
Enemies Revealed

I once more paced in my parlor, too enthralled and yet perplexed by all that I had experienced to sit down or rest. I had been escorted to my quarters for safety, with one guard stationed on the inside with me and two more outside the door. The guard that had temporarily taken over for London stood by the fireplace, trying not to look uncomfortable in the Princess' quarters. He wore the uniform of the Palace Guards, black breeches and a knee-length royal blue tunic with a gold center panel layered over a white shirt. The sword that had been presented to him upon induction into the position hung from his belt. He was young — but a few years older than Steldor — and quite unused to being assigned a task as important as protecting the Crown Princess of Hytanica.

"Do you know what is going on?" I boldly inquired, and the young man startled visibly as I broke the silence.

"I'm afraid you have a better idea of what this is about than I do, Your Highness."

He shrugged apologetically, but I could see curiosity in his eyes.

"If you don't mind my asking, Princess Alera... What exactly did happen in the garden?"

I stopped my pacing and relayed the entire story to him, including what London had called the intruder.

"Cokyri?" he repeated numbly, color paling.

"That's what London said."

"What are they doing here?"

"Well, actually, there was only one of them," I hastened to remind him.

"There's never just one of them, Princess."

"But what does this mean?" I grumbled in exasperation, feeling as though he were speaking in riddles.

A dramatic pause followed, and I would have laughed at his display of ridiculous histrionics had his next words not been exceedingly sobering.

"It means that the war could begin again."

I felt as though someone had dumped a bucket of cold water on my head, and I instantly understood why London had reacted so strongly. I knew enough of the tragedy and horrors of the war that I had no desire to experience such things firsthand, and most definitely not during the reign of my future husband.

"We haven't seen or heard from the Cokyrians in sixteen years," he continued. "The fighting stopped with no victory for either side, and no treaty signed, which means that the war could resume just as suddenly as it ended."

"How do you know all this?" I demanded, faintly irritated that this young guard could have grasped the significance of the intruder so much more readily than had I.

The guard straightened, puffing out his chest to show his pride in what he was about to say.

"When I was in training to be a Palace Guard, I was taught by some of the greatest men in the military, most of who are veterans of the war."

I nodded, then resumed my pacing, pressing my fingernails into my palms as I nervously clenched my fists. I drew up short at a rap on the door, but it was only a servant to prepare a fire in the hearth, as a chill was now descending upon the room. Eventually, I sat upon the plush sofa, and began to flip randomly through a book in a vain attempt to occupy my mind as the hours slowly passed.

Just when my tolerance for waiting had been exhausted, there was another knock on my door and I motioned to the guard to permit my visitor to enter. London stepped in and immediately dismissed the young man who had been standing in for him. The guard bowed to me and hurriedly departed, as London appeared to be in a rather foul mood.

"Who is she?" I clamored, springing to my feet, the book slipping from my lap and landing with a soft thud upon the darkly woven rug that covered much of the wood floor.

"I assume you mean the woman in the garden," London said, leaning back upon the wall by the door. His arms were folded across his chest and he seemed to be scrutinizing the rug's pattern, either in deep thought or out of a reluctance to encourage my interest.

"You asked me earlier if I had any idea who had intruded upon my 'precious garden.' I believe those were your exact words. Now I want to know."

London flinched as he became the target of my indignation.

"I'm sorry... about how I spoke to you earlier," he said sincerely, raising his eyes to mine, and my irritation slipped away.

"You were dealing with the existing circumstances," I hastily reassured him, moving conversationally closer. "No one can blame you for that. Now, won't you please tell me the identity of the woman?"

"Her name is Nantilam," he said, waving a hand impatiently, as if I were an irksome fly.

I scrunched up my face in concentration, for the name sounded vaguely familiar.

"Who?" I finally said, unable to dredge any details from my memory.

"Nantilam. I'm sure you've heard of her. She's—" London broke off abruptly and shook his head, scowling. "I've said too much already.

He pushed away from the wall and walked to the hearth, where he stooped to add wood to the fire.

"London," I pleaded, pursuing him for a few steps. "If you're worried that telling me will rouse my father's anger, I promise you that I will not discuss with him any information you share with me. I am well aware that he does not view these things as appropriate for the ears of a woman, and you would not be the only one with whom he would be displeased. Now, who is she?"

London straightened and appraised me for a moment before continuing.

"Nantilam is the High Priestess of Cokyri. You might say she's their Queen, except that she bears no marital ties to their Overlord. They are siblings."

"So what exactly is her purpose?"

He sighed, apparently recalling how little I knew about Cokyrian lifestyle.

"In Cokyri, females are held in higher regard than males, and women have historically ruled the Kingdom. Now, for reasons long since forgotten, the High Priestess and her brother, the Overlord, reign over Cokyri together. The Overlord is a seldom seen and greatly feared entity who protects and defends the High Priestess and the Cokyrian people. Nantilam rules Cokyri in all other respects."

"Why are the people so afraid of the Overlord?" I probed, puzzling over the particulars.

"He is not viewed as a person, like our King. He is a fierce warlord, evil and terrifying, sensationalized by decades of legends and myths. They say he has the power to wield black magic, to call it forth from his wicked soul. That he can kill you or worse with a wave of his hand. By 'they' I do not only mean the Cokyrians. Hytanicans also swear by these stories — soldiers who met him on the battlefield and never returned to the way they once were; few returned at all."

"Did you ever see him?" I uncertainly continued.

I knew little about London's past other than that he had fought in the war — he was, first and foremost, a soldier of Hytanica, and had been that before becoming a member of the King's Elite Guard. I had never asked about his life, and he had never volunteered any information.

London turned to gaze at the crackling fire, and did not respond for a long time.

"I did," he finally answered, but did not elaborate.

My inquisitiveness got the better of me, and I pressed further.

"What was he like?"

"We were talking about Nantilam," London said tightly, eyes once more on me, forbidding me to insist he recount more.

I yielded, abandoning my pursuit of information about the Overlord.

"Tell me what you can about the High Priestess," I requested, hoping I hadn't quashed his willingness to share what he knew. To my relief, he motioned for me to sit, then obligingly continued as I resettled upon the sofa.

"We don't know much. Despite all his secrecy, we actually know more about the Overlord than the High Priestess. As she was not involved in fighting the war, she has not been of particular importance to us... until now. Now we need to know what she was doing in the garden of the Hytanican Palace."

"Where is she?" I asked, attempting to process the information London was providing.

"I sent her to the dungeon, remember?"

"What will be done with her?"

He sighed, clearly tiring of my tenacious interest.

"She'll be kept in a cell overnight, and tomorrow she'll be brought to the Throne Room for questioning."

"Will I be permitted to be present?"

"Well, you are a member of the Royal Family." London ran a hand wearily through his thick silver hair. "However, your father could forbid your attendance."

I frowned, all too familiar with the restrictions brought about by my father's obsessive concern for safety.

"By next year I will be Queen. I must be prepared for that in every way possible, and that means learning about the enemy, doesn't it?"

"Yes, but you will not be King. It will not be left up to you to make important decisions for the Kingdom, so your knowledge of the enemy, as you call it, is inconsequential."

I was fuming inside. I knew London was right, and that my father in all likelihood would bar me from the Throne Room.

"I don't care," I sputtered, rather immaturely. "I will be there, no matter my father's opinions."

London gave an unconcerned shrug.

"You should go to bed," he advised. "Tomorrow will be a notable day, I am sure."

I rose to my feet as he turned to leave, for he was now off-duty.

"Goodnight, London," I murmured, then entered my bedroom as he exited my quarters.

I prepared for bed, confident that the Palace Guards outside my door had been posted until morning, for I knew Cannan and Kade well enough to realize that they would probably view the evening's developments as necessitating extra precautions. A short time later, I snuffed out my lantern and slid under my comforter, my exhausted body battling my restless mind, for the former sought sleep, while the latter wrestled with the best way to approach my father in the morning. My body eventually won out, and I fell into oblivion, with no firm plan of action at the ready.

"Father!" I called forcefully, and my voice echoed throughout the cavernous Throne Room, with its stone walls and floor, and twenty-five-foot high oak-beamed ceiling. It was just after sunrise, and the weak light that entered through the windows high in the northern wall did little to dispel the morning's somber atmosphere. I had risen early, determined to be present when the prisoner was brought in for interrogation, and had just begun my persuasive assault upon the King.

A spacious, raised marble dais was centered at the far end of the hall, and my father stared at me from where he sat upon his large, jewel-encrusted oak throne. My mother's smaller, but otherwise similar, oaken throne stood on his left-hand side, but was unoccupied, although whether by my mother's choice or my father's decree I did not know. Two vacant ornate chairs were positioned to the left of her throne, to be used by Miranna and me on those occasions when we attended my parents in the Hall of Kings, as this room was also known.

As I closed the distance between us, London at my heels, my father stood, his disapproving expression intensified by the austere faces of my ancestors in the life-sized portraits that hung on the walls to my left and right. On the wall behind my father, directly over the thrones and framed by banners in the Kingdom's colors of royal blue and gold, hung the royal coat of arms, a shield divided by an "x" into quadrants. The top section of the shield was red for military strength, with a golden lion to symbolize dauntless courage. The right section was purple for royal majesty and justice, with a silver crescent moon for hope. A blue tear signifying loss of lives in war upon gold for generosity made up the bottom section of the shield, with falcon feathers for obedience upon blue for truth and loyalty on the left.

My father, who looked resplendent in his robes of royal blue, the official crown of the King (a circlet set round with diamonds and four bejeweled crosses) upon his salt and pepper hair, glowered down at me as I came to stand before the dais. He had been stunned by my unconventional entrance, as had the dozen Elite Guards who stood six to each side of the thrones, as their expressions matched my father's exactly. Only Cannan, who stood on the King's right, seemed unperturbed.

"Alera!" my father said, making no attempt to hide his displeasure. "What is the meaning of this interruption?"

"I've come to witness the interrogation," I firmly asserted, "as I see no reason why I should continue to be confined to my quarters."

"But you must stay in your quarters," my father responded. "I will not have my daughter exposed to something as vile as the creature about to be brought before us."

"I am not a child. I will be Queen in one year. And I have already been exposed to her, for I am the one who was assaulted in the garden. Out of all those here assembled, it is I who most deserve to know the significance of this incident."

My father, mind already focused on the day's business, was momentarily at a loss for a response. He moved his mouth as if to articulate an argument, but no sound came forth. Before he could rally to deny my request, he was distracted by the opening of a door at the far end of the hall and Kade emerged into the room.

"Stay," my father irritably uttered, resettling himself upon his throne.

"Thank you," I said sincerely, and I took a seat in the chair closest to my mother's throne, London moving to stand behind me.

Two guards, holding the prisoner between them, followed Kade into the Hall of Kings through the door that I knew led to the dungeon. The dungeon was a wholly unpleasant place that I had only visited once in my life, thanks to London's willingness to satisfy a ten-year-old's curiosity. There were many cells with stone walls, dirt floors and thick wooden doors, each with a barred window barely large enough to show a prisoner's full face. It was dark, lit only by the dim torches along the corridor walls, and the dampness created a chill that could not be forgotten, even if you were fortunate enough to be released.

I did not know how the woman thrown to the cold stone before the King had been able to abide her time in our custody. Notwithstanding the deep circles beneath her eyes that gave evidence of a sleepless night, she was striking. Her eyes were large and many different shades of green, somehow stormy as the sea and bright as the spring at the same time. Her hair, though unkempt, was beautiful and as red as fire, falling unevenly to her rounded jaw, and her skin was golden as though she had spent her life in constant sunlight. She was clothed in black, her shirt and leggings made of a lightweight and fluid fabric. A most unusual silver pendant hung about her neck. It was narrow at its gold-tipped base, widening gradually in a graceful three-inch arc as it flowed upward, then banded with gold where it joined six overlapping pieces of silver that continued the gentle curvature, reminding me of blades of grass bending before a breeze.

"Tell us who you are," demanded my father, glaring down at our captive. He growled out the words with a commanding quality that he saved only for criminals and intolerably misbehaving daughters.

The prisoner, whose hands were bound in front of her, did not answer, and I stared in confusion at my father, for I would have thought it unnecessary to press her as to her identity.

I returned my attention to the woman as she shifted position, using her hands to push herself more upright so that she crouched on one knee, the other foot planted beneath her. Her head was bowed, although most assuredly not out of respect.

"Tell me now, Cokyrian, who you are," my father again ordered.

Still she did not reply, but slowly raised her head, meeting the gaze of her enemy evenly, almost challengingly, and there was an unmistakable aura of power about her.

"Need I remind you," my father said imperiously, "that you are in our control, and we therefore have the ability to do with you what we must to make you talk? You would do well to cooperate."

Finally, Nantilam spoke, her tone derisive.

"And you would do well to end this pointless interrogation and commence with the torture because you will not get any information from me, Hytanican scum."

The insult had barely reached my ears when I felt, more than heard, London move quickly forward from behind me to jump from the dais and land before the prisoner. With a swift kick to the chest, he knocked her backward off her feet, and I gripped the arms of my chair in alarm, terrified that London's hatred of Cokyri had seized control of his senses. I watched in horror as he dropped down beside her, one of his blades pressed against her throat, his deep indigo eyes boring into her stormy green ones.

"How did she obtain a weapon?!" Cannan was striding down the steps of the dais, jaw clenched in rage. He halted next to London and roughly pulled Nantilam to her feet. As London straightened, I barely registered, above the wild beating of my heart, the clatter of the small dagger the prisoner had been clutching in her right hand as it fell to the floor.

London reached out with one hand and jerked the silver chain from around Nantilam's neck, examining it thoroughly, for the pendant looked to have been broken. He then picked up the dagger and demonstrated how it fit into the portion of the pendant that dangled from the chain.

My father had risen slowly to his feet, and was now twisting the Royal Ring he wore upon his right hand in agitation, a mixture of disgust and fear upon his face. For an uneasy moment, I worried that he might lose his composure, but he drew several deep breaths, and the Kingly poise returned to his stance.

"Take her away," he ordered. "Bring her before us again at the end of the week with a looser tongue."

Kade signaled to his guards, who moved forward to grab the prisoner's arms and pull her away from London and Cannan. She did not resist as the guards roughly dragged her backward to the door leading to the dungeon, but kept her cool green eyes riveted upon the King.

As I waited for the furor about the incident to die down, I pondered the question my father had repeatedly posed.

"Father," I asked, when I finally had an opportunity to approach him. "Why did you demand to know her name? Wouldn't it have been better to ask her about something else since we already know who she is?"

My father's brow creased in bewilderment.

"We do not know who she is, or what she is doing in Hytanica.

All we know is that she is a Cokyrian intruding upon our home, and we intend to discover the reason." His frown deepened. "Why would you think otherwise?"

"I'm sorry," I mumbled. "I just assumed."

I left the Hall of Kings in a muddled state, wanting to ask London about this contradictory information, but he stayed behind, in deep discussion with Cannan about our captive. I knew, however, that he would soon return to duty as my bodyguard, providing ample opportunity for me to satisfy my curiosity and alleviate my confusion.

Chapter Four
Treachery Afoot

Though the interrogation had not yielded any new information about Nantilam, the next few days did indeed prove to be notable. Cannan, as Captain of the Guard, had promptly organized a search of the entire Kingdom for other Cokyrians who might have been aiding Nantilam in her as yet undetermined scheme. His second move had been to increase security in the Palace. No member of the Royal Family was to be left unguarded at any time, which meant that London was now essentially on duty twenty-four hours a day. In addition, Kade, at Cannan's direction, had posted Palace Guards around every corner, and areas that were already under guard were reinforced, so that it was impossible to be alone under any circumstance.

Once the initial flurry of activity had subsided, my father had tried several times to talk to me, no doubt about choosing a suitor and how that suitor should be Steldor. While I was confident he would never force me to marry Cannan's willful and arrogant son, I also knew he would not understand my resistance to the match. Most people, my father included, agreed with Steldor's opinions about himself, and it pained me to witness the adoration that was heaped upon him. Giggly girls were the worst, inflating his already over-blown ego a little more with each compliment they paid him. I harbored a small hope that someday he and his ego would just explode.

Ultimately, my father did manage to confront me about my marriage prospects. I was lounging on the sofa in my parlor in the early evening when there was a knock on the door.

"Should I get that, or do you want to pretend you're not here?" London asked, from where he was placidly leaning against the wall in the back of the room.

"You can answer it, if *you* wish to do so," I replied, with a sulky shrug, trying to act as it I hadn't heard his last comment. It was true that I would use 'that ruse on occasion when I was trying to avoid someone, and London knew I was not looking forward to a conversation with the King.

London either didn't pick up on my hint that I did not actually want him to go to the door, or he didn't acknowledge it, but either way, he walked forward and granted entrance to my father, who swept across the threshold before I had time to mentally prepare.

"Alera," he greeted me cheerfully. "With all that's been going on, I feel as though we've been dodging each other!" He chortled at what he considered to be a joke. "In any case, I'm glad to finally be able to talk with you."

"Shall I step outside?" offered London from his position by the open door.

"No, no. That's not necessary at all. I'll only be a moment." My father chortled again, his warm brown eyes sparkling. "Besides, you'd probably run afoul of one of your Captain's rules if you did. I wouldn't want to be responsible for getting you in trouble with Cannan!"

London closed the door and rested against the wall, arms crossed in the typical pose, and I straightened as my father came to sit beside me.

"As I was saying, Alera, it's wonderful that we're able to spend some time together. I intended to speak to you the night of your birthday, but things got a bit chaotic. Thank goodness for Cannan's clear head. If it weren't for him, I don't know what sort of mess we'd be in right now!"

I saw London bristle slightly in an uncommon show of spitefulness that Cannan was getting credit for controlling a situation that London had unquestionably handled. True, Cannan had now taken over, but London had played the key role on the night of the incident. All the same, he held his tongue.

"I've been wanting to talk to you about the selection of your husband," my father brightly continued. "I was delighted to hear from Lord Steldor that he greatly enjoyed the evening he spent with you, and I assume you had a pleasurable time as well. Tell me, has any other young man caught your eye?"

While almost any young man would have been better than Steldor from my point of view, I could think of no one whom my father would be willing to seriously examine. Steldor was clearly the heir apparent, as he had been groomed his entire life to be the successor to the King.

"I'm afraid not, Father."

"I will not conceal my thoughts from you," he responded, a satisfied air settling upon him. "I am content that Steldor is the only young man under consideration, and I am quite heartened that he has shown an interest in you."

I refrained from a grimace, having noticed that my father seemed far more concerned about Steldor's opinion of me than he was about my opinion of Steldor.

"Lord Steldor is... a remarkable person," I faltered. "But I am not convinced that he is the man I should marry."

"What can you possibly mean, Alera?" my father asked, genuinely shocked.

"I simply mean..." I was scrambling for a rationale other than the truth, which would never be viewed as sufficient by my father. "I see Steldor only as a friend," I finally said, trying to sound sincere. "Perhaps it would be better if he were to marry Mira."

My father scoffed at the idea. "Oh, don't be ridiculous," he said, with a disdainful wave of his hand. "If he married Miranna, he wouldn't be King."

"But she is better suited to his… personality," I argued.

"And he is better suited to be King than anyone else in this Kingdom." My father's increasing level of frustration was evidenced by the increasing animation of his hands. "And ability to rule is the primary basis upon which this decision is to be made."

"I understand that, Father," I glumly admitted, dropping my gaze to the floor.

He cupped my chin to raise my face to his, and I saw his countenance soften.

"It is surely not a big step from friend to husband; I insist that you seriously consider Steldor in that capacity."

"Yes, Father," I acquiesced, deciding it was best at this time to go along with his desires.

"Very good!" he exclaimed, clapping his hands together, his cheerful mood restored. "Then I shall inform him that you are receptive to his advances."

Before I had a chance to protest, my father stood and whooshed out the door.

"No," I whispered, and I could feel the color draining from my cheeks. "What have I gotten myself into?"

I caught the smirk forming on London's lips and rose indignantly to my feet.

"Don't you *dare* laugh," I scolded, with an irritable stamp of my foot.

"I wasn't going to," London insisted, though the smile did not fade from his eyes.

Feeling somewhat tense, I sent for Sahdienne, my personal maid, to draw a bath for me. My bath chamber served its functional purposes with a washbasin on a stand and a garderobe built into the side wall of the castle. What made it unique, however, was the large tub that was sunk into the tiled floor. Water was supplied to the room by pipes that ran within the walls to one of several wells serving the Palace, and was heated by virtue of the double-sided fireplace that served both my bedroom and the parlor.

As I bathed and continued my preparations for bed, London waited somewhat uncomfortably in the parlor. Until Cannan's recent orders, his assignment as a bodyguard had not required him to be within my rooms while I attended to such personal needs. Finally ready to retire, I dismissed Sahdienne, then opened my bedroom door a crack to murmur goodnight to London.

Slumber eluded me as I considered what the morning would bring, for the Cokyrian woman would be dragged before the King and Cannan once more, and I was resolute in my decision to be in attendance. Then something from the previous interrogation that had slipped my mind came rushing back, and I went into the parlor where London was reclining on the sofa.

Before I could speak, London was on his feet, causing me to shriek in alarm. His practiced eyes rapidly scanned the room for an enemy, then came to rest on me.

"What?" he asked tiredly, obviously irritated at having been disturbed for no good reason.

"How did you know?"

He stared at me, completely baffled.

"What?" he asked again.

"How did you know that she was the High Priestess, and that her name was Nantilam?"

As his brain wrapped around my question, his expression clouded over.

"I was mistaken," he gruffly stated. "It was simply a speculation that I unwisely made known to you. Now, can I get some peace or do you want me to read you a bedtime story?"

I rolled my eyes, as London was more sarcastic than usual at this time of night, then withdrew to my bed and fell into a fitful slumber. I woke while it was yet dark, and, after much tossing and turning, rose to get a drink of water. I poured myself a glass from the pitcher on my nightstand and took a sip. I knew I would not get back to sleep unless I was able to walk around and mull things over, but there was just one obstacle. I would never be able to get past

London, and I had an indisputable feeling that he would not embrace the idea of a stroll, for if I took a walk, he would have to accompany me.

I decided to chance it. Maybe my bodyguard had dozed off and would not wake to the sound of quiet footfalls. I slowly opened my bedroom door and tiptoed into the parlor. I was about to go into the corridor, amazed at my luck, when I glanced back to the sofa where London had been resting. He was not there.

I stepped closer to where he should have been, thinking my vision was distorted by the darkness, but the sofa was unoccupied.

"London?" I called softly, knowing that if he were anywhere nearby, he would hear me.

Only silence greeted me. London didn't materialize out of thin air; he didn't reply. I opened the door to the corridor and peered down its dimly-lit length, but he was not in sight.

I suddenly lost the will to go wandering, instead opting to curl up in my bed, worrying about where London had gone. Why would he have left me unprotected, against his orders? Had there been some problem that caused him to run off in the middle of the night? I lay in my bed for what felt like hours, at long last falling into a restless sleep, my dreams haunted by images of terrible fates that had befallen my bodyguard.

The following morning, I awoke and went straight to the bath chamber, not wanting to check on London for fear he had not returned. I dressed with my personal maid's help, electing to wear my silver and diamond tiara so I would have an air of authority for this second interrogation.

As Sahdienne curtsied and left, I walked into the parlor, where, to my relief, London relaxed next to the door into the corridor in his characteristic stance, back against the wall with his arms crossed. We surveyed each other for a short while before either of us spoke.

"What?" London smirked. "Did I put my shirt on backward or something?"

"No!" I said instantly, realizing I had been staring at him

wordlessly for an unprecedented length of time. "I just wanted to ask where you were last night."

London's smile at once disappeared. "I don't know what you're talking about," he said, looking somewhat ill at ease.

"I arose during the night, and you weren't here," I explained, uncertain how I could simplify it any further.

"I didn't go anywhere. I might have stepped into the corridor for a moment, but other than that, I was here all night. Perhaps you were dreaming."

"What?" I said in disbelief. "Pretty vivid dream, I'd say." I bit my lower lip in agitation. "Why are you lying to me, London?"

"I'm not lying to you!" London snapped in response, pushing away from the wall, his eyes flashing. "Are you accusing me of abandoning my charge?"

"No, of course not," I said, taken aback by his anger.

Abandoning his charge would mean disregarding every thing for which he stood, all the oaths he had sworn as a soldier of Hytanica and as a member of the King's Elite Guard. It would mean forfeiting his career, perhaps his life.

"I didn't mean to imply any such thing. I'm sorry if I offended you. I was just... curious," I meekly stated.

London did not utter words of forgiveness, and his voice still simmered with indignation.

"If you want to witness that interrogation, we'd better be going," he said.

I walked silently beside him down the corridor toward the spiral staircase, a resounding sensation of shame within my chest at how I had spoken to him, and at how he had reacted, though I knew he would pardon me as he always did. As we descended the stairs to the first floor, loud and disgruntled voices drifted to us from down the corridor to our right, and my father, Cannan, and four Elite Guards unexpectedly came into view.

"How can this be true?" My father's voice was frantic, and he was motioning wildly with his hands.

"She must have escaped during the night. When Kade went to get her this morning, she was gone." Cannan's response was calm, but worry lines creased his forehead.

"Is there a problem?" London queried, calling the attention of the others to us as we drew near.

My father cut in before Cannan could speak. "It would seem that our prisoner broke out sometime during the night and has fled."

"Has the area been thoroughly searched? She may not yet have been able to flee the Palace grounds." London was once again, without conscious thought, taking control of the situation.

"Yes, the search of the Palace and of the grounds has turned up nothing," Cannan said crossly, and I could tell by the twitch of his eyebrow that he was rankled by London's tendency to usurp his authority. "I've expanded the search throughout the city, and have alerted our border patrols, but so far, we have found no trace."

"How could she have escaped?" I blurted, unable to stop myself though I knew I was not the one who should be asking questions.

Cannan gave me a stern glance, telling me it was improper for me to inject myself into the discussion, but addressed my inquiry nonetheless.

"That is yet to be determined," he grumbled. "According to Kade, her cell was locked and intact, exactly as it should have been, except for the fact that she wasn't in it."

"None of this makes sense!" my father exclaimed, hands continuing to flail about. "Our dungeon is supposed to be escape-proof, with or without the protection of the guards!"

"I have asked Kade to summon for questioning any guard who was on dungeon duty last night," Cannan replied. "Unless the Cokyri really are as clever and cunning as myth suggests, the men should be able to provide some answers."

"Blame the traitor!" one of the Elite Guards who had accompanied Cannan cried out.

"Tadark!" Cannan reprimanded the young Lieutenant harshly. "Enough!"

"There is a traitor among us, rest assured," Tadark repeated defiantly. "The prisoner could not have escaped without help, and only someone who was already in the Palace would have been able to gain entry to the dungeon."

Tadark then dramatically addressed my father.

"My only request is that you sleep lightly, Your Highness, and be wary even in the presence of your most trusted guards."

"ENOUGH!" Cannan thundered, voice so severe that I momentarily felt sorry for Steldor if he'd ever had to endure the wrath contained in that one word.

"Yes, sir," Tadark sullenly responded, but it was clear he believed himself justified in making his point known. It was also clear he understood he was going to pay for his insolence later.

Since there would no longer be an interrogation, I returned to my quarters, the conversation in the corridor having raised additional worries in my mind, worries I desperately wanted someone to alleviate. How could our prisoner have escaped? As my father had said, it was nigh onto impossible to escape from Hytanica's dungeon. Had someone assisted her? But to what end? I shook my head in an attempt to clear it, but only succeeded in giving myself a dreadful headache.

The following few days were hectic, and a little jumbled in my memory. Cannan had again ordered heightened security in the Palace, and Kade had doubled the number of guards stationed at every post and on every assignment. Perhaps more disconcerting, my sister and I were forbidden to go outside the Palace at any time, even to visit the garden.

Cannan must have taken to heart the ill-advised conjectures of his young Lieutenant because he ordered that no member of the Royal Family was to be left alone with a single guard. This meant that I was given a second personal bodyguard, and it was my misfortune that the soldier who received the assignment was none other than Tadark.

Tadark was at least two inches shorter than me, and several inches shorter than London, with light, well-kept, sandy-brown hair and brown eyes. He was baby-faced, which gave him an innocent and boyish look, although I knew by age he had to be in his late twenties. Unlike London, he dressed in the uniform of the Elite Guard, a double-breasted royal blue doublet, white shirt, and black breeches, and was obviously proud to be among the select who had achieved the position. He wore the sword of the Elite Guard on his right hip, from which placement I surmised he was left-handed.

In many ways, Tadark was the exact opposite of London, for he was superstitious, and spoke often and at great length. While London tended to blend into the background, Tadark was constantly at my side, always telling me to "Watch out!" for this and "Stay away!" from that. London, as could have been predicted, thought Tadark's methods comical, but I did not. By the end of the week, I was ready to poison the annoying Lieutenant. I began to speculate as to how he had become a member of the Elite Guard, and resolved to ask London at my earliest opportunity.

As the week wore on, the morale of the Palace workers (the guards, servants, and cooks alike) began to drop as they started to suspect each other of having betrayed the Royal Family in some way. Only Cannan, Kade, the Deputy Captains in the Elite Guard, the King, and the dungeon guards directly involved with the incident knew the full details of the investigation, so everyone else was forced to piece the story together based on rumors circulating the Palace.

I was growing increasingly frustrated as London, a Deputy Captain, learned more and more about the situation while I was brushed aside and left maddeningly in the dark. Although I was a member of the Royal Family, I had no more ability to gather information than did the Palace staff, for Princess or not, I was but a woman, and as such had no need to be involved in military affairs. Then one day, during the following week, an idea came to me. Steldor, being the son of the Captain of the Guard and a military leader himself, most likely knew a good deal of information relating to the Cokyrian woman's escape. It was also true that his ego could be relied upon to blind him to the fact that I would be using him. As much as I, and probably London, loathed the prospect, the time had come for another date with Steldor.

Chapter Five
Of Stealth and Steldor

"Exactly why are you doing this again?" London asked, for the third time in the last half hour.

We were about to leave my parlor, as I was going to be spending the afternoon with Steldor in the central courtyard, but I turned to face him, irritated at his refusal to drop the subject.

"With all these new rules, the only way I could obtain my father's permission to go outside the walls of the Palace was to play upon his desire that I spend some time with Steldor."

I wasn't being entirely honest with London — though it seemed as if the Palace shrank in on me with each passing day, this was not the reason I had arranged another rendezvous with the Captain of the Guard's son. I needed to know what was going on, and Steldor was going to be my unwitting accomplice.

"So, you're willing to be alone with Steldor for hours just to get a little fresh air?" London succinctly said, one raised eyebrow punctuating his disbelief.

"London, you should be jumping at this opportunity, just as Tadark did," I pointed out, trying to distract him from the fact that I would be without a bodyguard for most of the day. "You are free of your duties for once and should be taking advantage of that, not trying to dissuade me from my plans. Go into the city! Do... whatever it is you do for entertainment! You finally have a day when you don't have to worry about me or my schedule. And remember, this wasn't my decision. It was the King's. He has somehow acquired the idea that Steldor is a little put-off by you, and thinks it would be best if the two of us spent some time together outside of your shadow. Besides, Steldor could protect me if the need arose, as could the dozens of guards stationed in the courtyard."

Guilt nipped at me for not telling the entire story — that I was the one who had told my father that Steldor was uncomfortable around London — but if my bodyguard were allowed to chaperone me as he had previously, he would figure out what I was attempting to do and spoil any chance I might have for success.

"I still don't like it," London said morosely. In a rare display of affection, he reached out a hand and brushed the backs of his fingers along my jaw line. "And I can no more stop worrying about you than I can stop my heart from beating."

I couldn't help but smile in response, despite my determination to stay firm.

"I know you don't like Steldor, or the King's decision, but you must comply with it."

"It isn't just dislike. I don't trust him. Have you forgotten what he tried last time?"

I put my hands on my hips in an exasperated posture, impatience welling within me.

"He won't try anything out in the open in broad daylight. He's not that idiotic. And besides, Madam Matallia has consented to act as our chaperone."

Madam Matallia, plump, but nevertheless pinched-faced, was the elderly woman who had been instructing Miranna and me in etiquette for the past twelve years, and in household management for the previous five.

"Madam Matallia?" London groaned, rolling his eyes. "She will be dozing under a shade tree within the first five minutes. And even if she's not, she adores Steldor. She'll purposefully drop her vigilance in the hope that he kisses you!"

I smiled to myself, as London wasn't the only one who knew of Madam Matallia's infatuation with Steldor. I had requested her as my chaperone specifically for her anticipated lack of watchfulness.

"And what of his *amazing scent?*" London mocked. "How will you ever resist him?"

Chewing on my lower lip in frustration, I made one final attempt to mollify my guard.

"I know what I am facing this time, so if he tries to kiss me, I'll slap him, alright?"

"Well, that would certainly be a new experience for him," London acidly declared.

As we left my quarters, London crossed his arms and sank into a stony silence. In an effort to dispel the tension, and as Tadark was not with us for once, I decided now was the time to ask about my younger guard's background.

"London, something has been on my mind of late. Tadark doesn't seem to fit the mold for an Elite Guard, and I'm hoping you can tell me how he became one."

London uncrossed his arms and smiled a little despite his somber mood, and the tension between us eased.

"Well, that depends," he said, casually running a hand through his silver hair.

"On what?"

"On which version you want to hear."

"There's more than one?"

London nodded, his smile broadening into a wicked grin.

"Do you want to hear the official version, the one Tadark claims to be true, or an eyewitness account from another guard?

"Begin with Tadark's, then tell me the other," I eagerly prompted, for I sensed I was about to hear an interesting story.

We had reached the spiral staircase, but rather than proceeding down it, London settled himself against the wall.

"The incident that led to Tadark's placement in the Elite Guard occurred a few years ago, and involved your mother. The Queen had been browsing the merchandise in the market, and was about to pay for a purchase when an imbecilic thief snatched her money pouch from her hands, bumping into her and knocking her to the ground. Her guards ensured that she had not suffered injury before pursuing the thief, so the cretin was given a head start... and then Tadark showed up on the scene. According to Tadark himself, he saw the thief assault the Queen, then gave chase, catching him, wrestling him to the ground and arresting him before the others could lend a hand."

I almost laughed out loud at the notion of Tadark acting so heroically.

Smiling broadly, I prompted, "And the other version?"

"The beginning is much the same," London said, enjoying the telling of the tale. "It is on the circumstances surrounding Tadark's arrival that the accounts differ dramatically. According to one of the Queen's own men, he and another guard gave chase to the thief. They were gaining ground on the young man when Tadark, then a City Guard, stepped out from a side street. It would be correct to say that the thief did not see Tadark soon enough to avoid a collision, and the two crashed into each other. The thief was knocked out, presumably from the impact of his head upon the ground. The other guards took him into custody as Tadark rose dizzily to his feet.

"Tadark and the unlucky thief were then brought before the Queen, who, naturally enough, assumed some act of bravery on Tadark's part. Upon her return to the Palace, she insisted that he receive recognition for his 'noble deed.' Cannan thereupon placed Tadark into the training program for the Elite Guard. I have always suspected that some other issue was preoccupying Cannan at the time; otherwise, he would have come up with something less grand as a reward."

London moved away from the wall, indicating with his hand that we should descend the spiraling stairs, and I obliged. As we stepped out into the first floor corridor, he finished his story.

"I would guess Cannan never thought Tadark would actually complete the training program, as about half of those who enter drop out. But somehow he made it through. Personally, I believe that someone made an appalling mistake in determining who was to be admitted to the Elite Guard that year, thus cursing us with the constant and aggravating presence of our dear friend Tadark. My only consolation is that he is unlikely to advance up the ranks of the Guard, always and forever remaining a lowly Lieutenant."

I was forced to stifle another laugh as we walked onto the intricately designed mosaic stone floor of the Grand Entry Hall and saw both Madam Matallia, clutching a basket of embroidery, and Steldor, casually flipping a dagger, awaiting me.

Palace Guards pulled open the twin heavy oak front doors, and Madam Matallia, her graying hair arranged into a precise bun, walked slowly and erectly over the threshold and out into the sunshine. Steldor fluidly sheathed his dagger and stepped forward to bow and kiss my hand, then smiled lazily at me, an unmistakable trace of tedium in his deep brown eyes. Despite the simple style of his belted green suede tunic, he was effortlessly stunning, and I felt quite plain in comparison to him despite my sweeping azure blue gown. I took the arm Steldor was now extending, wondering if he counted me as just another task on his schedule, then glanced back to assess London's reaction. My bodyguard, however, steadfastly refused to meet my gaze.

The central courtyard was one of my favorite haunts, second only to the garden. Lilac hedges lined the wide stone path that led from the Palace to the front gates, the point of entry into the grounds, and their profuse blossoms gave off a fragrance that clung to your clothes and your hair like mist to the low-lands. Majestic oak, white birch, and flowering cherry trees cast cooling shadows over the benches that were situated throughout the grassy expanse, while doors on both of the fifteen-foot-high side walls of the courtyard could be opened to provide access to the equally beautiful east and west courtyards. It was a lovely place to read, think, or simply daydream. Even being with Steldor could not dampen the joy I felt at being able to spend this lovely early June afternoon within the courtyard.

I came out of my reverie only to discover that Steldor was diligently reminding me of how incredible he was.

"So I thought, 'Why not?' and kissed her on the cheek," Steldor droned, an undertone of boredom again in his smooth voice. "I was not really attracted to her, but she was totally infatuated with me, and I saw no harm in paying her a little attention."

"Yes," I said sweetly, interrupting his monologue. "There are so many who would be pleased to receive a single crumb of your attention."

He wore a bemused expression for a moment, then continued, undaunted.

"She, of course, was delighted to be in my company. But then, who wouldn't be, given my handsomeness, heritage and charm."

I did my best not to laugh, knowing that he was completely serious, and managed to disguise my reaction as a girlish giggle.

Sensing an opportunity, I coyly said, "Not to mention how strong and brave you are."

I glanced around for Madam Matallia, who had perched herself upon a shaded bench (as London had predicted she would), and was conveniently out of earshot.

"I have no doubt that everyone admires you, and, of course, would trust you with important information," I boldly continued.

Steldor smiled arrogantly. "Well, I do hear about many things."

I couldn't believe how easily my scheme was succeeding.

"Oh, do tell me about something... official," I said, moving alluringly closer.

He put his arm around my waist, and I nervously hoped I had not given him the wrong kind of encouragement.

"What do you want to know?"

"Tell me something about Cokyri, perhaps about the Cokyrian woman who was our prisoner."

I wondered if he had caught on to what I was attempting to do, as he slowly said, "You want to know something about Cokyri?"

"Yes, I mean, you're so experienced and smart, you must have a theory as to how she escaped."

We stopped walking and Steldor turned to face me, eyes narrowed. I reached out flirtatiously to finger the silver wolf's head talisman that he wore about his neck, and he suddenly laughed. Placing his hand atop my own and pressing it lightly against his muscular chest, he began to belittle me.

"Well, I *am* experienced and smart, but really, Alera, it would be much simpler just to *ask* me if you want the details of the investigation."

I stared at his pendant as my cheeks began to go through every conceivable shade of pink.

"Then again, I do generally enjoy flattery… and your attempt to trick me into providing you with confidential information has been somewhat amusing."

To my mortification, he put his other hand under my chin, raising my deep brown eyes to his own.

"But you'll find it is difficult to match my wits."

I pulled my hand from his, stung by his words, utterly horrified and thoroughly embarrassed that I had been caught. Spurred by the threat of tears, I turned around, not wanting him to know that he had hurt me. Taking several deep breaths, I walked bleary-eyed toward a stone bench that was positioned beneath the branches of a white birch tree. When I reached it, I sat down in as dignified a fashion as I could manage, gazing stubbornly away from him and wishing that London would emerge to rescue me.

After a moment, Steldor walked over to sit beside me, but I resolutely refused to acknowledge him.

"Now, now," he said, in an unbearably patronizing tone, as if to a recalcitrant child. "There's no reason to be this upset that your little ploy didn't work."

When I remained adamantly nonresponsive, his voice softened, and he sounded as though he were offering me a treat.

"I know my father or the King would not talk about the affairs of the military with you, but I actually see no harm in satisfying your curiosity. After all, there is no use to which you could put the information."

He began to play with the hair that cascaded down my back. "All you have to do is ask."

My breath caught in my throat at the humiliating position in which he was placing me, but, seeing no other way to garner what I wanted to know, I reluctantly turned to face him.

"Lord Steldor, I would like to know the details of the investigation into the Cokyrian prisoner's escape."

"Very well," he acquiesced, far too pleased with himself. He relaxed in a stylized manner, resting his upper arms on the back of the bench, continuing to play with my hair. "Well, we have reached no conclusions as of yet, but I do know my father has redirected the investigation toward finding a traitor. The two dungeon guards who came on duty at midnight have confessed that they fell asleep in the course of their shift. As neither of these guards has ever shown neglect in his duties before, my father suspects treachery. He thinks that the guards were drugged.

"The guards were brought a meal about three hours after they reported for duty, and nodded off right after they ate. Both guards say they recall waking up just as the sun was rising, shortly before Kade came to retrieve the woman. That gives us the timeframe of the escape."

"And has your father focused on any person in particular?" I probed, thoroughly intrigued, my embarrassment forgotten.

"My father hasn't specified anyone, but the traitor would have to know the orders for the day that were issued by Kade to the dungeon guards. They vary day to day, and only the guards involved and the Elite Guard know the schedule for changing posts. If the traitor had known the orders, he could have drugged the food."

"So, our traitor would have to be someone in the Elite Guard?" I forced the sentence slowly from my mouth, for I could not truly conceive of any of the Royal Family's most trusted soldiers engaging in such an act of betrayal.

"In theory. Hence the doubling up of all the bodyguards. The drugging is also suggested by the fact that the keys were never noticed to be missing. As there were no signs of a forced breakout, the keys could easily have been used and returned while the guards were unconscious."

"That's frightening," I murmured, and a chill swept through me.

"Ah, never fear, Princess," Steldor said with a self-assured chuckle, putting his arm around my shoulder and drawing me near. "I'll protect you."

"I'm sure you will," I forced myself to say, slipping from beneath his arm to come to my feet, London's lack of trust in Steldor beginning to nag at me.

"Let's walk a bit, shall we?" I hurriedly invited.

I spent most of the afternoon with Steldor, sharing a bite to eat with him, and listening with feigned interest as he returned to making long speeches about himself. Eventually, we went back inside the Palace, I, at least, feeling a small twinge of guilt at leaving Madam Matallia asleep on her bench. Steldor accompanied me to the spiral staircase, but though he was willing to escort me further, I was able to convince him that no harm would befall me as I traversed the short distance from the stairs to my quarters.

Having successfully escaped from Steldor's parting embrace without a kiss, I trod lightly up the steps, picturing the faces of the Elite Guards in my mind as I considered the possibility that one of them was a traitor. I had known most of them for at least half my life, and I knew that in order to be inducted into the Elite Guard, a soldier's loyalty to the Throne had to be proven. What could have prompted one of them to betray the Kingdom he loved?

I heard muffled conversation coming from inside the library as I reached the second floor landing, and moved in the direction of the sound. As I approached the half-open library door, Tadark's unmistakable, and quite excited, voice reached my ears. I assumed that London was with him, since words were tumbling from Tadark's mouth in rapid succession, and only London would have had the patience to put up with his chatter for such an extensive period of time.

"When I was nine, I would steal my father's sword to play with. I never hurt anybody, but I got in a lot of trouble, believe you me. For some reason, I kept doing it though. I don't know why. I guess I was just destined to be a soldier. It was my dream to become part of the Elite Guard. You people inspired me to become what I am today. I made a lot of stupid mistakes when I was just a soldier, so I didn't think I'd make it, but I did! I remember hearing in military school about the training you have to go through to be in the Elite Guard, and I just thought, *Never*. Never would I survive that. But once I was in the training program, I didn't want to drop out, and so somehow I made it through."

There was a pause, and I pictured Tadark surfacing like a swimmer for air, as his speech had surely put a strain on his lungs. Then he continued, more slowly, his enthusiasm now tempered with curiosity.

"How did you survive it?"

Time slipped away as Tadark waited for London to respond. I guessed that London was reading a book and not paying any heed to what Tadark was saying.

"You're the quiet type, aren't you?" It was still Tadark who was speaking.

"Only around you," London replied absently, at last giving Tadark his due.

"Why's that? I really can't picture you talking much ever. You strike me as a bit... dull."

I covered my mouth with my hand in order to keep from laughing out loud, drawing odd stares from the guards and servants who passed me by.

"I just figure you talk enough for the both of us, Tad," London coolly explained.

"My name is Tadark!"

"What, you don't like the name Tad? I think it fits you. Tad."

"Don't call me that!"

"Whatever you say... Tad."

Tadark exhaled huffily several times, and I was certain London had returned to his book, at ease with Tadark's displeasure. After a moment, Tadark collected himself and attempted again to engage London.

"You want to know why I follow you around all the time?"

"Because we're stationed together?" London drolly inquired.

"Well, yes, but I mean other than that."

"Tell me, Tad. Why do you follow me around all the time?" asked London indifferently.

"Because I respect you. You're everything I strive to become — everything an Elite Guard should be."

"Oh, now I feel honored."

"I'd hate to think that you'd betray your King and Queen for your own profit."

Silence greeted Tadark's statement.

"What are you talking about?" London spoke as though to a helplessly feebleminded child.

"Someone has to have done it — released the Cokyrian prisoner. It could be you just as easily as it could be anyone else."

"There's no proof that anyone helped her escape."

"Oh, please," Tadark said, as though London had made a joke. "You know there's a traitor. I'm just saying that... *everyone*... is a suspect." Within *everyone*, he clearly included London.

"You're in no position to point fingers, Tadark. More often than not, the accuser is the guilty party."

London was incensed. I had never heard him use a deep, warning tone like the one he was using now.

"Don't push it with me. I can cause you a lot of problems, boy."

"'*Boy?*' Who are you to be calling *me* boy? You look younger than I do!" Tadark was almost squealing, his voice rising dramatically in pitch as he became increasingly overwrought.

A book tumbled to the floor, and I knew London had come to his feet.

"Attention!" London barked. "Have you forgotten that I am your superior officer?"

"No, sir, I haven't, sir," Tadark mumbled resentfully.

"I didn't hear you," London retorted, murderously calm.

"No, sir, I haven't, sir," Tadark repeated, with greater volume and clarity.

I decided to intervene before some horrible punishment befell my younger guard. I knew London, who generally followed no rules but his own, had to be infuriated to have called upon military protocol.

Swinging open the library door, I boldly hailed them. "I was heading back to my room when I heard your voices, and thought I might join you here."

London, uncharacteristically agitated, stood across from me in front of the library's large bay window, the book through which he had been paging forgotten at his feet, while Tadark stood uncomfortably before him at attention amidst several scattered armchairs. Along the right wall, a small brown leather sofa and several additional chairs were arranged in front of a large fireplace. On the floor, between the seating areas, was a large rug upon which I had frequently lain as a child, often entertained by drawings that London would make for me. Book-filled shelves formed legions of aisles on the left.

"At ease," London muttered upon seeing me, and the rigidity left Tadark's posture even as an embarrassed flush crept up his neck and a guilty look played upon his face. The two men glanced at each other and I could almost hear the question that had formed in their minds — *did she hear us?*

"Now boys," I teased. "Judging from your faces, you must have been discussing something I'm not supposed to know about."

There was an extraordinarily awkward hush following my statement.

"Don't be ridiculous," London said at last.

I decided to stop making them feel self-conscious.

"Well then, please resume your discussion. I'll just browse through the books as long as we're here."

My father had assembled a substantial book collection over the years, and had insisted that both of his daughters be not only *taught* to read, but *permitted* to read a wide variety of subjects. The books themselves represented years of painstaking effort by scribes, who copied the original author's words onto sheets of parchment that were then bound in leather or in elaborately designed metal covers. The Palace scribes and copyists worked in the far corner of the library, and sheets of parchment, rulers, quills, and bottles of ink could be seen upon the tables. The scribes also prepared official documents and proclamations, invitations for Palace events, and various other types of correspondence.

As I meandered down one of the aisles, I ran a finger lovingly over some of the volumes. Here were books of science, theology, philosophy, history, and medicine, along with vocabularies and encyclopedias. There were also compilations of short stories and folk tales, as well as poetry, romances, and plays. London, in all likelihood, had been reading one of the books of law, as he had a keen mind and knowledge of Latin. I was thankful that my father was a progressive man when it came to the education of his daughters, as we had been taught how to read, write, and do figures, in addition to the traditional feminine subjects of etiquette, movement, household management, embroidery, and music.

I continued to wander among the dusty tomes, not really in the mood to read, but needing some time to think without distraction. The library happened to be ideally suited to such solitary endeavors.

I was still unwilling to believe that there was a traitor among the Elite Guard, or any of the guards for that matter, but, as Tadark had said, there seemed to be no other possibility. I could not bring myself to doubt any of them, except perhaps Tadark, but he was too loud and foolish to get away with something as clever as this escape had been. Any of the others could have accomplished it, but I could not bear to lay blame on one of them. They were my guardians, and I trusted each of them with my life.

The only other option, one to which I clung desperately, was something of which Cannan had spoken when I had first learned of the Cokyrian woman's escape. He had mentioned something about the Cokyrians being famous for their stealth and slyness, and I hoped that this woman's flight was proof of that and not of a traitor within the Royal House.

Chapter Six
Secrets and Revelations

I needed additional information. Not about the breakout, but about the Cokyrian people. I ran through the list of those who might be able to tell me something, but turned up no one whom I would dare to ask. London would be dubious of my motives and Tadark was unlikely to know anything. I had already solicited Steldor and had no desire to do so again. My father, Cannan and Kade would refuse to tell me anything, and would view such a request from a woman as inappropriate. Settling upon a person whose knowledge of the Cokyrian people was uncertain, I walked back to where my bodyguards sat in tense silence — London perched on the deep padded sill of the library's sun-streaked window and Tadark in a brown leather armchair.

"I'm going to seek out my mother," I announced. "I have hardly spoken to her in weeks."

While this was not my true reason for wanting to spend time with my mother, it was accurate all the same, as I had seen her only occasionally at dinner since my birthday celebration nearly a month previously.

Both London and Tadark rose to escort me on my way to the quarters that my mother and father shared. I knew my mother would be there, as the sun was going down and it was her habit to retire early. She jealously guarded her rest so there would be no circles beneath her sparkling eyes or shadows upon her delicate face, for it would have been unacceptable for the King to have anything less than a beautiful wife.

My parents' quarters occupied the opposite corner of the second floor from my own, and consisted of five luxurious rooms: two primarily for my mother, two primarily for my father, and one large parlor used by both. It was thought unwise for the rulers of the Kingdom to sleep beside each other every night, as separation made it more challenging for an enemy to pose a threat.

I knocked on the ornate door to their quarters, and a young servant girl answered.

"Is my mother in her bedroom?" I asked.

"Yes, Your Highness," she responded with a demure curtsey.

I entered the luxuriously furnished parlor, leaving London and Tadark outside in the corridor with my mother's personal guards. Treading upon the woolen tapestries that covered the wood-planked floor and bespoke of immense wealth, I crossed straight to my mother's bedroom door and rapped lightly upon it with my knuckles.

"Come in," responded my mother's melodic voice.

I opened the door and entered the opulent room to find her sitting gracefully before the mirror at her dressing table, brushing her beautiful, long, honey-blonde hair. She was already in her nightgown, and her personal maid had drawn the heavy velvet drapes across the window that looked out over the garden.

The color dominating my mother's room was a deep plum that drew out the richness of the wood furnishings. Her bed had elaborately carved posts that matched the carvings on the adjacent wardrobe, as well as those on her dressing table. An expansive closet took up most of one wall, holding the wide variety of lavish gowns and robes that she possessed, and a heavy, locked trunk contained her crowns, tiaras and other jewelry. A large stone fireplace spanned most of another wall, with book shelves on each side. Padded plum velvet armchairs sat in front of the fireplace, draped with fur throws, while woolen tapestries adorned the walls and blanketed most of the floor.

My mother turned with a smile, gazing at me with blue eyes that were identical to Miranna's in every way.

"Alera, it's good to see you, my darling. I trust Cannan's restrictions have not been too stifling for you."

"I'm managing," I said truthfully, electing not to mention my escapade with Steldor. "I just wish that the mystery of the Cokyrian prisoner's escape would soon be solved."

My mother nodded sympathetically as she laid the hairbrush on the table.

"Tell me what you wish to know," she said, gliding to sit upon the plum velvet spread atop her bed.

I was momentarily nonplussed at my mother's insight, but I willingly moved to sit beside her.

"Don't be so astounded," she admonished lightheartedly. "I was the same way at your age — always wanting to know everything. But you mustn't tell your father that it was I who enlightened you."

"I won't, Mother." I scooted closer to her, eagerly adding, "Tell me what you can about Cokyri."

She laughed softly at my enthusiasm. Although more reserved than my father, she, too, had a kind and generous nature.

"I'm surprised you have to come to me for knowledge about Cokyri. No one knows as much about our enemy as London. I would have thought he might have shared a few things with you over the years."

I cocked my head, a bit confused. "Why would London know more than anyone else?"

"Oh," she said, apparently realizing that she had made reference to something about which I did not know. "It may not be my place to tell you."

My interest was piqued. "Tell me what?"

She pondered me for a long moment, and I feared she would not continue. With a whisper of a sigh, she relented, reaching out a hand to lightly push my dark hair away from my face.

"Years ago, toward the end of the war, London was a prisoner of Cokyri for almost ten months. There had been a ruthless battle in which our soldiers were greatly outnumbered. London was a Battalion Commander at the time, and when our soldiers were forced to retreat, he stayed to the end. When we went back to collect the bodies of our fallen, London was not among them, and we were left to assume that he had been taken for interrogation. The Cokyrians rarely took prisoners, and he is the only one who ever survived. Most of the information we have about the Overlord and the High Priestess has come from him."

My mother's lilting voice was sharply out of character with the seriousness of the topic about which she was speaking.

"He was a prisoner at the time the Cokyrians were stealing our children. He said they must have found what they were after, as they abruptly withdrew from our lands. All we really know is that they vacated their encampments and took flight. It was during the disarray surrounding the return of the troops to Cokyri that he managed to escape."

My insides had gone still, with the exception of my heart, which was thumping loudly inside my chest and stomach.

"What exactly do you mean when you say he was 'taken for interrogation?'" I asked slowly, anticipating the worst.

"We know little of what London went through while he was confined within Cokyrian walls," she said, patting my hand soothingly. "Those details were not something he wanted to share."

"But did they hurt him?" I pressed, knowing I should stop, but unable to do so.

I felt ill remembering how London had spoken of the Overlord. I did not want to think that he had incurred the Overlord's wrath, but it was inconceivable that he could have been a prisoner and not have been mistreated.

"As I said, we know little about what he endured," she said evasively.

It was clear that she hoped I would cease my inquiries if she refused to satisfactorily address them, but the determination in my eyes told her otherwise.

"He returned to us in a very strange state," she reluctantly continued.

"What do you mean by 'strange?'"

"He had no physical injuries that we could see, but it took months for him to recover."

"Well, of course it would," I reasoned, enormously relieved that my bodyguard and friend had not been tortured by the Cokyrians. "He'd just spent ten months imprisoned by the enemy. It would take a while to put such an ordeal behind you."

"Yes, it would," said my mother tentatively, as if expressing her thoughts were problematic. "But that's not the kind of recovery I'm talking about."

She raised a hand to delicately massage her forehead, as if encouraging the memories to surface, and I waited, bewildered, for her to carry on.

"He was terribly sick, but not from any illness that our doctors could identify. He acted feverishly, but his skin was colder than ice. He was delirious, unable to speak coherently or respond in any way to what was said to him. He screamed as if in terrible pain, but our doctors could not locate a source for the pain. He ate and drank little for weeks. The doctors bled him several times, but it made no difference, and they advised us he would die." She sat deep in thought for a moment. "We can't imagine the willpower it must have taken for him to return to Hytanica in that condition.

"When he awoke, he told us what he could, about his escape and about the Overlord. I'm afraid your father and Cannan quite besieged him the moment he returned to his senses. Everyone was concerned that he would slip back into the unknown illness that had incapacitated him for so long. Then I suppose he needed time to come to terms with the agony he had endured. He was withdrawn for many months, gradually returning to his former self."

I contemplated the pattern of the tapestry that lay on the floor, trying to make sense of the information my mother had provided.

"London has never mentioned any of this," I murmured.

"London is an especially private person," my mother offered by way of explanation. "If you ever choose to ask him about Cokyri, don't let your questions become too personal. Some things are better left buried."

I agreed, knowing that bringing any of this up with London would be terribly uncomfortable for us both.

"Goodnight, Alera," my mother said, giving me a light kiss on the cheek before returning to her dressing table to resume brushing her hair. "Do not let your curiosity lead you to err."

"I won't, Mother," I said. "And thank you."

I left her bedroom, taking my time in crossing the parlor to the door leading to the corridor. I had been so horribly naïve when I had asked London about Cokyri and the Overlord, on the night that the Cokyrian woman had been discovered in the Palace garden. I now understood to some extent why London never spoke of fighting in the war or his experiences with the Cokyrians. I very much wanted to know what he had suffered, but I would never raise the subject with him. I had to accept that I might never know.

I tossed and turned in my bed that night, with Tadark and London on duty in my parlor, plagued by disturbing images. London had claimed the sofa as his, which meant that Tadark would try to catch a few winks, rather gracelessly, in an armchair. It was usually the sound of Tadark's moaning and complaining that put me to sleep, but tonight the noise was wearing rather than calming in its familiarity.

As I lay in the darkness, I imagined the man reclining on my sofa to be starving in a Cokyrian dungeon, not knowing whether he would live or die. Our dungeon was a horrible place, and I dared not consider how the cruel Cokyrians housed their captives.

He had said he'd seen the Overlord. I had been frightened by the reality that such a person existed in this world. London had faced him. He had borne his fury. Or had he?

London had not sustained any physical injuries, but had only suffered from an unusual illness. Perhaps it was a Cokyrian illness — an illness of which Hytanicans had not heard and to which we had never been exposed. But if that were the case, the disease would have spread and the whole Kingdom would have become infected. And London should have died. The doctors had said it. Maybe the illness was unidentified, but surely a doctor knows when someone is going to die.

I did not know where this line of thought was taking me, but as I continued to sort details out in my mind, comprehension began to dawn. London knew Cokyri better than anyone in Hytanica. It was inconceivable that someone could have seen the Cokyrian Overlord and not also have seen the High Priestess. He had recognized Nantilam the moment he had seen her in the garden, and had told me who she was, then had tried to claim he was mistaken. Why would he withhold such information from Cannan and the King? And if he were reluctant to reveal what he knew, why had he shared it with me? I could only presume that my pledge to maintain his confidence had made him more willing to speak than he perhaps should have been, and that he had not thought my father would permit me to attend the interrogation.

And why would he lie to me not once, but twice? London had never lied to me before, but here, with the Cokyrians, came a side of him that I did not know or like. He had left my quarters during the night of Nantilam's escape, and though he had tried to convince me otherwise, I knew it to be true. I wanted to believe there was an explanation, but I had no faith he would tell me even if I demanded it of him. And then I came to a decision, one that made me both uneasy and regretful, but that I judged to be right. London might lie to me, but he would not lie to his King.

The next morning, I sent word to Lanek that I wished to see my father, and then visited our family Chapel, which was in the east wing just down the corridor from the Queen's Drawing Room. The

Chapel contained eight intricately carved pews, four on each side of a wide aisle, with a gilded alter and cross at the front of the room. A door to the left opened into a prayer room that contained many religious tomes and artifacts, and off of which was located the Priest's quarters.

At this time of day, sunshine filtered through the dramatic stained glass windows set high into the eastern wall of the Chapel. I sat on one of the front-most benches and bowed my head in unspoken prayer, soliciting strength and guidance as I carried out the decision I had reached. Then I departed, determined to see my father, London and Tadark joining me as I reentered the corridor.

I paced agitatedly in the small antechamber outside the Throne Room, awaiting entrance. The antechamber provided a waiting area for formal audiences with the King, and was accessed by walking under the Grand Staircase. There were three other points of entry into the Hall of Kings, one through the guard room that opened onto Cannan's office, another through the guard room that opened onto Kade's office, and the last through the King's Drawing Room. The King's Drawing Room was across the corridor from 'our private staircase and therefore gave my father easy access to the Throne Room from his quarters.

London and Tadark were with me, both in unusually good moods, or perhaps it just seemed so in comparison with my own. Both of them stood, despite the availability of several large brown leather armchairs, unwilling to sit down as long as I stayed upon my feet, although London, as always, rested his back against a wall.

"So what time is your appointment?" London teased, making fun of my father's need for highly unwarranted and extremely formal arrangements just to meet with his own daughter.

I gave no response and continued pacing, oblivious to the elaborate tapestries depicting victorious battle scenes that hung on the walls.

"It's rather ironic, really," London persisted. "The Princess can't see the King without an appointment. It would probably be easier for her to swim the Recorah River than to see her own father on short notice."

Tadark chuckled, though he snapped his head around as if worried that someone might have seen him act less than dignified while on duty.

London was much less serious than he had been the previous afternoon, and it pained me to be in his presence in light of what I was about to do. The military was his whole life. Was I prepared to destroy that? I shook my head. London would have a good explanation for everything, and if he didn't... then he had destroyed it himself.

Deciding I was in no mood to reciprocate his teasing, London moved on to his new pastime — antagonizing Tadark. While this was entertaining for both London and me, Tadark did not appreciate this particular pursuit.

Just when Tadark had finally conceived of a retort to a rather unkind comment of London's, the doors to the Hall of Kings were slowly pulled open, and I was motioned inside by one of the Palace Guards who stood just over the threshold. I felt inexplicably weak as I entered, aware that this was my last chance to turn from my decision, but no matter how I felt about what I had come to do, I believed I did not have a choice.

London and Tadark remained outside for the second time in two days as I stepped up to speak to one of my parents. I gave a small curtsey as I approached my father where he sat upon his imposing throne.

"To what do I owe the pleasure of this visit?" he asked eagerly, his deep brown eyes warm and bright.

I knew at once what he was expecting me to address, like a rush of cold wind hitting me in the face.

"It has nothing to do with choosing a husband or with Steldor," I uncomfortably disclosed.

His face fell ever so slightly.

"Well, then, what can be so pressing as to seek me out at this time of day? You know I have a busy schedule, Alera."

He had lost a bit of his good humor, and a scold had now crept into his voice.

"I think you'll find this of greater importance than today's business, Father," I asserted, beginning to twine my fingers anxiously.

His eyebrows drew together in concern. "Is everything alright? You're rather pale, my dear."

I took a deep, steadying breath.

"Do you have any leads as to the identity of the traitor?" I rather abruptly inquired.

"How do you know about that?" my father demanded.

"Word travels. The guards suspect each other."

"Still," he reproached, his scowl remaining, "this is not your worry. You needn't be afraid within the Palace, and you should not concern yourself with the military's business."

"Father, please," I begged. "Do you know who he is?"

He exhaled heavily. "No, we do not. But we will find him… if in fact there is a traitor," he hedged. "Do not fret, Alera. Cannan is taking care of everything."

My eyes passed over the Elite Guards who stood in their usual formation, six to each side of the King.

"Could we talk privately?" I softly inquired.

"If that is what you wish," my father responded, somewhat puzzled. He stood and stepped down from the dais, motioning me through the door to the side of the thrones that led into his study.

My father's study was warm and inviting, but a bit cluttered. On our left as we entered, shelves overflowed with books, and a large mahogany desk, littered with parchments, was straight ahead. Against the wall to the right was a large, luxuriously padded, brown leather sofa, upon which were strewn several additional books. The near right corner of the room was occupied by a fireplace, and several armchairs sat haphazardly in front of the hearth. In the far corner, between the sofa and desk, was a table that currently held my father's prized chess set. Rich tapestries hung on the walls, and furs were strewn on the floor to provide softness beneath the feet.

I crossed the study and sat down upon the sofa, my palms moist from nervousness. My father gathered the books and dropped them with a resounding thud upon the stone floor, then sat beside me, waiting for me to speak.

"London left me alone in my quarters on the night of the Cokyrian woman's escape," I blurted, without any preliminaries.

"What?" my father exclaimed in alarm. "Are you certain?"

"I woke up during the night and London was gone. I called for him — he was not there."

"You have no doubt of this?" my father pressed.

"I am certain, Father," I said, feeling somewhat queasy. "I would not have come to you if I were not."

"He knew he was not to leave you. Why did you not tell me this earlier?"

"Because London is my guard, and my friend. I was afraid of what might happen to him if I did."

My father reached out to lay a hand upon my own to quiet them, as I had been fussily clasping and unclasping them in my lap.

"And you no longer fear for him?"

"I fear for him," I said, head bowed. "But I could no longer hide this from you."

"Have you spoken of this to London?" My father's manner had now become grave.

"He lied to me, Father," I said disconsolately, raising my head to gaze upon his troubled countenance. "I know that he left, but he told me he was with me all night. He said that I must have been dreaming."

"Perhaps he is right. In any event, it becomes your word against his. Royal or not, you are but a woman, and London is a highly respected soldier of Hytanica."

He stood, and began to pace in front of the cold hearth. I exhaled regretfully, then resumed my confession.

"That is not the only reason I came to you. If you remember, I was the person who discovered the Cokyrian woman in the garden, and London was the one who put her under arrest."

"Yes, I remember," my father said, coming to a halt in front of me. "Of what importance is that?"

"London said something strange to me that night. He spoke of the woman as if he knew her. He said she was the High Priestess of Cokyri, and he told me her name, Nantilam. When you told me her identity was not known, I asked him about it, and he said he had been mistaken. He lied to me again, Father. I know he did."

My father said nothing, but stood deep in deliberation, distractedly rubbing the Royal Ring with the fingers of his left hand. I fidgeted ruefully as I waited for him to speak, feeling as though I had just betrayed the most important secret of my life, a secret I had promised to keep for someone I loved dearly.

"This cannot be," my father muttered under his breath.

"I know that he was a prisoner of war in Cokyri for ten months," I revealed. "He would know the High Priestess if he saw her."

"Has London told you——?" My father was clearly startled.

"No. He hasn't told me of his time as a captive in Cokyri. I spoke to Mother," I honestly explained at his baffled expression. "I went to her for information and she obliged. Be angry with me if you must be angry with someone."

He said nothing, but resumed his pacing.

"I'm sure London has an explanation for why he was gone," I continued tentatively, "other than what I know we're both thinking. He will tell you if you ask it of him."

"But nothing can excuse the fact that he left his post while under strict orders not to do so," he said grittily. "And any explanation he has will not justify keeping this woman's identity a secret."

He pivoted, then moved to open the door of his study.

"Guard!" he called. "Summon Cannan immediately."

"Yes, Sire," one of the Elite Guards responded before swiftly exiting the Throne Room.

"Alera," my father solemnly said, coming to sit beside me once more and enfolding my hands in his. "It's very important that you tell Cannan exactly what you told me."

I nodded. As much as it pained me to know that with every word I spoke, I condemned my bodyguard and friend further, I would tell the Captain of the Guard the truth.

After a few minutes, Cannan strode into my father's study.

"What is it, Your Majesty?" he inquired with a touch of urgency. "Your guard made it sound as if the Cokyri were marching on us as we speak."

My father stood and motioned to me, and I did as he had commanded, telling Cannan all that I knew. While Cannan's reaction to the information was difficult to discern, an occasional twitch of his left eyebrow told me he was just as shaken by this information as my father had been.

"London and Tadark are in the antechamber?" he finally asked, his dark, perceptive eyes fixed on me.

I inclined my head in confirmation, and he spoke to the Elite Guard outside the door to the study just as my father had done.

"Bring London and Tadark in, now."

Cannan glanced at my father, who indicated to me that I should rise and accompany them. The three of us reentered the Throne Room to await the entrance of my bodyguards. My father took the throne, while I sat in one of the ornate chairs to his left, Cannan standing on his right.

The guard did as he had been told, and soon both of my bodyguards were before us, Tadark plainly perplexed, London wary.

"Tadark, escort Princess Alera to her quarters," Cannan commanded.

"Sir?" the Lieutenant said, evidently expecting his Captain to give London similar orders. None came.

"Now," Cannan prompted.

I rose and went to Tadark, my gaze averted. I glanced sideways at London as I passed him, and he shot me a look that was filled with both fire and quiet resignation, a look that told me he knew exactly what I'd done.

Chapter Seven
No Explanation

I sat rather stiffly in an armchair in my parlor, too distraught to move. Since leaving the Throne Room, I had tried to eat, to read, and to work on embroidery, but as time passed without news of London, I had become less and less capable of concentrating. I longed to think of anything but what was happening in the Hall of Kings, but at the same time I could think of nothing else. It had been almost six hours, and the waiting had become unbearable. I wanted to know what London's fate was going to be, and yet I didn't, because I couldn't help feeling it would be my fault.

Tadark had several times taken a breath as if to say something, but had seemingly thought better of it each time. He wanted to ask what I had said to my father that was so confidential that London would be trusted with the information but not he. Though he had tossed accusations at London in the library, I knew it would never really enter his mind that my first bodyguard and his partner could be charged with treason.

London would *not* be charged with treason, I reassured myself. He would be able to explain everything, and he would return to being my guard before the day was out. I kept repeating the phrase over and over in my head — *London is not a traitor* — until it sounded hollow, and I was ashamed to discover that there was a part of me that doubted its truth.

I did not hear the knock on my door, but Tadark went to open it, granting entry to an Elite Guard I knew at first sight.

"Destari!" I exclaimed, rising from my seat as he advanced a few feet into the room. "What are you doing here?"

Destari bowed, then assumed a less formal stance. He was an unusually tall and muscular individual, who made Cannan look short, and Tadark childlike. He had raven hair, black eyes, a chiseled jaw, and thick eyebrows that gave him an intense and intimidating presence, but I had known him for my entire life and he did not frighten me in the least. Like Tadark, and every member of the Elite Guard other than London, he wore the proper uniform: a royal blue doublet, white shirt and black trousers.

"I have been assigned to be your secondary bodyguard for the time being," he said in his deep, resonating voice, and the bit of undigested food that remained in my stomach from lunch seemed to swirl queasily about.

"Where is London?"

Destari stared regretfully at the floor, and it was clear that it was a struggle for him to answer my questions, for he and London had been friends since military school, and had entered the ranks of the Elite Guard together.

"London has been relieved of his duties."

"What?" I uttered, shocked by this news. "Why?"

"You know why," Destari said, throwing a furtive glance at Tadark that told me to monitor what I said.

Tadark was evidently not deemed trustworthy enough to be told all the information in the hands of the Elite Guard, or at least he was not deemed trustworthy enough by Destari. From what I knew of Tadark, I didn't blame him.

"What I said doesn't prove anything!" I retorted recklessly, growing increasingly agitated as I absorbed the consequences of my actions.

"It proves enough," Destari flatly responded.

"What does that mean?" My mind was racing, frantically seeking some way to reverse what I had done.

"London would not allow doubts as to your credibility, so he admitted to knowing the identity of the Cokyrian woman. He also admitted that, on the night of her disappearance, he left your quarters, therefore abandoning his post, but he would not speak further. He neither confessed to nor denied assisting in her escape."

"I must speak to my father," I resolutely asserted, moving toward the door. I tried to step around Destari, who was blocking my path, but he would not budge.

"Destari, move this instant!" I ordered, with as much authority as I could muster, both my pitch and my volume rising.

"With all due respect, Princess Alera, it is getting late, and it would be better if you waited until morning to meet with the King," Destari irritably said.

"With all due respect, Destari," I returned heatedly, hands now gripping my hips, "get out of my way."

Tadark, who had been remarkably absent from this entire exchange, could restrain himself no longer.

"I'd have to agree with Destari, Princess," he began, but I cut him off.

"You have no say in this, Tadark!" I snapped. "I am sick of hearing your opinions!"

Tadark, brown eyes mournful as a hurt puppy's, shrank back, away from Destari and me, and I aimed my ire at the imposing guard once more.

"Unless you were given orders to keep me here, orders that I would nonetheless refuse to obey, you are overstepping your bounds. So move!"

I pointed emphatically in the direction in which I wanted him to shift, willing him to yield.

Begrudgingly admitting defeat, Destari stepped aside, and I stormed into the corridor, both guards reluctantly following. As I descended the Grand Staircase, the hopelessness of my quest tore at me, and my anger turned to desperation.

I entered the Hall of Kings, leaving Destari and Tadark in the antechamber, to see my father upon his throne, no guards in attendance. The waning late afternoon light coming through the high northern windows resulted in lurking shadows in the corners, giving the room an ominous feel.

"Father, what is going on?" I cried out as I swiftly approached.

"Alera," he said wearily. "I knew you would come when I sent Destari."

My father was despondently rubbing his jaw as I came to stand before him, the laugh lines upon his forty-nine-year-old face paradoxically giving him an aged and haggard appearance.

"Cannan and I acted on what you told us," he continued. "We had to do what we did — there was no other option."

"What will be done with him?" I choked, a horrible sinking feeling in the pit of my stomach.

"He is spending one last night in his quarters under guard. In the morning, he will be removed from the Palace grounds."

"But Father," I pleaded, hoping to affect him in some way. "London is not a traitor. He must have an explanation!"

"If he does, he did not share it with us. I cannot allow him to continue serving as a guard, much less one of the Elite Guards who protects the Royal Family, when his allegiance is in question."

"His allegiance lies with Hytanica!" I obstinately declared. I could not bear to think that London's loyalty could lie anywhere else. "He is *not* a traitor."

"Well, someone most definitely is!" my father countered, matching my tone and emphasizing each of his words with his hands. "Would it be easier to accuse some other member of the Elite Guard, when you have known most of them your entire life? One of them is guilty of treachery. Why could it not be London?" Taking in my tormented visage, his attitude softened. "I know that you are close to him, but I cannot run the risk of further betrayal."

"London has not betrayed us!" I repeated, more insistently. "There is good cause for his behavior of late. He just hasn't spoken of it yet."

"If he would not explain his actions to his King or his Captain," my father noted coldly, "then to whom will he speak?"

I sat down dejectedly on the marble steps of the dais. Although the answer was evident to me, I did not want to say it. If he would not explain his actions to his King, he would explain to no one.

"I want to see him, Father," I finally said, a dull ache in my chest where my heart had once resided. "I need to say goodbye."

I knew this could be the last chance I would have to see London. I had been forbidden to leave the Palace, and London would be forbidden to enter the grounds. I knew not how long this arrangement would last, and if there came a time for me to see or speak with him again, I did not know if he would oblige. I had ruined his entire life in one discussion with my father, and I would not have blamed him if he never forgave me.

"Very well," my father charitably agreed. "I will have him brought to you in the morning before he is taken from the Palace."

"Thank you," I murmured, rising to curtsey respectfully. I slowly departed the Throne Room, dejectedly returning to my quarters to try to rein in my feelings and bring order to my jumbled thoughts before I had to face London.

I awoke early the next morning, and sat apprehensively on the edge of the sofa in my parlor to await London's arrival. I knew he would be brought to my quarters as soon as the sun had risen, and I could not risk that I would miss him while I slept. Destari and Tadark silently attended me, Tadark standing awkwardly by the fireplace, and Destari, dark and brooding, near the door into the corridor.

There were so many things I wanted to say to London, but I would not have much time, and I was not sure how to say them. I did not know what his mood would be or if he would be willing to listen. But I had to try.

There was a knock on the door, and I sprang to my feet as Destari stepped forward. He swung the door open to reveal London, accompanied by a Palace Guard almost as tall as Destari and twice as thick. Apparently Cannan believed that someone of substantial size was needed to control London. While this would be true if he were set on resisting, it was completely unnecessary in this situation.

"London!" I exclaimed, as though I had experienced qualms as to who would be outside my door. "I was afraid you wouldn't come!"

"If it had been my choice, Princess, I would not have." His voice was bitter as he stepped into the room.

I was taken aback by his manner, though I had no right to expect he would greet me warmly. I glanced around the room to see that Tadark was in a snit — his rounded cheeks were steadily turning red, and his fists were balled at his sides. Though he appeared to be in an uproar over the way London had spoken to me, I knew that his antagonism really stemmed from the fact that he had borne the brunt of London's wit for weeks.

As for the guard who had come with London, he did not seem to care one way or another what London said or how he spoke to me, a Princess of Hytanica, and was likely as thick in his head as he was in his arms. Destari, who had stepped up beside his friend, looked uncomfortable, though he was not surprised or infuriated the way Tadark was. No one said anything, however, and it took me a moment to recover from the hurt I felt at London's harshness and formality before I could speak further.

"Would you leave us now?" I said to the three guards, as I hesitantly approached London where he stood just a few feet over the doorsill. Anything London said to me would be completely justified, and I worried that someone might interfere on my behalf. I needed to talk to London alone.

Tadark was predictably the first to assert an opinion.

"I'm not going to leave you alone with this criminal!"

He stood to his full and unimposing height, puffing out his chest in a feeble attempt to be menacing, then shifted uneasily as he read the deadly glare in London's eyes.

"Oh, be still, Tadark," Destari unexpectedly grumbled, reaching out to grab London's shoulder as if to hold him in position.

Tadark, looking horribly insulted, mumbled something indistinguishable under his breath.

Destari motioned impatiently toward the door with his head.

"Get into the hall."

Tadark wavered, then crossed the room to slouch resentfully past the older guards into the corridor, not daring to disobey a Deputy Captain.

"Take as long as you need," Destari said evenly, giving me a slight bow. "I will detain Tadark."

I nodded appreciatively, and Destari dropped his hand from London's shoulder. Stopping only to tap the thickly-built guard on the arm to remind him that he also needed to exit, Destari departed the room.

When all three guards had stepped into the corridor, I turned once more to London. He said nothing, but crossed his arms and moved to his left to lean as always against the wall, although this time his posture was unusually rigid.

"You must be angry with me," I ventured tentatively, not knowing where this conversation would lead.

"And why would I be angry with you, Princess?" London replied coldly.

"You don't need to address me so formally," I faltered. The way he was referring to me as "Princess" was making him feel distant and increasing my sense of desperation.

"I don't know what you're talking about, Your Highness. I am speaking to you the same way all of your lowly subjects speak to you. That's what I am now, you know."

"London, stop it," I insisted, guilt scorching the inside of my chest.

"As My Lady commands," he said with mock politeness, as though he were backing off rather than doing exactly what I had just requested that he not do.

"Please, London," I said more fervently.

"I'm not sure what you desire of me, Princess."

"London, don't," I finally implored with a stamp of my foot, unwanted tears searing my eyes. "I did what I believed best, and you're furious with me! Shout at me! Scream your heart out at me! Tell me I'm foolish and that I meddled in things that I shouldn't have! But don't just stand there and ignore what has happened between us!"

After my outburst, there was a silence that threatened to stretch into eternity. Then London straightened and stepped away from the wall, his jaw clenching and unclenching in subdued anger, and I involuntarily stepped back from him. His indigo eyes were now as hard as glass and a chill pulsated from him that was sufficient to rob me of breath. At last he spoke, his words as cutting as a knife.

"It's interesting to me — it is my life that has been ruined, and yet you act as though you are the one who is suffering. Perhaps you are not entirely convinced that what you did was necessary."

London had a gift for reading people like books. It was as though everyone's thoughts and feelings were laid out before him, allowing him to choose which of their insecurities to exploit. He had easily pinpointed mine — the one thing upon which I had dwelt since I had spoken to my father — had I done the right thing? My decision had seemed justified at the time, but now, in the aftermath, nothing was clear.

"I did what I believed best," I tremulously repeated, beginning to pluck at my skirt in my distress. "If I was wrong in my suspicions, you should have explained to my father and Cannan."

"Don't be a fool, Alera," London spat, his eyes now darkened by contempt. "There was no way for me to defend leaving your side against my orders. No matter what explanation I might have had, that was inexcusable."

"You could have told them the truth," I said daringly.

"I told them what I could."

"What does that mean?" I relentlessly pushed. "You've been branded a traitor, London! The truth can't be worse than that."

"Perhaps it is."

I was growing more distraught by the second. London was making no sense at all.

"What would you have had me do?" I demanded. "I went to my father because I could think of no alternative. If you know of some other action I could have taken so things would not have reached this end, I beg of you to enlighten me."

"You should have come to me," London said, as if that had clearly been the most logical course.

"I did!" I said in exasperation. "You wouldn't tell me anything. In fact, you lied to me twice! What was I to think?"

"If I had known what you were planning to do, I would have ... offered you assurances." London sighed heavily as he brushed back his unruly silver bangs. "You should have given me that chance."

"Then perhaps you would like to explain to me now," I mercilessly countered.

"It no longer makes a difference what I say," London said, almost sadly.

"Just answer one question, then. Did you help her escape?"

"This isn't—" London began, but I cut him off.

"Did you help her escape?"

"You don't know—"

"It's a simple yes or no question, and I wish you would just answer it. Are you the traitor? Did you assist in her escape?"

I glared at him, silently compelling him to respond honestly.

"I am not a traitor," he quietly declared.

The air thrummed with tension for a moment, then he continued, his heart obviously heavy.

"If you truly trust someone, then you trust their words and actions, even without explanation. You apparently don't have that level of trust in me."

I felt for a moment as if I were drowning. The only thing I found harder to endure than London's anger was his disappointment. I looked pleadingly at him, but his expression was unyielding.

"If there is nothing further you want of me, I will take my leave," he stiffly finished.

I grudgingly dismissed him, stepping into the corridor after him. As he and the guard assigned to remove him from the Palace strode away, I was gripped by genuine sorrow, instead of guilt, regret, or denial. I did not know when I would next see London, and I felt as though my heart were trying to follow after him. With each step he took, it pressed more painfully against my chest, trying to escape. I desperately wanted to run after him and somehow erase the events of the past day, but there was no way to fix what I had done.

The days that followed brought similar feelings of sorrow and regret, and I wished I could stop wallowing in my grief, London's comments about my self-pitying behavior continuing to ring in my ears. I found myself going through the motions of my day, working on embroidery and handwriting, receiving music lessons, visiting the Chapel for afternoon prayer, reading in the evening, without any energy or enthusiasm. Cannan had now lifted some of the restrictions imposed upon Miranna and me, so that we could again go outside the Palace accompanied by our bodyguards, but I had no desire to do so.

London's shoes were impossible to fill, and regardless of how I spent my time, something was missing from my life. I longed for someone to whom I could talk, but though Tadark and Destari were constantly around, neither of them made particularly appealing candidates. Destari was probably feeling somewhat the same as I, for he was a good friend of London's, but he was reserved and stoic, and I did not know him well enough to open up to him. As for Tadark, he couldn't resist talking about how he never really trusted London, how there had been something sinister about him, something that just didn't make sense. It was ironic that the person I really wanted to talk to about this was, in fact, London.

Two weeks after London's dismissal, on the nineteenth of June, I strolled with my mother and Miranna past the Queen's Drawing

Room and out of the Palace into the east courtyard, accompanied by the Elite Guards assigned to the Queen. Every few months, my mother would invite twenty to thirty young Hytanican women of noble birth to a gathering at the Palace. The purpose of these gatherings was to continue our etiquette training by testing our social graces. Sometimes the gathering was a garden party, often times it was a tea party, and once a year it was a holiday party. Whether my mother and the older women who helped her evaluate our skills knew it or not, it was also always a gossip party.

This afternoon, the event was a garden party that coincided with Miranna's sixteenth birthday. As sixteen was not an age that held special significance to the Kingdom, it was not to be heralded with a Palace celebration as my seventeenth had been. Nevertheless, my mother had decided to take advantage of her regular gathering to include a small tribute to her youngest daughter.

The east courtyard had its own distinct attributes, different from both the central courtyard and the west courtyard. While the west courtyard was relatively unspoiled, with crabapple and cherry trees growing among the wildflowers that spread at will, the east courtyard was statelier, as it was often used by the Queen for social functions. The middle area of the courtyard was paved with multi-colored stone that formed concentric circles around a large two-tiered fountain. Trees had been planted around the perimeter of the circle to provide shade and to create a sense of privacy. Flowers grew profusely between the trees and the exterior walls. On a day such as today, the air was thick with perfume, water in the fountain sparkled in the sunlight as it splashed into its basin, and numerous birds sang as they sat among the oak and elm trees.

Five small tables, each with a white linen tablecloth and five place settings, stood in close proximity upon the paved stones. The young women who had been invited had already gathered and were twittering among themselves like exotically plumed birds as they awaited our arrival. Four older women were also present so that one adult could oversee each table to ensure that our manners were impeccable. Galen's mother, the lovely Lady Hauna, was in attendance with her demure seventeen-year-old daughters, Niani and Nadeja; the sensible Lady Edorra had accompanied her vivacious daughter Kalem, also seventeen; the exceedingly proper Lady Kadia had accompanied easily excited sixteen-year-old Noralee; and bubbly fourteen-year-old Semari had come with sedate Lady Alantonya.

Miranna and I wove our way through the guests with our mother, greeting each in turn. When at last she approached her table and stood behind her ornate chair, all of the women moved to the tables as well, observing proper protocol by remaining on their feet until after the Queen had seated herself.

The tea service itself was quite formal and somewhat orchestrated. Biscuits and sweet cakes were served along with the hot drink. We were expected to sit up straight, arms in to our sides, no leaning over the dishes or elbows upon the table. Gentle women took small bites and ate slowly, and did not talk or drink with food in their mouths. In addition, only particular subjects were appropriate for a lady's delicate sensibilities, but given the level of scrutiny we were under, we tended to speak only when necessary.

It was when the formal tea ended that the real conversation began. Released from the table, and enormously relieved if we had survived without being chastised, we would walk and talk amongst ourselves, gossiping freely while the adult women chatted with each other.

I stood among a group of ten acquaintances that included Galen's twin sisters and Steldor's cousin, Dahnath, all of whom were dying to discuss the latest developments with me. Today's primary topics were, of course, the discovery of the traitor in the Palace, and a review of the young men in the Kingdom who might be appropriate as a husband for me.

"Tell us, Alera," began Reveina, a bold and serious brunette who tended to be the leader of our circle, "how was the traitor discovered? Rumor has it that *you* were the one who detected him and turned him in to the Captain of the Guard."

I did not know how to answer. It had been information provided by me that had led to London's dismissal, but I, at least, did not regard him as a traitor. I decided that this would, however, be too complicated to explain.

"I had observed some activities that were relevant to the investigation and, I suppose, played a small part in the decision to dismiss London," I simply stated.

"He was your bodyguard!" blonde-haired Noralee blurted, sounding scandalized, for she generally found everything to be shocking. "Doesn't it give you pause to think of all the times you were alone in his company, not knowing he was a threat to the Royal Family?"

A strong urge to defend London rose within me, but at the same time, I wanted this conversation to end quickly.

"I never felt unsafe with him," I firmly stated. "And he was never proven to have betrayed the Royal Family. He was dismissed for dereliction of duty."

"So do *you* believe he aided the Cokyrian prisoner in her escape?" Reveina followed up, her dark eyes narrowed, choosing to ignore my explanation for London's dismissal.

"I don't know what I believe," I said truthfully.

Just then Miranna and Semari noisily joined our group, drawing attention away from me, and I dared to hope my ordeal had ended, as the girls all politely extended birthday greetings to my sister. Unfortunately, this reminded several of them of *my* recent birthday celebration, and the discussion shifted to an examination of the Kingdom's eligible young men and their relative qualifications to be King. Thane, Corwin, Mauston, Taldon and a dozen others were discussed, then discarded.

Finally, Reveina declared, "We all know that there really is only one candidate. We just don't want to give him up to you."

Amidst a burst of giggles, several eager voices murmured, "Lord Steldor." There were also several sighs, as the girls thought longingly of spending time in his company, although Dahnath rolled her eyes, likely tired of all the adoration heaped upon her cousin. Dahnath, an auburn-haired beauty, was the seventeen-year-old daughter of Cannan's younger brother, Baelic, and was known for both her kindness and her rather studious nature. She probably was not as easily taken in by Steldor's charm as were the other girls.

"He is divine," Reveina gushed, voicing a collective opinion, and all except Dahnath agreed. To my consternation, even Galen's sisters, who were blonde like their mother, but with the light brown eyes and carefree smile of their brother, enthusiastically agreed.

"You are so fortunate to have him among your choices… and to have attracted his attention as well. He could marry anyone he wanted, you know," Reveina enviously concluded.

"The way he looks at you," added Kalem, the most boy-obsessed of the young women my age, her alabaster skin shining radiantly. "I hope some day a young man looks at me in that way."

Again, many heads nodded in agreement. This last statement struck me dumb, as I had always viewed Steldor as coveting the Throne, rather than being interested in me personally.

"Oh, Alera, you really are naïve," Kalem laughed, tossing her coarse dark hair. "He swoons over you just as we swoon over him!"

Although I disliked Steldor intensely, her observation brought a satisfied smile to my face.

At that moment, Lady Edorra, Kalem's mother, approached, and we immediately fell silent.

"The Queen is preparing to depart," she primly stated, glaring knowingly down her nose at us, thereby ending the gossip.

Feeling that my life was not in need of further examination, I glanced at Miranna to convey my desire to leave, and she and I departed shortly after our mother. As we passed the guard room to the right of the Grand Staircase, our bodyguards fell into step with us, and Miranna caught my hand.

"How are you, really?" she sincerely asked. "London's absence must be hard to bear."

"It is hard to bear," I confessed. "Every time I turn a corner, I expect to hear a sarcastic comment about something, but only encounter silence. He's been with me most of my life, and I feel adrift without him. I guess I relied on him for many things other than protection."

"I can understand how terrible you must feel," Miranna said sympathetically. "Halias has always been my bodyguard. Part of my life would be lost if he weren't with me anymore. But I'm sure it will get better with time. And you will see London again, someday."

Halias had become Miranna's personal bodyguard on the day of her birth. He, London, and now Destari, shared similar styles, in that they liked to keep their distance from their charges, to give them privacy. Tadark, on the other hand, hovered much too closely to us, as proven by the fact that he was currently hanging off my elbow. Miranna, like I, had a second personal bodyguard, but she had been fortunate enough not to get stuck with a Tadark.

"I suppose I will see him again. But I just don't know how to feel right now. His absence is a great one, one that no one can fill." Merely saying the words caused me fresh pain.

Tadark, who had a million remarks about London on the tip of his tongue these days and was always looking for an opportunity to let them spill from his mouth, could no longer restrain himself.

"London left his post in the middle of the night! *I* would never do such a thing!" he exclaimed, as though his ego had been dealt an enormous insult. "There was always something about him. I saw it the first time I met him, I did!"

"Tadark," I said, mildly irritated. "This phrase is probably meaningless to you as it is so oft repeated, but do be quiet."

"London wasn't half the bodyguard I am!" He said it as though he were trying to convince himself that his statement were true.

"*Now,* please," I said, striving to keep my tone civil.

Tadark stared huffily at me, then dropped back to fall in step with our other guards. I glanced back in time to catch the glare he received from Destari.

"I don't know how much more of him I can tolerate," I whispered to Miranna, returning my attention to her, and her face told me she understood completely.

As we approached the spiral staircase at the back of the Palace, I decided to step out the rear entrance and stroll in the garden. Although Miranna would have walked with me, I assured her such was not necessary, preferring to be alone.

I ambled along the garden's pathways, letting my mind become still as I beheld the array of plants: the stately elm, ancient oak, chestnut, and mulberry trees that provided cooling shade; the pear, lime, and orange trees that supplied us with rare and unusual fruit; the abundant lilies, violets, tulips, carnations, and roses that plied the air with fragrance; and the section of herbs that provided seasoning for cooking, and medicine for injuries and illnesses. Of course, the glorious foliage also attracted a multitude of birds, including nightingales, doves, magpies, finches, robins, starlings and wrens, that visited the garden at various times of the year, or called it home.

By the end of the afternoon, my mood had significantly improved. Although I continued to ache for London's presence more than I had ever longed for anything before, the beauty of the garden had assuaged somewhat my disconsolate feelings and I slept well that night for the first time since London had been removed from the Palace.

Chapter Eight
A Good Catch

"Alera!"

A shrill and exhilarated voice jarred me from my sleep. I sat up groggily and slowly pulled my eyelids apart. The drapes on my window were drawn together, making my bedroom as dark as if the sun had not yet risen, but my noisy intruder saw fit to remedy that, flinging aside the window coverings so that I had to squint to keep from going blind.

"Miranna? What...?" My body still demanded rest, and my brain refused to work hard enough to form a complete sentence.

"Have you heard the news? You won't believe it!"

Miranna sounded elated, so I assumed that the *news* to which she referred was not something bad.

"This early in the morning, I'd believe just about anything," I said, sounding a bit raspy from my deep slumber. "What is it?"

"You simply won't believe it!" my sister repeated, bouncing up and down on her toes in excitement, her strawberry blonde curls dancing merrily about her face.

"Yes, we've covered that," I grumped, sitting up so I could more readily examine her.

"Try to guess. You'll never guess! This is *so* exciting!"

"Mira, can't you just tell me?"

Miranna put on a little pout, but only for a few seconds, then she slipped back into her lively mood.

"You're certainly not a morning person, are you?" she said mischievously, her blue eyes sparkling.

"No," I confirmed, with utmost seriousness. "I'm not. Tell me what this is about, or I'm going right back to sleep."

"Listen to this," she bubbled, lying down on her stomach atop my bed, propping her elbows so that her hands held her chin. "The servants are whispering about it. Our soldiers have captured another Cokyrian within Hytanican walls! Cannan is bringing him in today!"

Miranna had succeeded in arousing my interest.

"Are you positive?" I probed, concerned yet fascinated.

"After I heard the rumors, I talked to Halias to find out if they were true. He said, 'Another one has been arrested within the city, but you didn't hear that from me.'" She dropped her pitch to imitate Halias, sounding surprisingly accurate, and I wondered when my sister had become such a good mimic.

"Just hope he didn't hear you from the parlor," I teased.

All four of our bodyguards were likely standing somewhat self-consciously about the parlor as we gossiped in my bedroom.

Miranna waved my comment off with a grin. "So, are you up for a little sneakiness?"

I pretended to be aghast. "Me? A spy? Never!"

We both laughed as Miranna went on to explain how she planned to spend the whole day in the central courtyard, *inadvertently* being present when the prisoner was brought into the Palace. My curiosity was too great not to join her, though we both recognized that Halias, at least, would know exactly what we were doing.

"He'll be fine about it," Miranna assured me, swinging her legs off my bed to sit up straight. "It's not like a swordfight is going to break out in the middle of the courtyard. There will be no danger. Halias knows that. Though he'll probably expect us to hide to save his skin. If Cannan sees we're there, he'll have Halias's head!"

"Destari's, too," I agreed, knowing Cannan would assign the

blame to the older and more experienced of his Elite Guards.

I found myself feeling almost jealous of Miranna's good fortune in a bodyguard, as I had on a few other occasions. Halias, who was similar in height to London, but with twinkling blue eyes, a broad face, a ready smile, and soft, dark ash-blonde hair that fell to his shoulders when not pulled back into a ponytail, was irreproachable when it came to protecting my sister, but tended to make even someone as relaxed as London look tense. He had always given Miranna a lot of freedom, asserting that his job was only to keep her safe and not to raise her, and his easy-going attitude made him very approachable, as well as immensely popular as an escort. Like Destari and London, he was a veteran of the Cokyrian war, having served as a Palace Guard, and was credited with uncovering a plot to kill the King.

Tired of my sluggishness, Miranna impulsively pulled my blankets off of me.

"Come on," she said, slipping from the bed and tugging impatiently at my hand. "I haven't the faintest idea what time Cannan will be bringing the prisoner in. For all we know, we may have already missed it!"

Deciding not to call for my personal maid, I scrambled from my bed and dressed with my sister's assistance. As soon as I was prepared, we rushed from my quarters and into the corridor, followed by Destari, Tadark, Halias, and Miranna's secondary bodyguard, a reserved Elite Guard a few years older than Tadark named Orsiett.

As we hurried toward the courtyard, I felt vaguely unsettled about our enthusiasm. I knew we should not be this enthralled about finding our worst enemy within our homeland. We were acting like children, with no appreciation whatsoever for what this discovery might mean. But when I remembered the few but intriguing facts I had learned about Cokyri in the previous weeks, and what a stir the capture of our other Cokyrian prisoner had caused, I could not contain my inquisitiveness. The only Cokyrian I had ever seen was Nantilam, the High Priestess, and this new person would be of a completely different status. I wanted to know what he would be like, the style of his dress, if he were a servant or a master. I also knew that males were inferior to women in Cokyrian culture, and our new prisoner was, according to Miranna and her informants, a man.

A warm wind caressed my cheeks as we stepped into the central courtyard, a welcome reminder that summer had arrived. It was late June, and though just yesterday it had been cool and refreshing outdoors, this morning it was warm and humid, with a promise of blazing hot weather as the day wore on.

Hytanican summers were notorious for sweltering days, with light rain often falling in the evenings. The weather was predictable in a most uncanny way, which was good for the crops grown by the farmers in the villages surrounding the walled city, and ensured that the rolling hills that marked our western border lay draped in green.

We stayed in the courtyard for hours, until I felt faint from the heat and was ready to abandon our mission, but Miranna wouldn't hear of it.

"The minute you go inside," she said, "Cannan will come marching up to those gates with the prisoner, and you will miss it."

She was referring to the exterior gates that permitted entry into the courtyard. The gates were locked to commoners most hours of the day, open only for a short amount of time during which anyone who had not been banished from the Palace grounds or the Kingdom itself could seek counsel from the King.

All at once, Halias spoke up. "They're approaching now. If you don't want them to see you, you'd better hide — and not behind that cherry tree."

He motioned to the thin trunk of a young tree that Miranna was moving toward as though to conceal herself.

Miranna changed course, and she and I maladroitly crouched behind the lilac hedges, peering through the irregular gaps in the branches to where the wide stone path leading from the front gates to the steps of the Palace lay, dirt-free and so white from the sun's rays that it was almost painful to view. Our bodyguards seemingly vanished, as I supposed they had been trained to do.

Drawn by shouts and the sounds of milling horses, our heads snapped toward the gates and we restlessly waited for them to open. Within a few minutes, they swung inward and Cannan strode between them, looking extraordinarily grim. He then turned to wait for his troops to dismount, as no animals were permitted in the courtyard, for a single spooked horse could seriously damage its beauty. The mounts would be brought to the Royal Stables, where they would be fed and groomed while their riders attended to business.

As my eyes roved over the scene before me, the movement of a particular soldier caught my notice as he roughly pulled a man whose hands were tied together behind his back off one of the horses. This soldier and another then approached Cannan, holding the bound man by his arms between them.

"That's him!" Miranna whispered to me, having taken in the same action. She gripped my wrist in anticipation.

I could not see the prisoner's face from where we were hidden, but he was wearing the white shirt and sleeveless brown tunic that was typical of a Hytanican villager, and if I had not known he were Cokyrian, I never would have guessed it. Nothing about him that I could see would have set him apart from all the other villagers frequenting the streets and businesses of our Kingdom.

I went behind Miranna and, continuing to stoop, moved down the line of bushes to the far end, so I could peer out to get a better glimpse of the man held captive between the large guards. As the gates closed and Cannan turned to lead his troops forward, I gained a more distinct view of the prisoner's face, and hastily stifled a gasp, for our prisoner was not a man, but a teenage boy. He held his head high, as though unafraid, but the way his eyes occasionally flitted between the guards at his sides and Cannan before him gave away his unease. His hair was thick and many shades of gold, as though the sun had unevenly bleached it. It was cut about an inch below his ears, and his bangs, which were slightly shorter, fell haphazardly over his forehead.

Miranna, plainly as astounded as I, moved to crouch next to me.

"He can't be any older than I am!" she exclaimed.

I cast my gaze behind the guards, and all thoughts of the Cokyrian youth left my mind as I caught sight of the light but confident stride, the muscular frame, the twin double-edged blades sheathed at the hips, the untidy silver hair partially obscuring mysterious indigo eyes — London was there, walking at the forefront of a half dozen soldiers as though he were one of them.

"What is he doing here?" I asked aloud, more to myself than to my sister.

"Who?" Miranna queried, obviously too enthralled by the young Cokyrian prisoner to observe anything else.

"London," I responded, pointing.

Miranna's gaze followed the invisible line stretching from my finger and landed on London, and I saw astonishment break over her face as well.

"What *is* he doing here?" She sounded as much at a loss as was I.

With no available answer, we returned our attention to the approaching soldiers, and it was then, as I studied the Cokyrian captive, that I noticed his eyes. They were steel blue, sharp and intense. Although his sun-tanned face had a youthful glow, his eyes were cold and unfriendly, as though he had vast experience in the world, and was now expecting the worst.

I unconsciously stooped lower as the troops passed. I watched in awe as London strode toward the Palace following the prisoner, just a few yards away from me, oblivious to my presence, and an unexpected flood of emotions threatened to overwhelm me — regret, guilt, sorrow, shame, and love for the man before me. The urge to run to him once again surfaced, and I had to turn away, though Miranna continued to watch, entranced, until the soldiers had passed between the thick wooden Palace doors.

"Curious about London?" said Destari's deep, resonating voice from behind, startling me so that I wheeled around. Miranna did the same, and we saw Destari and Halias crouching on the ground behind us.

Hearing the sound of booted feet scraping against bark, I turned my head to see Tadark tumble out of an oak tree, falling to the ground gracelessly and landing painfully on his rear end. He let out a wounded groan, and was unsympathetically shushed by Orsiett, who was walking up behind him.

Everyone stared incredulously at Tadark for a moment.

"Making furry friends up in the tree, were you?" Halias jibed, his blue eyes alight.

"No," Tadark sulked. "I wanted to see what was going on."

"Oh, now I understand!" Halias laughed. "You're a *scenery* guard, not a bodyguard!"

"Halias, we've been mistaken all this time," Destari added in his deep rumble, unable to pass up the fun. "It's not the Royal Family we're supposed to protect, it's the Royal Foliage!"

Tadark's cheeks burned and he bitterly muttered, "Leave me alone. You've made your point."

I watched the three guards in amusement, surprised to see Destari, who was usually quite serious, teasing Tadark as London would have done, and it struck me that Tadark somehow drew jests from people like a flower drew bees.

Destari returned his attention to me, and I suppressed my mirth in order to repeat my question.

"What is London doing here? Isn't he banished from the Palace grounds?" I forced out the words with some effort, as though the banishment would cease to be true if I refused to say it.

Destari opened his mouth to speak, but was interrupted by Tadark's moans as he inched closer to where the four of us sat, pulling himself along the ground as though in agony.

"Are you trying to make that inchworm feel good about itself?"

Halias ridiculed, pointing to a slow-moving specimen that was nonetheless crawling faster than Tadark across the grass.

Tadark made a noise that sounded like *humph*, and continued to scoot along.

"I think I broke something," he mumbled unhappily.

As he reached another tree, he sat up and leaned against its trunk, then plucked a blade of grass and began to fiddle with it between his fingers. Orsiett stopped by Tadark and also sat down, presumably too intimidated by the older guards to join us.

Destari chuckled, noticing as we all were that Tadark was monitoring the greenery rather than his charge, more or less proving Halias' statement to be true.

"You wanted to know about London, right?" Destari finally said.

I nodded earnestly.

"He's here because he is the one who discovered the Cokyrian in the city. He went to the Captain at his home and asked that in exchange for handing over the prisoner, he be allowed an audience with the King."

I made a noise of affirmation, for everything suddenly made sense.

"But how did he find that boy when no one else could, when the search of the Kingdom by all of Cannan's soldiers turned up nothing?" Miranna was bewildered.

Halias and Destari furtively glanced at each other, as if they were trying to judge how much they should tell us.

"During the war," Destari finally said, "London saw much of the Cokyrians. I suppose he developed a keener eye for Cokyrian mannerisms than the average foot soldier."

Miranna nodded, satisfied with the explanation. Unbeknownst to the guards, however, and thanks to my mother, I was mindful of the real reason London had greater knowledge of Cokyri than did anyone else.

~ ~ ~

Suspicion and apprehension rippled through the Palace that afternoon like the swift rapids of the river, but I cared not. I waited nervously outside the Throne Room, faint, inarticulate voices barely reaching my ears.

Miranna and I had eaten together, then she had left, as the day was getting late and she had other tasks to undertake. After we had parted ways, I had entered the antechamber, and I now paced ceaselessly, too anxious to sit down and too agitated to stand still.

As always, my bodyguards were with me. Destari leaned against the wall next to the door into the Grand Entry in London's characteristic posture, while Tadark stood uncomfortably in the middle of the room, shifting his weight from foot to foot. As he winced in pain, I remembered with some sympathy his fall from the tree, or, more to the point, his not-so-gentle landing.

Though neither spoke, I wished I could be alone. Even the dull sound of Tadark's fidgeting in the otherwise quiet room was a distraction to me, and though I very much needed to think, I seemed to have lost the ability to do so.

The time I might have had for reflection, however, was cut short by the creaking of the Throne Room doors as they were pulled open from the inside. London stepped between them and immediately took note of me, although his reaction to my presence was difficult to discern.

"Princess," he formally greeted me, tilting his head in respect as he came to a halt.

"Please, let's not start where we left off," I beseeched, wanting to avoid the pattern of our earlier quarrel.

An awkward silence followed, the only sound the breathing of the others in the antechamber, but I gratefully realized that the lack of a heated reply meant London's hurt had eased somewhat.

"You spoke with my father?" I finally chanced.

London nodded gravely, but did not otherwise answer.

"I hear you made a good catch," I nervously continued. "Is he pleased?"

"He is."

"And?"

"Your father is not a forgiving man."

I dropped my eyes to the stone floor. I knew it had been a fool's hope that London might be given his life back based on this one deed, but against my will, my heart had become set upon it. It was the only thing that could possibly begin to heal London of the betrayal I had dealt him, but any such hope had now been shattered by my father's obstinacy and mistrust. There was only one thing I could think to say.

"And you, London? Are you a forgiving man?"

"Some might say so." He said this in a way that was very near lighthearted, as if he meant to make me feel better. Then his tone darkened almost imperceptibly. "But some things are not so easily forgiven."

I managed to hold his gaze, though my head felt heavy with shame, and searched his familiar face for something more.

"London... I'm sorry." I did not elaborate, hoping my simple words would suffice.

"I know," he said dispassionately, and an uneasy silence fell between us.

London's eyes flicked to Destari, who was no longer leaning against the wall, likely having straightened the moment my former bodyguard had come into the room.

"I must go now," he said, then he crossed to his friend to say a few words before stepping into the Grand Entry Hall.

As London left, a sinking feeling of uncertainty as to when I would next see him once more overwhelmed me, and I waited for Destari to turn to me. Destari knew London better than anyone, and I desperately hoped to receive some reassurance from him.

"Will he ever forgive me?" I moaned as Destari's eyes met mine.

"I cannot say," he said evasively, black eyes murky and unrevealing. "London does not trust easily, and he does not forgive easily when his trust has been betrayed."

I pondered Destari's words for a moment, convinced he was hiding something.

"You speak as though you know of some other betrayal. Help me to understand him so that I can learn how best to seek his pardon," I implored.

Destari glanced warily at Tadark, indicating he did not want to speak in his presence.

"Tadark," I said sharply. "Remove yourself to the Entry Hall. We will be but a minute."

Tadark obeyed without comment, although he looked sullenly at the older guard as he hobbled from the room.

Destari cautiously assessed me as he tried to decide whether he should confide in me.

"I already know London was a prisoner of the Cokyrians during the war," I disclosed, hoping to persuade him. "If this relates to that time, you needn't keep anything from me."

Destari's heavy eyebrows rose slightly, and I knew he had expected me to be ignorant of London's history. After a few more moments of deliberation, he capitulated.

"The betrayal of which I am about to speak is related to that period in his life."

"Go on, please," I urged.

"Before London was imprisoned by the Cokyrians, he was betrothed to a young woman of noble birth," he stated simply.

Destari halted at my stunned expression. While I knew London had never married, I had always assumed that his devotion to the military had left little time for a personal life. Destari's revelation reconfirmed how paltry was my knowledge of London, and a crushing sense of remorse hit me at the thought that I had always been too self-absorbed to even be curious. I took a deep, steadying breath, waiting for my bodyguard to elaborate. With a measure of concern, he stepped forward and lightly gripped my elbow, directing me to an armchair. When I had seated myself, he resumed his tale, voice strangely hollow.

"A couple of months into London's captivity, the parents of his betrothed determined to have her marry another, as London was believed dead. She had already been pledged to him for a year-and-a-half, and her parents worried that at age twenty-two, her marriage prospects were becoming limited. She at first refused, as she was very much in love with London, but in the end, acquiesced to her parents' wishes. She was married to a much older man about two months before London's escape.

"As I assume you know, London was deathly ill upon his return to Hytanica, and so he did not immediately learn of any of this. When he was well enough to communicate, he began to ask for her, and it fell to me to tell him of her circumstances."

Destari rubbed the back of his neck as though he were reliving the unhappy memory.

"He did not take the news well, and I feared he might not be strong enough to survive this second trial. He was withdrawn for a long time, and in truth never came fully back to himself, becoming more guarded than he once was."

Destari sounded weary, as if just telling the story were exhausting.

"He has not, since that time, permitted himself to form deep attachments. Or at least, he has *tried* not to form strong attachments, but he did not count on the feelings he would develop for you as a result of being your bodyguard." Destari paused, shifting uncomfortably, before finishing, "London never really forgave his betrothed for doubting his return, and I don't know that he will ever really forgive you for doubting his loyalty."

I stared numbly at Destari, momentarily too overwhelmed by London's tragic past to respond. Finally regaining the ability to speak, I softly prompted, "Who was she?"

Destari frowned, then shook his head. "That is not for me to say. Perhaps someday London will be inclined to tell you."

I continued to stare at Destari, biting my lip as I debated whether to ask him the question upon which I had unendingly dwelt since London's dismissal from the military. Finally, I risked his anger.

"We both know London recognized the High Priestess. Do you think he released her?"

As I had expected, Destari glowered darkly at me.

"I don't know whether he released her or not, nor do I care. London has always acted in Hytanica's best interests, and if he did release her, he had good reason. He is not and never has been a traitor, and I would follow him without hesitation, even to my death."

I shrank under his glare, feeling horribly small and pitiful, for I did not have the same ability as Destari to simply take things on faith.

Destari and I left the antechamber in weighty silence, to be rejoined by Tadark in the Grand Entry. I could tell by Tadark's sulky expression that he was unhappy about having been excluded from our conversation, but he silently fell into step with us. Returning to my quarters, I prepared for bed, emotionally drained. As I lay inert in the darkness, beginning to drift toward sleep, I heard Destari's and Tadark's faint bickering. The only thing I could make out was Destari saying, "*My* sofa, *your* armchair."

Chapter Nine
Clandestine Meeting

I awoke later than usual the following morning and dressed with the assistance of my personal maid, Sahdienne, who had just brought my breakfast to my quarters. I entered the parlor to see Tadark standing by the table upon which the serving tray had been set, as though he had been ordered to guard the Princess' meal instead of the Princess herself, but Destari's looming form was absent. As Sahdienne departed, I took my breakfast tray and went to sit in one of the burgundy velvet armchairs.

"Where is Destari?" I asked, removing the cloth that covered my food to keep it warm, the delicious aroma of freshly baked bread and scrambled eggs wafting up to greet me.

"He was sent for by the Captain of the Guard early this morning," Tadark responded, still lingering by the table.

"For what purpose was he summoned?" I pressed, justifiably concerned in light of recent happenings.

"I don't know — I wasn't told anything," he said, trying to act nonchalant, although I could tell he was bothered by the fact that he had once again been left out of a meeting.

I shrugged and continued to eat my breakfast, hoping to conceal that my insatiable hunger for Palace politics was building.

Just as I put my utensils down upon my empty plate, there was a knock and Tadark opened the door. Destari entered and I could contain my curiosity no more.

"The last time I awoke to find one of my bodyguards missing, the outcome was disastrous," I said, somehow making a small joke out of London's dismissal. "I would like to know what's going on." I stood and walked toward the tall man, placing my tray back upon the table it had originally occupied.

"I'm to inform you that I am no longer your bodyguard," Destari answered, giving me a slight bow.

"And are you to inform me as to the reason you have been removed?"

I had grown a bit tired of Cannan and my father making decisions that directly affected me without even bothering to offer me an explanation.

"I was not instructed to tell you anything further," he rumbled, "but I suppose there is no harm in telling you that I've been given a new assignment."

An involuntary shudder rippled through my body as it came to me that with London gone and Destari re-assigned, I might end up with Tadark as my only bodyguard.

"Couldn't *someone else*—" I tipped my head toward Tadark, subtly hinting that I meant him, "—be given this new task?"

Destari shook his head slowly as he caught my meaning. "I'm afraid this is much too important to be entrusted to *someone else*."

I frowned in annoyance. "What is this assignment?"

"Perhaps you should raise your question with the Captain or your father," Destari suggested uncomfortably.

"I'm asking *you*." I adamantly put my hands on my hips. "I will learn what this is about one way or another, Destari. You may as well save me the trouble and tell me now."

He seemed unwilling to relent, but at the same time, appeared to recognize that his attempts at secrecy would be futile in the end.

"Have you not wondered where we are holding the Cokyrian prisoner?"

I heard Tadark shuffling around by the door and saw his eyes shift to Destari's face, his interest also captured by Destari's words.

"In the dungeon, I would presume," I said, already unsure of my statement as I read Destari's face.

"Do you see your father as the type of man who would imprison in such a place a boy of the same age as his youngest child?"

"No," I said, considering his words carefully. "Is it safe then to assume that he is being housed somewhere in the Palace proper?"

"That would be a fair assumption."

"And can I also assume that he will be guarded by someone with great experience?"

"That also is a reasonable conclusion."

I nodded gratefully. "One last thing, then."

Destari scowled at me as if asking what else I could possibly demand of him.

"Will I be assigned a new secondary bodyguard?"

"I'm afraid not," Destari responded with a knowing and sympathetic smile. "The Captain has decided that the measure of security we've been maintaining is no longer necessary, as... the traitor... has been identified. The members of the Royal Family will once again have only one bodyguard and he will return to a normal daily routine. Tadark will become your permanent guard."

I contained my groan of misery with some effort. I was relieved, however, that Tadark would no longer be protecting me twenty-four hours a day, as he was a bit more tolerable when taken in smaller doses.

"Well," I said, trying to sound lighthearted. "I appreciate that you took the time to tell me of your change in duty."

"You're welcome," Destari courteously replied, then he bowed and turned to leave.

"Wait!" Tadark cried sharply. "Aren't you going to tell us about your new assignment?"

Destari stared at him as though no expression he could form upon his face would quite convey what he was feeling, then walked out the door without another word.

~　～　~

I saw nothing of Destari or the Cokyrian prisoner as the days continued to pass, though I supposed the boy was being held in one of the guest rooms on the third floor of the Palace, away from the areas the Royal Family frequented. My father and Cannan could often be seen in deep discussion, most likely about their unexpectedly young captive, though they never said anything in my presence about what they intended to do with him. If not for Destari, I would have believed the boy to be starving in the dungeon with our other prisoners, though it should have occurred to me that my compassionate father would not allow a child to be confined within those dank walls. My father and Cannan needed to interrogate their captive, yet they would not want to subject him to torture.

As I considered these things, I felt relieved that I, unlike my father, did not have to make judgments as to the prisoner. He was young, yes, but also a Cokyrian, and though they would not treat him unkindly for the first reason, neither could they trust him. Hytanicans had only ever encountered Cokyrian adults and no one could imagine what this boy was doing here, if the Cokyrians had sent him as a spy or a messenger, or if he had for some reason fled his homeland. I was, of course, also frustrated by the lack of information I had been able to gather, but I supposed that this situation was held in stricter confidence than even the investigation of the Elite Guard had been. It was unlikely Steldor would know about this, I had been thankful to deduce, as it saved me from having to suffer through another afternoon with him.

On the morning of the fourth day after Destari had been assigned as the young Cokyrian's guard, I headed to the library, desiring a location to think where Tadark might hold his tongue. I was brimful of questions, yet could not concentrate, as Tadark was still bent on talking about London's incompetence. In fact, Tadark was in the middle of a tirade about London when I strolled into the library.

"Once in a while I would see a glint in London's eyes almost as though he were taunting me," Tadark was saying, and I fought the urge to tell him outright that London had actually *been* taunting him, when I saw my sister.

Miranna was sitting on the padded window seat across the room from me with her friend Semari, whom I had not known was visiting us in the Palace. They were quite clearly gossiping about something, because their voices were low and occasionally one of them would clap a hand over her mouth, aghast at something the other had said. They abruptly stopped talking, aware that someone had entered the library, and turned their heads in my direction to see who it might be.

"Come here, Alera!" Miranna said delightedly, waving me over with her hand. "We were just discussing the latest scandals!"

I smiled and moved toward the window, ready to contribute heartily to their conversation. When Tadark made to follow me, I waved him off with my hand, and he instead joined Halias by the fireplace.

"Miranna has just been telling me about the Cokyrian prisoner," Semari said as I settled into an armchair, her clear blue eyes glistening. "She claims he is very handsome."

She and Miranna giggled, and I readily concurred. The prisoner was undeniably attractive, though in a much different way from Steldor. Steldor had a polished style, with classic good looks and sophisticated taste. The Cokyrian was unique, with eyes that entranced in a moment, and a young but extraordinarily worldly face. While I had only seen him once, I sensed a deepness within him that Steldor would never possess. Not wanting to share any of these thoughts, I attempted to redirect the discussion to something of greater appeal to me.

"What do you suppose he is doing here?"

Semari did not share my interest.

"I don't care much about that," she scoffed. "But I do so want to meet him and ask him about Cokyri. I want to know what it's like there. I've never been into the desert lands of the east, or into the mountains, and can't imagine what it must be like to live in such a forbidding place."

"He can't be dangerous as are the adults of his kind, so it would be safe to talk with him, wouldn't it?" Miranna vigorously agreed. "He may well be our only chance to learn firsthand about the Cokyrians!"

Semari sat quietly, gnawing distractedly on a fingernail. Although she was almost a year and a half younger than my sister, her bubbly nature and love of all things feminine had made her Miranna's ideal match.

"What are you thinking?" Miranna asked.

Semari sighed in frustration, having discovered a fault in whatever she had been working over in her mind.

"We could never get to him in the dungeon. With all the guards down there, it would be impossible!"

I laughed to myself, as I knew something they did not. I bent forward and motioned for them to lean toward me, so I could murmur conspiratorially in their ears.

"Are you serious?" Miranna asked incredulously when I had finished.

I gave a self-assured nod.

Semari was gleeful.

"This is perfect," she gushed. "I know exactly what to do."

We huddled together so that our foreheads almost touched, and began to surreptitiously plot a way to meet the prisoner.

Semari, as had been planned for her visit, spent the night with Miranna, and the next morning we put our scheme into action. In order to discover where the prisoner was being kept, I chanced a visit to the guest wing that comprised the east half of the Palace's third floor. As I thought it probable that the Cokyrian was being housed in one of the rooms at the rear of the Palace, I avoided using my family's private stairway, instead using the stairwell located just off the second floor landing of the Grand Staircase to gain access to the upper floor. Although there were generally no guards posted on the third floor unless guests were occupying the rooms, I did not want to emerge from the spiral stairway and blunder into Destari.

My mission was to lurk in the guest wing for as long as it took to locate the prisoner's room, then return to the library where Miranna and Semari would be passing the time. The only disquiet I felt about my task was due to Tadark's constant and clinging company, but he became a potential obstacle only once.

"I don't understand what we're doing here," he said, bored with my chosen activity, or more precisely, lack of activity.

"You don't have to understand, Tadark. You just have to keep your mouth closed," I retorted.

"Are you doing something you're not supposed to be doing?" he asked distrustfully. "Destari said something about guest rooms..."

"I implore you to be quiet ...Tad," I needled, remembering how much he despised the moniker.

"Don't call me that." Tadark's brown eyes had narrowed resentfully.

"If you stop talking *right now*, I'll never call you Tad again."

He nodded, then stood back from me, and no further comments escaped from between his tightly compressed lips.

"Now, stay here," I instructed. "I will be back momentarily."

Tadark shrugged sulkily, for once content to do as he was told.

The guest wing contained seven rooms, five of which were located along exterior walls, and two of which were windowless interior rooms. A corridor led all the way through the wing so that I could start where I now stood and travel past all of the rooms, arriving back at my point of beginning.

I walked to the west, then turned north into the corridor that divided the guest wing from the servant's quarters. Coming to the end of the hall, I stealthily leaned around the corner to the right to peer down its length, looking for Destari. He stood with his back toward me outside the nearest of the two interior rooms, seemingly large enough to block the entire corridor. Though there was no sign of his charge, I had to assume I had discovered where the Cokyrian was being held. I considered the location, realizing that it made sense to house our captive in one of the windowless rooms.

I retreated to the front stairwell, and descended the steps to return to the second floor, Tadark trotting obediently behind. I hastened past the King's Dining Hall, then continued toward the library at the rear of the Palace, where I was to collect Miranna and Semari. They were seated together on the wide sill of the bay window when I entered, with Halias in front of them in an armchair, patiently indulging their desire to braid pieces of his long, blonde hair.

"Miranna, Semari, come with me!" I called eagerly. "I have something to show you!" They knew by my words that I had located Destari and the captive.

Semari and Halias stood, but Miranna remained seated for a moment longer, the brightness of her smile dimming slightly.

"Are you alright?" Halias asked as he moved his chair off to the side of the window, sounding a bit worried.

"Yes, I'm fine," she murmured. "Just a bit dizzy."

She got to her feet and began to cross the room with Semari.

"Now, what is it you have to show..."

Without further warning, Miranna collapsed, falling limply like a rag doll in the middle of the large rug on the library floor, her sentence left unfinished. I rushed forward, dropping to my knees at her side.

"Mira!" I cried, panic in my voice.

She lay on her side and her limbs began to quake, violent shivers soon consuming her whole body. Nonsense tumbled from her mouth in the same way it had when she had suffered similar attacks as a little girl. Semari was standing with her back to the library wall, her face stricken. Halias was at Miranna's other side in an instant, his blue eyes darting wildly between me and my sister, as this was not a danger from which he could provide protection. It had been twelve years since Miranna's last attack, and none of us was any better prepared to handle the situation over a decade later.

"Tadark!" I called to my horrified bodyguard, who was frozen by the door. "Fetch Bhadran! Tell him it's Miranna!"

Tadark raced from the room, off to find the doctor who attended the Royal Family.

"Quickly," I said to Halias, my words catching in my throat. "Find my mother."

Halias followed Tadark out the door without a backward glance, and Semari scurried after him to peek into the corridor.

"They're gone!" she whispered, turning to face me.

Miranna stayed her spasms and sat up, whereupon I helped her to her feet.

"We don't have long," I reminded them. "So we have to hurry."

Semari rushed out the door, her face flushed with excitement. Miranna and I followed, and, having successfully eluded our bodyguards, the three of us hastened south through the corridor toward the front of the Palace, then up the stairs I had previously used to reach the third floor. As I led our trio out of the stairwell, I turned east, then crept north until we could peer to our left around the far corner to observe the prisoner's room.

Semari retreated to the southern end of the corridor as Miranna and I ducked into a vacant guest room. It wasn't long before Semari let out an ear piercing scream. A few seconds passed and then we heard another.

As we had intended, Destari came hurtling around the corner to investigate, swiftly going past the room in which my sister and I were hiding and giving us the chance to slip out undiscovered. I clasped Miranna's hand and we moved stealthily through the corridor as Destari searched for the source of the screams.

I went directly to the door Destari had been guarding and turned the handle, stepping quickly inside. Miranna came in behind me, pushing the door with her hand so that it swung shut.

The Cokyrian was sitting cross-legged atop the bed in the sparsely furnished room, one of his hands shackled to the bedpost, but despite this, looking more relaxed than the last time I had seen him. He had bathed and changed into different clothing, black trousers and a loose white shirt, both of which were too big for him, the cumulative effect of which was to make him appear even younger. The only items on his person that were probably his own were the belt about his waist and the well-worn boots upon his feet.

He looked up when we entered, his deep blue eyes immediately appraising us, the lift in his eyebrows the only reaction to our unorthodox visit. In that instant, my tongue failed me. I had been concentrating so heavily on executing our plan that I had not given a single thought as to what I would say should we prove successful.

For a long and agonizing moment, Miranna and I stared at him, and he stared back at us. Finally, I introduced myself the way I would have to anyone else.

"Excuse our intrusion," I said, trying my best to sound pleasant and not unsure of myself. "I am Princess Alera of Hytanica, and this is my sister, Princess Miranna." I motioned to Miranna, who was standing beside me. "We deemed it time to greet our guest."

He continued to sit still, impassively assessing us.

"Forgive me for being forward, Your Highnesses, but I was under the impression that I am more of a prisoner than a guest," he finally said, voice smooth and polite.

"Prisoner or otherwise, you cannot deny that you are being treated kindly," I replied. "Since we have already introduced ourselves, common courtesy would dictate that you do the same."

He did not respond immediately, watching us warily, as if determining whether we represented some new interrogation technique.

"I am called Narian," he finally answered, though with a hint of suspicion.

"It's nice to meet you, Narian," I said.

Miranna had not yet uttered a word, apparently too stupefied that our strategy had worked to enter the conversation. She was not to be given the chance to speak, for at that moment, the door flew open, and Miranna and I just managed to avoid being hit. Destari stood in the corridor, face livid, black eyes glittering like shards of glass, grasping Semari's wrist in his left hand. He pulled her into the room behind him, glaring fiercely at everyone present, excluding Narian, who was obviously not at fault in creating the existing circumstances.

"What were you *thinking*?" Destari boomed angrily. "I would never have expected such rash behavior from any of you — especially you two!" he said, aiming his tirade at Miranna and me. "*Princesses*! Whatever made you try something this brainless? And just how were you planning to slip back out once you were inside? Did you actually imagine yourselves getting away with something as childish and irresponsible as this? You should be ashamed!"

He continued his rant for a moment longer, then stopped, as no one was listening to him. My sister and I were gaping at Semari and Narian, who were staring transfixed at each other. Though Semari's blonde hair was lighter and her skin fairer, their faces were strikingly similar, with full lips, straight noses and softly arching eyebrows. Their eyes, too, were a similar shade of blue, though Narian's were cold and unfriendly in contrast to Semari's, which were bright and innocent. The resemblance was so strong, in fact, that once I saw them together, I couldn't believe it had passed my notice.

"Kyenn?" Semari said tentatively, almost shyly.

Destari abruptly stepped forward.

"I'm taking you to the Captain of the Guard," he declared. "All of you."

Destari unshackled Narian, then marched us out of the room and west through the corridor toward the spiral staircase, keeping a distrustful hand on Narian's shoulder the entire way. As we approached the landing, we ran into Halias, who had evidently caught on to some of our plan and was not the least bit amused; and Tadark, who was quite perplexed, as he had not yet figured out what was going on.

"Destari!" Halias exclaimed in unmistakable relief when he saw the tall guard accompanying us. He approached, his relief instantly suffused by anger. "Where did you find them?" he growled, glaring pointedly at Miranna, Semari and me.

"In the prisoner's room," Destari fumed, his black hair and heavy brows making him especially formidable. "They took it upon themselves to meet him."

Halias gave Miranna a glower that would have made me tremble, but she only gave him a sheepish grin, peering apologetically up at him through lowered lashes.

Finally figuring out what we had done, Tadark gasped. He then glared at me, in an attempt to match Halias' look of disapproval, but it did not have nearly the same effect. I smiled serenely at him, and he widened his light brown eyes as if to intensify his enraged stare, but with his round, boyish face, only succeeded in making himself appear all the more ridiculous.

Halias continued to hold Miranna in his heated gaze as he informed Destari of the details of our grand scheme.

"Bhadran and the Queen are in the library, waiting for us to return," he finished.

"Then we should go to them at once," Destari concluded.

Halias moved to Miranna's side and Tadark to mine, as we descended the stairway and proceeded toward the door into the library, Destari following behind us with Narian. I was glad that, after my mother and father, it was Tadark to whom I would have to answer and not London. I hated to think what London's reaction to our plot would have been. I shuddered and pushed the extremely unpleasant notion from my mind.

We arrived in the library far too quickly for my liking. My mother and Bhadran rose from armchairs by the window the moment we entered, but did not speak. My mother was shaking her head at Miranna and me in disapproval, and I could not meet her gaze for shame.

Destari stopped by the door, not relinquishing his grip on Narian's shoulder, and motioned for Halias to join them. The two guards had a whispered exchange, and several times Halias glanced from Narian to Semari, who was standing meekly beside me examining the floor. As they finished, Halias seized Narian's upper arm and guided him toward the window seat. Pulling an armchair several feet away from where my mother and the doctor stood, he roughly pushed Narian into it.

"Sit," he commanded.

After Destari had departed to find Cannan, and Halias had replaced him temporarily as Narian's guard, my mother walked regally over to where Semari, Miranna and I stood bunched in the middle of the rug. Although she was as composed as ever, I couldn't help but dread what she would say to us.

"Miranna, tell me that you did not fake this entire thing," she said reprovingly, referring to the seizure Miranna had earlier appeared to suffer.

Miranna hung her head, her coppery-blonde hair falling forward like a veil.

"I'm sorry, Mother, but I cannot tell you that," she almost inaudibly said.

"I do not understand the three of you," my mother grimly continued, although she did not raise her voice above a conversational level. "What could possibly have possessed you?"

"We only wanted to see what he was like," Miranna replied, her face still obscured.

"We... weren't really thinking at all," I apologetically conceded, hoping my mother, who had recently told me of her own irrepressible girlhood curiosity, might sympathize with our desire.

"You're right. You didn't think this through at all." Her voice was devoid of its usual lyrical quality, and her blue eyes sparked in a rare display of anger. "We know *nothing* about this boy! You marched right into his room without a single guard to protect you. Do you not see how reckless you were?"

"He's my age, Mother!" Miranna protested. "What could he have done?"

Miranna had never been the type to accept that she had been wrong in her actions, and so she argued, often times making the situation worse for everyone involved. I fought for things I knew to be right, but was willing to acknowledge my errors. In this instance, we had not only crossed the line, but had left it far behind, and Miranna's audacity was completely intolerable.

"Foolish child!" my mother admonished, somehow sounding incredibly formidable while keeping her voice low so that no one could hear except we three. "If he were a Hytanican boy, he would be in his third year at the Military Academy! We do not know how they train their warriors in Cokyri, but if he had intended to do you harm, I believe he could have done so. You haven't the faintest idea with whom you are dealing. He is *Cokyrian!* None of you were alive during the war, but perhaps if you had been you would comprehend how brashly you acted today. If you had seen the death, the agony — if you had lost your entire family to those cold-blooded creatures as I did when I was young, then maybe you would have thought twice before entering that room."

Semari, Miranna and I stood still as death, barely daring to breathe, my mother's tongue-lashing somehow more painful than a physical form of punishment would have been.

"Your behavior calls for apologies to your bodyguards," she primly finished. "And I would strongly suggest that you seek forgiveness in the Chapel and say a prayer for better judgment in the future."

My mother turned from us and approached the doctor to tell him he had been called without good cause. After receiving her apologies, Bhadran bowed respectfully. Then he took his leave, shaking his graying head reproachfully as he passed us on his way out the library door. My mother reseated herself, and we glumly moved to stand beside her, eyes cast downward. Time passed in strained silence, then Narian spoke, quietly, but assertively, and I became aware for the first time that he spoke with a subtle accent.

"Why did you address me in that way before?" he asked. "Who is Kyenn?"

Semari tore her eyes from her hands and stared at him, hope illuminating her face, which was so uncannily similar to his own. I could draw no other conclusion than the one I knew was spinning in the minds of everyone around me.

Semari opened her mouth, but Halias cut her off.

"Don't say anything, Semari," he said brusquely. "There will be no conversing with the prisoner until the Captain arrives."

As if on cue, the library door swung open and Cannan strode in, followed closely by Destari, the dark and imposing bearing of the two men casting a further pall over the room. All attention shifted to the Captain of the Guard, but he said nothing, merely stopping to stand in the center of the rug. He first studied Semari, then shifted focus to Narian, then back to Semari, and again to Narian, his expression ponderous.

Destari, who had stepped up beside him, gravely asked, "What do you make of this, sir?"

"There is a clear likeness between them," Cannan allowed.

"Can it be?" Halias echoed, momentarily too distracted to use proper military protocol, but finally adding, "Captain?"

"I cannot think of another explanation. The King must be notified."

Chapter Ten
Back From the Dead

Rumors spread from person to person within the castle like a disease, stirring up questions and speculations that became my only source of information. My father was furious with both Miranna and me, but he was preoccupied with settling the issue of the Cokyrian boy's possible identity, and had not yet taken the time to discipline us. For this, I was exceptionally grateful.

The day after we had executed our plan, Semari had arrived back at the Palace with her parents. Neither Miranna nor I had been in attendance when they had met with Cannan and my father, and I had not since then been able to discover exactly what had transpired.

Miranna longed to speak with Semari, but she was afraid to ask Father's permission to pay her friend a visit lest she remind him that he had not yet dealt with us. I, too, wanted to know what had been determined about Narian, but the only people from whom I could receive accurate information were in the military, and none among them would be willing to speak with me.

My thirst for knowledge was likewise not to be quenched by my father, who finally broke away from his duties to deal with his errant daughters. He came to my quarters during the early hours of the morning, before undertaking his duties as King.

Tadark had reported to his post and was waiting in the corridor to learn of my schedule for the day. He rapped upon my door, then opened it to announce my father, who came in, looking unusually grim. I had just emerged from my bedroom into the parlor, and was sitting upon my sofa, brushing my long, dark brown hair. The humid morning air already had a stifling quality, which I felt even more keenly upon my father's arrival. I set down the brush and stood upon his entrance, but he bade me sit with his hand.

"Your actions of this past week have greatly disappointed me, Alera," he said, with little emotion. "I have lost much confidence in your decision-making."

"I know, Father," I said remorsefully, not dropping my head as I had done with my mother but meeting his gaze earnestly. "I'm sorry."

"I'm afraid 'sorry' simply isn't good enough this time," he said, not snappishly, but almost sadly. "You endangered not only yourself, but also your sister and her best friend. You made a very foolish choice, and I am not certain I can trust you to act less rashly in the future.

"What am I to do, Alera? You are seventeen years old, and yet you continue to play these childish games! You are to be Queen in less than a year. Given your age and upbringing, I should not have to be telling you to behave more sensibly."

He waved his arms distractedly as his agitation increased, while I sat in wretched silence, letting his criticism rain down upon me.

"Who is to govern beside such an unpromising Queen? Would she enable her husband to rule the Kingdom with a steady hand or distract him with her silly ploys?"

He glared sternly at me as though daring me to respond, but I knew there was nothing I could say. My throat had constricted, and I was incapable of thinking about anything but my own incompetence, which my father had just brought rather painfully into the open.

"A suitor must be chosen, Alera," he continued, beginning to pace in front of me, his brow damp with sweat. "You know who I want to succeed me. If another young man of quality does not soon present himself, then you will marry Lord Steldor, under my last order as King of Hytanica."

"But I cannot marry Steldor," I gasped, my brain finally jarred into action.

"Then perhaps you have another suitor in mind?"

He stopped and turned toward me, his tone telling me it was unlikely he would approve of anyone of my choosing.

"There is no one else, Father," I murmured, wringing my hands dejectedly, vague echoes of a previous conversation rebounding in my head.

"As I expected," he said unpleasantly, and I could not help but feel desperately inept. "I have taken the liberty of inviting Steldor to accompany you on a picnic outside the city walls. I have given him my permission to court you, and insist that you honestly evaluate him in terms of his qualities, and not based merely on your whims."

My father swung around to go, but I hastily called him back.

"Wait!" I cried, getting to my feet. "Miranna would enjoy such an outing as well. I pray you to permit her to come with us."

My father did not appear to be in a mood to compromise.

"A young man could be chosen as a companion for her as well," I continued in desperation, a pleading note in my voice. "Such an arrangement would place less pressure upon Steldor and me. And it would help me to relax in his company."

My father thought for a moment, and as usual, began to toy with his ring.

"Amidst all your terrible ideas, there is occasionally one of value," he finally conceded, a bit less sternly. "I will inform Miranna that she will be joining you and Steldor on your outing ten days hence."

He left the room without another word, and I sank back down on the sofa, the morning heat and my misery depleting my energy. After many minutes, it dawned on me that my father may have paid a visit to Miranna as well as to me. Even if he had not, my sister was someone who would empathize with my feelings.

Leaving my parlor, I hastened down the hallway toward Miranna's quarters. My sister's quarters also consisted of a trio of rooms, although she did not have a balcony as I did. Her parlor was similar to mine, with tapestries decorating the walls, rugs padding the floor, and a sofa and several armchairs to provide seating. The primary difference was in color, for Miranna favored blues, while my tastes ran toward rose and burgundy. Our bedrooms, however, were quite different, for hers was decorated more playfully, with a lacy spread and pale blue velvet draperies. The walls of her bedroom were not hung with tapestries either, as were mine, but with silks in softest hues of blue, yellow, green and pink. Ribbons in the same colors were hung in streamers from the four posts of her bed and decorated the edges of its canopy. A large number of lovingly kept dolls sat atop her bookshelf and dressing table.

Halias knocked on Miranna's parlor door as I approached, then opened it to grant me entry. My sister was sitting in a deep blue velvet armchair doing some handwork, but rose to usher me into her bedroom as soon as she took in my gloomy countenance. She plopped down on her bed and motioned for me to do the same.

"Is it Father?" she asked anxiously.

"Of course," I said, slumping down beside her.

"He spoke with me this morning about the need for me to act more prudently and to set a good example," she said ruefully, pulling a pillow into her arms and hugging it to her chest. "While it wasn't a pleasant conversation, he at least didn't strike me. How did he treat you?"

"He didn't physically punish me either, although that might have been easier to bear. Instead, he lectured me on my shortcomings as a daughter." I hesitated, then gushed, "He told me he fears I will be an incompetent Queen. He said that I am too old to be playing childish games and that he can no longer trust my judgment."

My eyes welled with tears as I said the words, though I was determined not to let them fall, for that would have somehow been an admission of the accuracy of his assessment.

"He doesn't know what he's talking about," Miranna simpered, shifting to take my hands in hers. "You will be an exceptional Queen. He should not base his opinion on this one incident."

"Father rules this Kingdom, Mira," I moaned. "He, better than anyone, knows the qualities that are necessary in a Queen."

"What we did was very unwise — even I see that now. But Father has overreacted. He has never before doubted your suitability as a Queen, and I'm sure in his heart he truly doesn't now."

"He also said that unless I soon find another 'man of quality' to be my husband, he will order me to marry Steldor." I removed my hands from hers, and began to fiddle with the lace that overlay her blue velvet bedspread.

This Miranna had not expected.

"Order you?" she dully repeated.

"Yes!" I exclaimed frantically, meeting her appalled stare. "What am I going to do? I cannot marry Steldor!"

"That doesn't sound like Father," she said, dismayed. She regarded me sympathetically for a moment.

"Father is just... under a lot of stress right now. I'm certain in time he will rethink his position... and regain his sense of humor." Her attempt to reassure me fell short, for her tone was not very convincing.

"And if he doesn't? Then what am I to do?" Panic was swelling within me. "I had hoped to marry for love — an intelligent and compassionate man — someone with the potential to become the greatest King in Hytanica's history! How much time will Father give me before he forces me to marry the man I detest?"

"Calm down, Alera!" Miranna worriedly insisted. "While I do not share your negative opinion of Steldor, I do agree that you should marry for love. Father will come round to that as well."

We sat in abject silence for a few minutes, then she abruptly scrambled to her feet.

"A change of scenery would do us both some good," she

declared. "Why don't we go out for a while? Leave both the Palace and our troubles behind?"

"A change couldn't hurt," I wretchedly agreed.

She twisted a strand of her strawberry blonde hair over and over with her left hand as she reviewed our options, then she flashed me a smile.

"I think today is Market Day — that should offer plenty of distractions. Come, sister, let's get some fresh air and take in the sights." She grabbed my hand and pulled me to my feet. "And we can scout for alternative suitors!"

I couldn't resist smiling at her suggestion, although I did not see my predicament as the least bit comical.

Two hours later, Tadark and Halias followed us out of the Palace, through the central courtyard and into the city. We proceeded for a short while down the thirty-five-foot wide main thoroughfare that cut the city in half, then turned west into the Market District. Here, shop fronts opened onto narrow streets, with similar types of businesses congregated together. As we strolled along, we perused the merchandise of the bakers, the spice-grocers, the apothecary shops, the tailors and the jewelers. Their wares were displayed on counters that doubled as the bottom halves of the horizontal shutters that closed the storefronts at the end of the day. The top halves of the shutters were propped up so as to provide the merchandise with some protection from the elements. Down one of the many side streets we could see the signboards for the shoemaker, saddle and harness makers, and tanners. Down another were the blacksmiths, armorers and sword makers. Yet another side street held the fish merchants, butchers and chandlers.

As we came to the last of the shops, the cobblestone street opened into a large grassy area atop a hill that sloped down into the training field just south of Hytanica's Military Complex. Here, temporary tents and stalls had been erected to accommodate the various vendors who brought items to sell or trade at Market Day.

Market Day was held once a week, and usually resulted in a teeming crowd. In addition to farm products such as fresh vegetables, animals, wine, ale and cheese, the craftsmen from the villages surrounding the walled city would come to sell their hand-made goods. As traveling merchants would also bring wares to sell, there was an ever-changing variety of items available. Furniture, tools, furs, glassware, exotic spices, rare oils and perfumes, pots and pans, laces and unusual fabrics were all part of the hodgepodge that was Market Day.

Miranna and I were both dressed in simple frocks that laced tight over the bodice before falling open to the ground to reveal white chemises. Our hair was down about our shoulders, but as the July day was hot, I found myself wishing I had copied Halias and pulled mine back into a ponytail. Such a hairstyle would have been in keeping with my garb, and befitting of a common woman, and would have aided us in our effort to blend in with the crowd, for shopping was more pleasurable when people did not constantly bow to us. Of course, no disguise in the world would have worked when our bodyguards were conspicuously present, so Tadark and Halias were also out of uniform, and, to Tadark's chagrin, Halias was allowing us further freedom to roam. As Halias, a Deputy Captain, outranked him, Tadark had no choice but to comply with his decision.

As we entered the throng of people surrounding the tents and stalls, we were bombarded by the sounds of vendors hawking their wares, customers arguing and negotiating, little children playing, and animals complaining in their various ways. My spirits immediately lifted, as I absorbed the energy that hung in the air in this fascinating place.

"Oh, look over there!" Miranna mischievously uttered, touching my arm and pointing over the heads of the milling crowd to a young man in his mid-twenties who stood beside one of the many vegetable stands.

"He's handsome — you could marry him!"

"I'm sure that would improve Father's opinion of me," I said, playing along. *"Sire, I would like to marry a vegetable merchant...or perhaps the servant of a vegetable merchant,"* I said with exaggerated formality, as though addressing the King.

"While he would not approve the match, it would be interesting to see his face when you asked him," Miranna said with a laugh.

We continued to work our way through the shoppers, scanning the wide assortment of items the villagers were attempting to sell this week. Miranna was replacing a scarf she had been examining at one of the stands when a familiar voice rang out from behind us.

"Mira!" Semari was slowly making her way toward us through the bustling swarm of people. She wore a long, light brown skirt decorated with braid, and a white blouse. Her cheeks were flushed, and her blue eyes danced with excitement.

"Semari!" Miranna cheerfully responded, giving her friend a hug as she arrived beside us. "How are you?"

"My father was furious when he was told what we had done, but I'm hardly even sore any more," Semari said, the smile on her face broadening, though it hardly fit her words. "And he's forgotten all about it now."

"Because of Narian?" Miranna pressed, jumping to the topic that had been foremost in our minds of late — the shocking resemblance between Semari and the Cokyrian youth.

Semari nodded energetically, and we moved off to the side of one of the tents so we could converse without being jostled by the milling shoppers.

"When the Captain of the Guard and the King met with us, the Captain asked my parents if they could identify him as their son... in some manner other than his appearance and his age. My mother recalled that Kyenn was born with an unusual mark behind his left ear, a mark in the shape of a jaggedly cut crescent moon. The Captain then examined Narian, and discovered the mark exactly as my mother had described it! How likely is it that two people would have the exact same birthmark, let alone such an unusual one?"

"Not likely at all," I said, captivated by her tale.

"The King and the Captain then acknowledged that he is the long-missing member of our family, my older brother."

"What are they going to do with him?" Miranna asked, likewise intrigued.

"Well, my parents want him to live at home, but he can't be completely trusted, so for now he stays under guard at the Palace. The Captain wants to slowly introduce him to Hytanican life, at the same time observing him, in case the Cokyrians did send him here for a purpose."

"Have you spoken with him?" Miranna persisted.

"Of course I have! The Captain has arranged for him to visit us each week. On the appointed days, Destari transports him to our home in the morning and returns him to the Palace in the evening. Destari and my father keep a close eye on him when he is with us, but there have been no real problems."

"What is he like?" I breathlessly asked.

"It's so thrilling to meet him, my long-lost older brother, but the situation is also very strange." Semari's tone became contemplative. "I have always been the oldest child in my family. It feels odd to be someone's younger sister. And from my parents' standpoint, it's as though he's come back from the dead."

I reflected on this for a moment. Semari's older brother, Kyenn, had been abducted just a week after his birth, and was believed to have been murdered, though his body had not been among those returned by the Cokyrians. The trauma Semari's parents, the Baron Koranis and Baroness Alantonya, had suffered had been so devastating that they still felt its pain sixteen years later, and had always been haunted by the uncertainty of what their son's true fate had been. It was almost inconceivable that the Cokyrian youth arrested by London could be their missing child. But their joy at his return had to be tempered by the horrifying knowledge that he had been raised in the land of Hytanica's greatest enemy.

"He is very quiet." Semari's voice drew me from my thoughts.

"He doesn't talk much at all, he just observes everything."

"Well, Hytanica must be quite interesting to him," Miranna conjectured. "The way we live is no doubt much different from life in Cokyri."

"I don't know if 'interesting' is the right description," Semari continued. "He acts almost condescending about the way we live… like he's disappointed, as if he expected more from us."

"What do you mean?" I queried in confusion.

"He's not exactly conceited," Semari said, trying to explain. "To give you an example — he was surprised, irritated almost, when he learned that I did not know how to handle a weapon; that the focus of my education and that of my sisters has been on etiquette and not Hytanica's history or its politics. He seemed to think our educations insufficient."

"Does he ever mention Cokyri?" Miranna asked, managing to divert us to the subject she'd been dying to discuss since we had begun chatting.

"As I said," Semari replied, "he doesn't say much. The only thing he's said is that while he was in Cokyri, he discovered he was Hytanican, and that's why he left to come here. He didn't say how he found out or anything else about his life there, and we haven't pressured him to tell us. My parents think he was raised as a member of the upper class, though, as he is quite well-mannered."

Just then, another aspect of the situation occurred to me. "What are you calling him? He apparently has two names."

"That is somewhat undetermined," Semari answered ruefully. "My parents want to call him Kyenn — he was born to them and that is what they christened him — but he insists that they call him Narian. My mother, though it dismays her, understands his preference and is willing to use his Cokyrian name, but Papa refuses. My father went to him and told him that he can introduce himself as Narian, or whatever he wants to be called, when he is elsewhere, but while he is under his father's roof, his name will be Kyenn. My brother replied that he would respond to no name except Narian, regardless of whose roof he was under.

"So as not to anger my father, the rest of us have also been calling him Kyenn, which only increases the tension all the more as he will respond to my mother's use of the name, but not my father's. He also directs any questions he might have, though they are few indeed, to her, and glares at Papa as if he were a simpleton if he deigns to answer on her behalf."

"London told me once that Cokyrian women, rather than men, occupy positions of power," I said thoughtfully. "Perhaps that is why he is willing to obey your mother but not your father."

"I suppose that could be the explanation."

Semari glanced down the street as someone called her name.

"I'm coming, Mother!" she returned, and then continued. "It's just that neither of my parents knows quite how to deal with him. My mother is not accustomed to being the center of attention, and she knows little about some of what he asks her. My father is the head of the house, and deserves to be treated as such, but at the same time, he does not want to be angry with Nar — Kyenn. My father's oldest son has come back to life, and all Papa wants is to get to know him."

Semari sighed, then finished, "Kyenn's attitude is difficult for all of us, but especially for my father, as he is not used to being someone's second choice."

This was an attitude with which no one in Hytanica would be familiar. I could not imagine someone showing greater respect for women than men, or treating their father as inferior to their mother. Both things would be completely unacceptable in Hytanica, and I wondered how Narian would ever fit into our world.

"I'm coming, Mother!" Semari repeated, as her name once again reached our ears over the crowd. "I have to go — my family is waiting. But maybe you can come for a visit to our country estate. There is a good chance that Kyenn will be there." She hugged us each in turn, and then ran off to join her family.

"She's incredibly lucky," Miranna sulked in the aftermath of her friend's departure. "The plan was for us to meet him and ask about Cokyri, and now he's practically living in her home."

"Life just isn't fair sometimes, even for Princesses," I teased, though feelings of envy were twisting my stomach also, for it was unlikely that we would be allowed to visit Semari at home while Narian was there. My father would insist upon giving the Baron and his family privacy so that Koranis and Alantonya could get reacquainted with their son, and their children could get to know their brother.

"We'd better return to the Palace," I said, noticing that the sky was clouding over in preparation for an evening shower. We were walking back through the cobblestone streets, Tadark and Halias in tow, when a different issue came to mind.

"Father has arranged another date for me with Steldor," I said drearily.

"Really? When?"

"Next week. I unfortunately had to use you to avoid being alone with him. Father is going to find an escort for you, and then the four of us will go on a picnic."

"Oh, that sounds splendid!" she exclaimed. "It will be enjoyable to get out of the city for an afternoon."

"So you're not upset with me?"

"Not in the least! I rather welcome Steldor's company. And I can help by drawing some of his attention away from you."

I still did not understand how Miranna could look forward to spending time with Steldor, but I wasn't about to argue with her. The more diversions there were, the less time would be available to the Captain of the Guard's son for bragging about himself.

Chapter Eleven
The Picnic

What had started as a simple picnic soon became an event requiring as much meticulous planning as a grand festival. First, there came the problem of finding a suitable escort for Miranna. My father spoke with most of the upper-class young men in Hytanica, but had difficulty finding one that he viewed as responsible enough to attend his youngest daughter.

My father also gave due consideration to how we would be transported, and where we would stop to eat. I had assumed we would spontaneously pick a site, but he was insistent on knowing exactly where we were going to be at all times. I began to think it would be simpler if he just came along with us.

And what about our bodyguards? Were both necessary to protect us? My father concluded that only one guard was necessary as we would be in Steldor's very capable hands. As Tadark refused to be left behind, and as he was closer in age to the rest of us, he became the favored one, despite the fact that Halias held rank over him. Neither Halias nor I was happy about this particular decision, but as long as the King was satisfied, there was nothing either of us could do about it.

My father directed our cooks to create a list of different foods from which we could choose for our picnic lunch. The resulting menu was pages long, and I picked the first few items that caught my eye, not having the willpower to review all the options.

By the time the day of the outing arrived, I was so tired of hearing about it that I was eager for it to be over. Miranna's enthusiasm continued to run high, however, due more to her infatuation with Steldor, I was sure, than with anything else.

It was the third week in July, and as the day was destined to be hot, Miranna and I had both chosen to wear long, full-cut skirts with short-sleeved white blouses. Her skirt was deep red with a sash of blue, and mine was green with a rainbow-hued sash. I had also braided my dark brown hair, while Miranna wore her blonde locks in a loose ponytail.

We left the Palace grounds in mid-morning, riding in a buggy that had been furnished by the Royal Stables and was pulled by a magnificent pair of black Friesian horses. The buggy had a high wooden seat over the front wheels upon which the driver would sit, with a double front-facing seat over the back wheels that was padded for comfort. The floor of the buggy was relatively low to the ground for ease of entry.

As Steldor would be handling the reins, it was assumed that I would sit beside him, and a pad had been laid on the normally bare wooden seat in recognition of this arrangement. My escort was casually but elegantly dressed in a double-breasted white shirt with gold buttons and trim, and black breeches. He wore black boots with a half dozen buckles running up the tall shafts. A dagger hung from his belt and a sword of his own design had been tucked on the floor beneath the front seat. His shirt sharply contrasted with his dark hair and eyes, and had no doubt been calculated to increase the intensity of their effect and raise the pulse rate of any woman within range. Even my breath had caught as I'd watched him strap our picnic supplies to the rear-facing jump seat at the back of the buggy.

Miranna's companion was a stocky young man named Temerson, whose height and eye color matched my own, but whose hair was cinnamon-brown. He was clad in the Military Academy's standard-issue brown tunic and sash over a cream colored shirt, and looked terribly out of place next to Steldor, although in truth he would have been rather cute if not subjected to such a comparison.

Miranna and Temerson occupied the back seat while Tadark rode his own horse so as to give us privacy. We were heading for a protected setting in the bend of the river, where trees promised shade, and the wide, rapidly flowing water would ensure a cool breeze. Even at a brisk trot, it would take well over two hours to reach our destination.

As we passed through the walled city, the horse's hooves made a pleasant clacking sound against the cobblestone of the wide thoroughfare. To the west of the thoroughfare lay the Market District, while to the east was the Business District, where money changers and lenders, taverns, inns, doctors and barbers did a lively business. Further away from the main street upon which we traversed, we could see church spires, the grainery, and innumerable residences. Ahead of us rose the thirty-foot high turreted stone wall that surrounded the city, with guard towers on each side of the gate as well as spaced evenly along its length. The city was home to about fifteen thousand people, with another twenty-five hundred living on farms and in villages scattered throughout the Hytanican countryside.

As we left the city, the stone thoroughfare narrowed somewhat into a dirt highway that wound its way through the countryside to the only bridge spanning the Recorah River. As we were headed toward the bend in the river, our route soon took us east off the highway onto a much narrower, and less traveled, country road.

The outing began smoothly enough, but I soon discovered that the mind-numbing planning for the picnic had made me even less tolerant of Steldor's ego. It helped that Miranna was present, but Steldor was flirting with me, not my sister. As the horses trotted onward, I tried my best to silently dissuade him by concentrating on the passing landscape.

Hytanica's rolling terrain was lush and green at this time of the year, and the fields of flax that would soon be harvested were dotted with beautiful pale blue flowers. As we drove along, we saw many farm hands hard at work in the fields, and Steldor would wave magnanimously to them on occasion.

Steldor was undaunted by my reluctance to interact with him, and proved quite capable of carrying an entire conversation himself. After another tedious monologue similar in content to the one he had delivered on the night we had dined together, he leaned conspiratorially toward me.

"So what's the name of your sister's friend?" he asked.

Temerson had introduced himself somewhat shyly to us all, but Steldor had been too busy being Steldor to pay attention.

"Lord Temerson," I supplied, Steldor's arrogance rapidly depleting my patience. "I assume you know his father, Lord Garreck, as he is a veteran Battalion Commander who has been teaching at the Military Academy for the past fifteen years, and his mother, Lady Tanda, is a friend of my mother's, and I presume, of your's."

"Ah," he replied. "So, Temerson," he said, glancing back at the young man with whom my sister had been unsuccessfully attempting to converse, "are you a student at the Military Academy?"

The inquiry was wholly unnecessary, given Temerson's age and apparel, but I suspected the military might be the only subject they would have in common.

I scrutinized Temerson while waiting for him to respond, and saw the look of a cornered animal settle upon his face. He opened his mouth, but no sound came forth, and he opted for woodenly nodding his head twice. It struck me that for someone with a naturally reticent nature, Steldor could be exceptionally intimidating, and probably doubly so to a young cadet, as Steldor was also a Field Commander. It was possible as well that Temerson had at some time been the object of Steldor's and Galen's razzing.

"The quiet type," Steldor remarked to me, as if Temerson weren't there. "Reminds me of another his age."

"And who would that be?" I asked, social graces winning out despite my determination to discourage him from talking.

"That Cokyrian boy."

"You mean *Hytanican* boy," I corrected, assuming that he knew the young man's true identity.

Steldor brushed my comment off. "He was raised Cokyrian. He thinks like them and behaves like them. That's all I need to know."

"Yes, but he was *born* Hytanican," I argued, hardly believing that Steldor would be so quick to judge Narian. "That's all *I* need to know."

"That's beside the point, anyway. All I was going to say is that he has barely spoken a word since we brought him to the Palace, and I find it rather odd."

"Perhaps he is just overwhelmed by all that has happened to him. He was captured by the people he undoubtedly fears the most, and now has been reunited with the family he's never known. I don't think I would be talking much, either."

"Or perhaps he doesn't speak because there is nothing going on in his head," Steldor said contemptuously.

I could tell my keenness to argue was beginning to annoy him, but I was rather enjoying his discomfort.

"Just because he's not about to divulge his life story at the merest implication that he should does not mean he is unintelligent, Steldor," I countered.

"Why are you defending him? You know no more about him than I do."

"Then why are you deriding him?"

"We clearly aren't going to agree on anything here."

"Actually, that's the one opinion of yours with which I will agree."

The rest of the trip passed without much discussion. Steldor and I did not converse further, and though Miranna tried several times to elicit a response from Temerson, nothing came of her attempts.

Steldor halted the horses beside a large oak tree near the river, and left Tadark to appropriately secure them. Temerson somewhat clumsily helped Miranna from the buggy and Steldor turned to assist me. I grudgingly permitted him to lift me to the ground. His hands were upon my waist as he set me smoothly down, but he did not immediately release me. Instead, his eyes bore into my own, and the blood drained from my face at the thought that he might kiss me. Then he smiled rakishly and dropped his hands, leaving me with the distinct impression that he had wanted to elicit such a reaction from me.

Tadark and Temerson began to remove the picnic supplies from the buggy, while Steldor supervised, unmistakably of the opinion that he was exempt from the work. He did, however, give directions as to where everything should be located, treating the picnic like some sort of military drill. When he directed Tadark to a specific spot to lay our quilt, I could restrain myself no longer.

"I would like the quilt to go over there," I called genially to the men, motioning to a grassy area closer to the river where several large willow trees stood, their tendrils gracefully trailing across the ground in the gentle breeze.

"No," Steldor said with an unbearably commanding air. "The quilt should be here."

Tadark was standing with two corners of the quilt in his hands, ready to lay it on the ground, but halted as we began to bicker.

"But this ground is smoother," I contended, walking over to the location I had chosen, remarkably willing to spend the afternoon arguing about this rather insignificant decision.

"We will have better shade here."

"But I'm standing *over here* and if we put the quilt *over there*, I will have to move." I gave Steldor a sickeningly sweet smile.

"Tadark already has the quilt halfway on the ground," he tried once more.

"But it will take minimal effort to pick it up and bring it to me. If Tadark does not wish to exert himself, surely you could manage it without undue strain."

Steldor studied me for a moment, obviously aware that he and I were engaging in some form of power struggle. Apparently concluding he could afford to lose this skirmish, he gallantly surrendered.

"As you wish. We will move the quilt to wherever you direct, Princess."

"Thank you," I said, smiling smugly to myself.

Tadark huffed as though moving the quilt were the most unreasonable thing I could have asked of him, but he nevertheless picked it up and brought it to where I stood. Temerson, who had been holding a large basket of food during our entire exchange, set it appreciatively atop the quilt, but did not say a word.

The men returned to the buggy, Tadark and Temerson to retrieve whatever drinks the cooks had supplied, and Steldor to again supervise the task, while Miranna and I settled ourselves upon the quilt. Miranna turned to me with an exasperated sigh.

"Why can't you treat Steldor with some decency?" she demanded.

"I simply am not in the mood to put up with his pretentious behavior," I replied defensively.

"Give him a chance, Alera," Miranna pleaded. "Has he really done anything so terrible today? And don't say he's egotistical. He's *Steldor*. That's a given with him."

"I suppose he really hasn't behaved too badly," I said petulantly. "If it will make the day more pleasant for you, I'll *try* to assume his intentions are for the best."

"See that you do," Miranna responded, somewhat placated.

Steldor was the first to return, strutting along in front of Temerson and Tadark, who were carrying wine flasks and goblets.

"I propose that we go for a stroll along the riverbank before we dine," Steldor said, his manner authoritative and, to me at least, incredibly maddening.

"I would prefer we eat first," I wickedly disagreed, in blatant disregard of the promise I had just made to Miranna.

"If we walk now, we will build up an appetite."

"I am hungry already," I insisted. "If we walk, I may faint."

Steldor seemed to know what I was doing, and his amused visage only rankled me more.

Unable to abide my obduracy, Miranna took control, rising to her feet to accompany him. She gave me a chilling look that told me to yield, and I exhaled in resignation.

"On second thought, a walk sounds lovely," I managed, though my tone was insincere.

I stood and promptly moved forward to grip Miranna's hand, pulling her beside me so I would not be forced to stroll alongside Steldor.

Tadark and Steldor joined us without delay, Tadark's duty and Steldor's pride not allowing either of them to let us get far ahead. Temerson trailed the four of us, too daunted by the company he was keeping to walk in-step with us.

The ground sloped gently toward the Recorah River, flattening as it reached the river's bank, thus permitting us to walk within a few feet of the racing water. Here where the Recorah changed course, no longer flowing south, but curving toward the western hills in the distance, its wide expanse narrowed, dramatically increasing the speed of its flow, and creating a white froth against the far bank. The one bridge that spanned the river to permit entry into our Kingdom was several miles to our west and was heavily guarded by Hytanican soldiers. Even though the war with Cokyri had ended sixteen years ago, my father and Cannan had not relaxed their vigilance, and patrols continued to ride Hytanica's borders while sentries kept twenty-four hour surveillance over the bridge.

Miranna and I began following the bend of the river, talking softly together. Steldor attempted to move next to me, but I was walking close to the water's edge with my sister firmly planted on my other side so he had no way to position himself. He chose not to try again, as that might have cast him in a foolish light, but drifted over to Tadark and began to talk just loudly enough for us to hear.

"So, you've become Alera's new bodyguard, have you?" he asked, a sly connotation to his words that I did not like.

"I have indeed," Tadark replied proudly.

"Let's hope you prove better than the *last* one."

"I most definitely am better!" Tadark confirmed. "London was not a good bodyguard. He couldn't keep track of Alera for a minute. I don't know how he came to be a member of the Elite Guard. He clearly wasn't fit to handle such important responsibilities."

"I agree," Steldor said with mock indignation. "I was never much impressed with him myself, unlike my father. The Captain was in such an uproar when we learned that London was the traitor. Personally, I don't understand why no one saw it coming, especially since he has always been a bit of a renegade."

"I saw it coming!" Tadark exclaimed, sounding like an excited five-year-old. "I knew there was something suspicious about him from the first moment I met him. I never quite trusted him, for his mind was often elsewhere, as if the Princess were not his first priority."

Unable to suffer more, I opened my mouth to defend London, but Miranna's soothing voice halted me.

"Just ignore them," she said serenely. "They don't know what they're talking about. Besides, Steldor is doing this on purpose. He wants to needle you. Don't give him the satisfaction of knowing he has succeeded."

With some effort, I regained my composure, knowing that my sister had spoken wisely. Steldor and Tadark continued to talk, but I did my best to shut them out, for their words hurt me and only increased the level of dislike I held for Steldor.

We circled around and returned to our picnic site, the baskets waiting for us upon the quilt. As Tadark withdrew toward the buggy, Temerson finally came to join the rest of us and we sat down to unpack the provisions. Our picnic fare of hearty breads, cheeses, cold soup, fruit, and wine looked delicious, but Steldor's presence had once again robbed me of my appetite. Even so, I was thankful we were eating as it brought all talk to an end.

As the meal drew to a close, Miranna turned to Temerson with a charming smile.

"Would you go with me to the river? I would like to rinse my hands in the water."

Temerson nodded slowly, his eyes growing large at having received such a request. Then he stood to accompany my sister, leaving me alone with Steldor. I thought there would be a very long, very tense silence, but Steldor had other plans. He sidled over to me and, placing one hand about my waist, swept me into his arms. I tried to resist, but he was strong and assured in his actions, and his intoxicating scent addled my brain.

"Don't be afraid of me, Alera," he murmured, voice intolerably indulgent. "I appreciate a little spirit in a woman." As his lips brushed my cheek, he continued, "At least this time we have a bodyguard who won't interfere."

"What do you mean by that?" I snapped, leaning away from him, his reference to London jarring me to my senses.

"The last time we had a chance to be alone, London rudely interrupted us, claiming that there was some *emergency* in the Palace."

He was now whisking the strands of hair that had escaped from my braid over my shoulders, lightly caressing my neck with his fingers.

"I would deem rescuing me from your unwanted advances to be an emergency," I said emphatically, pushing against him.

Steldor froze. I was certain that no one had ever before so much as intimated that his advances might be unwanted, and yet I had just bluntly told him that I had no desire whatsoever to be close to him. I could almost feel the heat rising inside of him as he angrily got to his feet, knocking me off balance so I tumbled uncomfortably onto my side.

"Here I am, alone with you, as affectionate and charming as

anyone could ever be, and you want none of it!" His voice had lost its honeyed quality, sounding lower, rougher. "There are many young women in Hytanica who would, without hesitation, give everything they have to win the attention I freely give to you, Alera."

After giving the picnic basket a swift kick, he stormed off to the river's edge where Miranna and Temerson were sitting side by side on a rock outcropping. Miranna had finally encouraged a bit of conversation from the timid young man, but as Steldor approached, Temerson fell silent.

Steldor artfully situated himself close to Miranna, unsheathing his dagger and placing one foot upon a boulder. As he casually flipped the knife back and forth between his hands, he began to shamelessly flirt with her. I was too far away to hear him, but his body language and the way Miranna blushed told me enough. My eyes narrowed as my dislike for the Captain of the Guard's son grew stronger with each giggle he elicited from my sister. I was positive that Steldor was trifling with her in an attempt to make me jealous, but while I was feeling many things at that moment, jealousy was not one of them.

Steldor's flirtations continued for many minutes, until Miranna glanced over toward me and understood what his motivations truly were. She abruptly stood and pointed over his shoulder.

"Look, an apple tree!" she exclaimed.

Steldor seemed momentarily taken aback that Miranna would have the presence of mind to notice an apple tree while under his spell. Then he unconcernedly shrugged and pivoted to face in the direction she was indicating, presumably deciding that, in her youth, she simply did not know how to respond to such a show of interest from someone as attractive as he.

"Alera!" Miranna called. "Come pick apples with me!"

Miranna walked toward me, followed by Temerson and Steldor, who had returned his dagger to its sheath. Steldor stopped beside me, wearing a shrewd expression, confident that his attempts to make me jealous had succeeded.

"Yes, Alera, come pick apples with us," he smugly said.

I motioned to Miranna and Temerson to go on ahead, then turned to Steldor.

"Perhaps you and Tadark should ready the horses for our departure," I suggested, trying to limit the amount of time I would be forced to spend in his company.

"Oh, hoping to leave so soon?" he asked acerbically, grasping my implication. "The King won't look for our return until late afternoon. We really shouldn't disappoint him."

He moved stealthily closer to me, his eyes locked on mine.

"The horses do need tending, though," I repeated, nervously giving ground as he advanced. "You and Tadark should lead them down to the river for some water."

For a moment I feared he was going to seize hold of me, and my pulse quickened in recognition of how easily he could assert dominion over me. Then he stepped past, the glint in his eye telling me he had once again achieved his intended effect.

"As you wish," he said flippantly over his shoulder. "Tadark and I will water the horses."

He strode toward my befuddled bodyguard, then gave Tadark a push in the direction of the buggy.

I trailed shakily after Miranna and Temerson, knowing I should not oppose Steldor so boldly, for women in Hytanica were expected to obey the men in their lives without question, or suffer the consequences. While Steldor was not yet my husband, he had my father's ear, and I suspected the King would permit him considerable latitude in dealing with me.

As I crested a small hill, I was pleased to find that there were, in fact, several apple trees. Miranna was standing beneath one of them as I approached, staring up into its branches. Just as I began to cast about for Temerson, I heard a *snap* and a startled yelp from high up in the tree. Miranna's mouth opened in alarm as the young man fell from above, landing right on top of her. They tumbled to the ground, then Temerson scrambled quickly to his feet.

"Are you h-hurt?" he asked as I rushed to my sister, his face turning scarlet with embarrassment.

"No, no, I'm fine," my sister reassuringly told him, although she winced as she shifted her body, and had not yet attempted to stand.

"Well, c-can I get you anything?" he stuttered in return, hoping to somehow make up for whatever injury he had wrought.

"Well, a sip of water might be helpful," Miranna replied, though she really needed no such thing. She simply wanted Temerson to feel like he was aiding her in some small way.

After Temerson had gone, I asked disbelievingly, "Are you sure you're not hurt?"

I was afraid that she might be downplaying her injuries so as not to worry anyone.

"Yes, I'm all right, really," she maintained. "Just a little stiff."

"What was Temerson doing in that tree?"

"He was trying to get that big apple for me — the ripe red one on that upper branch — and he fell," she explained. "Just help me up. I don't want to be a burden to anyone."

I reached for her hand and had her halfway to her feet when she cried out in pain and fell back again.

"What's wrong?" I demanded. "Where are you hurt?"

"I–I don't know," she said, as though every word cost her dearly. "I can't breathe."

"I'm calling for help," I informed her. "TADARK!" I shouted, turning to face the buggy.

Tadark was at my side in an instant, and I was thankful for his haste. Steldor was with him as well, having likewise responded to my urgent call.

"What's wrong?" Steldor queried, as though I had called for him and not my bodyguard.

I set my eyes on Tadark as I explained, "Miranna is hurt — we must return to the Palace at once."

The two men looked cynically at each other.

I've seen something like this before," Tadark said, blatantly suggesting that Miranna was faking her injury as she had previously faked her attack in the library.

Steldor clearly had been told of our earlier misadventure.

"Are you that desperate to get away from me, Alera?" he asked, a definite edge to his voice.

I, in turn, was furious. "Though this may come as a revelation, not everything is about *you*, Steldor! My sister is hurt, and I demand that you safely transport her back to the Palace."

Miranna's ragged breathing had become more regular, and Steldor interpreted this to mean that she had grown tired of acting.

"See," he said, motioning to my sister where she lay on the ground with her eyes shut. "She has improved. The game is up, Alera. Your little tricks will not work on me." Then he firmly added, as though speaking to a misbehaving child, "We will not return to the Palace until the appointed hour."

"Fine! I will take the buggy and bring her back myself! But I would start creating excuses, Steldor, because you're going to need something spectacular to explain *this* to my father!"

I bent down beside Miranna with my back to Steldor and Tadark. "Try again to stand and I will help you to the buggy," I softly said.

I guided her into a sitting position, although she gasped with the effort and I saw a single tear slide out of her left eye, where neither Steldor nor Tadark could see it. As she attempted to rise to her feet, a sharp cry escaped her lips. Then she collapsed, passing out from the pain. I barely managed to put my arm under her back and catch her, thus saving her from further collision with the ground.

After easing her down, I glared at the men with whom I was growing increasingly angry, willing them to do something. I was panicking on the inside as Steldor knelt beside my sister's limp form and pressed a hand against her ashen cheek.

"Her skin is rather cold and clammy," he acknowledged, his forehead now furrowed with worry.

"What do we do?" Tadark asked fretfully, shifting his weight from foot to foot as if he wanted to run somewhere, but was uncertain in which direction to flee.

"Gather up whatever supplies you can in the next few minutes and pack them into the buggy," Steldor told Tadark before turning to me.

"How did she come to be injured?" he demanded.

"She... fell," I lied, hoping to save Temerson from Steldor's wrath. Fortunately, he did not press for more information.

"Go to the buggy," he ordered. "I can carry Miranna."

I waited as Steldor easily lifted my sister, and then hurried after Tadark. Temerson was standing beside the picnic quilt, holding the cup of water he had retrieved, horror upon his face as he watched Steldor bearing his faint and pale date.

I stopped Steldor as he was about to try to position Miranna upright in the back of the buggy.

"Don't!" I snapped, hurrying to tug the quilt out from under the remaining picnic items, then carrying it to where he stood with my sister in his arms. "She needs to lie down," I instructed, moving past him and using the quilt to provide a pillow for Miranna on the buggy seat.

"If she lies down, there won't be enough space for the rest of us," Steldor pointed out.

"I can kneel on the floor and watch over her," I impatiently responded.

Steldor frowned at me, then laid Miranna smoothly down.

"You will ride up front with me," he said. "Temerson can kneel and tend to Miranna. The floor is no place for a lady, and I fear you would tumble from the buggy. One injured Princess is quite enough."

He called to Temerson to take up his place beside my sister, then assisted me onto the front bench seat.

"Abandon anything that cannot be transported with you on your horse," he called to Tadark, then climbed up beside me. With a snap of the reins, he sent the horses off at a gallop toward the city. As we rapidly covered ground, I silently prayed that Miranna had not suffered serious harm.

The enormous stone walls surrounding the city stood forbidding and cold against the steadily darkening sky as we approached our destination, and the first rumble of thunder reached our ears as Steldor pulled the horses down into a trot. The heavy gates of iron that controlled access to the city were raised at this hour of the day, and as we passed beneath their spikes, the City Guards on either side regarded us quizzically, in all likelihood having witnessed our somewhat reckless return.

We continued down the central thoroughfare toward the Palace at a slow, but steady, trot so as not to endanger anyone, for it was Market Day again and the streets were packed with people. Steldor brought the horses to a halt before the gates to the courtyard and lifted me to the ground as Temerson leapt from the buggy.

"Run ahead and tell the Palace Guards to summon the doctor," Steldor said to the worried young man. "I will bring Miranna to her quarters."

I went to my sister, laying a hand upon her damp forehead, meeting her agonized blue eyes.

"We'll have you in your bedroom in a few moments," I murmured.

Her eyelids flickered, but she did not otherwise respond. Steldor brushed me aside and scooped her into his arms, then proceeded through the courtyard gates and up the hedge-lined pathway that led to the Palace. By this time, Tadark had arrived, and he and I followed behind. As we approached the entry, I could see that Palace Guards were holding the double doors open for us.

"This way," I said, moving past Steldor as we stepped across the threshold to lead him up the Grand Staircase and on to Miranna's quarters. I opened the door into her parlor, and we went straight through to her bedroom, where he ducked beneath the pastel ribbons that streamed from the canopy over her bed to gently lay her upon the mattress' lacey spread.

"I'll be in the other room," he said, glancing uncomfortably about at the frilly and feminine room.

The Royal Physician arrived a short time later, along with my pallid mother. Temerson, flushed and frightened, followed behind them, although he waited in the parlor to keep company with Steldor and Tadark.

As Bhadran began to examine Miranna, he asked me to explain how the injury had been inflicted.

"She tripped and fell as we were gathering apples," I circumspectly said, attempting to make eye contact with my sister. I hoped she was alert enough to understand what I was attempting to do.

The man who had treated every injury and illness we had suffered throughout our lives looked skeptically at me, but did not comment, and I exited the room, for Miranna was now in highly qualified hands.

As soon as I reentered the parlor, Temerson turned his terrified eyes upon me, and I was filled with sympathy as I thought about the unfortunate circumstances in which he found himself. He had never before escorted a Princess, likely felt at fault for causing her some irreparable injury, and was anticipating that Steldor and perhaps the entire Royal Family would be furious with him. I wholeheartedly admired him for the simple fact that he had not fled. I smiled kindly at him, but then addressed Steldor, who was likewise worried, although whether about Miranna or his own skin, I could not tell.

"Thank you for your assistance," I said graciously, as light rain began to patter against the window. Unable to help myself, I added, "It would appear our picnic was ill-fated for a number of reasons."

He studied me carefully, no doubt trying to ascertain whether or not I would tell my father that he had delayed our return to the Palace by questioning our honesty, but he did not make the inquiry.

"How is she?" he asked instead.

"The doctor has not yet determined the nature of her injury, but she is awake and some rosiness has returned to her cheeks."

"Tell me again how she came to harm," he said, evidently dissatisfied with my earlier explanation.

I frowned at Temerson, warning him not to answer.

"She tripped and fell," I said. "She must have landed on top of something, perhaps a stone or a branch."

Steldor looked askance at me, then whirled on Temerson.

"You were with her. Is that how she was hurt?"

The color drained from Temerson's face, and I deftly interceded on his behalf.

"The injury *is* what it *is*," I said succinctly. "It is not really relevant how it was inflicted."

Just then Halias rushed through the door, his ash blonde hair falling about his shoulders rather than pulled back in its customary ponytail, his blue eyes uneasy.

"What is going on?" he urgently inquired.

"Mira suffered an injury as the result of a fall," I told him. "Bhadran and my mother are with her now."

"This is the last time she goes anywhere without me by her side," he steadfastly declared, with a reproving look at Tadark. "She does not come to harm when I am there to protect her."

Tadark glared at him resentfully, having taken offense to Halias' implied criticism of his ability as a bodyguard. Before he could reply, however, the bedroom door opened, and my mother glided into our midst.

"Our physician has given Miranna something to relieve the pain, and she is sleeping now," she informed us in her genteel manner. "She has bruised or broken several ribs, but will recover."

She smiled gratefully at Steldor and Temerson.

"Thank you for bringing her back to the Palace so quickly and for your kind ministrations."

Although my mother's voice was gentle, they understood that they were being dismissed. The young men bowed respectfully, then turned to leave.

"Temerson, a moment," I called to him. As both he and Steldor stopped, I said emphatically, "I only need a word with Temerson. *You* are free to go."

Steldor looked irked, but obediently departed nonetheless.

I approached the fidgety youth and quietly said, "Miranna's injury was an accident, and I will not put you in a position of blame. As she and I remember it, she fell."

His cheeks dimpled into their first smile of the day, then he bowed and left the room.

Later that afternoon, after I had returned to my parlor and Tadark had resumed his duties as my bodyguard, I informed him that I wanted to speak with him, and he warily entered my quarters.

"I believe my father would be desirous to know of the poor judgment you exercised earlier today at the time of Miranna's accident," I informed him, a gleam in my nearly black eyes.

His posture became more rigid, but he remained mute.

"Perhaps you are not fit to handle such *important responsibilities*," I continued, maliciously repeating his earlier criticism of London.

His sullen expression told me that he comprehended that his assignment as a bodyguard might be in jeopardy.

"Relax," I said, savoring the sudden power I wielded over my bodyguard. "If you don't cause me problems, I won't cause you problems. Understand?"

Tadark stared at me, brown eyes wide with indignation, as he absorbed the fact I had acquired some leverage over him.

"You are dismissed," I said, then smartly turned and walked into my bedroom, feeling that my day had just improved immensely.

Chapter Twelve
The Dignitary's Room

One week later, my mother called Miranna and me to the Queen's Drawing Room. This was the room in which she received visitors, met with household staff, and planned all of Hytanica's royal functions. I could not anticipate what she wanted from us, as we were rarely needed when she was meeting with visitors or staff, and I did not know of any upcoming events that would require the personal touch of the Queen and her daughters.

Miranna and I were not forced to wait before entering the Drawing Room as we were when going to see our father in the Hall of Kings, so we simply walked through the doorway. The Drawing Room was similar in size to our parlors, with two small cream brocade sofas and several rose velvet armchairs grouped together on the right side beside a wide bay window that faced the east courtyard. Our mother sat at a desk to our left, fussing with some correspondence. An abundance of fresh cut flowers stood in vases on the tables and in large pots on the floor to create a fragrant and heady ambiance.

"Oh, good," she said pleasantly when she saw us enter.

She stood from behind her desk and floated around it, taking a seat on one of the sofas.

"Come sit with me. We have many things of which to speak."

I sat in a plush armchair adjacent to the sofa, while Miranna gingerly sat down beside her.

"How are you feeling today?" Mother asked, helping Miranna to get settled upon the cushions.

Mira shrugged, wincing in pain.

"I'm feeling better, but not as well as I would like," she replied grimly.

"I'm sorry, dear," our mother soothed. "But I still can't quite see how you managed to injure your ribs in this way just by tripping."

A sly look passed between Miranna and me. The two of us had agreed that we would not tell anyone the true story of her injury, lest we condemn Temerson to some horrible fate that he did not deserve.

Remembering something, our mother stood to retrieve a bouquet of long-stemmed yellow roses from her desk, handing them to Miranna as she returned to her seat.

"These are for you, dear. Lord Steldor stopped by earlier to ask after you, and left these to brighten your day."

She then trained her clear blue eyes upon me.

"And how is the courtship proceeding?" At my averted gaze, she chastised, "Disagreeable women rarely make desirable wives... or Queens."

I glanced contritely at her, painfully aware that she and Steldor must have conferred about the attitude I had adopted toward him at the picnic.

"If one gives in to fate, life can provide greater pleasure," she continued in her lyrical voice. "Removing the thorns from a rose does not change the nature of the flower, but it does permit one to more easily enjoy its delicate scent."

I nodded once, acknowledging her subtle advice, although internally I seethed at Steldor's presumptuous attempt to use my mother to his advantage. Then I grimaced as it occurred to me that he might also have spoken with my father. If he had, my father would make his opinion known in a far less tactful way, and I knew his disappointment with me would intensify.

"There is another reason I called you here today," Mother said, seemingly satisfied with my receptiveness to her criticism. "Your father and I have decided to host a gathering in honor of Baron Koranis and Baroness Alantonya, and in celebration of the return of their son, Lord Kyenn. Since you are to be Queen, Alera, I want you to make all the arrangements, although I will review everything before it is finalized. Miranna, of course, may assist you."

I was stunned, to say the least. I had known that upon becoming Queen, I would have to assume all of the responsibilities that my mother carried, but I had not expected them to be given to me in such an abrupt fashion. I didn't even know where to begin when planning an affair such as this, and was glad that I would have Miranna's help.

"The event is scheduled for the third week in August, which gives you just under a month in which to make the necessary preparations," she continued. "The most pressing item is writing up a guest list and sending out the invitations, as they ought to be delivered by the end of the week."

"Who is to be invited?" I hoped she would have some list of names prepared to show us, but she did not.

"That is for you to establish," she said, lightly smoothing her up-swept golden hair. "Keep in mind that this celebration is to introduce Kyenn to the Hytanican aristocracy, so everyone of noble birth should be included. He has been adjusting remarkably well to Hytanican life so far — Cannan returned him to his family last week, and everything is going favorably. This is the final step to restoring him to the life into which he was born."

My mother continued her instructions, detailing what needed to be done, and by when. I felt that arranging this event was a blessing in disguise. As I had said to Miranna earlier, marrying Steldor was, for me, outside the realm of possibility. This celebration presented the ideal opportunity to seriously seek another suitor, one of whom my father would approve, and with whom I could at least have a civil exchange. Although Steldor would unfortunately be in attendance at the gala, as Cannan and Faramay were always on the guest list, I hoped that in a gathering of over six hundred nobles, I would be able to avoid him altogether.

Miranna and I were extremely busy during the next few weeks, and I found myself meticulously attending to the smallest of details. My father had made no attempt to talk with me about Steldor, and I thought perhaps neither my mother nor Steldor had discussed the picnic with him. I began to nurture the hope that a well-executed Palace function would redeem me somewhat in his eyes.

My duties included making selections as to the food and decor. This event would not include a formal dinner, but all the same, refreshments were a necessity. Accommodations also had to be arranged for guests traveling long distances, some of whom would be staying in the Palace, while others would be placed in guest houses within the city. Koranis and his family would not be among those occupying our third floor rooms, however, as Koranis, being a wealthy Baron, owned not only a country estate, but also a house within the city proper.

It also fell to me to ensure a thorough cleaning of the Palace, and servants could be seen sweeping floors, whisking away cobwebs from corners, polishing serving dishes, and readying a large number of oil lamps, torches and candles.

In my opinion, the most tedious task as we prepared for the gala was the fitting of my gown. Miranna and I were to have new dresses designed, to be worn specifically for the celebration. Miranna loved choosing new fabrics and styles for her clothing, and took pleasure in watching as the seamstresses created exquisite garments for her, but I regarded it as a rather tiresome process. I did not particularly care about fashion, and I would have preferred to have the seamstresses create my gown without me.

Our finished dresses naturally reflected our different personalities. My gown was fitted through the bust and waist, flaring out into a full skirt. The sleeves echoed the cut of the dress — fitted above the elbows, then flaring out to fall liberally over the wrists. Made of crushed silk in a light wine color, it was simple but pleasing to the eye. Miranna's gown, on the other hand, was fun and flirty. It was made of silk in a shimmering mint green that flowed loosely to the floor. Its empire waist was accented with colorful ribbons that hung freely, rippling when she moved, and that would be matched by ribbons woven into her hair.

On the evening of the event, when Miranna and I were impeccably groomed and attired, we made our way to the Dignitary's Room, the small room off the Ballroom where the King and Queen waited prior to making their formal entrances. As we walked, a queasy feeling pervaded my stomach — I had organized this affair and planned every aspect of the evening, and if the event did not go well, then my father's assessment that I was "an unpromising Queen" would be confirmed.

Halias knocked on the door of the Dignitary's Room, and when it was opened from the inside by a Palace aide I could see that Koranis and his family had already arrived. As the guests of honor, they would walk behind the Royal Family when we made our entrance into the Ballroom. Tadark and Halias would not wait with us in the Dignitary's Room, but would patrol among the gathered guests.

"All rise for Lady Alera and Lady Miranna, Princesses of Hytanica," proclaimed the Palace aide, announcing us to the Baron and his family.

As we entered, I saw that Semari was seated to the left of her mother, Alantonya, on the gold brocade sofa across from us against the far wall. Her sisters, Charisa, age twelve, and Adalan, age ten, sat to their mother's right. Nine-year-old Zayle sat tentatively on the edge of the raised marble platform in the far left corner of the room upon which stood a pair of regally styled and luxuriously padded royal blue velvet armchairs. Koranis stood to the right just behind the three wide steps that led up to the broad double doors that would be opened when it was time to step onto the Ballroom's elevated stage. One heavily-ringed hand hung by his side, the other held the inside edge of his ostentatious cream-colored dress coat, the sleeves and sides of which were thickly decorated with elaborate gold embroidery.

Narian stood on the opposite side of the room from Koranis, facing us with arms crossed over his chest, shoulder resting upon the wall, an occasional shift in his stance suggesting that he was discontented with his present circumstances. He was clad in a fitted dark gold coat in an unusual style that fastened off to one side, rather than down the middle, and had a scalloped bottom edge that fell at his hips. Only his well-worn boots seemed out of place. Made of oiled leather with a deep cuff below the knee, they had a somewhat higher heel and thicker sole than was typical of the boots worn by Hytanican men.

While I knew Narian's identity had been confirmed by the mark he bore upon his neck, the blue of his eyes, along with his straight nose and strong jaw line, also offered proof that he was the Baron's son. His thick and untidy hair connected him to Koranis as well, but only by its golden color, for Koranis' hairline was receding and every inch of the Baron was fastidiously groomed.

Alantonya and her daughters rose from their seats and curtsied before us, while Zayle stood and gave a slight, but very endearing, bow. Narian stepped away from the wall to bow as his father did, bent at the waist with head lowered in respect.

Alantonya was wearing a turquoise brocade gown over a scoop-necked gold chemise that had the effect of shading her blue eyes toward green. Gold ribbons crossed upon the gown's bodice, and several times banned the long, fitted sleeves. Her white blonde hair was pulled up off her shoulders, and she wore an opulent bejeweled pendant.

Semari's dress was similar in design to her mother's, but was simpler and less decorative, as was befitting a girl of fourteen. Her chemise was white with a ruffled neckline, and the gown was a beautiful shade of pale gold. Her hair, which was the same color as her mother's, was also drawn up off her shoulders, with small pastel flowers adding a playful touch. Her younger sisters wore simple blue frocks and their ash blonde hair fell halfway down their backs, while Zayle, with his flaxen hair, was dressed in dark trousers and a white shirt.

Koranis stepped forward to greet us.

"Your Highnesses," he said, giving each of us an additional tilt of his head, "allow me to introduce my son, Lord Kyenn."

He held his hand out toward Narian to invite him over, but Narian remained motionless, as if choosing whether or not he would comply. Just as we all began to feel self-conscious, he pushed away from the wall and came to stand by the Baron.

"Pardon my father," he said, inclining his head toward us, his thick hair momentarily obscuring his keen eyes, "but my name is Narian."

Koranis' eyes snapped to Narian's face, while Alantonya, who was just behind her husband, put her hand over her heart, revealing that she had been anticipating, no doubt with dread, that this issue might arise.

Narian raised his head to meet his father's harsh gaze.

"I'm *not* under your roof," he said, without a trace of disrespect, but simply as though he were stating a fact.

The silence that followed was unsettling for everyone except Narian, who was completely unperturbed despite the affronted look on Koranis' face. It was Semari who broke the awkward hush.

"Your gowns are gorgeous this evening," she complimented, moving forward and stepping around her father. "From what type of fabric are they made?"

We began to converse, the rather peculiar exchange we had witnessed between father and son temporarily forgotten.

A few minutes later, Koranis, having regained his tongue and his poise, approached Narian, who had resumed his earlier stance against the opposite wall. As Miranna and Semari were now talking primarily to each other, I was able to listen to Koranis when he spoke.

"This event is in celebration of your return to Hytanica," he stated in an unassailable tone. "Therefore, it will be your Hytanican name that is used tonight, and to which you will respond."

Narian met his father's gaze steadily, neither an acquiescence nor an objection leaving his lips, and my attention was irresistibly drawn to his deep blue eyes. Piercing, yet guarded, I once more pondered the lack of childish light everything else about him suggested should be there. While he was lean and obviously strong, his body had not yet matured into the well-muscled physique of Steldor or any of the bodyguards protecting my sister and me. And Koranis physically overshadowed his son, standing several inches taller and weighing half as much again. If not for those intense eyes and his inscrutable expression, he would have passed for a normal Hytanican youth, not yet fully grown, enjoying carefree days with his friends, and creating terrible worry lines upon his parents' faces.

My parents, wearing robes of royal blue that were banded and stitched in gold, joined us shortly thereafter. They were accompanied by Cannan and their personal guards, although the latter took up posts in the corridor. Lanek preceded them into the room, introducing the King and Queen in his usual manner.

"All rise—" He paused momentarily as everyone was already on their feet, "—for his Highness, King Adrik of Hytanica, and his Queen, the Lady Elissia."

Once more Alantonya and her daughters, together with Miranna and I, curtsied, while Koranis and his sons bowed. Just as he had when my sister and I had arrived, the Baron then stepped forward and addressed my parents.

"Your Majesty," he greeted my father, then turning to my mother, "My Queen. It is my pleasure to introduce to you my son, Lord *Kyenn*."

He said the name with an emphasis that was lost on my parents, and followed it with a warning look in Narian's direction.

Narian came away from the wall, a shadow of a scowl briefly upon his features. He said nothing, however, but bowed his head respectfully to my father and mother.

"Your Highnesses," he murmured.

Though he had seemed insolent to me moments before, he now sounded timorous, as if in awe of the grand company among whom he stood.

"It is delightful to finally meet you on such an amicable basis. I am afraid our previous encounters were a bit less civil," my father said with his typical cheeriness, and the slight rise in Narian's eyebrows implied that the King's jovial nature had not been revealed on the other occasions when they had met.

"Indeed, Your Majesty. I am honored you feel that way," Narian replied courteously, every bit the perfect gentleman. There was not a trace of his earlier attitude toward his father, and I was disturbed by his chameleon-like ability to adjust his personality.

My father's smile broadened, and I could tell he was impressed by Narian's comportment. Most Hytanicans viewed Cokyrians as ruthless thieves and murderers; therefore, such respectful conduct was not to be expected from a boy who had grown up among them. While my father did not easily succumb to closed-minded notions, some part of him believed Cokyrians to be so insufferable that even he expected less of Narian because of where he had been raised.

I myself did not share those opinions, perhaps because I knew little of Cokyri and the horrors of the war, but still I was perplexed by the young man. While we knew nothing of his upbringing, his pattern of speech and excellent manners provided proof that he had been well-raised, and yet his demeanor suggested a harsher childhood. I glanced at Cannan, whose dark eyes seemed to be taking stock of Narian, and realized that he, too, was struggling to figure out the mysterious boy.

Lanek departed, as it was his role to inform the King when all of the guests had arrived, and my father and mother took up their seats on the raised platform in the corner of the room. Semari, Miranna, and I resumed our small talk as our parents conversed, and the younger children moved to sit on the sofa. Cannan stayed by the door, looking as formidable as ever in an embossed black leather military jerkin, his interest held by Narian, who once more stood with shoulder against the wall.

I wanted to ask Semari about her older brother as I had that day in the marketplace. Had anything changed now that he was actually living with them? Had he spoken further about his past? But I refrained, as to do so would have been rude, especially with Narian nearby.

After about half an hour, Lanek returned, and the aide who granted him entry swung the door wide so that the Elite Guards in the corridor could follow after us when it came time to enter the Ballroom.

"Sire, the nobility have arrived and await your pleasure," Lanek reported with a deep bow.

"Very well, and thank you," my father said. He stood, then motioned toward the double doors across the room from him. "It is time to greet our guests."

My mother stood as well, and after smoothing her gown and her hair, linked arms with my father as she always did when they made public appearances. Cannan pushed open the wide double doors and then stepped through them to make way for Lanek. The diminutive man marched up the steps onto the stage-like platform and took a deep breath so he could generate sufficient volume to be heard throughout the hall as he announced my parents.

"All hail the King, King Adrik of Hytanica, and his Queen, the Lady Elissia," he shouted, and hundreds of eyes turned toward us and then were lowered in respect, as those gathered bowed or curtsied.

My parents stepped regally forward and Miranna and I followed, moving to stand beside our mother. We would not receive a formal introduction as had the King and Queen, but all the same, the people knew who we were and were bowing to us as well.

"Welcome," my father proclaimed, starting his introduction as he always did. "On this occasion, we honor a family that has, for many years, served this Kingdom well, and in so doing has earned my friendship, as well as that of my Queen and our daughters. I would like to present to you the Baron Koranis and his wife, the Baroness Alantonya; their daughters Lady Semari, Lady Charisa and Lady Adalan; their youngest son, Lord Zayle; and the young man whose startling return has provided the impetus for this gathering — their oldest son and first-born child, Lord Kyenn."

Koranis and his family stepped forward on my father's right as they were introduced, and now, as the King finished his speech, the guests gave a vigorous round of applause.

Cannan led my parents down the set of stairs on the Ballroom side of the stage, and the rest of us followed, the guards who protected the King and Queen bringing up the rear. A seating area with two thrones had been readied off to the right of the platform, and my parents would spend most of the evening there, greeting guests and speaking to those who sought an audience with them. Less ornate chairs had been set in the same area for Miranna and me, though neither of us was likely to use them. While my father would no doubt expect me to wait for Steldor, I was dead set on avoiding the young man who had permission to court me, intending instead to mingle with the crowd in a desperate effort to find an alternative suitor. Narian and his family would also move among the aristocracy, making less formal introductions and engaging in polite small talk, although the younger children would quickly run off to find their friends.

Tonight the Ballroom was arranged so that two long refreshment tables lined its sides, with the area in the middle occupied in part by a dance floor. The rest of the space was left open, providing an area for people to meet and chat. As the purpose of the gathering was to welcome Narian into Hytanican society, the colors that dominated the decor in the room were Hytanica's royal blue and gold.

Walking with Miranna through the vast hall, I scoured the crowd for what my sister kept referring to as "a good catch." It wasn't long before young men were coming up to me everywhere I turned, having taken my glance in their direction as an invitation to approach me. While I desperately needed to find an alternative suitor, I soon tired of the monotonous interactions. Every young man to whom I spoke had apparently been taught to greet me in the same way: "Good evening, Princess Alera. You look beautiful tonight... and what lovely weather we are having."

Even Miranna, who was far more boy-obsessed than I, was growing weary of these clumsy flirtations. She took the opportunity to escape the boredom, however, when she spotted someone she knew across the room close to one of the long refreshment tables.

"Oh, look!" she exclaimed, taking my hand in her own and tugging it excitedly. "There's Temerson! I must go speak with him."

After pinching her cheeks to raise their color and fluffing her long curly hair, she sashayed off toward the bashful sixteen-year-old, who was managing to exude a sophisticated air in an ivory doublet and dark brown trousers. As Miranna approached, however, I saw his eyes widen in panic, and I wondered if he knew that he was fast becoming her favored escort.

Unfortunately for me, my sister's departure meant that I would now have to brave the guests on my own. I began to move back toward my parents, not to speak to them so much as to take a break from the males who had been swarming around me. As I made my way, I stopped to greet Faramay and Cannan, who was now at his wife's side.

Baroness Faramay was, without dispute, the most beautiful woman I had ever seen, but, unlike her son, was gracious and kind, and completely oblivious to her own beauty and its effect on people. Her chocolate brown hair fell around her lovely oval face in thick curls that moved when she turned her head, sweeping gracefully across her delicate cheekbones, shoulders, and back, and drawing attention to her whether she sought it or not. She had blue eyes that were large and striking, and though she was almost forty, her fair skin was smooth and glowing. Her dress was of lavender silk with a fitted square-necked bodice and long gathered skirt, complimented by puffed sleeves in deep purple that were trimmed with lavender ribbons above the elbow and at the wrist.

It would be clear to anyone who had seen Steldor that Faramay was his mother, as the resemblance between them was plain to see. Needless to say, it was also clear why Steldor's looks were so dazzling. Though Cannan was a handsome man, his wife was an arresting beauty, and Steldor had been blest with many of her physical features. The only similarities between father and son were their chiseled jaw lines, the deep brown of their eyes and hair, and their powerful physiques.

All at once, Faramay's face lit up as she took in something over my shoulder. I swiveled and saw Steldor, accompanied by Galen, half-way across the room, surrounded by a group of adoring girls who were giggling and blushing at every utterance that came forth from their mouths.

"Oh, there's my angel!" Faramay said, with the eagerness of a doting parent. "Doesn't he look fine this evening? I don't believe I've seen that doublet before. It must be new. It looks splendid on him, don't you think?" she remarked, to no one in particular.

She was correct; he did look splendid. His emerald green doublet was more fitted than his casual clothing, subtly accentuating his impressive build and dramatizing his dark features. Faramay did not appear to notice that her son was unrelentingly flirting with all of his female followers, as her judgment was clouded by the love she possessed for her only child.

"Shall I get his attention?" she asked, raising a dainty hand to wave without waiting for my response.

"No!" I said, somewhat impolitely, not quite ready to deal with Steldor. So far this evening, his tactic seemed to be to play along with the games of the other girls in an effort to make me jealous, an approach with which I was quite content. I did not care with whom he flirted as long as he left me alone.

Faramay cast me an odd look, and I hurriedly clarified my answer.

"I would prefer to have the pleasure of his company a bit later this evening," I said, hoping to placate her, whereupon she returned to simply observing Steldor, her enamored expression a testament to how completely devoted she was to her son.

As Faramay continued to fixate upon Steldor, Cannan spoke, taking me by surprise, for he had been on alert for signs of trouble and had not thus far contributed to our conversation.

"Please forgive my son his antics, Princess Alera," he said, the volume of his deep, full voice lowered so that Faramay would not hear. "I'm afraid he has some growing up to do."

I nodded, uncertain how to respond. I understood then that Cannan, unlike his wife, was cognizant of Steldor's faults, and my esteem for the Captain of the Guard increased all the more. I wished I could trust that Steldor would grow to become like his father, but as that transformation seemed unlikely, I remained unwilling to gamble my chance at happiness by marrying him.

I parted from Cannan and Faramay a few moments later, but as I looked ahead at the large group of people surrounding my parents, I rethought my destination, instead opting to visit the dance floor on the other side of the Ballroom to my left. While I had no desire to dance this evening, I generally appreciated the music and was curious as to who was courting whom.

My eyes were on the musicians as I approached, for they seemed to be enjoying themselves as much as the dancers. They performed using a variety of instruments including mandolins, lutes, a dulcimer, the flute, and various types of recorders and drums. Depending on the instruments used, the sound ranged from beautiful and haunting to fast and wild.

Standing at the edge of the dance floor, I couldn't help but smile at the absolute delight on the faces of every individual spinning in the arms of another. As the couples moved around the crowded floor, my gaze came to rest upon Miranna and Temerson. They were by no means the most refined couple present, and at times it was difficult to know who was leading and who was following, but they were laughing and smiling and having more fun than anyone else I could see.

My spirits lifted appreciably as I listened to the music and beheld the dancing. My good mood evaporated, however, when I glanced behind and saw Steldor gradually making his way toward me.

I scanned the room for an escape route, some way I could flee without making known such was my intention. I began to move leisurely away, hoping he did not know that I had seen him. When his progress was impeded by several parents keen on introducing him to their daughters, I hastened to the back of the Ballroom, where the wide-open balcony doors beckoned.

As I stepped out into the warm late-August air, I looked over my shoulder to confirm that Steldor was still being hindered. Satisfied that I had eluded him for the time being, I turned, expecting to be alone. I was not.

Chapter Thirteen
Confrontation

My heart began to thump much too loudly as I saw Narian leaning back upon the railing, his hands resting on either side of him on the dark wood, barely visible in the sudden change from the brightness of the Ballroom to the moon-lit balcony. A slight smirk curled his lips, belying his otherwise serious demeanor.

"I didn't mean to startle you, Princess Alera," he said apologetically, straightening to give me a small bow, his face smooth and unreadable now that his smile had vanished. His speech was refined, with a faint, but pleasing accent, and his tone was rehearsed, as if he had been taught precisely how to speak to people of substantial status.

"You are forgiven, Lord Narian," I said, addressing him formally as I endeavored to regain my composure.

Unwilling to show my unease, I glided to the railing several yards from where he stood and rested my elbows upon its weathered surface. He casually moved closer to me, turning as well to face the railing, taking up a posture similar to my own.

"Think me impudent, if you will," he said boldly, "but I must inquire as to what a Princess is doing out here on this balcony in the middle of such a grand gala."

I tossed my hair over my shoulders and gazed at him, drawn to his intense blue eyes. Unable to pull away, I stared into them as though I might break through the floor beneath my feet if I looked anywhere else.

"I have my reasons," I cautiously answered, acutely aware of his proximity. "On occasion I come out here to avoid the crowd."

My skin was beginning to prickle, and I felt totally disconcerted, although I could not have identified good cause for my reaction. Irritated at myself, I posed an inquiry to him.

"Now I must ask what the guest of honor is doing out here on this balcony with so many people inside clamoring to meet him?"

"Avoiding the crowds or avoiding that dark-haired gentleman?"

Narian lightly side-stepped my question and I felt unnerved by both the intrusive nature of his statement and the astuteness of his observation. How could he have known Steldor had designs on me? Had he, for some purpose, been watching me? Despite the warning now flashing through my brain, I could not bring myself to break away from him, for he fascinated me as much as he unnerved me.

"Lord Steldor might have something to do with it," I confessed. "He is the son of Cannan, the Captain of the Guard." I half-expected some sort of reaction at the mention of the man who had arrested him, but there was none. "He wishes to take my hand in marriage."

"And you do not return his affections," Narian stated, drawing the natural conclusion from what I had told him. He turned his body toward me, one hand now resting on the railing.

"No," I said honestly, pivoting so that my position was the mirror image of his.

Although I felt I had said too much already, I was compelled to continue by his attentive and undistracted focus upon me. Here was someone other than London who was actually listening to me, rather than brushing me aside because I was a woman.

"I do not want to marry him. It is what my father desires, not I. Steldor is hot-tempered and spoiled, and I do not see him as making a good King, now or in the future. But my father will see to it that Steldor becomes King, irrespective of my feelings."

I stopped, simultaneously embarrassed that I was pouring out my deepest secrets to someone I barely knew, and perturbed that he had so easily inspired me to share such confidences with him. This was not a topic about which I readily spoke, and I had not voiced my opinions about Steldor and my father's edict that we be wed since London had departed.

"I'm sorry," I fumbled. "I should not be saying this to you."

"There is no need to seek my pardon," Narian replied. "I, too, despise having my life laid out for me."

I knew he had pinpointed my feelings with his presumably casual statement, but was not about to concede this, for I did not like the idea that my thoughts could so effortlessly be discerned, especially by someone so young.

"If my words have implied that I am dissatisfied with my obligations as Crown Princess of Hytanica, I assure you I meant no such thing," I said defensively.

"I understood no such thing," he responded with a hint of a smile, as though he knew something I did not. "Duty is important. But at some point the choice you will face is whether to carry out your duties or live your life."

"And what would you know of such matters?" I pressed, quite unsettled by his uncanny ability to distill the truth.

He stared at the flickering lights coming from the lanterns in the city for a moment before responding.

"We should go back inside," he said. "I'm sure someone has noted the absence of the Crown Princess and the guest of honor."

I nodded, not foolish enough to be disappointed by his evasiveness.

"Shall I escort you back to your parents?" he asked, extending his arm to me.

"Perhaps it would be best if we went in separately," I suggested, my thoughts flying to Steldor and his temper.

Narian, as if reading my mind, asked, "Are you afraid of Steldor?"

"No!" I exclaimed, not willing to admit that the man I detested was the reason I dared not be seen with him. "I do not fear Steldor."

"Then are you fearful of what people will think?"

"Of course not."

"Then it will be my honor to escort you."

Having no further basis for objection, I accepted his arm and together we walked through the balcony doors to rejoin the celebration.

As soon as we entered the Ballroom, my eyes connected with Steldor's, and I halted, knowing there would be no escaping this time. He had evidently seen me move toward the balcony and had come to find me, and now stood but fifteen feet away. I could almost feel the anger beginning to simmer inside him as he took note of my hand nestled in the crook of Narian's arm. He strode to where Narian and I stood, then abruptly put his arm around my waist and twisted me so forcefully away from my companion that I could not have forestalled him even if I had anticipated his action.

"I can take it from here, thank you very *much*," he spat as he pulled me to his side.

"Steldor, let me go," I said, fighting against him.

He did not comply, instead wrapping his arm more tightly about me, which meant he'd had too much to drink this evening, as he would normally have had the good sense to release me.

As practiced as he was at hiding his emotions, Narian could not disguise his disdain in the face of Steldor's appalling behavior.

"It would seem that Princess Alera does not welcome your advances," he said grimly, trying to draw Steldor's interest.

Steldor glared at Narian, then suddenly pushed me behind him so I would be out of the way.

"And who are you to speak for the Princess?" he retorted.

"She spoke quite clearly for herself, though you did not heed her."

Steldor's dark eyes narrowed menacingly. "Stay out of this, Cokyrian," he growled.

The heads of the people around us had begun to turn, and the surrounding area had become rather still. Pleasant banter had ceased, as everyone's attention was now transfixed upon Steldor and Narian.

"Was that supposed to be an insult?" Narian asked, having suffered no offense whatsoever at being called a Cokyrian.

"No," Steldor snarled as he took another step toward his young challenger. "That was a warning."

"Then consider me warned." Narian did not yield as Steldor continued to approach him with clenched fists.

Quivering with resentment due to the rough way Steldor had handled me, and fright due to the malice I had seen in his smoldering eyes, I cast about for someone who could intervene and prevent the clash between the two young men from becoming more heated. I saw no one in the immediate crowd who would be of help, as the guests were too entranced by the unfolding argument to think about putting a stop to it. While Steldor's friends, Galen, Barid, and Devant, had joined the surrounding circle, they had no interest in interfering. To the contrary, their faces showed that they were relishing the action. For the first time since he had become my bodyguard, I desperately longed for Tadark, but then just as desperately hoped he would stay away, knowing he would be ineffectual at best and might make the situation worse.

Narian and Steldor were now standing less than two feet apart, and the horrific thought that Steldor might strike Narian flashed through my brain. Steldor was almost four inches taller and more heavily muscled than his challenger, both things that caused me to believe Narian might actually be in danger. The fact that Steldor was capable of overpowering almost anyone in Hytanica was an additional reason for me to fear for Narian's safety.

"Steldor, that's enough," I implored, coming up beside him and grasping his arm, to no avail for he ignored me.

"Come with me, my Lord, and we can talk," I persisted, now tugging on his arm to get his attention. "This really isn't necessary."

He jerked away from me, and I stumbled back in alarm.

"What?" he said scornfully, jerking his head toward Narian.

"Your pretty boy can't take care of himself? He needs to be saved by a *woman?*"

"You will not speak to the Princess in such a manner," Narian interjected unexpectedly, authoritative in a fashion I would not have thought possible. "If your fight is with me, then you will address *me.*"

Steldor rounded on Narian, his rage rising to the point where it was almost an audible rumble.

"Perhaps you should run off to Mama and Papa before you get hurt," he taunted.

He shoved Narian in the chest, trying to push him backward, but Narian merely shifted his weight to absorb Steldor's prod. As Narian stood his ground, Steldor's eyes burned, and I knew he was dangerously close to exploding.

"Did you hear what I said?" he demanded, jabbing Narian with increasing force.

"I heard what you said," Narian replied steadily. "But perhaps you should be more concerned about *your* father than about mine."

Steldor faltered and his eyes flicked warily over the crowd, as if worried that Cannan might be among the spectators, then returned to rest on Narian's face. A flush began to creep up his neck, for Narian had somehow deduced one of his only vulnerabilities.

I began to feel ill, knowing that Narian was too brave, or perhaps too foolish, for his own good. I feverishly searched the vicinity, and finally caught sight of several guards engaged in amiable conversation near the western wall. In the midst of them I saw Destari, and I frantically willed him to notice my plight.

At that moment, he glanced in my direction, then immediately stepped away from the other guards to stride toward me. Tall enough to peer over the heads of the other guests, he assessed the situation and quickened his pace. He obviously had no idea how anything had started or exactly what was happening, but all the same, Steldor was involved, and everyone in the military knew of the young Commander's fiery temper.

"I said, MOVE!" Steldor thundered, and Narian assumed a fighting stance with his forearms in front of his chest and his left foot a half-step ahead of his right. As Steldor employed his full weight to drive him back, Narian deflected his lunge with ease.

Steldor looked momentarily stunned, then balled up his fists to strike his adversary. Fortunately, it was then that Destari stepped between them and put a hand on Steldor's chest, restraining him.

"This is not the place for such conduct," he admonished in his deep and powerful voice.

Steldor forcefully thrust Destari's hand away in another attempt to get at Narian, but Destari more firmly gripped him by the arm. Steldor fixed the Elite Guard with a glare that contained all the loathing he could rally, then landed one great shove upon his shoulder.

"Get out of my way!" Steldor scowled.

Destari, who, as a Deputy Captain, was Steldor's superior officer, became a much fiercer opponent, as his black eyes glistened and his stare became threatening.

"If you were a wise man, you would *not* try that again," Destari warned.

Steldor took a small step back to distance himself from the towering guard, and as he did so, glanced past Destari's shoulder, and I saw his resolve weaken. Though his anger did not diminish, his face subtly paled, and I followed his gaze to where Cannan, composed yet dangerous, now stood just outside the circle of people surrounding us. Cannan must have seen that trouble was brewing, and had come to deal with whatever the problem might be. I suspected that by the time he had drawn near, Destari had arrived on the scene, and Cannan had decided to let him handle things so Steldor did not have to suffer the indignity of being reprimanded by his father in front of all these people.

"You need to cool off," Destari said to Steldor through gritted teeth, not raising his volume. "Go. And that's an order."

With one final vindictive glower at the Elite Guard, Steldor turned and, motioning to his friends to join him, stormed off, to where I knew not.

I thought about Steldor's reaction to his father, and, knowing what I did about Cannan's status and his temperament, could understand Steldor's reluctance to cross him. Cannan was a confident and decisive man of action, who was known to have a formidable temper, although it was much better controlled than that of his son. I did not know of a single person who was not somewhat intimidated by the Captain of the Guard, and Steldor had grown up answering to him. As Cannan had an uncanny ability to see right through people, it was inconceivable that he was taken in by his son's charm as were most people. Steldor also had to deal with the fact that Cannan was not only his father, but his military leader, and, in that role, would tolerate no disrespect.

For a brief moment following Steldor's ignominious exit, Destari and Cannan locked eyes, then both of them scrutinized Narian, attempting to sort out what they had just seen. What manner of sixteen-year-old boy would challenge Steldor, much less do so without a sign of trepidation?

Narian did not acknowledge Destari and Cannan, but simply held out his arm once more to me.

"Shall we?"

I clutched at him, feeling weak in the knees, and for a moment leaned upon him.

"Are you all right?" he asked, and I could feel his breath upon my cheek.

"Yes, of course," I murmured, then I straightened, giving him a feeble smile. "Let's just move on," I said, utterly desperate to escape from the unpleasant situation.

As we walked toward the front of the Ballroom, people continued to gawk, although they resumed their activities upon our passing. The entertainment was over, and there was no need to waste such a delectable evening.

Having recovered my poise, I bid Narian thanks and a polite

goodnight when we reached the sitting area where my parents were holding court. Koranis and Alantonya were nearby, and immediately motioned their oldest son over for additional introductions. As he joined them, I wondered who he truly was, for I knew his name and little else. How could he, a boy one year my junior, be so courageous? Grown men quaked in the face of Steldor's temper, but Narian had not so much as flinched. Perhaps he had underestimated Steldor's skill, or overestimated his own, and all in my defense.

I was flattered, though I supposed his actions had nothing to do with me personally. As Semari had told Miranna and me in the market, he had an unusual amount of respect for women, and had no doubt been offended by Steldor's treatment of me on that basis alone. As I mulled this over, I realized how unaccustomed I was to being taken seriously. I had been taught all my life how to be a Lady, a submissive being (though my conduct was sometimes viewed as less than appropriate), and the rapt attention Narian had paid to my opinions on the balcony had been a bit disconcerting.

I looked around and saw Miranna pushing her way through the crowd of people, coming in my direction. I nodded my head toward the door to the corridor, and, after making sure she had seen my gesture, excused myself from the celebration, informing my parents that I had developed a headache and that it was necessary for me to return to my quarters. After meeting with me, Miranna would return to the Ballroom, but I was beginning to feel as though I would drown in its heavy air.

As a guard pulled one of the double doors open for me, I stepped into the corridor and inhaled deeply, noticing for the first time how unbelievably stifling the Ballroom had become with so many people occupying it. Where I now stood, it was cool and, more importantly, quiet. All I could hear was the faint hum of conversation through the thick wooden doors.

Miranna joined me a few seconds later, the babble of the guests momentarily loud as she stepped out beside me.

"Tell me everything!" she breathlessly demanded, her voice trembling with barely contained curiosity. She clasped my hand and eagerly led me onto the landing of the Grand Staircase. "All I saw was Steldor as he stormed off, and you taking Narian's arm, but judging from the muttering around me, the three of you created quite a stir."

I relayed to her the entire story, beginning with my hasty escape to the balcony and my interlude with Narian, and finishing with our courteous goodbyes once we reached the front of the Ballroom.

Miranna laughed and playfully tugged at her curly hair.

"What?" I asked, unable to see the humor in the evening's events.

"Well, sister, it appears that *you* are being fought over," she said with a grin.

"Oh, nonsense," I responded, waving her comment away.

"It's true! Perhaps Narian could be the man of your dreams, standing up to your enemy to defend your honor."

"You're ridiculously infatuated with romance," I said flippantly.

"Perhaps," Miranna admitted, but her smile remained. "All the same, I'm going to arrange an outing to Semari's country home for the both of us. Perhaps we'll get another glimpse of your champion."

I shook my head, believing it better to let Miranna poke fun than to waste my breath arguing.

"And how about *your* suitor?" I said, expertly changing the subject.

"Who, Temerson?"

I flashed a mischievous grin of my own. "You two were quite a pair on the dance floor."

Miranna's cheeks began to pink and her clear blue eyes shone.

"I may have lost a few toes tonight, Alera, but nothing you say can put a damper on my mood."

"Is there something you're not telling me, Mira?" I teased.

"No," she replied with a shy smile, "but he blushed horribly when I kissed him on the cheek as we parted."

"Mira!" I exclaimed in feigned disapproval as she giggled. "Can I conclude, then, that you are having a particularly good evening?"

"Yes, indeed, and I will continue to do so, if I ever get back inside. I'll speak to Mother in the morning to make the arrangements to visit Semari."

Her face once again lit up in anticipation of rejoining the festivities. She did a graceful pirouette and said an airy goodnight, then reentered the Ballroom, brushing her fingertips through her hair as the doors closed behind her.

Just after Miranna's departure, Tadark tumbled through the doors to see if I were in need of an escort. As he would be off-duty as soon as I retired, I gave him leave to enjoy the rest of the celebration. Having dismissed him, I walked alone through the corridors, savoring the tranquility, my mind returning to Narian. I had formed several new impressions of the young man over the course of the evening, many of which were contradictory, and none of which shed light on his obscure past. While I did not live in Miranna's romantic fantasy world, the idea of seeing Narian again was very appealing.

Chapter Fourteen
Enigma

The buggy jostled us uncomfortably as we slowly made our way to the country home of the Baron Koranis and his family, for the road had become pitted from the rain the night before. Miranna sat beside me, surveying the passing landscape as the horses trotted onward under the guidance of a Palace Guard, our bodyguards traveling with us on horseback. I stared straight ahead, excitement stirring within me, mixed with a hint of annoyance at the way Tadark rode outlandishly close to my side of the buggy. I supposed his zealousness was due to the fact that Koranis' estate lay along the eastern border of our Kingdom, in the direction of Cokyri.

Miranna had arranged everything so that our mother and father were under the impression that we were making this journey to visit Semari. If either of our parents had known our true purpose, we would not have been allowed to go.

I felt a twinge of guilt, not about permitting Miranna to mislead our parents, but about causing Alantonya the effort of preparing for and fussing over our arrival, just so that we could get another look at her eldest son, whose privacy we would indisputably be invading. While we always enjoyed the company of Semari and her family, Narian was truly the inspiration for this get-together.

In spite of Miranna's encouragement, it was impossible for me to think of Narian as a suitor. One year younger than me, he was not even an adult by Hytanican standards. Age was not, however, my only concern.

Narian was an enigma, a complete and total mystery to me, to my father, to his family, and to Cannan. There was simply too little known about him for me to put much faith in him. And after the incident at the celebration in his honor… though it had happened five days previously, it was as fresh in my mind as if it had occurred yesterday. I could see his youth plainly, but I could sense no youthful innocence within him, and that profoundly disturbed me.

After another half-hour, our driver brought the horses to a halt in front of Koranis' country home. Halias and Tadark dismounted and helped us to the ground as my eyes roamed over the property. I had only been to this country estate a few times in my life, for although I was compatible with all members of Koranis' family, I was not especially good friends with any of them as Miranna was with Semari. My sister had come here often while we were growing up, but I had rarely accompanied her.

The house itself was large and well-crafted. It was wood-framed, filled in with wattle and daub, and stood two stories tall upon a stone foundation. It had glass windows that could be covered by shutters to block the light and help regulate the interior temperature. To the right of the main entrance, the house was rectangular, while the left came forward in an "L"-shape. The cream-colored exterior was partially covered with vines and topped with a dark brown tile roof, and the grass surrounding the multi-colored stone path leading to the door was lush and green.

I barely had time to acclimate to my surroundings when Semari rushed through the front door and over to Miranna and me. She curtsied politely to us both, then discarded all formality as she began jabbering enthusiastically to my sister. It did not upset me that she concentrated upon her best friend. On the contrary, I was quite content to view the scenic land and take in the fresh air in relative peace.

A few moments later, Alantonya more sedately came out of the dwelling, followed by Charisa and Adalan, who stood behind her while she waited patiently for us to approach.

"Your Highnesses," she said in greeting, dropping into a low curtsey, her younger daughters imitating her movement.

She invited us into the house where we took up seats in a tastefully decorated parlor and began to engage in idle small-talk. In less than an hour, a servant entered to announce that tea was ready to be served, and Alantonya informed us that we would be taking our refreshment in the backyard. As she ushered us through her home, we passed several lavishly furnished rooms that shamelessly gave notice of Koranis' immense wealth. I looked over my shoulder for Narian one final time as we stepped out the rear door of the dwelling, but was once again disappointed. I had hoped to catch sight of him, but as far as I could tell, he was not at home.

Before us on the soft, green grass was a small circular table set for six. A large maple tree obligingly provided shade from the mid-afternoon sun. Although the days were still hot, they were becoming less humid as the end of August approached, and the evenings now had a definite chill. As we seated ourselves around the table, I gazed out across Koranis' property. To my right, under the cloudless sky, lay vast farm fields, while to my left and before me, the land sloped toward the forest, and I marveled at the unsurpassed beauty of this property.

The small-talk continued, although Charisa and Adalan said not a word, probably afraid they might make some glaring error in etiquette. I sincerely complimented Alantonya on the loveliness of her home, then inquired about the property itself.

"Does the Baron own all the land reaching from here to the forest?"

"Yes," Alantonya replied, sipping her tea. "Lord Koranis owns in excess of a hundred acres, most of it cleared for farming. He inherited some of the land, received some as a gift from the King, and purchased the rest. But he also claims part of the forest. When he first took over the property, he hired some villagers to cut trails through the woods for safer passage on horseback. That's where he is right now — out riding with Kyenn and Zayle."

I nodded in interest, now understanding Narian's absence, though I could not help but be dismayed by it. We had primarily come, after all, to see *him*. We finished our tea, then Alantonya stood with a warm smile.

"Semari, perhaps you and the Princesses would like to walk along the riverbank. It is a lovely afternoon, and a stroll will put a blush into your cheeks."

"Yes!" Semari happily agreed, tugging at my sister's hand. "It's not far into the trees, and it's so pretty there!"

Miranna stood and she and Semari skipped away from the house, my sister's wavy red-blonde tresses bouncing up and down upon her back in odd juxtaposition to the side-to-side swishing of Semari's straight white-blonde locks. Halias, who along with Tadark, had maintained a polite distance during tea, followed after them, while I remained a moment longer to thank our hostess.

"It was my pleasure," Alantonya responded with a small curtsey. She then beckoned to her younger daughters to accompany her into the house.

I hastened after the other girls, Tadark as always at my heels, and though I was not dressed for such an excursion, soon caught up with them, for they were dilly-dallying along. I was wearing a puffed-sleeved white chemise topped by a wide, billowy, cotton overskirt in blush pink with a white underskirt, and a matching panel-bodice that laced up both sides. On my feet were pliable, thin-soled, goatskin leather shoes. Miranna was similarly attired, although in pale yellow.

The three of us, bodyguards trailing, ambled down the hill together and entered the woods, taking care to follow the winding, leaf-strewn, tree-rooted path where water still puddled, for the sun could not easily reach the forest floor. The dampened foliage and earth emitted a slightly musty fragrance, a smell I always associated with the earthworms that rose to the surface in the garden after it had rained.

A short while later, Semari led us to the right on a rockier trail that soon opened directly into a narrow clearing that bordered the swiftly-flowing river. The trees hung over the edges of the clearing, their trunks obeying the invisible boundary but their leaves and branches unable to be contained. The open space between the woods and the river was only about twelve feet, and while the closeness of the trees ensured refreshing shade, it also seemed to magnify the sound of the rushing water.

I had forgotten prior to our visit that Koranis owned property along the Recorah River, yet we now stood beside the splashing and tumbling torrent. I looked into the dancing water and saw that it was deep here, even along the rocky edge, so deep that it would have risen above my head had I stepped forward a few paces.

I was pulled out of my reverie by the sound of Semari's giggling. She was tugging at Miranna's arm, and the two of them again began skipping away, following the Recorah downstream. Once more, I followed hurriedly after them.

Semari and Miranna stopped next to a cluster of rocks and boulders that stood sentinel next to the river, the craggy tops of the stones rising above the churning rapids. Semari perched on top of one of the boulders and Miranna joined her, but I chose to stand a few feet away, not daring to be so close to the roiling water.

The trees grew even nearer to the river here, giving the area a somewhat ominous feel. I gazed further upstream and could see the ruins of the old bridge that had once existed to provide passage to the east. It had been burned decades ago during the war and had never been rebuilt. Across the Recorah from where we stood, the terrain became rocky and foliage more intermittent as the land stretched into the foothills of the Niñeyre mountain range. This inhospitable area was sparsely populated, primarily by nomads, for it became windy and dry as one moved away from the water. This was the land the Cokyri had to cross to enter our Kingdom, as they claimed the high desert area of the mountain as their own.

Miranna, growing restless atop the boulder, rose to her feet and took a step forward, peering down into the swirling water.

"What are you doing, Mira?" Semari asked, shifting to get a better view of her friend.

"I'm seeing if I can spot any fish," Miranna explained. "Temerson told me that they sparkle when the sun shines off their scales."

"You won't see any fish in this part of the river," Semari giggled. "The water is moving too fast."

"You may as well come down," I called apprehensively to them. The last thing I wanted was for my sister to plunge into the Recorah.

I glanced over at Halias and Tadark, who had moved down the tree line with us and were talking at the edge of the clearing. Tadark was sitting on his heels near a large willow tree, but Halias had remained on his feet, eyes fixed on his charge.

"As you wish," Miranna said grudgingly, dropping her hands to the rough stone surface to make the short climb down less arduous. Just as she did, I heard the *chink* of something metal as it ricocheted off the rock and splashed into the water.

"Oh no!" Miranna exclaimed, leaning forward. "My bracelet! It's fallen into the river!" She dropped to her knees, preparing to reach for it.

"Get down from there now!" I snapped, my over-protectiveness as her elder sibling kicking in full force.

Miranna looked at me petulantly, but then slowly began to climb down.

"But what about my bracelet? I can see it — it's right there, caught between two of the rocks."

She and Semari approached me, a definite pout upon my sister's face. I again glanced at Halias, whose stance had notably relaxed now that Miranna's feet were securely on the ground. I deliberated about whether to call him over to retrieve my sister's lost jewelry, then settled against it. While the younger girls deemed this incredibly important, I thought it rather trivial, and would have been embarrassed to make anyone attempt this ridiculous retrieval task, especially a member of Hytanica's Elite Guard.

"I'll try to reach it," I finally groaned.

I moved forward and pulled myself, with a distinct lack of grace, up to stand on top of the rock outcropping, then took a stumbling step toward the river. I crouched down, for the surface of the boulders was sharp and uneven, and with more caution than I had employed before, continued to advance.

I could see Miranna's bracelet directly below me, shimmering with sunlight in the shallow water that had pooled between the last of the bleak gray rocks that tumbled into the water. As I could not reach it from my current position, I sat and began to ease my way downward, using the jagged edges of the stones as footholds. When it looked to be within my grasp, I seized the best handhold I could find and leaned forward, straightening my arms as I stretched to rescue the bracelet from the clutches of the Recorah.

I wasn't close enough. Grimacing with frustration, I released my handhold very slightly, trying to gain another inch.

Things happened quickly then. My fingers were vainly grasping air and my arm was waving about as if independent of my body, desperately groping for something to hold me in place, but there was nothing to which I could cling to keep from plummeting into the frothing water below. As the river consumed first my left shoulder, then my hips and legs, I vaguely heard the sound of a high pitched shriek, either from Miranna or Semari, but the water splashing into my mouth prevented me from uttering any similar cry of distress.

The raw torrent swirled around me, threatening to pull me under, and I sputtered and flailed in panic, certain I would drown. Just as the current was about to sweep me away from the boulders, I was half-dragged onto the rock by a pair of strong arms. My dress, which was now soaked and extraordinarily heavy, seemed reluctant to leave the river behind, but this did not hinder my rescuer. My first coherent thought, strangely, as I coughed and fought to pull air into my burning lungs, was that London had somehow materialized to save me. When my breathing eased, I looked into the face of the man upon whom I was leaning for support, and felt a shock as intense as the one the cold water had just dealt me.

Narian. Narian had pulled me from the river. I hadn't known he was there, yet somehow he had been near enough to reach me, and agile enough to rescue me, without falling into the water himself.

"Where did you…?" I muttered in bewilderment.

"I came down the path," he stated simply, jumping nimbly off the rock pile. "I saw you falling."

As he turned to offer me a hand, Halias brushed him roughly aside, and lifted me to the ground. The Elite Guard had evidently seen me plunge into the water, but had not been close enough to help me. Narian must have been very close indeed to have reached me before I had yielded to the river's strength — much closer than either of the bodyguards and definitely closer than the path.

"Are you alright, Princess?" Halias asked urgently. "Are you hurt?"

"I'm fine," I assured him, although my heart continued to pound in recognition of the danger in which I had placed myself, and I shook from the chill of the water.

Miranna and Semari, who had been hanging on to each other as though afraid they might fall into the river as well, now rushed to me to ascertain if I had suffered injury. Miranna impulsively hugged me, having concluded that I would live, and then she and Semari began to laugh in relief. Even I had to chuckle a little bit at what had undeniably been a graceless entry into the water. I caught a flicker of amusement in Narian's usually intense eyes as well, and was surprised for a moment at how different he looked when he relaxed.

As Miranna began to wring the water out of my long hair, Halias removed the royal blue doublet he wore as a member of the Elite Guard, so that he stood in his white shirt, and insisted that I put the garment on for warmth. As I did so, I stared down at my skirt. It was rumpled and dripping, and grime from the rocks had collected among its thick folds. I glanced at Narian and saw that his dark shirt and breeches were wet where he had held me against him.

Halias, too, was now gazing at Narian, although there was a much edgier expression upon his face than on mine. I realized that this must be confounding for both him and Tadark, who had stopped a few feet away, too shaken to step forward (I was, after all, *his* responsibility). They had been trained to notice and react the moment a disloyal eye flickered in the direction of a Royal, and yet they had been effortlessly skirted by a sixteen-year-old boy. And, on top of it, this boy had just saved the dignity, if not the life, of one of their charges.

"What is going on here?" A man's voice loudly hailed us, and a breathless Koranis, followed by Zayle, emerged from among the trees, the two having come down the path. Koranis' eyes widened as he passed Tadark and took in the entire scene.

"My goodness, Princess Alera," he exclaimed, "what has happened to your gown?"

He fleetingly looked at the others gathered around me, then a frown creased his brow as he noted the condition of his son's clothing.

"I fell in," I quickly said, motioning toward the river with my hand. "Nar — Kyenn rescued me." I glanced at Narian to see his reaction to the name I had used for him, but his face was inscrutable. "I am quite indebted to him."

"You should return to the house without delay," Koranis decreed, somewhat needlessly, given my sodden appearance. "You will need to change, and we are certain to have something that will fit you." He gazed at Narian, then finished, in his somewhat overbearing manner, "Kyenn and I will accompany you, as it would appear he needs to change as well."

"Thank you for your ministrations but don't let this ruin the afternoon for everyone else," I said resolutely. "I am completely unharmed, and there is no need for you to accompany me to the house, as the Baroness will be there to assist me. I would much prefer that you take some respite from your day rather than inconvenience yourself further."

"Oh, please Papa!" Semari implored. "Won't you stay for a little while? You and Zayle have only just come."

Koranis paused indecisively, and I recalled what Semari had said about her father having been told to keep an eye on Narian. Most likely concerned that letting his son walk through the woods with the Crown Princess of Hytanica would be unwise, Koranis turned to Halias, seeking his opinion. At Halias' encouraging nod, he smiled indulgently at his daughter.

"I suppose I could stay for a short while," the Baron pronounced. "Kyenn, you will return to the house with Princess Alera and her bodyguard."

I could tell from Narian's expression that he detested his father's dictatorial air, just as I could tell from Tadark's wide brown eyes that the prospect of being my only defense against Narian was making him feel ill. It was obvious from my bodyguard's reaction that talk of the recent confrontation between Steldor and Narian had circulated among the Palace force.

"You're not truly frightened of a teenager, are you?" Halias muttered irritably to Tadark.

"No," the younger guard asserted indignantly, standing up tall and puffing out his chest like a small and very offended owl.

Halias saw right through him and added, his words barely audible, "My God, Tadark, he's not even armed! How did you get into the Elite Guard anyway, with such a core of cowardice?"

I was once again amazed at Tadark's ability to provoke the most tolerant of people. It was practically impossible to anger Halias, and here Tadark had done it as effortlessly as a bird taking wing. Even London, with his gift for finding people's weaknesses, had never been able to truly rile Halias.

"Come, Tadark," I interposed before their exchange could become more heated. "I would like to return with some measure of haste."

Tadark's cheeks colored slightly as he stepped forward to lead the way. I followed behind, wondering where Narian had gone, for he had departed the moment Koranis had told him to do so, although I was sure he hadn't acted out of obedience. Perhaps he did not like the company gathered in the clearing, or perhaps accompanying me didn't appeal to him in the least. But as Tadark and I came to the end of the narrow trail that connected to the main path, I saw Narian leaning against a tree, waiting for us. Tadark shot the young man a distrustful glare as he came to walk beside me, then dropped behind us in order to better monitor Narian's conduct, his left hand tightly gripping the hilt of his sword.

We made our way through the trees without speaking. I was eager to say something to Narian — I had never been so intrigued by a person in my life — but he seemed content to maintain the silence between us, the only sounds being the incessant sloshing of my skirt and squishing of my shoes.

I grabbed fistfuls of my skirt in an attempt to make my movement less hindered as Narian lithely moved ahead of me, but to no avail. It continued to cling uncomfortably to my skin and my undergarments, causing me to stumble over and over. I moaned in annoyance, longing to break free of the woods. I knew from the sunlight that filtered through onto the path that the trees were becoming less dense as we advanced, and could only hope I didn't fall before we came to trail's end.

"Do you always dress like that?" Narian had halted fifteen paces in front of me, a disgruntled expression upon his face.

I stared at him as if a stream of profanities had just come from his mouth rather than the simple question he had actually posed, astounded that he had spoken.

"I'm generally tidier," I said, eyes shifting to my disheveled clothing as I pushed my damp, limp hair away from my face.

"I meant, do you always wear those impractical skirts?" he clarified, scrutinizing me as I labored to move toward him without tripping over the heavy tent that hung around my legs.

"Impractical?" I repeated, unsure whether he had meant to insult me or not.

"Well, yes," he said pointedly. "You no doubt would have drowned from the weight of your gown had I not been there to prevent it."

"I'm afraid I didn't consider the risk of falling into a river and nearly drowning when I chose my wardrobe," I snipped, stopping a few feet in front of him.

"Well, what did you consider?"

"I don't know!" I said, bridling at the subtle criticism in his tone. I uttered the first thing that came to mind. "The weather!"

"The weather?" he repeated, raising a derisive eyebrow.

"Well, what would *you* have had me take into account?"

"Self-defense. Cokyrian women only wear dresses at formal functions, and even then they bear weapons. You have no ability to conceal a weapon at all."

"That's what *he's* for," I countered, waving in Tadark's general direction.

"He is your only protection?"

"Yes, on an outing such as this," I confirmed, perplexed by his interest, but certain I was about to put an end to this debate. "At larger affairs, multiple guards watch over me."

"Tell me," he murmured, taking a step closer. "How would your guard protect you now?"

His nearness was disconcerting and I began to worry that Tadark was daydreaming.

"From what would I need protection?" I asked slowly, unable to look away from his keen blue eyes, which were boring into my suspicious brown ones.

A flash of light, a glint of metal in the sun, told me before he readied it to strike that he held a dagger in his right hand. In stunned disbelief, I saw the blade come toward me. Terror flitted through my brain as I grasped that I might actually again be in mortal peril. Then Narian stooped and slashed off the front of my skirt below the knee so that my leggings were exposed rather indecently to the air.

I stood frozen, too horrified to move. Tadark was at my side in an instant, his sword drawn and pointed as if he were protecting me, although I knew he would have arrived too late had Narian actually intended to do me harm.

"You will step away from the Princess," Tadark commanded.

Narian stared unflinchingly down the length of the cold metal, then relented and moved backward so that I was beyond his reach. Skillfully flipping the dagger so that he held the blade, he extended the weapon to my bodyguard, who glowered at him distrustfully.

"I assume you're going to demand that I relinquish my weapon," Narian calmly explained.

Tadark said nothing, but warily snatched the knife from Narian's proffered hand.

"It is of no great loss to me," Narian continued, sounding indifferent, as Tadark tucked the dagger away in his belt. "A Cokyrian is never without weapons."

I wasted no time puzzling over this last statement, for heat was rapidly rising inside me.

"Look what you've done!" I railed, frustration emanating from the very pores of my skin. "My dress is ruined!"

Narian surveyed me, unaffected by my outburst.

"You'll find walking to be much easier now," he said. "And I must say, Princess, that there wasn't much hope for your gown anyway."

I opened my mouth, expecting a suitable comeback to emerge, but none came. Before I could gather my wits, he started once more down the path, and I followed silently after him, shaking my head in awe of his nerve. But, I grudgingly had to admit to myself, I didn't stumble once.

Chapter Fifteen
Unappealing Proposals

M y Lady, Lord Steldor awaits you in the garden."
"Thank you," I said to the young Palace Guard who had
been sent to the library to find me. I had been lounging, reading a
book, and simply letting my thoughts wander. As the guard hurried
away, I groaned inwardly, though my feelings were no doubt
written upon my face. Steldor was not the person I wanted to see.

In fact, the only individual on my mind was Narian. I could not
escape from the image of his knife drawing near my flesh, or erase
the knowledge of how easily he could have harmed me before
Tadark arrived to stand between us. Narian was completely correct
regarding my protection — in a scenario such as the one I had faced
two days previously, the sole person who could have defended me
was me, and I barely possessed the ability to flee with some
semblance of coordination.

I thought back to how he had snatched me from the river. I
could have drowned — my own bodyguards had been too far away
to rescue me. But Narian had been there, having somehow bypassed
Tadark and (more impressively) Halias. How long had he been with
us before he had saved my life? Had he simply been standing among
the trees, observing the three of us as we made fools of ourselves?
Would he have revealed himself to us if my clumsiness had not
made it necessary? How could he have gotten close enough without
any one's notice so that he could reach me before I had been

swallowed up by the water? These questions haunted me, despite my efforts to divert my attention elsewhere.

Tadark had ignored my strangely introverted attitude of late, too humiliated by his own blunder in underestimating Narian to bring up the incident. I, too, kept silent about it, preferring to ponder the mystery Narian presented on my own.

I stood slowly, and unenthusiastically began to make my way to the garden to meet with the man of my nightmares. I had not seen Steldor since the evening of the event held in honor of Narian's family, and still had no inclination to do so. Narian was almost Steldor's exact opposite, and having spent time recently with the former, I suspected that I would have a harder time than usual abiding the latter's ego.

I ambled through the corridor, in no rush to get to my destination, then walked down the family staircase, Tadark beside me this time rather than behind. My last visit with Narian had substantially increased my bodyguard's vigilance, inside as well as outside the Palace. He would not accompany me into the garden, however, as my father and Cannan deemed Steldor to be just as capable of protecting me as any bodyguard.

I saw Steldor as I entered the grounds, a short way down the path from me. He had evidently come from the Military Base, as he was garbed in a black leather military jerkin with deeply-etched scrolling over the shoulders and front, sword at his side. As I approached, I saw that he held in his left hand a bouquet of flowers that I instantly recognized as having come from the garden in which we stood — obviously an impromptu addition to whatever he had planned for me.

"You're especially radiant today, Princess Alera," he said, bowing and kissing my hand in his usual way, apparently hoping that the cheap flattery he used on other girls would have a softening effect upon me. He extended the hand in which he held the bouquet. "These flowers pale in comparison."

I wanted to roll my eyes, but I suppressed the urge and half-heartedly took the flowers.

"What do you want, Steldor?" I bluntly inquired, his outrageous behavior of a week ago uppermost in my mind.

"Perhaps we should walk," he suggested, making a sweeping motion with his hand toward the garden pathway.

"I'd rather not."

A shadow of displeasure fell upon his features at my outright refusal, and I knew his thoughts had tracked my own. "You're not making this easy for me," he complained.

"And why should I make things easy?"

"Really, Alera," he said, voice thick with condescension, "you cannot honestly believe my actions at the Palace celebration to be unjustified."

I raised an eyebrow as if to say, 'Oh, can't I?' but he unabashedly continued.

"I admit I may have overreacted somewhat, but you can hardly claim my anger was unprovoked."

"And what exactly did I do to provoke you?" I asked, my jaw set, not willing to let him get away with blaming that fiasco on me.

"You must get past these childish games!" he suddenly admonished, running a hand through his dark hair in frustration. "You know very well we are courting. Could you have possibly thought that I would react in any other way? Being seen with another man will not change the fact that we are to marry. It's time you accepted that, and began acting in an appropriate manner."

I was momentarily nonplussed for this was the first time marriage had come up in conversation between us. Both of us knew the expectations held by our parents and the Kingdom, so we had not felt the need to discuss the matter specifically. It was assumed, by Steldor at least, that we would in the future be wed. I had a different opinion.

"That wasn't quite the proposal I envisioned," I said dryly, giving him a withering look.

He sighed in frustration. "Do you want me to get down on one knee, Alera? Is that it? If that will cause you to see things as they are, then I will gladly do it."

"That will hardly be necessary, as you would only dirty your knee to hear an answer you would not welcome," I said scathingly.

Then I forged ahead without care as to the consequences.

"I believe *you* need to get past the childish assumption that everything will fall neatly into place for you, because the truth is, the expectations of my father, of my mother and sister, of the *Kingdom*, cannot force me to marry you. In order for you to marry me, my Lord Steldor, I would have to say 'I do,' and quite frankly, I don't!"

I brandished the bouquet of flowers he had given me in his face.

"My only regret is that my flowers had to die in vain!"

I hurled the bouquet at his chest, then turned and stalked down the path, a triumphant smile pulling at the corners of my mouth at his affronted expression.

As I reentered the Palace, the same guard who had informed me of Steldor's request to meet with me was talking with Tadark.

"Your Highness," he said respectfully when he saw me, giving a slight bow. "The Captain of the Guard requests to see you and your bodyguard in his office. He said it was of some importance."

I nodded to the guard, dismissing him, and my victorious feeling was eradicated by dread. Cannan had never before sent for me, and I could think of no reason for him to want to speak with me now. Did this have something to do with the courtship between his son and me? Should I add Cannan's name to the growing list of people I had apparently disappointed? The list that included London, my father, mother, and Steldor?

Tadark and I walked through the King's Drawing Room to gain entry into the Hall of Kings, continuing across its floor to the Captain of the Guard's office, which was located near the antechamber. As we entered Cannan's domain, I saw Halias standing in the back of the room, though Miranna was nowhere to be seen.

The furnishings in Cannan's office were dark and imposing, much like the man himself. Various types of weapons hung on the walls or were confined in glass-fronted cabinets. A map of Hytanica hung on one wall, next to a map of the entire Recorah River Valley that identified neighboring Kingdoms as well as our own. The Kingdoms of Gourhan and Emotana lay to our south, across the Recorah River. To our west, Lake Resare, fed by a tributary of the Recorah River, marked our boundary with the Kingdom of Sarterad. I involuntarily shuddered as I noted the identification of the Kingdom of Cokyri in the high desert area of the Niñeyre Mountains to the north and east of our borders.

Cannan, as Commander of Hytanica's military, had to be the busiest man in the Kingdom, for the heads of each of the Military's five divisions were under his direct control. This meant that the Major in charge of the Reconnaissance Unit; Kade as Sergeant at Arms in command of the Palace Guard; the Master at Arms who headed the City Guard; the Colonel who was Headmaster at the Military Academy; and the various Battalion Commanders who led the Armed Forces all reported to him. In addition, the members of the King's Elite Guard were under his authority.

The Elite Guard was charged most specifically with defense of the King and the Royal Family. There were three ranks within the Elite Guard, but even the lowest rank was above those soldiers in the Palace Guard, the City Guard, and the Armed Forces, so that an Elite Guard could take command of the necessary troops if circumstances warranted. London, Halias, Destari, and the other Elite Guards who held the rank of Deputy Captain were the highest ranking officers in the military aside from Cannan, followed by the Colonel in charge of the Military Academy. Next came the Sergeant at Arms, the Master at Arms, the Commander of the Reconnaissance Unit, the officers at the Military Academy, and the Elite Guards at the rank of Major. The lowest ranking Elite Guards were Lieutenants, as were the Battalion Commanders. Steldor, Galen, and the other Field Commanders were under the authority of one of the Battalion Commanders, and directly led the troops on the battlefield.

Cannan sat behind his austere, heavy oak desk, studying several sheets of parchment. The only other items that lay before him were his sword, which was to his right, and a couple of quills and a bottle of ink. Behind and to his left side, the door to the armory stood ajar, revealing a wide variety of weaponry. A second door that I knew led into the guard room by the Grand Staircase was closed. Cannan raised his head as I entered, but did not rise.

"Please be seated, Princess Alera," he said, motioning to the wooden chairs across from him on the other side of the desk.

As I complied, Tadark moved to stand on my right side, Halias taking up a similar position on my left, neither sitting while in their Captain's office, although there were several chairs available.

Cannan did not waste time with small talk.

"I understand that you visited the country estate of the Baron Koranis two days ago. Tadark has informed me that you spent time with his son. What was the nature of your exchange with him?"

I was taken aback at his interest, but nonetheless answered his question, albeit somewhat hesitantly.

"We discussed what he called the impracticality of my clothing."

"Tell me more," Cannan prompted.

"He said that I should be able to defend myself; that Tadark's protection was—" I glanced uncertainly at my bodyguard "—inadequate." Tadark bristled slightly but remained mute. "He told me that Cokyrian women wear dresses only on formal occasions and that they always bear weapons."

Cannan mulled over my words for a moment, then changed the topic slightly.

"Tell me about the dagger. Did you see where he had it concealed?"

"No," I replied, feeling quite inadequate for I could provide very little useful information. "It was just there in his hand."

Cannan did not seem disappointed by my answer.

"Can you think of anything else that would be important for me to know?" he continued, and his words gave me hope that this inquisition was about to end.

I concentrated for a moment, then recalled something I had not fully appreciated at the time, but which now gave me great pause.

"He did say something rather odd to Tadark as he offered him his knife," I said, recognizing halfway through my sentence that I was likely contradicting whatever story Tadark had woven as to how he had managed to disarm Narian. "He said, 'Cokyrians are never without weapons.'"

Cannan nodded, then directed a question to Halias.

"And do you have any explanation for how this boy managed to get near enough to the Princess to rescue her from the river without somehow alerting you to his presence?"

Halias' light blue eyes flicked in irritation in Tadark's direction, as he apparently had not known before this moment that the younger guard had informed their Captain of this particular aspect of the incident.

"I have no explanation, sir," Halias said, automatically coming to attention, "but I can assure you that we were vigilant in our protection of the Princesses. I know of only one other person who could have accomplished this, and he ought to be standing in Tadark's place."

The silence that followed was deafening. Tadark gave an offended huff, and Cannan shot him a silencing glare before turning back to Halias, his countenance stony.

I was dazed by the boldness of the bodyguard's statement. Halias, unlike London, had never been one to challenge authority. He did his job in protecting my sister, but was generally content to trust his Captain and the King to make important decisions. Now, as he looked unflinchingly at Cannan, I realized that Destari and I were not the only ones who still trusted London, regardless of how damning the evidence against him might be.

Cannan had not broken eye contact with his Deputy Captain,

and I slowly became conscious of the fact that Halias' assertion could be treated as insubordination. But just as I began to fret, he again shifted his scrutiny to me, letting Halias' defiance pass unaddressed.

"You had an exchange with Lord Narian on the balcony at the Palace celebration last month," he said, and I felt as though I were once more under interrogation. "What did you discuss then?"

I shifted uncomfortably, unsure of what information he was hoping to obtain from me. I thought back to the evening when I had stood beside Narian on the balcony, all the while feeling that none of this was Cannan's business, but too in awe of him to say so. Just as I concluded it would be best to tell him what I could, I remembered that I had confessed to Narian my disapproval of, and extreme dislike for, Steldor.

"Well..." I said, trying to phrase the information in such a way that I would not be forced to share my opinion of Steldor with his father, "we talked about the importance of duty."

A shadow of a frown fell on Cannan's face, as though he were contemplating what would have prompted us to confer on such a topic.

"I see. Go on," he finally commanded.

"He told me that he despised having his life laid out for him," I sheepishly replied, examining my shoes, knowing, though no one else did, that my complaints about my obligations as Crown Princess had inspired this declaration from Narian.

Cannan, if aware of my discomfort, chose to ignore it.

"Interesting," he said. "Did he say anything else?"

"Yes... that at some point, I would have to choose between carrying out my duties and living my life." I winced at Cannan's penetrating look, then quickly finished, "After that he offered to escort me back inside." I did not elaborate, knowing everyone in the room was knowledgeable as to the succeeding course of events.

A long silence followed, as Cannan sank into thought, unperturbed by what I might be feeling. In truth, I found myself humbled and humiliated. Did the Captain somehow view my encounters with Narian as inappropriate? Perhaps he shared Steldor's opinion of my conduct, that I should be approaching my responsibilities more seriously and not be wasting my time speaking to sixteen-year-old boys? I was desperate for this line of questioning to end, and fidgeted nervously with the folds of my skirt until Cannan spoke once more.

"I want you to return to Baron Koranis' estate to visit Narian and his family several times during the next month. You will report to me on anything Narian tells you about Cokyri and his upbringing there."

His candid request, or more accurately, his outright order, perturbed me.

"Are you suggesting that I spy for you?" I inquired apprehensively, my stomach beginning to tighten uncomfortably.

"No," he smoothly replied, unfazed by my response. "I simply want you to interact with him and relate to me any information he volunteers."

I still was not happy with the idea.

"I don't want to betray his trust," I ventured, though I sensed my attempt to dissuade Cannan would be futile.

Cannan was silent for a moment, as though deciding whether he owed me an explanation. Then he spoke placatingly.

"You must understand that what Narian has told you of his past in your two brief meetings exceeds what he has revealed to any other person. In order for *us* to trust *him*, we need to learn about his life in Cokyri. Who raised him? What has been his training? How did he learn of his true identity?"

Cannan's tone now became insistent, and his eyes held mine.

"It is imperative that we discover what we can about his background. He seems to be more open with you than with anyone else, and it behooves us to take advantage of that fact."

I nodded solemnly, feeling rather childish for attempting to argue with him.

Cannan stood and planted his hands on the wood surface before him, brushing the sheets of parchment aside. He then spoke to the three of us, his voice unassailable.

"No one other than those in this room and the King has knowledge of this plan, and no other is to learn of it." Addressing me, he continued, "You may choose to invite Princess Miranna on your return visits to see Narian. In fact, to avoid scrutiny, I would strongly suggest that you do so. But, she will be kept ignorant as to your true purpose."

Cannan's eyes flicked to Halias' face as well, and he allowed a transitory pause to emphasize his point.

"That is all," he bluntly finished, straightening to his full height. "You may go now."

I rose as Tadark and Halias turned to escort me back to my quarters. Having had few dealings with the Captain of the Guard in the past, I was impressed by the measure of authority he had exhibited, even toward a member of the Royal Family. He was confident in a much different way from his son — Steldor was conceited, while Cannan was decisive. The deep respect I had for him made me feel as if *I* should have bowed prior to leaving his office.

It was early September, and this time my mother was hosting a recital in the Music Room of the Palace. She had invited two dozen young noble women, accompanied by their mothers, to share their accomplishments in voice and with the harp and flute. Miranna would be one of the young women demonstrating her talents on the harp, but my mother had not approached me with a similar request, perhaps thinking I had endured enough stress over the last month as a result of the Palace function I had successfully orchestrated.

I was thankful that this gathering had such a specific aim, as it meant there would be little time for gossip. I dreaded the questions that would be flung at me with respect to the altercation between Narian and Steldor that had taken place just two weeks previously.

The Music Room was adjacent to the Queen's Drawing Room, and likewise had a bay window that yielded a view of the east courtyard. Two rows of benches had been arranged so that they faced away from the window toward the front of the room where the performers would sit or stand. I glanced outside as I selected a bench, and could see that summer was rapidly giving way to fall, as the flowers in the courtyard were beginning to forlornly wither and die, while the leaves on the trees were taking on vibrant hues. As I seated myself, dark-eyed Reveina, ever the leader, slid in on one side of me, boy-obsessed Kalem on the other.

"So tell us," said Reveina, her voice eager, but hushed. "What exactly happened between Lord Steldor and the Cokyrian?"

She brushed back her sleek brown tresses as she leaned intimately toward me.

"Yes, we were in the Ballroom that evening, but did not witness the quarrel. We've heard so many conflicting versions of it that we want to know the truth from you," Kalem excitedly added, her glistening blue eyes framed by her coal black hair.

"His name is Lord Narian," I said tersely. "And he is Hytanican, not Cokyrian."

Neither my comments nor my argumentative manner dampened their enthusiasm.

"Did Steldor strike him? Did he strike Steldor?" Reveina was persistent. "We've heard both versions, and tend to believe the first, but the second would be so ..."

"Worthy of gossip?" I finished.

"Yes, of course," laughed Kalem.

I glanced toward the front of the room, longing for the performances to begin. As Miranna, who was to play first, was not yet ready, I attempted to put a stop to the speculations as best I could.

"There was no fight at all," I said softly, but firmly. "Steldor had just consumed more ale than he perhaps should have, and had become a little jealous. He did not like me speaking with Narian, although it was to be expected that I would converse with the guest of honor." I was being as tactful about the incident as I could. "Sorry to disappoint, but no one hit anyone."

Their faces dropped, and their lips formed a pout, as if they had at least expected I would make a good story out of it. Before they could say anything further, the first notes of the harp caught my ear and I was saved by the start of Miranna's solo.

The recital continued for another two hours, alternating between singers and instrumentalists. Right before the last vocalist of the day, I stood and excused myself, hastily exiting the room so I would not have to deal with any further inquiries. I knew my mother would view my behavior as rude, and that I would suffer a reprimand later, but that was a price I was definitely willing to pay.

Chapter Sixteen
Abhorrent Deeds and Successful Missions

By the time Miranna and I paid another visit to Koranis' country estate, harvest time was upon us. From mid-September through October, crops such as wheat, barley, rye, and oats were gathered and stored, grapes were harvested for wine, honey was collected, and fruit, including the apples in the Royal Orchards, was picked. It was the most anticipated time of the year, culminating in a week of celebrations at the end of October that included feasting and dancing, along with a Tournament and Faire.

As we crossed the countryside in our buggy, I idly considered what Narian would think of the upcoming festivities. I doubted he would be as enthused as the rest of the Kingdom, for if he had been disappointed by almost everything else he had seen in Hytanica, as Semari had indicated, then I supposed he would look askance at the harvest festival as well. Even so, I could not help but hope that after partaking of the most thrilling of the year's celebrations, he would prove to be more impressed with Hytanica than he had yet been.

Miranna and I chatted politely with Koranis and Alantonya upon our arrival at the Baron's estate until we were interrupted by Semari's enthusiastic greeting as she bounded out of the house. Alantonya politely took advantage of her daughter's materialization to retreat into the home, suggesting before she did so that we take another constitutional, though she firmly reminded us to stay far away from the river. Koranis also chose to take his leave, apparently overwhelmed by the excited chattering of the two younger girls, but was intercepted by Tadark as he began to walk toward the stables. Curious as to what business my bodyguard would have with the Baron, I stepped away from my sister and her friend so as to position myself for eavesdropping.

"I believe this belongs to you," Tadark was saying, sounding very self-important, and extending the dagger Narian had wielded after my fall into the river.

"Yes, that is mine," Koranis affirmed, sounding bewildered. "I assumed I had lost it. However did you come by it?"

"It wasn't lost, sir," explained Tadark, sounding almost gleeful. It was obvious he knew that he was about to cause trouble for Narian, and was enjoying the small bit of revenge he could exact for the embarrassment the young man had dealt him at our last visit. "I took it from Lord Kyenn the last time we were here. I brought it to the Captain of the Guard as I did not know it was yours."

Koranis stared blankly at Tadark for a moment.

"I remember having it when we were out riding and thought I must have dropped it. But if Kyenn had it..." A flush crept over Koranis' double-chins as comprehension dawned.

"Kyenn!" he angrily called, turning to face the house.

After several minutes, and another urgent call, Narian sauntered out the front door, apparently not feeling the need to hurry in spite of the insistent quality of his father's voice.

"In what manner did you come by my dagger?" Koranis demanded as Narian came to stand before him.

"I extracted it from its sheath," Narian coolly answered.

"Then you are a thief, boy, and I will not tolerate a thief in my home!"

Koranis, who had assumed a stern posture, almost imperceptibly flinched as Narian's piercing blue eyes locked upon his own. Tadark, who was smaller in stature than the other two men, now looked cherubic, undisguised joy shining upon his boyish face.

"Perhaps a good whipping is in order to teach you respect for other people's possessions," Koranis asserted, although his words, strangely enough, came out sounding more like a proposal than the imposition of a punishment.

There was silence in the aftermath of the Baron's statement. Even Semari and Miranna's prattling had died away as they watched father and son in fascination. I could not tear my attention from the scene, as the golden-haired pair stared at each other, Narian's lean and muscular build in sharp contrast to Koranis' over-fed and over-fussed appearance.

Narian casually appraised the Baron with definite disdain in his eyes, showing no sign of remorse or concern in the face of Koranis' threatened penalty.

"I wouldn't try that if I were you," he cautioned, his voice barely audible.

Koranis took a small step back from his son, realizing as he did so that the two of them had attracted our full attention.

"Get back into the house," he blustered, quickly dismissing Narian. "I will deal with this later."

Narian shrugged, then unhurriedly reentered the home.

Plainly perturbed by Narian's attitude, Koranis turned to my bodyguard and curtly said, "Thank you for returning my weapon to me." He then continued on to the stables, leaving an extremely disappointed and pouting Tadark behind.

Miranna and Semari soon resumed their chattering, but I was staggered by what I had just seen. In Hytanica, the father was the undisputed head of the family, with absolute dominion over his wife, his children, and their lands and possessions. Yet I could not shake the feeling that Narian had been the one threatening Koranis, rather than the other way around. This was all the more disconcerting as Narian had neither shown signs of anger nor aggression. Rather, he had seemed to be coldly sizing up a foe, and the shocking notion that Narian held power over Koranis entered my head.

It wasn't long before Semari, Miranna and I took Alantonya's suggestion and again traipsed through the trees along the path to the river, Halias and Tadark in our wake. To my disappointment, Narian was not with us. I had taken advantage of his presence in the house to invite him to accompany us, but he had not responded, leading me to the disappointing conclusion that I would not see him further on this day. I had hoped that simple curiosity would entice him on our walk, although part of me suspected that he viewed us as tedious and uninteresting.

As soon as we reached the clearing through which the Recorah flowed, Miranna and Semari rushed ahead, their giggling becoming fainter as they approached the water. Halias went after them, but I hung back, preferring to enjoy the scenic landscape from a safer distance.

I examined my surroundings, searching for a shady spot where I might sit, and spied the gnarled, exposed root of an ancient oak tree. As I moved toward it, I was startled to see Narian leaning against a tree but a few feet to my left. He was clad in a black shirt, this time topped by a leather vest, and black breeches, colors that enabled him to fade into the shadows cast by the dense trees. It occurred to me as I contemplated him that the High Priestess at the time of her capture had likewise been dressed all in black.

Tadark had seen Narian as well and now clung annoyingly to my side, and I knew something had to be done. I stopped and turned to him, attempting to conceal my irritation.

"If Lord Narian is to be relaxed enough to talk to me, you are going to have to give me some room."

My bodyguard looked torn, but then motioned forward with his hand to indicate that I should continue without him. After glancing toward the younger girls, who were being entertained by Halias as he demonstrated the proper way to skip rocks, I changed course and began to move slowly toward Narian, knowing that there was no way to conceal that I desired to speak with him. Narian examined me as I came closer, but made no move to begin a conversation when I reached him. I decided to cut straight to the point.

"I've been thinking about what you said to me on my last visit… about protecting myself," I began, feeling enormously self-conscious due to the lack of friendly small talk preceding this exchange. Cannan might be accustomed to a measure of bluntness in his speech, but I was not.

"You were right," I admitted, trying not to let my discomfort show. "There may come a time when my bodyguards will be unable to defend me. It would seem wise that I learn to defend myself."

I waited to see what his reaction would be, but he continued to survey me impassively, and I awkwardly cleared my throat.

"I can think of no one to teach me these things, except… you," I clumsily finished.

He nodded, as if understanding how I had reached this conclusion, but his succinct reply irritated me.

"I can't do that," he said matter-of-factly.

"Why not?" I demanded, planting my hands on my hips in mild frustration. "First you tell me that I must be able to protect myself, then you refuse to teach me the necessary skills? Women in Cokyri know how to defend themselves. You said so yourself!"

He smirked, the same smirk I'd seen on the balcony. "Women in Cokyri wear breeches."

I was silent for a moment, slowly grasping the implication. "You want me to… wear breeches?"

"Only if you wish to learn defense," he replied, raising an eyebrow ever so slightly, and I had the unmistakable impression that he was issuing a challenge.

"Then I will do so," I said decisively.

I waited for him to offer a pair to me for my use, but he said nothing, the gleam in his startlingly blue eyes telling me he knew exactly what was on my mind, but that he would not give me anything unless I specifically requested it. And that I was not about to do.

"When next I come," I said obstinately, "I will bring breeches."

How I was going to accomplish this was beyond me at that

moment, but I cared not. I would not give Narian the satisfaction of having a Princess of Hytanica request to borrow a pair of his trousers.

We returned to the Palace before dusk, although the pale shades of evening were beginning to brush the sky, and slowly walked up the courtyard path and through the large front doors into the Grand Entry Hall. I began to climb the left side of the winding double staircase, expecting Miranna to follow, but she made some comment about wanting to stroll in the garden as she was feeling stiff from the buggy ride.

I wavered, debating whether I should join her, when the sound of a door opening and closing and footfalls other than my sister's reached my ears, and I saw Steldor emerge from the guard room to the right of the staircase, from which one could gain access to Cannan's office. Not wanting to be seen, I hurried up the stairs to Tadark, who had already reached the landing. Steldor stood in the entryway for a moment, then proceeded in the same direction as Miranna, settling the question of whether I should follow after my sister. I instead elected to continue on to the library.

"You're not actually going to wear breeches, are you?" Tadark asked disbelievingly when we reached my destination.

It was obvious that he had overheard at least part of my talk with Narian, and I feared that he might include mention of my plan to the Captain of the Guard when he next made his report, which would mean both Cannan and my father would learn of my intentions. That would put an end to any possibility of acquiring a pair, which in turn would paint me as foolish in front of Narian when I returned empty-handed, not to mention that it would leave me with no one to teach me self-defense. The time had come to refresh Tadark's memory as to something I had not mentioned since the day of the picnic.

"Yes, I am," I said with assurance, "and you are not to say a word about it... to anyone."

"It is hardly appropriate for a Princess to wear a man's clothing," he said, trying to persuade me to change my mind.

"Your opinion isn't relevant, Tadark, and this will not get back to the Captain or my father," I declared, preparing to deliver my final blow. "Or I will be forced to inform them of your errors in judgment when Miranna was injured at the picnic."

His face paled and I felt a twinge of pleasure in knowing that I had succeeded in securing his cooperation.

"Fine," he grudgingly muttered, crossing his arms.

Feeling rather proud of myself, I began to ponder the problem of how to obtain the trousers. Concluding that I needed a co-conspirator, I decided to find Miranna in the garden after all.

I left the library and descended the spiral staircase, making my way to the rear entrance of the Palace. Tadark pulled open the heavy oak doors for me and I stepped into the waning sunlight. As I looked down the row of unlit torches, I saw Halias leaning against the wall not far from where I now stood, in a posture that brought London to mind

"Where is Mira?" I asked, for he generally would have been walking with her.

"She is by that fountain," he said, smiling in greeting and pointing down the path directly in front of me.

I turned to approach the fountain he had indicated, leaving Tadark in Halias' company, and as I did so, saw that Miranna was not alone.

Her back was to me, but over her shoulder, I could clearly see Steldor's arrogant, but incredibly handsome, face. He was almost six inches taller than Miranna, and based on his expression, took note of me before my sister had any idea that I was present. He was quite openly flirting with her just as he had been down by the river on the day of our picnic. On that day, he had been attempting to settle the score with me for refusing his advances. Now, as his dark eyes burned into mine over my sister's back, a sly sneer curved his lips, and he did something even I would never have believed him to be capable of doing. Wrapping an arm around my sister's waist, and placing his other hand upon her upper back, he pulled her smoothly toward him, then gave her a long and lingering kiss on the lips.

I was too thunderstruck to react as Steldor stepped back from Miranna. She swayed on her feet, visibly overcome by his romantic gesture, but he moved around her without a further glance.

"Princess," he murmured as he swaggered past me, his tone in that single word revealing how infuriatingly satisfied he was with himself.

Miranna turned in confusion as he sauntered away, not understanding his abrupt change in attitude, and I knew the moment she saw me, for her eyes widened in horror. She could no doubt sense my cold fury, though it was directed at Steldor rather than at her. I walked toward her without speaking and with no design to be vindictive, although the slightly hysterical darting of her eyes and her tiny backward step told me that she believed otherwise.

"Alera," she squeaked, her hands flying to her tormented face. "When did you...?"

"I saw the kiss," I said simply, saving her from having to stutter out the rest of her question. I was not angry with her — there was little she could have done to prevent Steldor's deplorable action. She was also relatively infatuated with him, and to have her first kiss come from someone over whom she swooned had probably been thrilling.

I could see that she was on the verge of tears.

"I'm sorry!" she said plaintively. "I'm so sorry! It was childish of me to be flirting with him. I'm sure I gave him the wrong impression. Steldor is yours — I had no right to kiss him, and you have every right to be upset with me."

My sister seemed to be oblivious to what Steldor had truly intended to accomplish by kissing her and was therefore blaming herself entirely.

"It's all right, Mira," I said sincerely, cutting her off before she could continue with her unnecessary apologies. "Steldor is not mine, nor have I ever desired that he be mine. He can kiss whomever he wants, as can you. You have nothing to feel guilty about whatsoever."

She shook her head. "I just feel so dreadful, Alera. Is there anything I can do to make it up to you?"

"Once again, don't bother about it. I am *not* upset with you. But..." I trailed off, determining how best to say what I had in mind. "There is something you can do."

"What? I'll do anything. Just find it in your heart to forgive me."

"Mira, I forgive you," I said impatiently, then brazenly announced, "I need breeches."

"Breeches?" she repeated, baffled enough to momentarily forget her guilt over the incident with Steldor. "Whatever for?"

"Well," I said, coming to the conclusion that honesty was the best course of action, "Narian is going to teach me some basic self-defense, and he said he'd only do so if I wore breeches. That's where I need your help."

"He's teaching you... to defend yourself? But isn't that what our bodyguards are for?"

I almost chuckled at how similar my sister's observation was to what I had told Narian on our first visit to Koranis' estate.

"Do you want to help me or not?" I asked, knowing that delving into the details of my request's origin was not relevant to her decision, and would only delay her answer.

"Of course I'll help," she said right away, just as I had known she would.

"Good."

I glanced toward our bodyguards to check that they had not moved within listening range, then pulled her down to sit beside me on one of the garden benches.

"Now, the issue is how to obtain them. We could try the laundry, but I doubt any of the guards' or servants' trousers would fit me, and I *know* Father's wouldn't."

"Perhaps we could take Tadark's," Miranna innocently suggested. "His breeches would probably be closest to fitting you."

"But how would we remove them?" I blurted, the heat rising quickly in my face as I realized how scandalously I had spoken.

Miranna stared at me for a moment, joining me in my deep blush. Then we were both seized with the giggles, and any vestiges of tension dissipated.

"I think, sister," Miranna finally gasped, "that it would be wiser just to purchase a pair."

"I agree," I said, becoming more serious. "But how will we do that? No one will see it as proper to sell trousers to a Princess, and I don't think we will be able to fool Halias and Tadark as to our activities for long."

Miranna absently twisted a curly lock of hair as she ruminated over my question, then she smiled.

"We'll commission someone to buy them for us," she said decisively.

"Like whom?"

"I don't know — but there are plenty of young boys in the marketplace who would be willing to earn some extra money by making a purchase for us. Market Day is only three days hence. We should go and make our purchase then."

I was impressed by the simplicity and yet utter brilliance of my sister's idea, and somewhat embarrassed that I had been unable to come up with it myself.

The following days crept past. Miranna was exceedingly attentive toward me, despite my constant declarations that I was not angry with her, and together we created a plan to acquire a pair of breeches without raising anyone's suspicions as to what we were doing. By the time Market Day arrived, we were ready and willing to put our strategy into action. As usual, we dressed like villagers so that we would not stand out amongst the crowd, and left the Palace before midday. Our bodyguards were once again out of uniform and walking unobtrusively behind us, thanks to Halias, who was likely restraining Tadark.

Miranna, having an uncanny ability to spot young men across great distances, was scanning the crowd for the boy who would play the most important part in our scheme — the buyer of the breeches. We needed someone to whom we could talk without our bodyguards becoming suspicious. Unfortunately, we did not generally socialize with those outside of our immediate circle of upper class young men and women. Two Princesses chatting with a market boy might seem rather odd.

Strolling beside me, Miranna let out a gasp, then grabbed my lower arm to pull me to a standstill beside her.

"What is it?" I eagerly inquired, thinking she had fortuitously located our quarry.

"Look," she said furtively, indicating where I should glance with a jerk of her head. "It's Steldor and his friends."

I peered in the direction of her nod, and my gaze came to rest upon Steldor, who was the tallest and most handsome of the group and had a particular quality that called all eyes to him. As I took in his three friends, I realized that Barid and Devant were standing on either side of a cringing young man who wore the belted, knee-length, gold suede tunic, cream shirt, and brown trousers of the City Guard. Steldor and Galen were particularly imposing figures, clad as they were in the belted, black leather military jerkins that displayed their rank as Field Commanders, and the young guard was clearly struggling to present a brave front. Steldor, who stood in front of his prey, was jabbing him in the shoulder in a way that told me whatever was coming out of his mouth was less than kind, and he wore a nasty grin. After a moment, the four friends burst out laughing and Galen clapped Steldor on the shoulder as if congratulating him on a well-spoken insult, while the guard's face turned red with resentment and humiliation.

Taking Miranna's hand, I moved us out of the flow of shoppers, and we watched in morbid fascination from twenty feet away as

Galen lightly pushed Steldor aside and stepped forward to drape an arm around their victim's shoulders in insincere amicability. He said something as well that elicited a few chortles from his cronies, going so far as to pat the guard's flaming cheek in definite mockery. After that, he began to point at the dagger hanging from the young man's belt, presumably criticizing it in some way, then had the nerve to unsheathe it, fluidly disarming the guard and no doubt adding to his embarrassment.

The guard at once tried to snatch back his knife, but Galen tossed it to Steldor, who caught it smoothly and flipped it around once in his hand. The young man pulled away from Galen and, with an ineffectual lunge, tried again to reclaim the weapon. Steldor held it away, laughing at his victim's plight.

It was then that Steldor became aware of Miranna and me, as well as of Halias, who had begun to walk purposefully toward him and his friends to break up their fun. Without a word, Steldor extended the dagger to the City Guard, his sadistic grin gradually becoming smug, an expression with which I was all too familiar. The guard hastily snatched and sheathed his weapon, glancing distrustfully between the two Field Commanders. Steldor then signaled to his three friends, and the four of them began to walk away from the young man they had just remorselessly shamed. As they did so, Steldor turned to me and bowed, a sardonic gesture that unmistakably indicated I should be applauding the show. As he strode quickly after Galen, Barid, and Devant, I could just see the self-assured smile once again spreading across his features.

"Oh, he is unbelievable!" I exclaimed, beginning a potentially lengthy rant.

"Yes, he is," Miranna cut in, "but I think I see the exact person we need."

She pointed in the direction of Steldor and his friends' retreating backs, and I saw Temerson darting around the group of four men whom I had just gone from disliking to despising. Temerson appeared jittery, as if expecting to be their next target, but the tension left his body as the group hurried by.

Miranna fluffed her hair, then clasped my hand and pulled me forward. I cast Halias a grateful smile as we brushed past him, and he gave me a slight nod of acknowledgement.

Temerson's back was toward us as we approached, and he jumped when Miranna tapped him on the shoulder.

"P-Princess," he stuttered, then, seeing me, added "ce-es. What are you doing here?"

Miranna smiled at his flustered reaction.

"We're shopping," she gently teased.

His face reddened at the absurdity of his question.

"Well, yes — I mean, what-what else would you be doing? I only meant, that, well, why are you *here*, talk-talking to *me*?" he stammered, tripping over his tongue as he tried to clarify himself.

"Because we're friends, aren't we?" Miranna answered, her tone so sweet and gentle that I had to look away lest I laugh.

Temerson's brown eyes widened and his eyebrows shot upward, indicating both his delight and astonishment at her statement.

"I, uh, I, um, err, I mean... okay."

I could tell Miranna was now also trying not to laugh, as she did not want to embarrass our potential ally.

"I'm glad that's straightened out," she said, then cautiously continued, "I'm afraid we don't have much time to talk, but could I ask you for a favor?"

Temerson's head bobbed up and down vigorously.

"Yes, anything!" he said, finally delivering a sentence without a stutter.

Miranna placed her hand upon his arm and leaned forward to speak secretively to him, just in case there was a chance Halias or Tadark might overhear. As she finished, he stepped back from her, cocking his head to the side.

"Seriously?"

"Seriously," Miranna confirmed.

While Miranna's request was a bit unorthodox, I was positive he would undertake it, if for no other reason than the gratitude he felt toward us for never disclosing the true cause of Miranna's injury at the picnic.

"We would appreciate it if you didn't tell anyone about this," my sister said, stealthily slipping a small pouch of money into Temerson's hand. "The breeches are for a friend of ours, who is about your height, but very slight in build."

"If that's what you want," he said in confusion.

"Thank you," Miranna said gratefully. "We have to go, but if you'd bring them to the Palace later today or tomorrow—"

"To the P-P-Palace? Me? B-By myself?" Temerson was alarmed.

"You'll be fine," Miranna reassured him. "Ask for me — I'll tell the guards I'm expecting you."

Temerson nodded tentatively as he murmured, "I can do it," though whether he was speaking to us or to himself was unclear.

However fretful he had been about completing his task, somehow Temerson managed it. Less than two hours later, as I sat upon the sofa in my parlor, Tadark in a chair across from me and a chess board on a small table between us, Miranna rushed through the door without knocking. She held a brown parcel in her hands and was beaming mischievously. Halias entered a step behind her, plainly perplexed by her lively mood.

I scrambled to my feet, ignoring Tadark's miserable moan of defeat as he comprehended that my last move had made me the victor in the game he had been reluctant to play in the first place, and Miranna and I triumphantly entered my bedroom. We perched upon my bed, and Miranna nimbly untied the cords that crossed over each other to encircle the package from both directions. She hastily pulled the wrapping away, and the first thing that we saw was a long stemmed pink rose lying atop the package's contents. My sister's cheeks took on the color of the rose's petals as she carefully lifted it toward her face, breathing in its delicate fragrance.

"I guess 'okay' wasn't enough of an indicator that he wants to be your friend," I said lightheartedly, knowing how much Temerson's simple gesture meant to my sister. It was sweet and romantic, and I knew Miranna would be gushing about it to Semari for weeks.

I reached into the package and pulled out the remaining item — my breeches. They were made of lightweight wool, dark brown in color, and felt rough and coarse in my hands. I got to my feet and held them up to my waist, the fabric falling almost to my ankles.

"The length is workable," Miranna observed, "but we may have to cinch in the waist somehow." She smiled widely at me. "Well, do you want to try them on?"

I eagerly agreed, and Miranna hurried over to assist by unlacing the back of my dress.

Chapter Seventeen
Self-Defense

"Here, see? I have them," I said, lifting my breeches up for Narian's inspection. "Now you have no basis for objection to teaching me self-defense."

"I can object as long as you're not wearing them," he stated dryly.

My cheeks colored slightly and I hoped he could not see my discomfiture.

"I'll need to change."

I glanced around and the pink of my cheeks deepened. We were standing in a clearing in the woods that we had reached by virtue of a fifteen-minute hike on another narrow path. We had left Miranna and Semari at the river, Halias having distracted the two of them so that we could inconspicuously make our departure. While I would have preferred a shorter walk, we had to be far enough from the Recorah so that neither of our sisters nor Halias might accidentally stumble upon us. The worst part of our chosen site was that there was no place for me to change with the exception of the woods surrounding us.

Tadark, who stood not three feet from my side, nonsensically close in light of the admonition I had given him on our last visit, had begun to glare alternately at me and at Narian, already not liking the way this afternoon was going. I was not particularly enamored with the situation myself. My discomfort increased dramatically at the thought that, without my sister or my personal maid, I would have to ask either Tadark or Narian for help in unlacing the back of my gown. Opting for the lesser of the two evils, I directed my request to Narian. At his nod, I turned around and he gathered my long brown hair together, draping it over my left shoulder.

"You should put your hair up or braid it in the future," he critiqued as he loosened my laces. "Or better yet, cut it."

I glanced at him, but was unable to determine if he were serious, then walked toward the woods in as dignified a fashion as I could muster.

"I insist that both of you turn your backs!" I called over my shoulder.

I dodged behind some trees, and after glancing toward the clearing to make sure Narian and Tadark had obeyed my wishes, removed my dress. I pulled the breeches on as fast as I could, not wanting to have an encounter with someone while only half-clad. Having brought no shirt to wear with the trousers, I tucked in my chemise. While this was somewhat bulky, it had the benefit of taking up some of the extra space in the overly large garment. Despite this, the breeches would have fallen to my ankles had it not been for Miranna's inspired thinking in sending some of her hair ribbons with me to use in tightly cinching the waist.

Regardless of the ease with which I could move while wearing men's clothing, I found the breeches to be extremely uncomfortable in more than one way — having always worn skirts in the past, the somewhat rough fabric of the breeches against my legs made me desperate to shed them in favor of my usual garb. The thought of emerging in such an outfit in front of my bodyguard and a young man I barely knew was also quite unnerving. The absence of a heavy skirt covering my legs made me feel exposed.

Knowing I was too far committed to change my mind and retain any dignity, I walked back into the clearing and over to face Narian and Tadark, who were standing side by side. Tadark shifted self-consciously, not wanting to look directly at me as though I were indecent, yet unable to look elsewhere because of the utter ludicrousness of my appearance. Narian did not seem bothered in the least, although in truth it was probably stranger to him to see a woman in the garments we wore on a daily basis than it was to see me clothed as I now was.

Narian stepped forward and to my right so that he stood between Tadark and me, and I could see the narrowed brown eyes of my distrustful bodyguard over his shoulder. Gripping my right elbow, Narian pulled me across the front of his body so my back was to his chest. I stiffened instantly at his proximity, for although he was only an inch taller than me, I was keenly conscious of his lean and muscular build, and my own vulnerability.

"No need to be so tense," he said, near enough to whisper in my ear. I could feel his breath as it passed over my cheek, and a shiver swept my body.

He pulled my forearms up so they were in front of my chest, and I balled my fists, recognizing the fighting posture he had assumed when he'd been forced to defend himself against Steldor.

"Put your feet shoulder-width apart," he instructed. "Move your left foot forward, just a little."

He turned my body away from him, then stepped back almost on top of Tadark to examine my posture, and I released the breath I hadn't known I'd been holding

"This is the basic fighting stance," Narian informed me. "Hold your left arm a little higher, and relax your muscles. The stiffer you are, the slower you'll move."

He scrutinized me once more before continuing, his voice brisk and authoritative.

"Now, the first thing you must learn is to always be aware of your surroundings. When you enter a room, you must take note of all who are present, and you must register every exit through which you could make an escape if it became necessary. The opportune moment for an enemy is the moment you let your guard down."

Without warning, Narian twisted to seize Tadark, and with

great force, pulled my bodyguard toward him so that he was thrust across Narian's hip and thrown to the ground. With a grunt of pain, Tadark landed on his back at my feet, head toward Narian, his usually well-kept sandy brown hair now in disarray.

"Any questions?" Narian asked, without extending a hand to help Tadark to his feet, as if my bodyguard were merely a prop to be used for demonstrations.

Tadark sat up and glared at Narian resentfully, face ablaze with furious embarrassment. I was astonished at Narian's audacity, and couldn't help but conclude he had been letting Tadark know who was really in control. In any case, I had to concede that he had very emphatically made his point.

Narian strode toward a large tree at the edge of the clearing. He stepped behind it and reappeared a moment later with a sheathed half-sword in his hand that was similar to the long-knives carried by my former bodyguard, though this one was fancier and newer than London's had been.

Tadark was on his feet by the time Narian returned, ready to charge full-speed at him, a battle cry upon his lips. He resisted, recognizing Narian was not presenting a threat, for which I was quite thankful, though more for Tadark's sake than anyone else's. But however grateful I was for Tadark's self-restraint, I was troubled by the fact that, for the second time, Narian had managed to acquire a weapon.

"Where did you get that?" I asked uncertainly, seeing how firmly Tadark was clutching the grip of his sword.

"I borrowed it," Narian disclosed, unsheathing it and holding it out to me.

"From whom?" I persisted, taking the sword rather awkwardly as I had never held a weapon before.

"Koranis."

I raised a skeptical eyebrow and was sure Tadark's expression mimicked my own.

"And does Koranis *know* that you borrowed his sword?"

Narian cocked his head and cast his eyes upward, as if picturing what Koranis might have been doing at that exact moment.

"He may by now. So I suggest we not waste our time," he said without remorse, stepping around me to adjust the position of the sword in my hand.

Now that I was gripping the weapon correctly, he began to teach me some basic movements. I groaned in frustration as I struggled to follow his instructions, for I made mistake after mistake. Finally, he permitted me to take a break, and I rested, perspiration dampening my forehead despite the coolness of the mid-September day.

"Why is this so easy for you?" I asked, then blushed at my own idiocy. A typical Hytanican boy of Narian's age would have had sufficient military training to instruct me, if so inclined, in the same things Narian was endeavoring to teach.

Narian didn't view my inquiry as irrelevant as did I, and answered simply, "I've had weapons training."

"I suppose your training has been similar to that of Hytanican boys," I said, thinking out loud. I waited for him to confirm my statement, then realized that he would have little knowledge of our military schooling.

"Hytanican boys enter the Military Academy at fourteen, so you would be in your third year had you grown up here."

He gave me an odd look, as though uncertain as to my interest, then seemed to perceive my curiosity as simply that — curiosity.

"When I was fourteen, I'd already been in training for eight years," he informed me.

I gave no response, hoping that none was necessary, as I was unable to formulate one. If he were telling the truth, he had begun his training at age six. *Six years old.* Were all Cokyrians taught at such a young age? I could not imagine what military skills one could teach a six-year-old, and the only clear thought I processed was that his answer explained why Cokyrians made such fearsome warriors.

"You were sent to military school when you were six?" I finally asked, incredulous. Hytanican boys lived at the Military Academy during the training year, and I tried to imagine being separated from my family as a six-year-old.

"Not exactly."

"Were you taught by your father then?"

I mentioned the only alternative a Hytanican youth would have had for learning such skills.

Narian gave a short and mirthless laugh.

"*Father* is not a fitting name for the one who instructed me."

His words were vague, but I could tell he did not wish to discuss it further. He proceeded to teach me several more defensive moves, and by the time my sister and I returned to the Palace that evening, my arms and body were too sore to lift a cup of tea.

It was but a week later when Miranna and I climbed into the buggy to begin another journey to Koranis' estate. As we traversed the countryside, I could see villagers hard at work in the fields, bringing in the crops. I myself did little to assist with the preparations for winter, but all the same, the approaching harvest celebrations were a source of excitement for me as well as for everybody else.

The week-long Faire, and the Tournament that was scheduled for October twenty-ninth, the last day of the festivities, were the most exciting and captivating of our revels. The Faire drew vendors from surrounding Kingdoms, who brought with them unusual wares and exotic foods, while the Tournament was the climax of the celebrations. The Tournament attracted young men from significant distances to participate in the archery, knife-throwing, and axe-throwing competitions. Others came for the horse racing, while the most skilled entered the combat events. All were enticed by the generous prize money posted by the King. I wondered if Narian, with his obvious military training, would have an interest in observing the fighting events.

As we arrived at Koranis' home, I knew by the way Tadark's jaw locked that he remained adamantly opposed to the idea of Narian instructing me in self-defense. I, on the other hand, was looking forward to Narian's teaching, and had once again brought my breeches. I had briefly debated wearing the trousers underneath my regular clothing, but did not want their roughness against my legs during our journey. To simplify changing, however, I was wearing a basic skirt and blouse, and my hair hung down my back in a single long plait so it would not draw Narian's criticism.

After greeting Koranis and Alantonya, my sister and I, accompanied by Semari, Narian, and our bodyguards, went off to enjoy the day. As the weather was continuing to cool, Alantonya had suggested that instead of visiting the river, we pick berries down at the forest's edge. We took several willow baskets to fill, as the berries would be plentiful at this time of year.

To save ourselves from having to haul brimming baskets of fruit back to the house, we concluded it would be wise to make use of the buggy. Halias handled the reins, to spare our poor driver the boredom of sitting in the buggy while we picked the berries, and I sat in front with him. Miranna and Semari were in the seat behind with the baskets at their feet, and Tadark rode his own mount. Narian received permission to ride Halias' cremello and was thus saved the effort of saddling one of Koranis' horses, and with that, the six of us were on our way.

The leaves on the trees and bushes were turning color, painting Koranis' estate in gorgeous tones of deep gold, orange and russet. I had not thought the Baron's land could be any more beautiful, but the mixed palate of the forest was breath-taking.

The berry bushes were not far from the beginning of the path we followed to reach the river, perhaps less than a quarter mile. Upon reaching our destination, Halias tied the horses and helped me down from the buggy, but before he could extend the same courtesy to Miranna or Semari, they had jumped to the ground, each carrying a basket, and had run toward the forest's edge.

I glanced under the back seat of the buggy where I had hidden the package containing my breeches prior to leaving the city. As Narian had not attempted to speak with me, I did not know if he was in the mood to give instruction this day. Thinking he perhaps was not, I picked up a basket, intending to join the younger girls, but froze as I saw Halias approach Narian where he had dismounted from the cremello stallion.

"I am to check you for weapons," he informed Narian. "The Captain of the Guard's orders."

Without objection, Narian rolled up his left shirt sleeve, and pulled a dagger from a sheath strapped to the inside of his forearm.

"You will find no others," he said as he handed it to Halias.

Halias gazed steadily into his eyes for a moment, then tucked the blade into a saddlebag and went after the younger girls. Narian nonchalantly approached the wagon, and I fought the urge to ask if the weapon he had just surrendered to Halias had been "borrowed" from Koranis.

"Retrieve your package from under the seat and tell your guard to bring his horse," he murmured in my ear as he brushed by me.

I nodded, impressed by how observant he was, then retrieved the package and surreptitiously tucked it into my basket.

"Take your horse with you," I said to Tadark, who was standing nearby.

At the inquisitive lift in his eyebrows, I shrugged, indicating that I knew no more about the request for the horse than did he. He scowled in response, surmising that this had been Narian's idea, then trudged over to his mount to grudgingly untie it, startling the animal in the process.

Narian was standing fifteen feet from where Miranna and Semari were picking berries. Halias was between Narian and the girls, with his back to us. As I moseyed toward them, not wanting to draw notice, Narian disappeared into the woods. I peered into the trees to see where he had gone and perceived a narrow trail that slowly widened as it reached further into the forest. With one final fleeting look at the people to my right, I entered the woods and began to follow the path. A few moments later, Tadark approached me from my left, leading his horse, having ducked into the trees some distance away from the others so as not to attract attention. Ahead, down the trail, I could see Narian waiting for me.

"Where are we going?" I asked as I approached.

"To the clearing," he replied, his tone telling me he viewed my question as superfluous. "You'll need to wear those breeches again."

He turned and hiked on. Beginning to feel the weight of my skirt as I climbed a small slope, I called to him, panting from exertion.

"Perhaps I should change now. It would make all this walking much easier."

He stopped and turned to face me, obviously consenting. I moved into the cover of the trees and changed with haste into my breeches, emerging this time without a moment of indecision. After I had deposited my skirt into the basket and placed both in Tadark's custody, I began to follow Narian once more.

When we reached the clearing, Narian walked behind the same tree from whence he had previously obtained the half-sword, but when he emerged this time, he held a long, coiled rope. He gave the rope to me and went to Tadark's horse.

"We're not going to be fighting today, if that's what you wish to ask," Narian volunteered, addressing the issue that had been running through my mind and yet managing with his simple statement to fill me with dread.

"Then what are we doing?" I queried apprehensively as he started to strip the saddle and pad from the horse's back.

Tadark's body went rigid and his eyebrows dove toward his nose in a scowl, showing his offense at Narian's subtle disrespect — taking charge of his mount without pausing a moment to seek permission.

After putting the saddle on the ground, Narian took the reins from Tadark and led the horse toward me as I stood in the center of the clearing.

"Surely women in Cokyri don't ride horses," I hedged, hoping I was wrong about his intentions.

"The woman who raised me is one of the best riders in our

Kingdom," he informed me, and I noted that this was only the second time he had referred to someone who had been present during his childhood. I was too absorbed in my own predicament, however, to give his statement further consideration.

"You don't expect *me* to get on that creature, do you?" I sputtered, ready to refuse with all my strength of will.

"Do you expect me to continue teaching you?" he countered, taking the rope from my hand and attaching it to the horse's bridle.

I frowned, not liking where this was heading.

"I do," I said in trepidation.

"Then I suggest you get on the horse." There was the slightest trace of impatience in his manner.

He tied the reins together and slipped them over the animal's neck, laying them upon its withers. The horse was dark bay, with a black mane and tail, and although it stood calmly enough, I was certain I could detect an evil gleam in its large brown eyes. It snorted and pawed the ground, as if to substantiate my belief.

"I don't particularly like horses," I informed Narian nervously, though I sensed that nothing I said would deter him.

I gazed at him almost pleadingly, but he simply stood beside the animal, absentmindedly patting its neck, his steely eyes commanding me. With a deep breath, I reluctantly acquiesced and stepped up to the beast, then waited for him to lift me onto its back.

He did not. He simply bent his knee toward me while holding the reins under the horse's chin, offering his leg as a step so that I could mount by myself. As much as I wanted to, my pride would not let me back down, even though it seemed to me that the dark and menacing animal had grown incredibly large in the last few seconds. If Narian thought I could mount this beast by myself, then I would not prove him wrong. I put my left foot on his leg and hoisted myself upward, balancing a moment before proceeding.

"Take hold of the mane," he instructed, and I did as I was told, wrapping my fingers into my mount's coarse hair. Surprisingly, I managed to jump up on the first try, though I landed on my stomach across the horse's back. I fought to avoid sliding downward, employing all my strength so that I was finally able to swing my right leg over the animal and sit up straight.

I couldn't help but beam triumphantly at my accomplishment. Tadark, who was standing at the edge of the clearing over by the saddle, gazed askance at me, but I ignored him, looking instead at Narian, who was shaking his head in mild amusement.

Narian began to lead the horse and before I knew it, had extended the rope so that the dreaded beast was walking briskly around him in large circles.

"Sit up straight, but don't stiffen," Narian said to me, his voice light and soothing. "You can let go of the mane. You won't fall."

I relinquished the horse's mane, to which I had subconsciously been clinging quite tightly, and rested my hands on my thighs. I began to think myself silly for having been so afraid of riding, feeling quietly secure now that I had mounted on my own and was sitting on the back of the moving animal without having suffered serious injury.

"Let your legs stretch down," Narian directed, falling silent when I obeyed.

As I relaxed, my hips moved with the horse's gait, and I began to feel as if riding was an improvement over walking. Although I hated to admit it, I was actually enjoying myself, and I bit my lip to keep from smiling. Narian, however, never encouraged my efforts with praise, but simply gave instructions and made corrections when I was doing something wrong. His next directive, however, rekindled my anxiety.

"Hold onto the mane again," he said.

I latched onto the horse's thick locks immediately, but before I could question his abrupt instruction, he urged my mount into a slow trot with a soft *cluck* of his tongue.

Instinctively, I leaned forward into the animal's neck, cleaving desperately to its flowing black mane, certain I would fall. As I flopped about like a fish trapped on shore, I wanted nothing more than for my riding lesson to end.

"Sit up," Narian brusquely commanded. "You have to sit up straight and move with the horse, just like before."

"But that's impossible!" I insisted, my voice breaking every time one of the horse's hooves connected with the ground.

"It's not impossible. You simply have to try. Now use your hands to push yourself upright."

I did no such thing. I was too petrified to move, let alone attempt to follow his instructions, lest I go crashing to the ground. My pride and my determination not to disappoint Narian had long since deserted me, and now surviving was the only thing upon which I concentrated.

"Alera, you're not listening to me," Narian said, irritation lacing his words.

"I can't!" I cried in a panic.

Narian brought the horse to a halt and began to saunter toward me, casually coiling the rope around his hand. I sat up shakily as he approached. *Maybe he's given up on me*, I thought feverishly, silently begging him to help me dismount.

He untied the end of the rope from the bit and tossed it to the side.

"Move forward," he commanded.

"What?" I asked, perplexed.

"Slide up," he repeated, annoyed at my failure to comply.

I slid toward the horse's withers, uncertain as to the need for his request and definitely disappointed that the lesson was not coming to an end. But before I could venture a guess as to what he was planning, he had grabbed the mane and swung effortlessly onto the horse's back, landing behind me. Placing a hand on my waist, he pressured me to shift toward him so I would again be correctly situated on the horse's back.

He reached around me and took the reins in both hands, clucking so that the horse moved back into the trot. I was tense now for two reasons — the horse's trot was no more comfortable the second time around, plus Narian was sitting so close to me that I was forced to lean against him.

If I had been flustered before, however, what he did next put me into shock. He dropped the reins, which were still tied together so they would not fall to the ground, and rested his hands upon my hips.

"You are too stiff," he said, his tone mild now in comparison with the disapproval he had previously shown. "Just sink into the horse's gait, and let your body move with it."

With his hands he began to guide my hips in following the rhythm of the horse's legs, and a tingly warmth spread from his palms throughout my entire body.

The trot now felt much smoother and was easier to ride, and I once again had to work to suppress a smile of accomplishment. We rode in circles just as I had while Narian had been on the ground, the horse apparently responding simply to the pressure he applied to its sides with his legs. He turned our mount around to trot in the other direction, the quickness of the animal's motion startling me, but with his hands resting steadily on my hips, I was not frightened.

"This isn't so tricky after all," I said, proud of my new abilities.

"You may yet prove to be a rider," he replied, "but we have one last lesson for today."

I didn't know whether to be pleased or upset.

"And what lesson is that?" I asked with some misgiving.

He gave a short laugh, and then released my hips to wrap his right arm around my waist. Without further warning, he pulled me sharply to the left so that we toppled off the horse. I shrieked in alarm as the ground came up to meet us.

Narian twisted so that I landed mostly on top of him, my cry becoming stuck in my throat by the jolt of the impact. I was too dazed to react for a moment, then realized that my position on top of him was hardly proper. I scrambled to my feet, horrified.

"What sort of lesson was that?" I shrilly demanded.

I could scarcely believe that after he had *promised* I wouldn't fall, he had deliberately made me do so. I was too flabbergasted to be angry, though I knew that emotion would emerge with time.

Narian had propped himself up onto his elbow and, to my utter astonishment, began to laugh. His face was alight and he looked like a different person altogether, his cheeks slightly flushed with happiness, his blue eyes bright and unguarded. My anger and incredulity were shut out for an instant as I saw a genuine smile upon his face for the first time since I had known him.

"You're... laughing," I said, strangely not offended by the fact that he was clearly laughing *at me*. Instead, I was curiously touched. He had always hidden his emotions and I felt privileged that I was the one around whom he felt he could drop his cold pretenses.

The smile faded as Narian came to his feet. He regarded me almost fondly for a moment before his countenance became shielded, as if his sudden display of emotion had been a mistake.

"Now that you know you can handle a fall," he said simply, "you'll be less worried about it in the future."

It was then that I heard Tadark's outraged stomping as he advanced on Narian. He stopped directly in front of the young man, his left hand resting on the hilt of his sword.

"Get away from the Princess!" he barked, though the distance I had created between myself and Narian when I had leapt up was several feet, and Narian was making no attempt to draw nearer.

Narian's face did not change, except that his eyebrows raised in amusement, as Tadark, posturing like a child in the throws of a temper tantrum, began to berate him fiercely.

"This is so vastly improper I can barely stand it! Women in breeches, women on horseback! And a Princess, no less! I don't know what you were thinking — she could have been injured! She could have died! Your behavior is reprehensible," then rounding on me he added, "both of you! I don't care what you say, Princess, and I no longer care whether I lose my post over this or not — no more of these *lessons*! You could have been hurt! Not to mention how horribly unbecoming it is for a Lady of the Royal Family to be... to be..."

He gestured violently with his hand to indicate my appearance, his face red, jaw clenched, and eyes bulging, unable to find the correct descriptive words.

"And you," he said, swiveling again and pointing an accusatory finger at Narian, "were sitting much too close to her!"

That said, Tadark marched over to his not-so-lively steed, which was munching grass, and roughly snatched its reins. He led it over to where I had mounted and tossed on the saddle, fastening it with a vengeance.

"We're going back," he pronounced, leaving no room for argument.

I shot Narian a rueful look, hoping Tadark had not offended him, but he showed no reaction and simply began to follow after my blatantly antagonistic bodyguard as he led his horse forward onto the path. I knew that I should be outraged by Narian's conduct, but I actually was resentful toward Tadark for interrupting us and ending the lesson.

We stopped halfway back so that I could change, then continued on our way. We reached the edge of the forest just as Miranna and Semari, bored with berry-picking, were beginning to search for us.

"Oh, there you are," Miranna said, her eyes flitting from me to Narian suggestively. "Where were you?"

"We went for a walk," I explained smoothly.

"With Tadark's horse?" she asked in bewilderment.

I motioned toward Tadark as if to say that he was the reason the horse had accompanied us.

We sat in the shade to eat some of the delicious raspberries and blackberries that Miranna and Semari had picked, then the younger girls scrambled into the buggy and we packed the baskets around their feet. I winced as I climbed up to sit on the hard wooden front seat beside Halias. Horseback riding, or perhaps falling, had made me quite sore.

"Is anything wrong, Princess?" Halias asked, hearing my sharp intake of breath, a hint of concern in his blue eyes.

"No, I'm fine. Picking the berries was just more strenuous than I expected it to be," I glibly said, though the odd look he gave me was a reminder that he was well aware that I had trekked in the woods with Narian while the younger girls had been gathering the fruit.

Chapter Eighteen
Sees All and Tells All

We stayed a short while at Koranis' home before beginning what, for me, was a wholly unpleasant trip back to the Palace, as the jostling inherent in the buggy ride did nothing for my aches. Miranna glanced inquisitively at me several times, but did not dare press me for information given the closeness of our bodyguards, and with a Palace Guard as our driver. Upon our arrival, I retreated without delay to my rooms, utterly exhausted. I instructed Sahdienne to prepare my bath, and was taking a soothing soak in the warm water when there was a faint knock on the door to my quarters.

I would have had Sahdienne answer the door, but I had dismissed her after she had readied my bath, and Tadark was off duty, as I had no plans to go anywhere else this day. I waited, on the chance that my would-be visitor would simply leave, but the knock was repeated with greater insistence. I hurriedly dressed in my nightgown to walk through the parlor and open the door myself, knowing who I would find on the other side.

Miranna instantly sprang across the threshold, then seized my hand and pulled me into my bedroom, settling herself upon the bed. I sat laboriously beside her, my muscles stiff and sore, knowing without doubt what she wished to discuss.

"So tell me what you were *really* doing today," she said, confirming my supposition.

"You probably wouldn't believe me if I told you," I replied, with a slight chuckle.

"Try me."

I grinned, anticipating her reaction.

"I was given my first horseback riding lesson."

Miranna gasped, wide-eyed. "Well, that's unexpected."

"It was for me as well," I admitted.

Miranna smiled slyly, romance obviously on her mind.

"Well, is Lord Narian a good teacher?"

My cheeks pinked as I recalled the unexplainable pleasure I had felt when Narian had been sitting behind me.

"Can I assume then that you've been enjoying your lessons?" she teased, reading me with ease.

Hoping to save myself from further embarrassment, I lightly said, "They're quite unlike anything I've experienced before."

"Sounds to me like Steldor may have acquired some competition."

The smile slowly faded from Miranna's face, for she knew Steldor was not a good topic to broach around me, but could not take back the words.

My detestation for Steldor gained control of my tongue.

"With or without competition, Steldor has no chance of winning my affections," I crossly declared.

"Have you spoken to Steldor since... we were together in the garden?" she asked, obviously uncomfortable.

"No," I snapped. "Nor do I have any desire to speak with him. I'd prefer he keep his distance."

If possible, Miranna's face fell even further, her eyes dropping to the cream-colored spread atop my bed. I understood then that she viewed herself as at least partly responsible for my negative feelings toward Steldor, perhaps thinking she had "come between us." I immediately regretted having entered into the subject, not only for my sake, but for hers as well.

"My objections to Steldor originated long before the incident in the garden. You are not responsible for the way I feel about him," I gently reminded her.

She raised her head and I patted her hand encouragingly, which was enough to reawaken her playful mood.

"And do you have objections to Narian?" she cajoled.

I mentally revisited my rationale for why Narian could not be counted among my suitors — I had said that he was too young for me, although in truth the youthfulness that was evident in his face was belied by the lack of childishness in his manner. I could not fathom what kind of upbringing could compel someone to act so much older than his years. And then there was the fact that we knew next to nothing about his past. I had a difficult time placing my trust in someone about whom so little was known.

Now I knew not how to answer Miranna. I had seen a different side of Narian today. I had glimpsed within him someone to whom I could relate, perhaps someone I could befriend. But just as quickly as that part of him had emerged, it had vanished.

I sighed as I tried to figure out how to best express my thoughts.

"I don't know how to feel when I am around him," I finally confessed. "I've spent quite some time with him now, but yet he won't let me see who he really is. He is always so serious, so aloof and distant. Today was the first time he has truly relaxed, and it was only for a fleeting moment."

"What happened?" Miranna queried, and I realized I had forgotten to tell her the details of the day's visit.

"I fell off the horse," I said, knowing there was no way to make that particular event sound dignified, "and he actually laughed."

For some reason, I did not want to tell Miranna that Narian had been on the horse with me and had, in reality, pulled me from its back.

"You weren't hurt, were you?"

"No, just my pride. But in that moment, Narian seemed so open — I had never seen him like that before. I couldn't help but feel something for him."

"Feel what?" Miranna asked, for once genuinely curious and with no hint of romance.

"I don't know," I said, the truth gnawing at my insides. "It's all so confusing."

Miranna's sly tone returned.

"Do you find any other young man likewise confusing?

"No, he's very unique."

Miranna smiled sweetly.

"What?" I demanded, irked by the way that smile suggested she knew more than I did.

"I've never heard you talk about anyone this way before," she giggled, and I could not assert differently. "You may as well accept it, Alera — you have another suitor."

Before I could respond, Miranna hopped off the bed to bid me a cheerful goodnight, and then pranced from the room. A moment later, she exited my quarters, pulling the door noisily closed behind her, leaving me alone with my muddled thoughts.

The following morning when Tadark came on duty, he brought with him a message that we were to report to the Captain of the Guard's office. I knew that Cannan would demand to hear about my visits with Narian, and as we walked the corridors, I tried frantically to decide what details I could relate. I was unwilling to divulge to him most of what I had told Miranna, for the information was either too personal or too objectionable.

We arrived at Cannan's office much sooner than I would have liked, as my mind was still in turmoil. The last time I had been in this office, I had felt as though I were being interrogated, and I was not looking forward to a similar round of questions. All such worries flew from me, however, when I saw Destari standing in Cannan's office near his desk. As Destari had not been involved in any of my visits, I did not think Cannan could be planning to discuss Narian.

Cannan bade me sit in the same chair I had occupied during our last meeting, and I felt a twinge of unease. Tadark did not follow me all the way into the room, but faltered by the door as if he were not permitted to cross the threshold.

"You are dismissed, Tadark," Cannan said, and Tadark quickly departed.

As my brows knit together, Cannan again turned his attention on me.

"Destari is replacing Tadark as your personal bodyguard. I assume this will be a satisfactory arrangement?"

"Yes," I said, but could not stifle my curiosity. "Why is Tadark being replaced?"

I had known that problems would result if Tadark carried out his threat to put a stop to my "lessons," but had never seriously believed that he might be dismissed from his post due to my activities.

"Tadark asked to be reassigned," Cannan frankly replied. "He informed me that personal conflicts had arisen that were compromising his ability to protect you."

A dreadful sinking feeling engulfed me, and my pulse hammered painfully in my temples. Tadark *had* spoken to his Captain. How much did Cannan actually know? Was he knowledgeable of the things Narian had been teaching me? And if I withheld that information from him, would I be caught lying to the Captain of the Guard?

I swallowed painfully, but said nothing, hoping neither Cannan nor Destari would notice how overwrought I had become.

Thankfully, Cannan did not wait long.

"You've been to Koranis' estate several times over the last few weeks," he proceeded in his business-like manner. "What can you tell me?"

I stalled before replying for as long as I dared, knowing I was risking a rebuke, then said, "Narian doesn't say much, especially about Cokyri. I've learned very little."

"I asked *what* you have learned, not *how much* you have learned," he succinctly stated, with a touch of impatience. "I will judge the importance of the information myself."

I knew then that I would have to tell him *something*. I did not think he was angry — he just did not allow anyone to evade him. However, I was determined to conceal as many details of my visits as I could.

"Narian mentioned some things about his military instruction," I reported, nervously entwining my fingers. "He told me he began training when he was six."

Cannan said nothing, but his expression commanded me to go on. I had expected some reaction from him, but his bearing told me he knew there was other information to be garnered. I squirmed inside, as his unmistakable power, coupled with his dark hair and eyes, made him tremendously intimidating.

"I don't know the nature of his training," I continued, hoping to placate Cannan without having to reveal too much, "but he gave the impression that he was not sent to a school, at least not at that age. He spoke of one teacher, but the man was not his Cokyrian father. He also made reference to a woman having raised him, but he did not call her mother."

As I relayed this information to Cannan, something else came to me.

"In fact, he has never mentioned a mother, father, or a family in Cokyri."

Cannan nodded. When I did not speak further, he stood to dismiss me.

"Very well then. You will no longer meet with Narian as you have been these past weeks, although more *conventional* visits are, of course, permitted."

I froze, momentarily staggered. There was no denying any further that Tadark had told his Captain *everything*. My reaction was not only due to Tadark's tattling, however. It was actually, to a much greater extent, due to Cannan's lack of umbrage. The fact that he had not thought it necessary to specifically address my unorthodox excursions in our conversation gave me hope that he had also considered it unnecessary for my father to be informed of them. He simply intended to make the point that nothing escaped his knowledge, and in that he had succeeded.

"Thank you," I said meekly, as I likewise rose to my feet, knowing Cannan would catch my true meaning.

Later that afternoon, Miranna sought me out in a state of poorly restrained excitement. She rushed into the tea room on the main floor where I was sitting by the bay window, warming my hands on my cup and absentmindedly watching the chilly rain falling in the expansive west courtyard. I was in a rather pensive mood that was perfectly complimented by the weather. Waving a scroll of parchment beneath my nose, Miranna exuberantly announced, "We've received an invitation to Semari's birthday celebration! And it's only two weeks away!"

My expression mirrored her enthusiasm, but for an entirely different reason. I had been more disappointed than I had cared to admit by the fact that my meetings with Narian had effectively ended. Though I knew an occasional visit would be permitted, Cannan had deprived me of the only available justification to see Narian that would not draw questions from my father. Not to mention I would now have to deal with Destari's much more assertive presence. I knew I would be permitted no latitude while Destari was on guard, whether or not he had been informed of my recent activities. This celebration, as I saw it, would provide me with a chance to see Narian in a different but completely legitimate context, one that would arouse no one's suspicion.

I took the invitation from Miranna and unrolled it, glancing over the details. The event was to be held on October twelfth, with activities and games such as tag, footraces, and apple-bobbing in the afternoon, followed by an evening of feasting and dancing. As Semari was reaching the age of fifteen, I knew this would be an elaborate affair. At fifteen, young women in Hytanica came of courting age, although marriage before the age of eighteen was generally discouraged.

Miranna gleefully snatched the invitation from my hand as soon as I had finished, and skipped out the door.

"I simply can't wait!" she called as she disappeared from sight.

The two weeks until Semari's party flew by, as preparations for the upcoming harvest festival generated a maelstrom of frenzied activities throughout Hytanica. It was exhilarating to simply roam through the city and observe the changes as merchants and businessmen positioned themselves to earn a sizeable profit off the large number of visitors that were certain to arrive.

The site for the Faire was the grassy area that was the location for Market Day. Here, additional tents for vendors had been set up and small stages were being erected at intervals among the tents for use by performers. The shop-fronts in the Market District were being cleaned, and I noted several freshly painted signs identifying some of the establishments. The taverns, inns and public bath houses in the Business District were also being readied for a large influx of guests.

The land just west of the Faire sloped down to the flat military training field of approximately fifteen acres that would be the situs of the Tournament. The field was south of the sprawling Military Complex that lay to the west of the Palace. The Military Academy, with its main classroom and office building, stables, barracks and officers' housing, made up a little less than half of the Complex. The rest of the buildings served Hytanica's permanent military and included offices, meeting rooms, a dining hall, the infirmary, a stockade, an armory, stables, barracks and officers' quarters. Both the school and the Military Base used the field for military maneuvers, although it was being marked out at this time to serve the needs of the Tournament.

When the day of Semari's birthday was upon us, Miranna and I traveled in luxury in a Royal Carriage to Koranis' estate as part of a large contingent from the Palace. My parents led our caravan in their private Royal Coach, as they thought it probable that they would return to the Palace at an earlier time than their daughters, and a third carriage bore the King and Queen's personal assistants. A dozen Elite Guards, including Destari and Halias, rode alongside the carriages on horseback, while twenty-some Palace Guards brought up the rear. As my parents were not particularly interested in the games mentioned in the invitation, we left the Palace so that we would reach our destination in the late afternoon, just before the feasting was to begin.

The weather was noticeably cooler and the days were noticeably shorter, which persuaded the trees to shed their leaves and put additional spring into the horses' trots. Given these seasonal changes, the carriages had been stocked with fur throws and several lanterns for use during the journey home.

As we arrived, I could see that grooms were stationed along the side of the house to take charge of the horses and carriages, while servants were available to escort guests to the back of the home. A large, multi-colored, open-sided tent had been erected on the flat area atop the leisurely sloping hill in which to serve the feast, and a planked floor had been laid for the dancing. As we ambled toward the tented area, I could see that long rows of tables had been arranged inside the tent, with one raised table at the far side that was perpendicular to the rest, at which the Royal Family and the hosts would sit. The high table was draped in royal blue cloth and several of the Kingdom's royal blue and gold flags fluttered behind. Cooks were busy setting out food-filled dishes at a table draped in white linen at the near end that would be used for serving. While some guests were milling about the area, most had strolled down the gentle slope to watch or participate in the variety of games taking place at the forest's edge.

Koranis, resplendent in all his finery, and Alantonya, a more understated match, came to greet us. While my father and mother talked with them, I glanced around the grounds of the estate with an eye for one person in particular, but I did not see Narian anywhere. I did not dare ask Koranis and Alantonya as to his whereabouts, as to do so would have been rude in light of the fact that this occasion was in Semari's honor. Such an inquiry might also have aroused my father's interest.

As Miranna and I began to walk the grounds in search of Semari, I continued to sweep the throng for her older brother. As it turned out, Semari located us, and came prancing our way with a large and inviting grin upon her face, her blue eyes bright and her cheeks rosy. She was dressed in a high-waisted, full-skirted, russet gown layered over a white chemise with long, full sleeves, and her white blonde hair hung in a ribbon-entwined braid down her back.

"I'm so glad you could come!" she exclaimed, clutching Miranna's hands.

Before Miranna could return her greeting, Semari had begun to pull her down the hill toward the place where another round of horseshoe toss was beginning.

"You'll never guess who's here!" she eagerly exclaimed.

I looked toward the group of boys and girls surrounding the designated area for the game and saw among them the young man with reddish-brown hair whom my sister had come to favor. Clinging to his arm was a boy about half his size and half his age, presumably his brother.

Semari and Miranna joined the group, Miranna smoothing her skirt and adjusting her hair in anticipation of talking with Temerson. Her gown was dark green, with a bodice that laced together in the front over a ruffle-necked white blouse. Her strawberry-blonde hair was loosely pulled back and tied with a green ribbon, although a few curly strands had escaped to fall softly across her cheeks.

I was attired in a flared, deep blue velvet gown with a square-necked, white satin brocade stomacher. The shoulders were puffed and slashed, and the sleeves were tightly laced from elbow to wrist, extending over the back of my hands to a point. My dark hair had been swept up off my shoulders and was encircled by a delicate tiara consisting of two parallel silver bands set with alternating sapphires and diamonds. Although I knew Narian did not necessarily appreciate the way in which Hytanican women adorned themselves, I had taken special care with my appearance this evening.

I had elected not to go with Semari and Miranna, as I knew their chattering would center around the male species, a subject I did not want to discuss. Looking back toward the house, I saw that Cannan and Faramay had arrived and were approaching my parents, evidently having elected to forego the games just as we had. I had already determined that the man I reviled was not currently on the grounds, and his absence from his parents' side gave me hope that he had chosen not to attend.

As most of the guests had gathered at the bottom of the hill, I went to join them, and my parents and their friends soon followed. I did not spend much time greeting those around me, for I wanted to find Narian. As I perused the area, I saw Cannan break away from my father and mother, and, leaving Faramay behind, begin to walk in my general direction. Confused as to what he could possibly want with me, I glanced over my shoulder and realized that he had made eye contact with Destari, who stood approximately ten feet away.

Destari did not move as his Captain arrived. Judging from their serious demeanors and their hushed tones, the issue about which they spoke was of some importance. Unfortunately, even though they were not far from me, the incessant prattle of the people in the area made it difficult to distinguish a single word, regardless of how hard I strained my ears.

Their conversation complete, Destari and Cannan began to walk toward the edge of the forest. While I had not expected my bodyguard to stay at my side all evening, given the vast number of guards who had accompanied my parents and were now scattered about the estate, the way in which he had taken his leave had been rather official, and therefore intriguing. My curiosity burning, I determined to find out where Cannan was going and what was so important that he needed to have Destari accompany him.

Chapter Nineteen
Never Without a Weapon

I followed Destari and Cannan toward the tree line as casually and inconspicuously as I could, weaving my way through the other guests, and though their destination seemed clear, it took me a moment to locate Narian, who was dressed once more in dark colors, leaning against the trunk of a large maple tree. Narian had an uncanny ability to hide in the open and thus pass undetected by almost everyone, including me, but apparently not by the Captain of the Guard. The sixteen-year-old was indifferently observing the celebratory activities, but shifted his gaze to Destari and Cannan the moment they began to approach him, as though he had been solely monitoring their movements.

I could see no harm in what Narian was doing, and so could not understand why Cannan would want to meet with him. I found myself worried for Narian's sake, but he moved away from the forest's edge and toward the two soldiers, no sign of misgiving in his stride. This time, as I inched closer so that I was on the fringe of the crowd, I was able to overhear their discussion.

"I have been informed that you have quite a talent for acquiring weapons," Cannan brusquely stated. "I hear it told that you are never without one. So, tell me, are you now armed?"

"I am," Narian replied, without hesitation.

The Captain bowed his head in appreciation of receiving an answer as straightforward as his query, then his eyes flicked toward

Narian's hip, where he would have held a sword or dagger, finally moving down to check his boots.

"I see no weapons," he pronounced, with a measure of skepticism that sprang from the fact that Narian had been disarmed by his own men when he had been taken prisoner. Still, it could not be denied that the young man had managed to acquire a weapon on at least three previous occasions.

"I have them," Narian said simply.

"Is there a problem, gentlemen?" interrupted a self-important voice I recognized as belonging to Koranis. The Baron was lightly panting, his thinning blonde hair dampened with perspiration, as he hurried over to the two men confronting Narian.

"Are you aware that your son has been obtaining weapons?" Cannan asked, without taking his eyes off Narian.

"Surely you overstate the situation," Koranis blustered indignantly. "As you well know, he took a dagger from my person several weeks ago, but was duly punished. There have been no other such incidents."

As Cannan gave a small shake of his head, Koranis rounded on his son.

"What weapons are these? Where have you been getting them?"

Narian shrugged, decidedly unruffled.

"Some are my own. Others are yours."

Koranis' affronted frown deepened, and he looked from Destari to Cannan as if trying to assess their reactions.

"That's impossible," he muttered, evidently concluding that he needed to defend himself. "I keep all my weapons in a locked trunk in my bedroom."

"Perhaps you need better locks," Narian responded with not-so-subtle disrespect.

"This is absurd!" Koranis contended, face shading toward maroon, clearly insulted by the fact that Cannan and Destari did not doubt Narian.

Narian ignored Koranis, presumably deeming his father no

longer worthy of his time, and addressed Cannan, his tone disdainful.

"You can hardly expect the rabbit to keep up with the fox."

Koranis let out an offended breath, too appalled by Narian's audacity to formulate a response. Fortunately for everyone involved, the Baron did not see Cannan incline his head toward Narian as if telling him that he understood his point.

"We will be requiring a location apart from your guests," Cannan informed Koranis. "Narian was about to show us the weapons he carries."

Narian's eyebrows lifted, as if he were trying to recall when he had so agreed, but he said nothing in protest.

Koranis huffed a few times, unaccustomed to taking orders while on his own property, and unquestionably piqued that Cannan had not referred to his son as Kyenn. But he chose not to make his complaints known.

"We can go around to the front of the house," he indicated with some measure of grace, and began to lead the way.

Cannan, Destari, and Narian followed, while I trailed a fair distance behind, utterly fascinated, and praying my presence would not be discovered. The four men reached the top of the hill and I allowed a few minutes to pass before pursuing them, knowing that once I left behind the bantering guests, my movements would be easier to detect. When I felt relatively safe, I sidled up to the side of the house and peered around the corner to look into the front yard.

"Any weapons you may have in the home are of interest to me as well," Cannan was saying. "Go and retrieve them."

Narian stood a few feet in front of the others, facing them.

"None of my own weapons are in the house," he said. "I could, however, retrieve Koranis' for you."

"That won't be necessary," Cannan said dismissively, ignoring once more Narian's show of disrespect for his father.

"I need a target," Narian stated, and Cannan motioned to an oak tree thirty feet from where I was hiding. As the group of men moved toward the tree, I pulled back to avoid being seen, but to my mortification, did not move fast enough.

"Princess, you may as well come out," Destari called irritably, and my heart began to pound as I anticipated how irate Cannan would be at my behavior.

I stepped out slowly, knowing there was no use in pretending that my presence by the house had been a coincidence. I approached the men, my eyes on the imposing Captain of the Guard, trying to gauge his reaction. To my utter relief, he turned away without a word, and it occurred to me that he saw no point in issuing an order for me to leave, as he could not ensure that I would actually obey without assigning Destari as my escort.

I moved to stand beside my bodyguard. The house was to our backs and the tree was to our right, roughly twenty feet away. Narian watched Cannan for an indication that he should commence the demonstration, showing no reaction to my unorthodox arrival. At the Captain's nod, he deftly reached into the pouch hanging from his belt and secured a small handful of powder which he threw to the ground before us.

The flash was blinding. My hands flew to my face and I stumbled backward, and would have fallen had Destari not seized me by the shoulders and pulled me into the protection of his arms. As I squinted through my fingers at the thick swirling smoke, I began to feel dizzy. The scent of the substance threatened to choke me, though it did not taste or smell exactly like smoke. It was sweeter, and with every breath, my eyes grew more unfocused.

The haze finally began to clear, although my mind remained clouded for a few moments longer. When I could think coherently again, I saw Koranis shaking his head back and forth, and Cannan scanning the area before him, for Narian had taken advantage of our disoriented state to slip from view. Then we heard a resounding *thunk*, and our heads snapped toward the tree where a knife now protruded at eye level. Destari loosened his hold on me as we all turned to look to where Narian stood behind us.

"If you want to examine the dagger, I have another," Narian casually commented, arresting Cannan's walk toward the tree to retrieve the weapon. He then knelt down and adeptly extracted a second knife from the heel of his left boot. Cannan, having reversed direction, held out a hand, and Narian extended the grip of the weapon to him. I involuntarily tensed as the Captain checked the blade, which was relatively narrow and only about six inches in length, but designed to do maximum damage, as it had jagged tines along its edge to tear flesh to shreds. Narian walked to the tree and jerked the other dagger from its trunk, returning it to its place, as he waited for Cannan's reaction.

"So the thicker sole and heel on your boot allow for a hidden sheath for the blade?" Cannan queried, obviously intrigued, as Narian returned to stand before him.

Choosing to let his actions answer the question, Narian took the second knife from Cannan, then quickly reinserted it into the heel of his left boot.

"And this powder — let me see it," Cannan commanded.

Narian untied the pouch from his belt and passed it to him without objection. Cannan opened the pouch and removed a small amount of powder, then rubbed it cautiously between his fingers. The substance sparked dangerously, but there was not enough of it in his hand to create the same effect we had just witnessed.

"Is every warrior in Cokyri equipped with similar weaponry?" Cannan queried, a twitch of his eyebrow the only indication that Hytanican soldiers were not equipped with weapons such as these.

"Not everyone."

Cannan waited for Narian to elaborate, but when he did not, handed the pouch to Destari for further examination.

"Other than the weapons we took from you when you were arrested and that are in my possession, have we now seen your arms in their entirety?" he grimly inquired.

"No," Narian shamelessly replied.

For the first time, the Captain of the Guard appeared to have lost his patience. Narian was not being particularly forthcoming, and I knew from personal experience that when Cannan asked something of you, he expected you to comply, and to do so without delay.

"Then show us whatever else you have," he ordered, his jaw rigid.

Narian held Cannan's eyes for a moment, then reached toward his belt, lightly brushing the dark stitching with which it was adorned. He pinched the end of one of the stitches between his thumb and forefinger, and withdrew a sharp, slender dart. I held my breath, inexplicably terrified of that tiny needle.

"Poisoned darts," Narian explained, holding the barb up for all to see. "If I removed this wax from the tip and pierced your flesh, you would be dead within minutes."

A look flashed between Cannan and Destari, and I heard Koranis murmur anxiously, "God save us." Then Cannan held out his hand for the dart.

"And is there an antidote?"

Narian shook his head. "The poison affects the body too swiftly for an antidote to be effective," he grimly stated.

"And you wear these next to your own skin?"

"Cokyrian warriors are willing to live dangerously in service to their Kingdom and, if necessary, to die as a result," he confirmed without emotion.

"And are you among them?" Cannan pressed.

Narian unflinchingly met the Captain's commanding eyes, but did not answer.

"I will keep these items for now," Cannan said, handing the dart to Destari as well. "I would like our alchemists to examine the substances."

Destari carefully wrapped the dart in Narian's soft leather pouch before tucking both into the shaft of his own boot. Cannan then turned on his heel to stride toward the rear of the house, an exceedingly troubled Koranis a pace behind. Stopping abruptly,

Cannan once more faced Narian.

"You will report to my office at the Palace in two days," he instructed. "Our military would be well-served by learning as much as we can from you about Cokyrian weaponry and fighting techniques. I will return all of your weapons to you at that time, including those taken upon your arrest."

Cannan turned to Koranis in response to the Baron's sharp intake of breath.

"Your son has had the opportunity to kill a number of my guards and your family several times over, not to mention certain members of the Royal Family," he inexorably stated. "As he has not shown any inclination to harm anyone, I believe he can be trusted."

Koranis, his face drained of color and his blue eyes wide with alarm, unwisely attempted to challenge the Captain's decision.

"That is easy for you to say, as he does not live in your house! I want him off my property, *tonight!*"

Cannan glared at Koranis, and I could see a rage building within him that was entirely out of proportion to Koranis' demand. He stepped menacingly toward the Baron, who recoiled from him until he collided with the side of the house. Moving directly in front of the cowering man, Cannan leaned toward him, supporting himself with one hand upon the wall.

"You are pathetic, an empty imitation of a father," he spat, glowering down at Koranis with pure loathing in his voice. "It is extraordinary that Narian is alive, a miracle that he somehow returned to Hytanica. There is no justice in the fact that of every grieving father in the Kingdom whose son was stolen by the Cokyrians, it is yours who found a way home. You, who would thrust aside this blessing for which the rest of us would kill. You fail to appreciate the gift you have been given."

Koranis cringed and tried to slide sideways away from the Captain of the Guard, but Cannan grabbed him by his dress coat, almost lifting him off the ground.

"The sight of you sickens me," he seethed, the controlled quality of his deep voice making him all the more terrifying. "I would give anything for it to have been my son who returned. I would have embraced him regardless of how he had been raised or by whom."

With that, Cannan released the quaking man and stepped back from him, although his deadly glare did not abate. It was a testament to the level of fear that gripped Koranis at the thought of Narian's continued residence within his home that he dared to speak again.

"I have a wife and four younger children to protect," he blubbered. "I cannot run the risk that you may be wrong."

When Cannan showed no reaction to Koranis' statements, the Baron slowly straightened.

"Take him with you, enroll him in the Military Academy, do whatever you think best. Just keep him away from me and my family."

Despite his attempt to regain his poise, Koranis sounded as though he were pleading. Even though I did not know exactly what I was witnessing, I began to inch closer to Destari, as concern for the Baron welled within me. I thought it entirely possible from Cannan's threatening posture that he might do the man harm. I glanced skyward in prayerful thanks when the Captain, shaking his head in disgust, took another step away, seeming to recognize himself that he needed to keep Koranis out of his reach.

Gesturing toward Narian, Cannan coldly admonished, "Like it or not, you have an obligation to the boy. If you won't let him live here, then I will move him into your city residence."

He paused, and when he continued, there was a hint of resignation in his words.

"I know what it is like to have a son who is headstrong; who, like yours, has taken my weapons and horses without permission, and who has cost me innumerable sleepless nights. Still, I would not relinquish a single moment of time with him."

I could once again hear anger rising inside Cannan, although he did not make a move toward Koranis.

"You, on the other hand, have not even tried to reach out to your son. I feel no compassion for you, and have but one regret — that I ever entrusted him to your custody."

Cannan looked almost yearningly at Narian for a long moment, and I thought I saw a flicker of the same emotion in the young man's eyes. Then the Captain abruptly returned his attention to Koranis.

"You act as though Narian is a disappointment when it is, in fact, he who has been cheated. Narian deserves a better father than you."

Cannan then turned and strode down the hill. Without waiting to see what I would do, Destari took hold of my arm above the elbow and pulled me alongside him as he followed the Captain, leaving Koranis alone to face his son. If not for Destari, I would likely have remained rooted in place, reeling from shock. I struggled to comprehend what I could only interpret as a revelation on Cannan's part that he had lost a son to the Cokyrians.

I regained my voice as Destari and I joined the guests who were now gathering at the top of the hill and beginning to enter the tent. Alantonya had apparently stepped forward in her husband's stead to call the guests to the feast.

"Did Cannan have a second son?" I weakly inquired.

Destari drew me aside, clearly disgruntled by my question.

"Yes. Like a number of others in Hytanica, the Captain had an infant son who was abducted and killed by the Cokyrians, and whose body was among those returned for burial by our enemy. Now, let the matter rest."

Fully acquainted with my persistence when my interest was aroused, he added, "And never raise such a question around Baroness Faramay."

I nodded, but continued to cling to my bodyguard's side for a few moments longer, quietly absorbing this startling information. Then a new strand of thought began to form. Was this why Faramay sometimes seemed so fragile? Was this why she devoted so much attention to Steldor? I also couldn't help but wonder how different

Steldor's life would have been if his brother had survived. I couldn't imagine my life without Miranna. A wave of sympathy crashed over me for Cannan, Faramay, and even for Steldor, although he probably had few memories of his younger sibling.

I thought of the Captain's face as he had harangued Koranis, and suddenly understood the reason Cannan had, right from the beginning, treated Narian so well, and so differently, from our other prisoners. Was this also why he had so readily taken Galen, a fatherless boy, into his heart?

And what of Narian? Was he, at the age of sixteen, already a Cokyrian warrior? His vague words seemed to suggest as much. I shivered as I thought of the weapons I now knew he had carried concealed on his person the entire time he had been in Hytanica. I remembered the first time I had met him, when Miranna, Semari and I had briefly eluded our bodyguards, and recalled that he even then had been wearing his boots and belt — the only articles of his clothing that Cannan had let him retain. I once again felt as if I did not know him at all. Did he ever truly let anyone get close to him? The only thing I knew with certainty was that there were more things in the world of which to be afraid than I had imagined.

As my mind continued to whirl, I became conscious that Destari was observing me, a measure of concern upon his face. I smiled feebly at him before venturing away from his side to enter the dining area.

Chapter Twenty
The Greater Sin

My appetite had diminished almost to the point of nonexistence, but I dutifully joined the line of people at the serving table and allowed my plate to be filled with food, for it would have been impolite to refuse the elaborate feast. In addition to a variety of breads and cheeses, the serving table held steaming platters of roast pig and chicken; smoked fish; beets, turnips, beans and other vegetables; a selection of fruits, including apples, plums, pears, strawberries, raspberries and blueberries; and baskets of nuts such as walnuts and hazelnuts. Small sugar sculptures of animals, served only at the finest of gatherings, had been prepared for dessert. Jugs of wine, ale and cider had been set on the dining tables.

As I exited the serving line, my eyes fell upon Steldor, accompanied by Galen, and my flickering hope that he would not attend was extinguished. They were standing at the end of one of the long dining tables, their plates of food seemingly forgotten in front of them on the wooden tabletop. Galen, wearing a long-sleeved white shirt and black trousers, was casually flipping a dagger between his right hand and his left, in a manner that I had come to associate with Steldor. Steldor stood by him with one booted foot upon the table's bench, resting his elbow upon his knee. He was wearing a long-sleeved, black suede leather jerkin with extended shoulders, the lacing of which was open to reveal a white shirt, and black breeches. The grip of the silver sword that hung at his side was wrapped in black leather overlaid with silver wire, and the pommel was set with rubies that might have given it a sophisticated quality were it not for the winged and barbed guard that gave notice of its power. His dark apparel suited his dark features, and gave him a mysterious and brooding look. In spite of my jaded feelings toward him, and my much subdued mood, he took my breath away. Just then he glanced at me, only to quickly avert his eyes. Although I was almost too indifferent toward him to care, his reaction surprised me, and I was rather pleased to discover that I held some sway over him.

I held my head high and chose a path through the tent toward the high table at which my family would dine. My parents were already seated, and were being individually attended by servants. My route was calculated to take me between the long tables that were furthest away from Steldor and Galen, so I would not have to risk a conversation with either of them. As I proceeded, however, I saw my strategy spoiled.

Galen moved away from Steldor and began to walk toward me, coming down the same aisle that I had entered, but from the opposite direction, so I would have no way of avoiding him without making blatant that such was my desire. I did not know Galen well, but any friend of Steldor's was not likely to be held in high esteem by me. As he approached, he absently played with the hilt of his sword, then stopped in front of me, making no attempt to disguise that he had planned to intercept me. He bowed his head in respect, his wavy ash-brown hair shifting fluidly with his movement.

"Princess Alera, may I guide you to your table?" he politely inquired.

I was not inclined to trust him, knowing that there had to be a purpose behind his solicitousness. Then I consented, permitting him to take the plate from my hands and carry it for me. It was a short walk between where we now stood and the table at which I would sit, so whatever he intended to say or do, he would have to accomplish it with a measure of haste.

"How are you finding the evening?" Galen asked genially, walking beside me, completely unharried.

"I am glad for the respite from my usual duties," I said. Unable to resist putting forth the insinuation that I was quite content to maintain my distance from Steldor, I continued, "I have found the festivities to be quite entertaining and the companionship *thus far* to be quite pleasant."

Galen caught my implication, and dropped his volume to begin a more private dialogue as we arrived at the table to stand only a few feet from my father's seat.

"I'm afraid Lord Steldor has found it quite the opposite, My Lady, for he cannot enjoy himself until he knows he is forgiven."

I met Galen's serious brown eyes coolly, hardly believing what I was hearing. Had Steldor actually been too cowardly to approach me himself to apologize? Or was such an act of contrition beneath him? Or perhaps he suspected I would refuse to listen to him, but would not as readily brush Galen aside. Regardless of Steldor's motives, I knew I was being manipulated, and I scowled in annoyance.

Galen reached into a pouch that hung from the belt at his waist and removed from it a stunning silver pendant necklace. He laid it across the back of his hand to show how the silver of the pendant swirled fluidly around to cradle at its center a tear-drop-shaped sapphire. The necklace was beautiful, expensive, and a perfect companion to my gown. I marveled as to how my erstwhile suitor had managed this feat. Perhaps, I reflected cynically, he had purchased several necklaces with different gemstones so he would have one that matched any gown I might have worn. Or perhaps he had an informant. Knowing how infatuated the majority of the female population was with him, I had no doubt that my maid would have been easily charmed into revealing my planned attire.

"Steldor wishes me to give you this as a token of his affection and as an indication of his longing to mend his relationship with you,"

Galen said disarmingly, offering the necklace to me in such a way that anyone watching would see its splendor. "He would be honored if you would wear it tonight, but if you refuse, he will accept your decision with grace and humility."

I understood the real alternatives with which Galen was presenting me. Wear the necklace, and Steldor would assume that all was forgiven; refuse, and he would leave me alone for the rest of the evening. Making my choice, I gazed at Steldor for a moment as if to first tell him that I intended to decline, before informing his friend of the same, but I vacillated, temporarily at a loss for words, as I observed Steldor's demeanor. He had not moved, and was atypically alone. One hand was resting on the table beside him, and he was drumming his fingers upon it inattentively. His expression was not haughty, nor was his stance. Rather, he looked more vulnerable than I had ever seen him in my life, as if he were actually troubling himself over the nature of the conversation Galen was having with me, and an entirely unexpected sense of compassion swept through me. Steldor did have some fine qualities, a fact that escaped me on most occasions, for I could generally not see past his intolerable conceit. But now, as that aspect of his personality was subdued, I almost wanted to make peace with him. *We might make a good couple, after all,* I told myself, as I pictured us together. *If there were some way to contain his ego.*

As I returned my attention to Galen, I saw my father wink at me, and I came to understand how clever and cunning Steldor and Galen could actually be. They had expertly executed their scheme. It would have been just as simple for Galen to give me the necklace before we'd reached the table, or to do it at a later time in the evening, but instead he had waited to be in the presence of my father. I knew my father had heard the essence of our exchange, and that if I now refused Steldor's gift, I would not only be disappointing Steldor; I would be disappointing the King.

I bit my lower lip in frustration, finally assenting, briefly turning my back to Galen so that he could fasten the pendant around my neck. I glanced once more toward Steldor, whose attention was now upon me, and saw his face brighten as I agreed to accept the gift. To my dismay, I also saw a return of his typical air of condescension.

"Thank you, My Lady," Galen said, and I scoffed internally that he was even expressing gratitude on behalf of his friend. "Steldor will greatly appreciate your gesture." Then he strode away to return to Steldor's side.

I did not track either of them further, but took my seat to my mother's left as my father beamed happily at me. My mother turned to me as well to admire the necklace.

"He does have exceptionally good taste," she commented in her lilting sing-song manner, "in women as well as jewelry."

I shrugged, then picked half-heartedly at the meat and vegetables on my plate. A short time later, I saw a somewhat ashen-faced Koranis hastening toward our table, but I did not see Narian. What had happened between father and son after they had been left together in the front yard? It appeared that Narian, at least, would not partake of the feast. In truth, I was no longer certain that I wanted to see him, for his display of weapons had terribly disturbed me. I reviewed the past couple of hours in my mind, feeling as if the entire evening were spinning out of control.

I excused myself from the table after eating a few bites of my meal, and strolled out of the tent to where the musicians were setting up to play. Casting about for Miranna and Semari, I spotted them sitting on a bench along the edge of the dance floor. Judging from their rosy cheeks, they were cheerfully gossiping about something. The nature of their chitchat became clear as I saw them look longingly toward a group of young men lounging in the shadows, a group that included Temerson. Temerson's brother had remained with him, although the boy was now accompanied by Zayle, Semari's younger brother, and judging from the jostling and teasing going on between them, a friendship had been born.

Dusk was now upon us, and torches were being lit that would, with or without the moon's assistance, bathe the dance floor in a romantic glow. As the musicians began to play, several couples moved onto the wooden planking and began to step with the music. I stayed on the sidelines as I had at the event in Narian's honor, content to admire the graceful movements of the others. I saw my mother glide into the midst of the other dancers, accompanied by my boisterous father, and idly pondered whether Temerson would have the nerve to ask Miranna to dance, or if she would have to take the initiative herself. My reverie was broken by an altogether too familiar, and definitely unwelcome, voice.

"Would you grant me the honor of a dance, Alera?"

Steldor had stepped into place beside me, and with a slight bow, was now offering me his hand.

I did not extend mine in return, but unblinkingly watched the scene before me.

"Hardly," I snipped.

As I was determined not to look at him, I had to imagine his reaction to my rather presumptuous rejection, and tried to picture the frustration and confusion that was presumably clouding his face. Galen had apologized for him, after all, and I had supposedly forgiven him. So why was my mood so cold?

"You would receive my generous gift, yet deny me a simple dance?" he asked manipulatively.

To that, I had no answer. The gift of the necklace, though likely a somewhat insincere gesture, was magnificent and expensive, and having accepted it, I could not with a clear conscience refuse to dance with him. He seemed to read my thoughts, although in truth he had planted them, and took my hand without another word.

He was an excellent dancer. He moved with such ease and grace that it was difficult for me to match him. Perhaps we could have more effortlessly moved as one had I been at all content in his arms.

Though at first we danced as would acquaintances, Steldor soon realized that many eyes were upon us and decided to publicly confirm that we were courting. With a very smooth motion, he pulled me closer to him, and I instantly went rigid. He continued to dance as elegantly as before, but my movements were becoming increasingly ungainly.

"I have learned that you've made several visits here of late," Steldor remarked softly, although there was a hint of malice in his tone, no doubt stemming from his conjecture that I had been coming only to see Narian. He did not know, of course, that his own father had commissioned me to spend so much time with Koranis' eldest son.

"Tell me," he continued, expertly maneuvering us around the dance floor, "do you tire of playing nursemaid?"

Indignation immediately flared within me at his gibe toward Narian.

"Only when I'm with you," I retorted.

He cocked his head at me, in neither anger nor amusement, but in some new emotion I could best interpret as consternation. The song ended, and I turned to leave, pleased that I had delivered the final blow, but he slipped his arm around my waist.

"Not so fast," he murmured, though the malevolence in his voice had been replaced by pained resignation. "We need to establish some sort of truce."

The musicians began another piece, and once more Steldor and I danced, the elegance of his movement increasingly hindered by my resistance to the pressure his hand was exerting upon my back.

Without further ado, Steldor lamented, "I don't understand you. You seem to be set wholeheartedly against me, and I don't even know what I did to garner such resentment."

I could hardly believe what I was hearing.

"You kissed my sister," I said reprovingly.

"Before that!" he exclaimed, as if the point I had raised were irrelevant. He dropped his volume, conscious of the couples surrounding us. "Since the day we met, you've exhibited nothing but contempt toward me. What could I have possibly done so long ago to offend you?"

I distinctly remembered my first impression of Steldor, as my opinion of him had not changed much over the years. I had been ten at the time, and he thirteen, and yet he had already possessed the ego of a young peacock.

"It's nothing you did," I hissed, dying to unleash my anger as I had in the garden in the aftermath of Narian's ill-fated celebration at the Palace. "It's simply... who you are!"

"What does *that* mean?" Steldor demanded, completely baffled.

I was sure no one had ever dared to tell him there was something wrong with his character.

"It's your attitude," I admonished, the loathing he had inspired within me on countless occasions quickly surfacing. "The way you walk, the way you talk... even the way you *breathe*."

He raised a sarcastic eyebrow as if telling me I could do better by way of explanation.

"Honestly, Alera, the way I breathe?"

I exhaled in frustration.

"Even now, you're unbelievably condescending!"

Though I was growing passionate in my speech, I managed to regulate my volume.

"You treat everyone as if they are beneath you — Miranna, the guard in the market, Temerson, Narian, *me*! You can't even deign to apologize for yourself, so forgive me if I'm a little disagreeable."

I tried futilely to pull away, but he held me in position, silently fuming. I felt trapped, and the deadly glare he fixed upon me was most unsettling. As my discomfort grew, so did my resolve to withdraw from the dance floor, and I remained stiff and unwilling in his arms as he continued to try to dance with me.

Suddenly, he snapped, "Damn it, Alera, you won't even let me lead!"

He gestured with a hand from my body to his, making known the distance I insisted on creating between us. His voice was low, but heavy with rancor.

"This dance exemplifies our entire relationship! You are more than 'a little disagreeable,' Alera. You can't conceive that anything I do has merit, is good, is right, *has potential*. At least my so-called arrogance has foundation — I can do the things of which I claim to be capable, so that I do not boast, but rather state fact. You, on the other hand, oppose me without thought or reason! Better to be justifiably arrogant than to be irrationally contrary. If it were not the case that we must marry in order for me to assume the Throne, as is your father's desire, I would not suffer your company, and I don't think many men would."

The second song ended, but Steldor did not release my hand. With an affectation of pleasure upon his face, he led me away from the other couples.

"Now, won't you join me at the refreshment table?" he said, with forced pleasantness in his voice as well.

Stung by his criticism, and unable to refuse lest I prove his point, I let him guide me to the table a few yards away, for once not fighting the arm he slid around my waist, then waited uncomfortably for him to bring me a glass of wine. I hated that he was at least partially correct about my behavior toward him, and wracked my brain for a way to escape the beastly circumstances in which I now wallowed. As Steldor returned to my side, I noticed Miranna doggedly approaching us, and a wave of gratitude swept over me. She moved smoothly behind Steldor and tapped him on the shoulder.

"Lord Steldor, would you care to dance?" she sweetly asked, an innocent smile curling her lips.

He glanced between us in mild annoyance, no doubt aware that Miranna's objective was to rescue me, and I feared he would turn her down.

"By all means, feel free to dance with Mira. It will, after all, give you another basis on which to compare the two of us," I nastily goaded him. "As you have flirted with us both and kissed us both, I would assume dancing with us both would be of interest as well."

His eyes narrowed slightly, then he gulped down his wine and thrust the empty goblet into my hands.

"A gentleman will always satisfy a Lady's desires, even should it enable him to make such comparisons," he acerbically replied.

Shifting his attention to Miranna, he gallantly bowed.

"I am honored by your request," he said, extending his arm so that he could escort her onto the dance floor.

While I was relieved to see him walk away with Miranna, I was dumbfounded by his gall, as he had intimated that both my sister and I sought his attentions, and I began to feel desperate to leave the gathering. After locating Destari, I instructed him to prepare one of the three Royal Carriages for departure. I then hastily thanked Koranis and Alantonya for their hospitality, noting as I did so that Koranis had recovered his self-important air, finally seeking out my parents to inform them that I was returning to the Palace. My father, in particular, looked disappointed, but he held his tongue. Shortly thereafter, and due in no small part to Miranna's continued insistence that Steldor dance with her, I was happily settled into a coach and on my way home, Destari riding his horse alongside the carriage while several additional guards followed behind.

We had not traveled far when I dimly became aware of the sound of an approaching horse, traveling at a leisurely canter. Destari motioned for my carriage driver to halt and rode out to meet the rider who had successfully intercepted us. As only an occasional muffled snatch of conversation reached my ears, I was not able to identify the speakers, and I began to worry that Steldor had pursued me. My disquiet was allayed a few moments later by Destari, who returned to the carriage and spoke to me through the window in the door.

"Lord Narian is here and requests to see you, Princess."

I nodded, puzzled but not displeased, and Destari opened the door, taking my hand as I stepped to the ground. I walked toward Narian, who had alighted from his impressive dappled gray steed to stand fifteen feet away, reluctant to enter into the midst of the guards who had protectively surrounded my carriage.

Although I knew I should be wary of him after what I had witnessed only a few hours previously, my reaction was in fact quite different, as I felt a light and tingly sensation at being in his presence.

"Shall we walk?" Narian invited, still holding his horse's reins and seemingly unwilling to speak freely in front of my guards.

"Yes," I murmured, holding up a hand to Destari to indicate that he should not accompany me.

"Will you bring me one of those lanterns?" I asked, motioning to the oil lamps hanging from the front of the carriage.

Destari retrieved the one nearest him, silently handing it to me.

"We'll return in a short while," I said, feeling compelled to reassure him.

Again, Destari did not object. I could only assume that he was unperturbed due to the amount of trust Cannan had shown toward Narian by allowing him to retain possession of his weapons.

As soon as Narian and I were out of earshot of the others, he irritably stated, "I presume our meetings, and your lessons, are at an end."

"My permission has been withdrawn," I casually replied.

With a sharp laugh he halted, and his horse shifted restlessly behind him.

"I forgot — you need permission for everything."

I turned toward him, unsure how to respond, and unable to read his mood. I held up the lantern so I could see his face, but his expression was inscrutable.

"I know you are not familiar with the types of weapons I carry," Narian continued, sounding for once ill at ease about the topic he was broaching. "I asked you once if you were afraid of Steldor, but perhaps I should ask if you are afraid of me."

It did not take me long to answer. "I perhaps should be, but I am not."

"I would never hurt you, Alera."

His mesmerizing blue eyes captured me, then he looked away,

as if he'd said something improper.

"Unless you count causing me to fall off a horse," I jested, attempting to lighten the mood and make our exchange less awkward.

Narian's eyes danced as if he were reflecting upon a particularly humorous memory, and a slight smile played upon his lips. As if on cue, his horse snorted and shook its head impatiently, and he gave it a pat on the neck before indicating with his hand that we should resume our aimless stroll.

"And how are things between you and your father?" I hesitantly inquired after we had walked a few additional paces.

"Koranis fears his own son," Narian said contemptuously, his voice hardening. "As you heard, he wants the Captain of the Guard to enroll me at the Military Academy; until then, I am to move into his residence in the city. He intends for me to leave with the Captain tonight, and chose to oversee my packing. He does not trust that I will only take those things that are my own." He glanced sideways at me. "Of course, this means that I will be living closer to the Palace."

When I did not reply, his mood darkened, and I knew another more serious remark would follow.

"You didn't appear to enjoy Steldor's company tonight."

I gave little thought to how Narian had seen me with Steldor, let alone discerned my feelings, as I was growing quite accustomed to his keen observations.

I laughed shrewdly.

"I don't ever *enjoy* Steldor's company."

"Then why do you endure him?" Narian demanded, sounding both confused and frustrated.

"I really have no choice," I declared, confident he would acknowledge the difficulty of my circumstances.

"You always have a choice."

His words were blunt and devoid of sympathy, and I stared at him, without an inkling of what to make of our brief encounter.

Our walk had taken us in a loop, and we were now returning to the lighted vicinity of the carriage.

"Steldor has most assuredly noted my absence by now," I said, "so I had better continue to the Palace before he opts to pursue me."

A playful glint flashed in Narian's eyes as we came within a few yards of the coach.

"He may find that rather difficult, as I borrowed his horse."

I shook my head in disbelief as Narian mounted the powerful animal.

"Borrowed?"

Narian only smirked.

"Good night, then," he said, before galloping into the darkness in the direction of Koranis' estate.

Chapter Twenty-One
Divided Heart

"So tell me, did Temerson ever work up the courage to ask you to dance?"

This was the first my sister and I had visited since Semari's birthday celebration five days earlier, and we were sitting in my parlor, I upon my sofa, and she in an adjacent arm chair.

"No," Miranna chuckled. "But Perdic, his eight-year-old brother, did."

I laughed along with her, picturing Temerson's face as his own brother asked a Princess to dance when he could hardly speak to her without stuttering.

Miranna and I were spending the afternoon together, working on the embroidery of the handkerchiefs we were to give out before the Tournament. The mid-October sky was gray and overcast, and the logs smoldering in the fireplace were necessary to chase the chill from the air.

It was tradition that each Princess who was of courting age would choose an escort for the Tournament and the dinner the evening before by delivering a personally embroidered handkerchief to the favored young man. While Miranna and I were given leave to stitch whatever design we fancied on our handkerchiefs, I had, since the first time I was escorted at the age of fifteen, simply sewn my name into the corner. Miranna's design would be more elaborate, but then, embroidery was more to her liking than it was to mine.

"I actually danced a couple of times with Perdic," Miranna was saying. "He's a sweet boy, though he's much bolder than his brother. Zayle, who spent most of the evening with Perdic, also requested a dance, which made Semari laugh." She smiled warmly at the memory. "Eventually *I* asked Temerson to dance!"

"And, of course, he agreed," I said good-naturedly, admiring my sister's confidence.

Our conversation was abruptly ended as my parlor door swung wide and my father bounded across the threshold, beaming cheerfully.

"Ah, both of my daughters, I see! Excellent! Not interrupting anything, I hope?" he asked, bustling into our midst.

"Not at all," I said, returning his smile. "Join us, Father."

My father sat beside me on the sofa, then he took in our activity.

"Ah, the handkerchiefs," he said, grinning from ear to ear. "And who will be so lucky as to receive yours, Miranna? The same boy from last year, perhaps? He was quite charming, if I recollect correctly."

He winked, and Miranna's cheeks turned pink.

"No," she said, knowing that Father's thoughts had traveled to potential suitors for her, though she would not be of marriageable age until she turned eighteen. "I was planning on sending mine to Lord Temerson."

"Isn't he the boy I chose to accompany you on the picnic?"

My father's face grew even brighter at Miranna's nod.

"Excellent. Comes from a fine family," he said, then added teasingly, "I really do have a knack for these things."

He turned to me, patting my hand affectionately.

"You will be interested to know that Steldor is going to be involved in a fighting exhibition at the Tournament. Cannan has arranged a mock battle between Steldor and Lord Kyenn to show the people some Cokyrian fighting techniques."

"Why Steldor?" I blurted, immediately besieged by dread on Narian's behalf.

My father interpreted my words in a way that I had not intended.

"You will only be deprived of your escort's company for a short period of time. What grounds are there to deny such an opportunity to the best fighter in Hytanica, especially when he volunteers for the good of the event?"

I looked at my father blankly, and he glanced to Miranna as if begging her to allay my concerns. He was clearly under the impression that the reason for my anxiety was that I could not bear to be apart from Steldor.

When Miranna shrugged, but otherwise remained mute, my father spoke again, his spirits dampened by my reaction.

"Well then, there's another item to discuss. I noted that things went quite well between you and Steldor at Semari's birthday. That was quite an extravagant gift he extended, and I was happy to see you accept it. Your mother and I were also quite heartened to see the two of you dance."

My father's deep brown eyes brightened, as his zest for his subject rose.

"I think the time has come to make it known to the Kingdom that you and Steldor are to be wed. I've talked with the priest about a betrothal ceremony, and I have arranged for it to take place within the next few days so that the engagement can be made known at the Tournament."

My lips parted in shock, unable to believe that he thought I was on good enough terms with Steldor to be betrothed. Steldor would embrace the idea, but I could hardly stand to consider it, as evidenced by my sudden strong urge to bolt from the room.

"I can't," I faltered, hoping I sounded less distraught than I felt.

My father frowned, perplexed.

"Whatever do you mean, Alera?"

"I mean... that I can't. I can't pledge myself to Steldor. I... am not convinced he is the man I should marry."

A strained silence fell in the room, the only sound an occasional hiss from the fireplace.

"Why not?" my father demanded, exasperated.

I searched for a way to express my feelings, for I knew the simple fact that I abhorred Steldor would not disqualify him as a candidate. All I could think to do was to tell my father what I had confided only to my sister.

"I feel... an attraction... to someone else," I said lamely.

"You are *attracted* to someone else?" he repeated incredulously, gesturing with his hands in agitation. "Who is this person?"

"I do not wish to say. But the fact that I am drawn to someone else would suggest that Steldor is not the ideal match for me."

I prayed I did not sound disrespectful. Nonetheless, my father did not react positively.

"This is preposterous, Alera," he said, becoming irritated. "If you will not tell me who this young man is, then I must assume that he is someone of whom I would not approve, in which case you would not be permitted to marry him. Unless this other man possesses the qualities necessary to be my successor, whether you are *'attracted'* to him or not is irrelevant. You must marry a *King*."

"I implore you, Father. Just give me a little more time."

He looked at me critically for a moment, then relented.

"Granted," he said, "but I expect you to use the time wisely. We are six months from your eighteenth birthday and the day when you will wed, and a decision must soon be reached regarding your husband."

He then harshly rebuked me.

"In fairness to Steldor, it is deceitful to receive such a splendid gift as that necklace with a divided heart."

My father stood to leave, then faced me again, his unusually stern visage making him seem older, and I became cognizant of the extent to which his dark brown hair had been replaced by gray. In that moment, I realized how important it was to him to step down from the Throne.

"Alera, notwithstanding this other person, you are to bestow upon Steldor the honor of acting as your escort for the Tournament and the dinner preceding it."

That said, he exited the room, his steps noticeably less buoyant.

As his footfalls faded from my hearing, frantic thoughts flashed in my head, but strangely, the one that plagued me most was the fighting exhibition my father had mentioned. Why had Steldor volunteered? His opinion of Narian was no secret to me, and I doubted it was to the Captain. Cannan must have deemed his son trustworthy, but I could not conceive that Steldor's motivations in participating in this simulated fight were completely innocent.

I glanced uncertainly at Miranna, who was viciously twisting her coppery-blonde hair, and knew that she was having similar thoughts.

"Now men really *are* fighting over you," she said.

Criers and heralds who had been sent forth several weeks ago to publicize the approach of the Tournament began to return over the next few days, and vendors and merchants arrived to unpack and set up their displays. Everyone intending to sell merchandise had to check in with the Keeper of the Faire to pay a fee and be assigned a location from which to operate. Inns began to fill and business at the taverns boomed as excitement reached a fever pitch.

The morning of the first day of the Faire dawned crisp and clear. Miranna and I worked our way through the gathering crowd to the grassy area where Market Day was normally held. Tents for the sellers spread from here toward the Military Complex and the Palace to the north. A smiling Halias and a grim Destari accompanied us, but this time they were in uniform and stayed at our sides, as there was a much increased potential for jostling and thievery amidst such a teeming crowd.

As we wandered among the tents, a happy uproar bombarded our ears, as laughing, shouting, and bargaining blended into a cacophony of sound. Above the hubbub, we would occasionally catch an unusual accent or a foreign tongue, or the music of minstrels and musicians. I cocked my head slightly, believing that I had heard a Cokyrian accent. Was Narian nearby? I thought it possible, as he had been living in the city since the night of Semari's birthday celebration, but I did not catch a glimpse of him.

In addition to the sounds, the sights of the Faire overwhelmed us, as there was an astounding variety of merchandise for sale. Wool, cotton, silk, and linen cloth were available in a myriad of colors, including violet, bright red, green, blue, yellow, rose and gray, with strands of gold or silver woven into some of the fabrics. Hemp for nets, ropes and bowstrings; furs and skins; and embossed leather was also in abundant supply. Spice vendors busily measured out small amounts of unusual seasonings such as cinnamon, pepper, saffron, ginger, nutmeg, clove, cumin, and mustard for their eager buyers, and purveyors of rare oils and perfumes did the same. As we moved with the flow of people, we saw jewelry, swords and daggers, pots and pans, magnificent tapestries, hand-crafted candlesticks and chests, hand-carved ivory and ebony figurines (including chess pieces), valuable books, sumptuous and exotic clothing, and rare carpets, all of which were available for purchase.

The inevitable scuffle, as well as a brawl or two, would occasionally break out in the pathways between the tents, to be quickly subdued by City Guards who were patrolling the grounds in large numbers. It was important to the success of the Faire that merchandise be protected from theft and damage, and that the safety of sellers and buyers alike be ensured.

Perhaps our favorite aspect of the Faire was the entertainment, with the large variety of tempting treats for the palate a close second. We laughed at the antics of tumblers and jugglers, and gaped in awe at the magicians who could swallow swords and fire. The smells of prepared food, wine and ale whetted our appetites, while unusual sweetmeats, uncommon cheeses, and exotic tastes, such as chocolate, fed our souls.

We returned to the Palace that evening quite fatigued, but exuberant, our senses battered by the sights, sounds, and smells of the day. We were determined, however, to venture forth again, and our next few days followed the pattern of the first, as it took a good deal of time to fully appreciate the Faire. We would wake in the morning ready to meet the challenge of the day, and fall into our beds utterly exhausted in the evening.

As the Tournament drew nigh, more visitors began to arrive. The Inns were now overflowing, and some city residents made extra money by renting out rooms in their homes, while the King permitted travelers to pitch tents on the open ground near the Palace or outside the city walls. Most of these new arrivals were coming to participate in the Tournament games, lured by the generous prize money and other rewards the King posted for the winners.

On the day before the Tournament, Miranna and I did not attend the Faire, as I was needed to oversee the final preparations that were underway in the Palace for the traditional pre-Tournament dinner. As with the celebration for Koranis and his family, my mother had turned the event over to me, something I had taken as a high honor, as it implied my skills were adequate in this respect. My primary tasks had been planning the food that would be served and the evening's merriment.

The dinner would be held in the cherry-paneled King's Dining Hall on the second floor, with approximately four hundred guests in attendance. The guests were those who had paid their entry fee to participate in the Tournament, as well as their ladies. The King's Dining Hall could seat at least a thousand people, with ten long, oak tables running the length of the room. Three dozen candlelit chandeliers provided lighting, as did numerous oil lamps hung by chains from the walls. At the far end of the hall, a high table was set perpendicular to the rest for the Royal Family and our escorts. Decorations were minimal, for this dinner was less formal than most hosted by the King. Spirits tended to run high, wine flowed freely, bragging was boisterous, and entertainment was plentiful.

On the evening of the feast, Miranna and I awaited the arrival of our escorts in the second floor lesson room, which doubled as a parlor, with Destari and Halias outside in the corridor. I was wearing a gown of burgundy velvet that laced across the bodice, then fell into a wide circle skirt, the richness of the color complimenting my loose, dark brown tresses. The sleeves echoed the cut of the gown, fitted between shoulder and elbow, then opening wide to drape over the hands. Miranna's gown of deep blue velvet captured the blue of her eyes, and was styled with a fitted waist and gently flaring skirt. Its full sleeves narrowed at the elbow to lace tightly down to the wrist.

It wasn't long before Steldor, self-assured and resplendent in a black doublet with gold stitching in a diamond pattern on the front, and Temerson, scared and uncomfortable in an ivory doublet, arrived. Steldor had tied the kerchief he had received from me around the hilt of his sword, as tradition dictated that the men honored with the handkerchiefs were to display them in some way. Temerson carried no sword, and I could not at first perceive what he had done with Miranna's kerchief, but then saw it tied about his left wrist.

Steldor took the lead, which seemed to suit Temerson, strutting into the room to kiss my hand as he always did. Dispensing with small talk, he extended his arm to me.

"May I have the honor?" he asked.

I nodded warily, uncertain what to expect from him, as we had not parted on the best of terms two weeks previously. We immediately left the room to walk down the corridor to the Dining Hall, followed by Miranna and Temerson, and our bodyguards. As we proceeded, I ruminated over Steldor's atypical behavior — he had neither flippantly complimented me nor tried to engage me in conversation.

My thoughts flew apart when the door to the Hall was opened and the sounds of the raucous guests hit my ears. As we proceeded down the center of the room toward the high table, the noise briefly subsided as heads were lowered in respect. Wine and ale were being served, but the feast would not begin until the King and Queen had arrived. Steldor, ever the perfect gentleman, held my chair out for me as I took my seat, then poured and offered me a glass of deep red wine.

A trumpet blast from the far end of the Hall told me that my parents were about to enter, preceded, as always, by Lanek. I chuckled softly as I realized even Lanek could not have been heard above this group of revelers, and had therefore been forced to resort to trumpets.

"All rise for King Adrik and his Queen, the Lady Elissia," Lanek announced.

The room fell silent as those gathered in the Hall stood for the entrance of the King and Queen. My smiling father, in a gold brocade dress coat with an attached royal blue cape emblazoned with the royal crest, greeted people as he proceeded; my serene mother, in a royal blue velvet gown with a gold brocade underskirt, walked regally at his side. A dozen Elite Guards followed in pairs, moving to stand in a row behind the high table with Halias and Destari, their royal blue doublets adding vibrant color to the rich, cherry-paneled wall. Cannan and Kade, and a number of Kade's Palace Guards, prowled the perimeter of the room, watching for signs of trouble. Stepping onto the platform on which the table sat, my father positioned himself behind his chair to open the evening's revels.

"Let the feast begin!" he heartily called.

A shout went up from the celebrants as servants began to bring heaping platters of food to the tables.

The feast went on for hours, with several courses being served. My father spared no expense, as legs of mutton and veal, chicken, venison, pork and beef were laden on the platters amid the array of breads and vegetables. Sugar wafers, oranges, apples, pears and cheeses were served as dessert. Wine and ale were consumed by the barrel.

As the meal came to an end, the merriment began. Tumblers

and acrobats worked their way up and down the aisles, while jugglers and jesters performed at the front of the room between our table and the others, to be later replaced by singers and musicians.

Throughout it all, Steldor played the part of the solicitous suitor, filling my wine glass, plying me with sweets, pointing out clever tricks and antics, and identifying some of the men who would be the best competitors on the morrow. To my continued astonishment, he did not brag or boast, but genuinely took pleasure in the available entertainment, as well as in bantering with the guests. Whether due to the wine or his change in approach, I found myself enjoying the evening, and perhaps even his companionship.

Just when it looked as though one too many barrels of drink had been opened, as some participants were threatening to start the competitions right in the Dining Hall, my father stood. Trumpets again sounded to call attention to him.

"My good Lords, depart and get some rest, for the sun shall soon rouse you, and the Tournament games will begin," he announced, indicating that the feast had come to an end.

With that, he and my mother departed the Hall, followed by Steldor and me, then Miranna and Temerson, with the Elite Guards bringing up the rear. My parents and their guards turned down the corridor toward their quarters, while my sister and I, with our escorts, returned to the lesson room, Destari and Halias at our heels. Behind us, I could hear the riotous sounds of our departing guests.

I turned to Steldor as soon as we were within the lesson room, intending to dismiss him.

"As we must also rise early, I will bid you a good night," I said, rather abruptly.

"Keep me company a moment longer," he said, as Temerson bowed and hastily departed.

Steldor's voice was silky smooth and his dark eyes seemed to shimmer.

"We should not be together without a chaperone," I

automatically responded, beginning to wring my hands.

"I only desire a few minutes, and your bodyguard is outside in the corridor."

I glanced at my sister, hoping for some assistance, but all she gave me was a reassuring smile. With a flip of her bouncy hair, she stepped out of the room, leaving me to alone to deal with Steldor.

Steldor studied me for a moment, and then reached out to still my nervous hands. I jumped at his touch, and he smiled in bemusement.

"Are you really that terrified of being alone with me?"

When I did not answer, he lightly continued, "It appears you have given some thought to our conversation at Koranis' estate. I'm sure you will agree that our time together is quite pleasurable when you do not continually resist me."

I stared at him, his ability to put all blame on me for the problems between us robbing me of speech. As I struggled to formulate a response, he affectionately stroked my long, sleek hair.

"May I kiss you goodnight?" he asked, once again catching me completely by surprise, and I knew my face gave full notice of my jumbled feelings.

"Just one kiss, I promise," he teased. "I won't expect anything more."

It came to me then that he thought I was reluctant to be alone with him due to my lack of experience with men. While that was part of the reason, it seemed to have escaped him that I did not like him or trust him. I decided not to correct his misconception, as he was at least taking a gentlemanly approach.

I nodded my head unenthusiastically, and he stepped closer to place one hand on each side of my face in a gentle caress, his seductive scent washing over me. Then he joined his lips with mine.

"Sleep well, Princess," he said, removing his hands and stepping away from me. "I will return to escort you to the Tournament field in the morning."

He bowed deeply and departed, leaving me slightly off balance as I had not anticipated such tenderness from him, and highly unsettled by the knowledge that I had enjoyed both his kiss and his touch. I followed shortly after him into the corridor where my bodyguard was waiting.

"Goodnight, Destari," I murmured, overcome with weariness.

As I drifted toward my quarters, the foreign notion that I had just had a pleasant time with Steldor broke over me, and I had to admit to myself that he could, in fact, be good company. Unfortunately, I had no idea how to ensure that the Steldor with whom I had just spent the evening would be the Steldor I was being pressured to marry.

Chapter Twenty-Two
The Legend of the Bleeding Moon

On the morning of October twenty-ninth, the Royal Family rode in two carriages to the bowl-shaped Tournament site west of the Faire. The King and Queen rode in one carriage, and Miranna and I, with our escorts, rode in style in another. Our bodyguards and numerous other Elite Guards rode alongside on horseback.

The weather was sunny, but cold and breezy, and numerous fur throws had been provided for our use both as we traveled to the Tournament site and within the Royal Box. While the spectators would most likely feel the chill as the day wore on, such weather was well suited to the competitions, as it would exhilarate the participants and spur them on to more heroic feats.

The viewing box that had been constructed for the Royal Family and their guests sat on top of the hill that sloped down to the military training field where the events would be held. The box was entered from the rear, and had walls with large, open windows and a roof to provide some shelter from the elements. The exterior was draped with silk in royal blue and gold, and tapestries were hung on the inside to provide additional insulation against the chilly fall air. The Royal Box would be full, as it would hold not only my family, our escorts and our bodyguards, but visiting Royalty from two of our neighboring Kingdoms, Sarterad and Gourhan. Emotana's sovereigns had sent regrets and would not be in attendance.

Cannan's wife, Faramay, had also been invited to join us, as she would otherwise have lacked an escort, and Lord Garreck and Lady Tanda, Temerson's parents, would be our guests as well. Finally, Koranis and Alantonya would sit with us, serving to ratchet up the tension in the box, although my father seemed oblivious to the strained relationship between the Captain and the Baron.

On the north side of the field, a large viewing stand had been built for the comfort of the Lords and Ladies who would attend the event. The stand was a three-sided roofed structure, open in the front, with tiered seating. It had likewise been draped with royal blue and gold silks. The grassy hillside would provide plenty of seating for the thousands of commoners who would throng to the site to watch the contests.

The field itself had been marked out to meet the needs of the Tournament. An oval track had been established, and was roped on both sides of its twenty-five foot width, ready for the horse races. On the inside of the near edge of the oval, and slightly to the left of the Royal Box, a large stage had been erected for the one-on-one combat competitions. To the north of the stage, targets were set for the archery tournament, and would later be replaced by targets for the knife-throwing and axe-throwing events. To the rear of these areas, but still within the oval, several large tents had been pitched for use by the participants as they readied themselves for the games. Billowing silk banners indicated which tents had been assigned to each Kingdom: royal blue and gold for Hytanica, black and silver for Sarterad, Gourhan's crimson and white, and Emotana's black and forest green. Water for drinking and washing had also been provided, and doctors were available to treat the injured.

By the time we entered the Royal Box, competitors were already on the field preparing for the contests, Lords and Ladies in colorful raiment of lush velvet and embroidered silk had begun to fill the viewing stand, and the citizenry were gathering on the hillside. I knew the audience would continue to grow as the day went on, as the archery, knife-throwing, and axe-throwing competitions were first, followed by the more daring and perilous horse races, finally culminating in the fighting events: first hand-to-hand and then with swords and other weapons. The noise level would also increase throughout the day, as the crowd would enthusiastically extol its favorite competitors and be equally vocal in its jeering of those it abhorred, the abundance of wine and ale tending to inspire avid crowd participation.

The opening of the Tournament was heralded by trumpets and drums, and my father stood to formally address the crowd, deepening the pitch of his voice so that it boomed across the hillside.

"Honored guests, valiant competitors, and loyal citizens of Hytanica, I bid thee welcome to this auspicious Tournament. Competitors, I exalt thee to be brave and daring, yet honorable and true, and I pray you will be safe from injury. To the people in attendance, I encourage thee to rejoice with the winners, commiserate with the losers, but above all, to loudly cheer."

My father paused dramatically before exuberantly proclaiming, "Let the Tournament begin!"

The archers, proudly displaying the silks of their respective Kingdoms, approached the competition area as the cry of "Let the Tournament begin" was repeated across the hillside. They eyed their targets and made final adjustments to their bows while waiting for the contest to commence.

I located Lanek on the Tournament field, as he would be announcing the events. It would be his responsibility also to provide commentary throughout the day, and he would no doubt be quite hoarse by the time evening fell. As the archery began, Lanek called out the distances to the targets, the marks of the archer's arrows, and the names of those who would be advancing. With each succeeding round, targets would be moved further away to provide an ever increasing challenge for the competitors.

Steldor's mood had not changed much from the previous evening, and he continued to use his inexhaustible charisma to enchant the King and Queen, as well as the other Royals in the Box. If anything, he was even more charming and witty than he had been at the pre-Tournament dinner. While his ability to ingratiate himself with my parents taxed my patience, his mood in every other way suited me perfectly.

From archery, the Tournament proceeded to knife-throwing, followed by axe-throwing, with Lanek continuing to announce distances to targets and accuracy of throws. After a break for lunch, the horse racing began, and by the time the first winner crossed the finish line, the hillside was packed with vocal spectators. The horse racing involved much jostling among the competitors, which sometimes resulted in fallen riders and occasionally downed mounts. While there were some injuries, all of the toppled riders were able to limp off the track amid shouts from the crowd, most without assistance.

Friendly repartee continued to fill the Royal Box throughout the day's contests, although Koranis would glance warily at Cannan on occasion, careful to maintain some distance between himself and the Captain of the Guard. Of course, Cannan's reaction to Koranis' presence was far more difficult to ascertain.

As the increasingly dangerous fights with weapons began, conversation among those in the Royal Box gradually fell off, although the crowd on the hillside voiced their opinions as vociferously as ever. Competitors would fight one-on-one in several different modes during this part of the Tournament. First would be wrestling, then hand-to-hand combat, followed by combat with swords and other weapons. Although weapons used in the fighting events were blunted in an attempt to prevent harm to the competitors, injuries were frequent, but thankfully rarely fatal.

The men involved in the fourth-to-last battle, one Hytanican and one clad in the black and silver of the Kingdom of Sarterad, were called forth by Lanek, and they climbed the few stairs on either side of the stage, drawing their swords.

Steldor had been intensely concentrating on the fights and was mildly startled when Cannan put a hand upon his shoulder and motioned to the door of the Box. Steldor stood, then made a point of offering me words of consolation before departing.

"I am afraid that I must leave you now, as the time to fight the *Cokyrian* draws nigh." He bowed and kissed my hand, then continued to hold it, knowing full well he had irked me by the manner in which he had referred to Narian.

"Don't worry, I won't be gone long," he glibly continued. "I know you will miss me terribly, but perhaps Miranna will be able to console you."

He released my hand, then gave my parents and the other Royals a respectful bow before politely leaving to prepare for the exhibition.

After he had departed, talk resumed, centering mostly upon the fight that would soon take place between him and Narian. The Cokyrians were the most feared warriors in the entire Recorah River Valley, and the exhibition we would soon see provided a rare chance for the public to gauge their skills. Though it was known by everyone in the Royal Box that the flow of the fight had been plotted from first thrust to final parry, no one except Cannan had ever witnessed it, and the air tingled with anticipation. Adding to the sense of danger was the knowledge that, unlike the weapons involved in the competitions, Steldor's and Narian's would not be blunted. Cannan had wanted to preserve the authenticity of the fight, and was willing to trust to the skills of the young men involved to prevent injury. I, too, felt on edge about the upcoming event, though my feeling was more accurately described as dread than anticipation.

Destari's whisper jarred me from my musings.

"Excuse yourself and come with me."

I looked at him in confusion, but seeing his dark and serious expression, did not argue. I rose, depositing the throw that I had draped over my legs on my chair, and approached my father, lightly placing a hand upon his shoulder.

"I feel a need to move about for a few moments," I said. "I will return shortly."

My father nodded, not shifting his attention from the sword-fight occurring on the stage below. As I moved toward Destari, I saw Temerson's mother, Lady Tanda, touch my bodyguard's arm to get his attention.

"How is London?" she quietly asked.

"He is fine," Destari replied, with a hint of what presented itself as disapproval. "He has survived far worse than this."

After glancing at me to ensure that I was complying with his directive, Destari slipped out the door. He waited for me just outside the Box to extend his hand in assistance as I hurried down the steps.

"Follow me," he said as soon as my feet were on the ground, and before I could inquire after his strange behavior, he had begun to walk briskly in the direction of the Faire grounds.

I trailed after him, almost jogging to keep pace with him. He led me through the maze of vendors, paths teeming with people, to a heavily draped gold and maroon tent on the outskirts of the Faire near the cobblestone streets of the Market District. The front flaps of the tent were spread open around a long table covered in old and expensive artifacts. I frowned, drawing my cloak securely about me, thinking it unlikely that Destari had brought me here to see ancient relics, but unable to imagine what his real purpose had been.

Behind the table sat a deathly thin, middle-aged man with olive skin, short scruffy hair, and bulbous black eyes. His long, crooked nose jutted forth from his face, bobbing up and down as he motioned us into the tent, while the rest of his body remained immobile in the chair.

I nervously followed Destari, then waited as he pulled aside one of two hanging tapestries that served as dividers between the front and rear sections of the tent.

"Destari, what—" I began, but then swallowed my words as my

eyes swept the shadowy back section of the tent, lit only by a small, open flap in the cloth ceiling. Crates that had previously contained the vendor's merchandise were stacked in the corner, and leaning against them with his arms crossed over his chest was someone I had not seen in many months.

"London!" I exclaimed, shocked, yet delighted, to see my former bodyguard.

Only the dust particles wafting through the air in the steady stream of light from the ceiling flap separated us, and the thrill that surged through me would have caused me to run and embrace him had not my good sense returned. London was far from a physically demonstrative person, and would not appreciate my show of affection under the best of circumstances, which these were not.

I stepped hesitantly forward, Destari at my heels, aware that London and I had not spoken since the day of Narian's capture, at which time nothing had been resolved between us. While I was elated to see him, he probably did not feel the same pleasure to be with me.

"Princess Alera," London said in greeting. "Glad you could fit me into your schedule."

His familiar sarcasm was like music to me, serving as an abrupt reminder of how sorely I had missed him. I stopped a few feet away, shifting self-consciously as I thought back to all that had changed between us, at a loss for what I should say next.

"You look well," I faltered clumsily.

"As do you, Princess."

I averted my gaze, disheartened by his continued formality, and stared for a moment at my shoes. Regaining my composure, I tried again, with greater sincerity than I had managed before.

"Truly, how are you?"

"I'm fine. I always land on my feet." He smirked as he chided, "I hear you've managed to dispose of yet another bodyguard."

I could feel the heat rising in my cheeks, but London did not seem to notice.

"I am sorry for causing you pain," I said, as I earnestly searched his indigo eyes, "but can't we put this behind us?"

"Whatever suits the Princess," he casually responded, and I was relieved to hear a slight tease in his voice. After a glance at Destari, who now stood beside me, he more seriously added, "This wasn't intended to be a social gathering anyway."

A brief and somewhat awkward hush transpired, during which London ran a finger along the dusty edge of one of the pine crates.

"Destari tells me you've become friendly with Koranis' eldest son," he ultimately continued.

I should have known Destari would be keeping London informed as to my activities — after sixteen years of monitoring my every movement, it was without doubt difficult to let old habits die — but I suspected London had pieced together more information about my visits with Narian than even my bodyguard knew.

I shrugged noncommittally, giving no other response.

"And what is your opinion of him?" London lightly asked, equally unrevealing as to his purpose in pursuing this topic.

I knew there was no point in trying to deceive London.

"I enjoy his company," I confessed. "He fascinates me."

"You ought to be wary of him," London replied, his tone darkening.

"Why?" I demanded with a scowl. "Because he was raised in Cokyri?"

"No," London said steadily, "because he is not who he appears to be."

"I could say the same thing about you," I retorted.

He cocked a cautionary eyebrow at me, and I immediately regretted my words, once again lapsing into silence.

After a moment, London pressed, "Have you found no reason to distrust him?"

For some unknown and unwarranted reason, I was piqued by the way London was speaking about Narian.

"I confess that there is little I actually know about him, but based on what I *do* know, I have no cause for concern."

London shook his head. With a disparaging smile, he said, "You see and yet somehow you are blind."

He ran a hand through his untidy silver hair before proceeding, his manner grave.

"At the end of the war, the Cokyrians stole from us forty-nine infants and killed forty-eight, keeping and raising only Narian. Have you not wondered why? How many children do you know who begin their military training at the age of six? And how many have a private teacher?"

London stared piercingly at me, though I knew he did not require an answer.

"This boy somehow managed to bypass Halias and Tadark without making a sound, moving stealthily enough to escape the notice of two Elite Guards; well, one-and-a-half." Despite the seriousness of his lecture, London still could not refrain from a jab at Tadark. "How many sixteen-year-olds would have that ability?"

He pushed away from the crates, manner more fervent, words hanging, as did his breath, in the frosty air.

"He manages to acquire weapons at will against our best efforts to ensure that he remains unarmed — as you may or may not know, the knife Narian used to cut your dress was taken directly from Koranis' person, apparently before he discovered the ease with which he could break into the locked weapons trunk in the Baron's bedroom."

London let these facts sink into my besieged brain, then continued, "You were witness to the weaponry he carries — he is armed beyond reason, not only with the weapons of a soldier, but the weapons of an assassin. As you learned at the celebration held in his honor, and as I discovered the day I arrested him, he has no fear of injury or mindfulness of danger."

He glanced at Destari for confirmation. "After a century of war with the Cokyrians, we know what to expect, and this is not it."

A somber silence pervaded the tent. I was certain Destari had heard some of this before, but considered all together it made quite an impression. My cheeks burned even as my body shivered, and I snuggled deeper into my cloak. I knew he was completely correct in that there was something about Narian that simply did not ring true, but I could not comprehend what he was attempting to tell me, nor could I believe that Narian meant harm to anyone in Hytanica.

"If Cokyrians are known for their stealth, how is Narian any different?" I dared to ask, snatching at threads in my desperation to avoid the truth.

Destari, who still stood at my side, exhaled in exasperation at my refusal to accept what was so blatantly obvious.

"You trust those you barely know, yet have no faith in those who would willingly lay down their lives for you!" he said sharply, his heavy brows drawing close to shroud his black eyes.

He moved to stand next to London, and it felt as though they were uniting against me.

"I don't need to hear this," I said stubbornly. "I'm old enough to make my own judgments."

London scoffed. "Your own judgments, yes; wise judgments, hardly."

Unable to stand for more, I turned and stalked toward the tapestry behind me, frenzied enough to want to rip it to shreds rather than to simply pull it open, but London's words stopped me in my tracks.

"You won't stay long enough to hear the news from Cokyri?" he slyly asked.

"What do you mean?" I warily asked, peering over my shoulder at him.

Destari, who now stood between London and me, likewise stared at him.

"I have just returned from a rather long journey into the mountains in the east," London said cagily. "I discovered some remarkable things."

"You've been in Cokyri?" Destari exploded, in an unusual outburst of anger toward London. "Have you learned nothing over the years?"

"Alera, have you heard tell of the bleeding moon?" London tenaciously continued, choosing to ignore his friend, and showing no sign of remorse or regret.

I shook my head slowly, unable to articulate a response. London had gone *willingly* to Cokyri? After spending ten harrowing months there as a prisoner, he had returned to the enemy's land of his own accord, somehow managing to pass undetected? The idea was unfathomable to me, but I did not have long to dwell upon it.

"After I captured Narian and his identity was discovered, I became suspicious," London stated, his posture relaxed, although his voice was taut. "As time went on and Destari kept me apprised of Narian's activities, I began to ask myself the same questions I posed to you just moments ago. I canvassed Hytanica's records for information on the year of Narian's birth, as much of that time was lost to me."

I realized that he was making a vague, and uncommon, allusion to his time as a prisoner in Cokyri.

"I read descriptions in scroll after scroll of a 'bleeding moon' that hung in the sky for months, but I could not discern its significance.

"In frustration I traveled to Cokyri, and accessed what records I could, just as I had in Hytanica. After several days, I finally came across a single document, written centuries ago, that gave an account of an ancient legend, the Legend of the Bleeding Moon."

London straightened to his full height and planted his feet, no longer casual in his stance.

"The account held that the Kingdom of Hytanica was built on sacred ground, and that because of this she would forever be protected from her enemies. We all know Cokyri should have been able to conquer Hytanica during the war, and the legend dispels the mystery of why they could not do so. According to this legend,

Hytanica can only be defeated by one of her sons, who bears the mark of the bleeding moon."

His eyes flicked between Destari and me, assessing our reactions.

"Sixteen years ago, Narian was born a son of Hytanica under a nighttime sky that was ruled by what our own scrolls describe as a bleeding moon, and I'm sure you know of the strange birthmark upon his neck," London said pointedly.

My heart lurched wildly in my chest, though I still did not understand the importance of London's discovery.

"What does this mean, London?" I asked, almost terrified to hear his answer, suspecting that my face looked as grim as Destari's.

"It means that nothing Narian says can be ignored. It means that whatever Narian's intentions are in Hytanica, he has a destiny to fulfill in Cokyri. It means he is the weapon that can bring Hytanica to ruin."

London's tone was heavy and dark, and I reeled as though I had been physically battered by his words. Nothing made sense, and yet everything made sense. As I tried to steady myself, one clear thought emerged and slowly came from my mouth.

"But even if everything you have said about Narian's past is true, he must have a choice!"

I glanced frantically between London and Destari, hearing Narian's own voice echoing in my head. "*You always have a choice,*" he had said to me on the night of Semari's party.

"He can turn from that destiny, can't he?" I desperately repeated, feeling as though I were suffocating in the stale atmosphere of the tent.

"Perhaps." London took a deep breath before continuing. "The Cokyrians are desperate to ensure Narian's return. They are determined to reclaim him, no matter the cost. At the time the High Priestess was captured in the Palace garden, Narian had already been missing for ten days."

"Why seek him in the Palace garden?" I asked weakly, hoping

that by concentrating on a different aspect of this entirely implausible scenario I could somehow make it untrue.

"She was not looking for Narian in the garden."

London hesitated, as though he did not think it wise to reveal more.

"She came to the Palace to find me," he reluctantly admitted, apparently concluding he had no option but to explain further. "She sought my assistance in locating Narian. I am indebted to her for my life, though it is in a way you would not understand."

Destari cleared his throat, although he was unable to rid his voice of tension.

"Shouldn't this information be brought to the Captain and the King?"

"The information comes from me, so they will not trust it," London bitterly responded. "The time for them to know will present itself, but meanwhile, we keep a watchful eye on Narian."

"And of what do you think he is capable?" Destari asked suspiciously, disclosing his belief that I might seek to spend time with Narian.

"His current capability is not what keeps me up at night," London said brusquely. "Regardless of whatever plans Cokyri has for him, he is only sixteen, not fully grown or trained. He has also been treated most kindly here in Hytanica, so I do not believe he poses an immediate threat to anyone. My concern lies in what he may become should he return to Cokyri, whether he goes voluntarily or is taken by force. If he returns, Hytanica's fate may be sealed. We must do all we can to ensure he does not end up back among the enemy." London fixed his gaze upon me. "You would do well to stay away from him, Alera."

I nodded feebly, swaying on my feet as a wave of dizziness hit me. Taking note of my condition, Destari stepped forward to lightly grip my upper arm as London spoke to him.

"It's time you returned to the Royal Box, as Alera's continued absence may draw questions."

I made no attempt to move, mind now as numb as my body, and Destari finally nudged me toward the tapestries with his hand. As I began to pass through them, I stopped and turned halfway around to face London.

"When will I see you again?" I asked, indescribably saddened by the knowledge that he could not accompany us.

"I don't know," he said, but something in the depths of his eyes told me he felt as I did. "I'm not exactly welcomed at the Palace."

Chapter Twenty-Three
The Exhibition

Destari and I made our way back to the Royal Box, sorrow at my separation from London now also a part of my jumbled set of emotions. Destari's hand on my upper arm continued to steady me until we came into sight of the guards posted around the entrance, and I moved forward to climb shakily up the steps. I tried to act normally as I reseated myself beside Miranna, again pulling the fur throw lying on the chair over my lap.

My sister's blue eyes opened wide as she assessed me.

"Are you alright, Alera? You're as pale as a ghost!"

"I'm fine," I assured her, but she reached out to tuck the throw around my legs, concerned that I had caught a chill. When I said nothing further, she went back to talking with Temerson, and I took several deep breaths in an attempt to calm my nerves.

I wanted to embrace the excuses and rationales I had created in my head for every unknown that surrounded Narian, but none of them could withstand scrutiny. London's information had finally completed the puzzle that Narian represented, but this was not something I wanted to accept.

Realizing that I had been staring at a crack in the wooden floor, I lifted my head to find Cannan closely observing me. I managed an artificial smile, and forced myself to look out across the Tournament field. Just as I did, a young man dressed in crimson and white tumbled off the stage after receiving a particularly nasty blow from his opponent, and the King and Queen of Gourhan moaned in defeat. The crowd on the hillside erupted into cheers and applause, apparently favoring the victor, who wore the colors of Emotana.

"Who won?" Miranna asked, breaking from her conversation to survey the outcome. "Oh, I was supporting him!"

I was certain Miranna hadn't the faintest familiarity with either of the competitors and had selected this one for whom to cheer because he was more handsome than the other. Whatever her motives, she was now applauding enthusiastically. As Emotana's Royalty were not in attendance, she soon realized she was applauding alone, and her enthusiasm waned.

As Lanek announced the victor's name for all to hear, the fighter on the stage gave a deep bow, and I realized that this had been the last contest of the day. When the crowd had quieted somewhat, the man hobbled off the stage, having been wounded during this battle or a previous one, while his unfortunate opponent was carried away, presumably to the physician's tent some distance down the field.

The trumpets blared again, drawing attention to Lanek as he climbed onto the stage so that he would be visible to the crowd despite his small stature. Steldor and Narian mounted the steps on either side of the platform and waited for him to make his announcement. Both Steldor and Narian were wearing dark trousers, white shirts, and tall leather boots. Each had slipped his arms into a leather breastplate that strapped in back and provided minimal protection for the chest. I assumed that Cannan felt there was little risk of injury, and did not want heavier armor to hinder their movements. Daggers hung at their sides, and each held a long-sword in his right hand. Steldor's sword was his custom-made blade with the leather grip and ruby pommel. Narian's sword also had a grip wrapped in black leather and wire, but was devoid of decoration, with a narrower and less wieldy blade.

I scrutinized Narian, but could detect no uneasiness in his carriage. As I next examined Steldor, who was as confident as ever, and whose motives I did not trust, I wished that Narian would be warier of his opponent. Though I doubted that Steldor would intentionally try to harm Narian under these circumstances, I could not quell the warning sounding within me. Narian was noticeably smaller than Steldor, and I couldn't help but fear for his well-being.

"And now, for the climax of this year's Tournament, the much heralded fighting exhibition between Lord Steldor, son of Cannan, the Captain of the Guard; and Lord Narian, son of the Baron Koranis," Lanek bellowed.

Koranis stiffened at the manner of Narian's introduction, although he said nothing. Did he object to the use of the name *Narian* rather than *Kyenn?* Or did he simply no longer desire to claim Narian as a son?

"Lord Steldor will be using his Hytanican weaponry," Lanek continued, "and Lord Narian will be using the weapons of Cokyri."

Excited muttering rippled through the crowd at the mention of the Kingdom where Narian had been raised, to be quickly replaced by the usual banter on the hillside and in the stands. His role fulfilled, Lanek hurried down the steps to make way for the fighters.

Steldor and Narian nodded to each other from their respective sides of the stage, then advanced on each other, readying their swords. Crossing blades briefly as they met in the center, they began some simple combat maneuvers, increasing their speed as they fell into the rhythm of the somewhat repetitive activity.

My tension eased as I viewed the routine fighting upon the stage, content for it to remain exactly as it was, though the crowd shifted restlessly, craving something more.

Steldor pulled back from Narian, and, responding to the crowd's discontent, tossed aside his sword with an insolent sneer. Narian also took a step back, but made no move to change his weapon.

Steldor drew his double daggers from the sheaths at his hips and flipped them expertly, catching the handles so that the blades extended from the backs of his fists. Lowering his hands, he advanced on his opponent. Without stopping or breaking eye contact, he deftly raised the weapons, crossing them in front of him, and thrust them toward Narian's chest.

Narian reacted faster than I would have thought possible, dropping his sword to catch Steldor's wrists so the blades came to rest threateningly above his shoulders.

My apprehension grew as Steldor leaned toward Narian and muttered something indistinguishable, and then pushed him forcefully backward off his feet.

Steldor retreated two steps, and then waited with his hands at his sides, shifting his weight from foot to foot. I glanced around the box to judge the feelings of the others, but saw only that everyone was fiercely focused upon the stage.

Gathering his feet beneath him, Narian slowly and resolutely rose, eyes boring into Steldor. As he came upright, he pulled out his own double daggers, which fit around his knuckles so that the blades arched over his hands, then nimbly moved forward. Positioning himself so that he could strike with his left leg, he planted a solid kick against Steldor's chest. Steldor stumbled back a few paces, and then nodded approvingly at Narian, as though satisfied with his response.

The crowd's attention was now riveted on the stage where the fighters had begun circling each other, Steldor exhibiting a cocky and menacing swagger, while Narian kept lower, catlike in his movement. I shifted fretfully, gnawing at my lower lip, though it was conceivable that this change in style had also been planned in advance in order to play well to the crowd.

As the fighters completed their circle, Narian dipped his inside shoulder forward ever so slightly. Seizing the opportunity, Steldor flipped the dagger in his right hand over again, then swiftly advanced to strike Narian in the temple with the butt of the knife. As he did, Narian dropped low and turned his head with the blow to avoid its full impact, then swiftly spun to his right, slashing

Steldor above the knee with his blade. Bleeding from the gash in his leg, Steldor backed off and Narian rose to his feet, blood trickling from his temple.

The watching crowd had fallen completely silent, no longer sure if what they were seeing was a demonstration.

"I daresay these two young men are getting a little carried away," my father said with an unconcerned chuckle.

I could not understand his cheerfulness. Steldor's first blow had not been restrained, and Narian had meant to draw blood. I glanced over at Cannan, who was standing and glaring at the stage, jaw clenched, his arms crossed upon his chest. Faramay was also anxiously eyeing Cannan, obviously aware that something was wrong.

I returned my attention to the fight, now sitting on the edge of my seat, tightly gripping the arms of my chair as I began to pray soundlessly for Narian's safety. Steldor had been the victor in every Tournament fighting competition he had entered since coming of age at eighteen, and was renowned as the best fighter in the entire Recorah River Valley. It was not a question of who would emerge triumphant at the end of this fight — the only uncertainty was how badly Narian would be beaten.

Tiring of their game of cat and mouse, Steldor and Narian suddenly ran at each other. As they came together, Steldor stabbed at Narian with his right blade, but Narian deflected it and likewise redirected Steldor's left hand, follow-up thrust. After pushing both of Steldor's daggers away, Narian circled his right arm down and in, slashing vertically up the center of his opponent's breast plate and almost cleaving it in two. Steldor drew his arms protectively in to his chest, and Narian immediately brought his left arm across Steldor's body, hooking him by the shoulder with the barbed edge of his blade and pulling him around. As he rotated, Steldor extended his right hand, cutting Narian across the shoulder.

Faramay gasped as the two came apart and spatters of blood flew from their weapons. Both of the young men now had dark stains forming on their white shirts.

Looking down the row of people, I saw Koranis and Alantonya sitting side by side, Alantonya utterly mortified, Koranis somewhat vindicated. My father was frowning down at the stage, continuously twisting his ring, finally disturbed by what he was seeing, while the faces of the visiting Royals registered equal parts confusion and concern. Beside me, Miranna's fingers were pressed against her cheeks, ready to creep up and hide her eyes, and Temerson had tentatively put a hand on her back to reassure her. My mother, Faramay, Lady Tanda, and Lord Garreck wore equally appalled expressions. Only Cannan's stance and countenance had not changed in the least.

As Steldor regained his balance, he turned his left blade over so both of his knives extended from the tops of his hands, and thrust toward Narian, driving the daggers underneath the younger man's arms. Pressuring the base of his fists into the center of Narian's back, between his shoulder blades, Steldor forced him downward until his arms flared out and up, then brought his right knee up to connect violently with Narian's chin.

Steldor pulled his arms away, shoving Narian one final time toward the ground. Narian caught himself with his blades so that he somehow kept his feet, but his head hung forward, heavy bangs hiding his pain from view. Steldor, unmistakably smug, took one step back, and glowered down at him.

"Stay down, Narian," Cannan muttered. "Don't get up."

Narian breathed deeply for a few moments, then abruptly slid his legs forward between Steldor's and kicked outward, forcing his adversary to splay his legs shoulder-width apart. Narian then sprang to his feet and with Steldor now at his eye level, slashed through both of Steldor's shoulder straps. With a thud, Steldor's already damaged breast plate fell to the ground. Thundering footsteps on the stairs of the Royal Box told me that Cannan had decided it was time to put an end to this fight.

Steldor pulled his left leg in and shifted his weight onto his left foot, then spun around to plant a solid side kick against Narian's chest with his right leg, once again knocking the younger man off his feet. Absorbing the fall, Narian rolled onto his upper back, and then snapped forward to land in a crouched position. Steldor faced Narian, settling his weight, right dagger held up, left held low, awaiting Narian's next move. His smugness had died away to be replaced by unbreakable concentration on the battle at hand.

I could see Cannan roughly pushing his way through the masses, his progress slowed by excited spectators. Narian caught the disruption in the crowd as well, and thrust his daggers to the side. At first, I thought he was going to concede the fight to Steldor, before Cannan could intervene, but he instead ran at his opponent. He pulled Steldor's arms away from his body, and with surprising agility used Steldor's thigh as a step, pushing himself off the ground to plant his right heel forcefully against his adversary's chin. Steldor's head whipped back and he fell hard, the stage shuddering with the impact, his blades flying away from him, as Narian flipped over to lightly land on his feet.

Faramay's hands had gone to her mouth in horror, and mutters filled the Box at this strange new development. The tension was palpable, and the air felt thick, making it difficult to breathe, and I prayed that Cannan would soon intercede.

For a moment, Steldor did not move, obviously stunned to be the one flat on his back, then his muscles slowly tensed as a fierce and uncontrollable rage ignited within him. Raising his arms, Steldor slammed his clenched fists upon the floor of the stage and rose forebodingly to his feet.

Striding furiously toward Narian, Steldor brought his right arm down and back and launched a deadly uppercut at Narian's jaw. Narian grasped Steldor's arm and pushed upward to avoid the blow. Wrapping his right leg around Steldor's, he then pulled Steldor's feet out from under him, using the momentum of the punch to send his adversary slamming against the ground once more. Pinning Steldor's right arm with his left hand, Narian pressed his knee into

Steldor's chest, rendering his foe helpless against his final move. As Cannan broke through the last line of people and rushed toward the stage, Narian drew back his fist and threw a punch toward Steldor's windpipe that would have taken Steldor's life had he not pulled it at the last second.

The silence was absolute. Everyone was frozen — Cannan at the edge of the platform, Narian with his fist suspended above Steldor's throat, the spectators on the hill and in the boxes. It was as though time had stopped.

Narian slowly retracted his hand and rose to his feet. His eyes met Cannan's, and his expression was so unfeeling that it sent chills down my spine. Glancing around, he seemed to recall that he had been involved in an exhibition, and dispassionately examined his defeated opponent, who was struggling onto his elbows, before extending a hand to help him to his feet. Steldor glared frigidly at Narian, then grudgingly accepted his assistance. As Steldor came to his feet, the first applause reached my ears, then the sound grew louder until the entire crowd was cheering madly.

Steldor and Narian gave subdued bows before exiting the stage in opposite directions, doing their best to hide their injuries. Steldor, limping slightly, walked away with nothing but a fleeting glance at his father, who directed his gaze at the Royal Box as if making a decision, then followed after his son. For the first time in memory, the Captain of the Guard had looked pale and somewhat shaken.

A soft moan captured my attention, and I looked to my right at Faramay, who was on her feet, frantically hanging on to the edge of the viewing window with pallid hands. As my mother turned to her to offer assistance, Faramay fainted, her legs crumpling beneath her. Tanda and Alantonya went to her aid where she lay on the floor, fanning her face, and my mother dispatched a guard to fetch some water.

With Faramay providing an unexpected diversion, I rushed from the Box without a word to anyone, my head spinning. What had I just seen? Steldor, the best fighter the Recorah River Valley had ever seen, defeated by a sixteen-year-old?

Narian's unusual weapons had frightened me, but that was nothing compared to the raw emotions that now clawed at me. I was frustrated and furious with myself for my naiveté, and felt somehow betrayed by him — I had trusted him to a large extent and had been at his mercy many times. Now, when I thought of the peril in which I had unwittingly put myself, I was almost traumatized enough to join Faramay on the floor.

I hastened down the slope through the milling crowd, my cloak billowing behind me, scowling whenever my progress was impeded.

"Alera!" Destari called, plainly in pursuit.

I did not slow down, but he nonetheless overtook me.

"Where are you going?" he growled, stepping in front of me and putting a hand on my shoulder to force me to stand still.

"I need to see him," I said, trying in vain to move past my bodyguard.

"Lord Narian?" he asked in disbelief.

"Yes!"

Destari matched my obstinate glare, but then deemed it futile to try to argue with me. Instead, he took me by the arm and began to forge a path through the spectators, who gave way to the large and powerful guard. We crossed the short span of field to the tents that had been used by the participants to prepare for the competitions.

As we wove through the tents, we saw healers tending to wounded fighters, but did not see Narian or Steldor among them. Destari impatiently intercepted one of the doctors to determine Narian's whereabouts, and we were directed to a medical tent where Narian's wounds were being dressed. Destari ducked his head and stepped inside to make known my arrival.

As I entered, Narian was sitting on a wooden bench, his blonde hair damp with sweat, and his loose-fitting white shirt pulled down off his shoulder so that his wound could be cleansed, stitched, and bandaged by the physician who was examining him. He rose slowly to his feet when he saw us, pushing the doctor's hand away and returning the bloodied sleeve to its rightful place.

The physician bowed respectfully to me on his way out, and I requested that Destari likewise leave us. My bodyguard's eyes narrowed in distrust.

"If you need me, I'll be right outside," he muttered, begrudgingly exiting the tent.

I was now alone with Narian, and we stared warily at each other. Then I found my voice.

"Who are you?" I demanded confrontationally.

Narian did not reply, but watched me like a hawk watches its prey. My frustration mounted.

"Are you the one of whom the legend speaks?" I pressed insistently. "Are you here to destroy Hytanica?"

As Narian gazed at me, I could see his affected indifference fading.

"I did not come here for that reason," he said straightforwardly, and I could tell that my unexpected knowledge had unsettled him, "though it is the legend that brought me here."

I nearly rolled my eyes, scoffing.

"Then, pray tell, why are you here, if not to *fulfill your destiny*?"

There was true conviction behind Narian's words when next he spoke, my hostility having spurred him to explanation.

"I did not know of the legend or that Hytanican blood runs through my veins until six months ago, when I learned of both through a discussion that was not intended for my ears. I came here only to discover my heritage, perhaps find my family, but that is all. I did not come here to harm anyone."

My racing heart began to calm as I listened to him, and a wave of compassion swept over me for the young man who in age was my sister's equal but who in all else was years beyond.

"Is it your plan to return to Cokyri?" I asked, my anger dissipating, replaced by a strong sense of foreboding.

"No," he said, slowly shaking his head. "There is something here that binds me, something unconnected to my resentment toward the people who raised me and who lied to me." His eyes captured my own, the longing within them achingly clear, then he steadily finished, "But Alera, if ever I do find myself back in Cokyri, the Overlord will be difficult to refuse."

A tremor shook my body as I grasped the reality of Narian's situation, and to whom he would have to answer.

"The Overlord?" I murmured, barely able to speak.

Narian stared blankly over my shoulder for a moment, then again gazed at me.

"The Overlord was and is my teacher. He is the one who trained me, as well as the one I serve."

A wave of nausea swept over me, and it took most of my strength to stay on my feet. London's description of the Overlord sprang unbidden into my mind — *"He is an invisible warlord, evil and terrifying. They say he can kill you or worse with a wave of his hand..."* — and I thought of London's condition after having escaped his clutches. Narian had faced the Overlord almost every day since he was six, learning his methods and skills.

"I did not choose this to be my fate," Narian went on, his countenance softening, the horror upon my face apparently causing him distress. "You need not fear me, Alera."

There was a trace of hopelessness in the short laugh that preceded my next words.

"Needn't I? Perhaps now you mean me no harm, but should Cokyri reclaim you, what then?"

His face shut down, his rare show of emotion disguised and contained. In exasperation, I turned to leave, but his hand caught my upper arm, preventing my departure. Before I could react, his other hand was upon my waist, pulling me toward him, and his vivid blue eyes captured my deep brown ones. As my heart began to pound once more, his lips met mine, lightly at first, then more insistently, and I succumbed to his embrace. I melted against him, my hands upon his back, all reason having abandoned me. After several moments, our lips reluctantly parted, and he briefly leaned his forehead against mine. Then he stepped back, his hands on my hips to create a little distance between us.

"I will never hurt you," he promised.

As my good sense returned, I stumbled away from him, then shakily turned and exited the tent, thoroughly unnerved by the passion that had just flared between us.

Destari gazed skeptically at me as I appeared at his side, but said nothing, simply choosing to lead me back to the Royal Box where the awarding of the prizes had begun. It would normally have been my responsibility to assist my father in this ceremony, but my sister had been called upon in my absence. As I approached the Box, my father gave me a knowing look, a look that revealed he had assumed I had gone to check on Steldor. I climbed the stairs and moved to stand beside Miranna, who eyed me curiously. As the names and deeds of the winners were announced by Lanek, I joined in extending congratulations, my father awarding bags of gold, while Miranna and I bestowed elaborate figurines. Ebony falcons went to the winners in archery, knife-throwing and axe-throwing; gilded horses to those who had triumphed in the races; and goblets of gold to the victors in the combat events.

As the Tournament closed, I returned to the Palace with my family. Sensing my agitated frame of mind, Miranna did not press me for information, for which I was thankful. I begged off from the small dinner my father always hosted for the Tournament winners, claiming fatigue, and retired to my quarters, unable to feign a festive mood.

I prepared for bed, then sought sleep, but was plagued with terrible thoughts about Narian and the legend. Narian had been raised by the Overlord to destroy my homeland and all that I held dear. He claimed that he did not intend to harm Hytanica, but what choice did he have? Just as it was my destiny as Crown Princess to become Queen, so was it his destiny to fulfill the legend.

But as I unendingly sorted through all I had learned, I placed two fingers against my lips, recalling the pressure of his kiss. I had felt such extraordinary happiness in his arms. How could someone with such a horrifying fate evoke such tender feelings from me? How could I desire the company of a person who was doomed to become my enemy?

With no answers to these troubling questions, I longed to escape into oblivion, but sleep came slowly and provided no rest when finally it arrived.

Chapter Twenty-Four
It's Tough to be a King

The guards pulled open the doors that led into the antechamber and Steldor emerged from between them, absolutely magnificent in his long-sleeved, black leather military jerkin and black trousers. His black boots with the half-dozen silver buckles on the shafts were so polished that they glistened, his distinctive long-sword was sheathed at his left side, and a dagger hung from his belt on the right. With a practiced pace, eyes straight ahead, he began the long walk up the center of the Hall of Kings toward the Royal Family, the only sounds his footsteps against the stone of the floor and the crackle of the logs burning in the large fireplaces on the eastern and western walls. My parents, in their royal blue robes and official crowns, sat upon their thrones, my father's personal guards standing in their usual formation, while Miranna and I sat to the left of our mother, Halias and Destari behind our chairs, all of us watching Steldor's advance.

Three days had passed since the Tournament, giving Steldor time to recover sufficiently from the injuries he had acquired during the so-called exhibition. The only remaining sign that he had been in a fight was the faint bruising along his jaw line. Cannan, who stood beside my father's throne, had requested this audience with the Royal Family, presumably at his son's behest, though I, at least, suspected that Steldor had not been informed of the meeting until after it had been arranged. The purpose of the audience had not been divulged, but it took no scholar to ascertain it.

As Steldor arrived before the dais, he fell to one knee, bowing his head to the King.

"Rise," said my father, his aspect for once stern as he confronted Steldor.

Steldor stood, saying, "Have I permission to speak, Your Majesty?"

"Granted."

Nodding his gratitude, Steldor began, voice rich and strong, dark eyes upon my father.

"I humbly come before you to ask forgiveness for my behavior of late, particularly at the Tournament during the fighting exhibition. I acted rashly, Sire, and allowed my temper and my competitive nature to overpower my reason. I deserve the disgrace I have brought upon myself, but that I have brought disgrace upon you and your family is inexcusable."

Letting his admission resound for a moment, Steldor shifted his attention to me.

"I also ask pardon from Princess Alera," he smoothly continued, "as I was unable to fulfill my duties as her escort following the incident."

His apology did not move me in the least, and I let my scorn show upon my face. He had obviously concluded that as long as his father was forcing him to apologize to the entire Royal Family, he should at least do so eloquently, and at that he was succeeding. I could already feel my father's resolve breaking down, and knew Steldor would have been wholeheartedly forgiven even if those had been his final words, which they were not, for he was once more addressing the King.

"I would also like to express regret on my father's behalf for administering *unnecessarily* to me when he should have returned at once to His Majesty's side." One eyebrow arched slightly in irreverence as his eyes flicked to Cannan. "While duty to a son is important, duty to a King is supreme."

Cannan looked mildly disgruntled, but definitely not surprised, as though this jibe had been expected.

"And so," Steldor finished, dropping again to one knee, "in deep remorse, and as an act of contrition, I offer my resignation as a Field Commander to my King."

He hung his head, the very image of penitence, and I pondered cynically how many times he had rehearsed this highly effective performance.

Steldor had made an offer my father would never accept, but which made him the most repentant man who had ever lived. I could scarcely believe his audacity, much less my father's gullibility, as the King stood to speak, his face now benevolent and forgiving.

"That will not be required, young man. Your apology is received without reservation."

"Thank you, My Lord," Steldor replied, his tone solemn and a touch too respectful as he slowly lifted his head, peering artfully through his thick, ebony lashes.

My father extended his hand so that Steldor could rise and kiss the Royal Ring, pleased with the way Cannan's son had shouldered the blame for the exhibition gone awry, although anyone who truly knew Steldor would have felt the smugness radiating from his very being. With one final, graceful bow, Steldor turned smartly on his heel and walked with the same steady cadence away from us and out the antechamber doors.

One week later, at mid-afternoon, my mother, Miranna, and I were having tea in the small room designated for that purpose on the main floor of the Palace. We sat at a quaint table in the room's center, bathed by the rays of sunlight entering through the bay window, and enjoying the west courtyard in all its late fall splendor.

Our conversation covered a wide variety of topics, from the latest and most unusual raiment we had observed upon the nobility attending the Tournament, to old friends and acquaintances my mother had encountered at the Faire. Thankfully, Steldor was not mentioned, nor was my slightly distracted state of mind. I tried to avidly participate in the friendly chitchat, but had difficulty concentrating, as had been the case ever since the exhibition.

I had not seen nor contacted Narian since we had kissed on that day, and I wondered if he was as confused as was I. My response to his kiss had made my feelings for him quite clear to me, but I could not understand why or how these feelings had evolved. And I had departed immediately — without a word. What if I had given him the opposite impression, that I did not return his affections?

My thoughts were interrupted by a knock on the tea room door, and Destari granted entrance to Orsiett, the Elite Guard who had been Miranna's secondary bodyguard during the search for the traitor, and who was now working as an aide to Cannan.

"Destari," Orsiett said briskly. "I need a word with you."

Destari exchanged a concerned look with Halias before stepping into the hallway with Orsiett and closing the door behind him. Halias shrugged in reply to our inquisitive stares, then scowled irritably at one of the Palace Guards who accompanied my mother everywhere, as he was leaning toward the door in an attempt to surreptitiously hear the discussion taking place on the other side.

The guard was forced to pull away, however, to avoid a collision with the door as Destari hastily reentered the room.

"Halias, we are to escort the Princesses and the Queen to their quarters without delay."

As he stepped to Miranna's side, Halias asked, "What is the urgency?"

"A Cokyrian has come to the Palace to speak with the King."

"What?" my mother whispered, reaching distractedly to touch her honeyed hair, her blue eyes uneasy. She moved protectively closer to Miranna, placing a trembling hand upon my sister's shoulder.

"We do not know yet why she is here," Destari informed us. "She arrived under a white flag. The three of you are to return to your quarters until the purpose of her visit has become manifest."

Halias did not speak, but stared straight ahead, the clenching of his jaw made particularly apparent by the fact that his hair was pulled back in its customary ponytail. We left the tea room surrounded by guards, Miranna worriedly watching her bodyguard, then finally glancing to me to find the reassurance she craved. I had none to give. I could hear nothing but the thrum of blood in my ears. Everything I knew about the Cokyrians suggested that they acted, they attacked, they *slaughtered* without warning. Why had they now decided to come and talk? My thoughts flew to Narian. Had they come, as London had predicted they would, to reclaim him? And if that were the case, would we be able to keep him safe?

Miranna and I were allowed to keep together in my rooms, but my mother was taken to her own quarters for security's sake. If the Cokyrians did intend to use some form of trickery to harm the Royal Family, keeping us separate would make it more problematic for them.

Upon the passing of a little more than two painstaking hours, Orsiett returned and informed Miranna and me that we were to report to my father's study. Accompanied by our bodyguards, we proceeded down the spiral staircase and into the King's Drawing Room, Orsiett breaking off to head down the corridor to our right. From the Drawing Room, we entered the Hall of Kings, and crossed its expanse to reach my father's study through the door to the east of the thrones.

My mother was already seated upon the sofa, and my father's form was filling the armchair beside her. He was leaning toward her attentively, one of her hands in his, serious expressions on both of their faces. As we entered, he motioned for us to sit as well, and Miranna chose the other half of the sofa, while I sat in an armchair. Destari and Halias remained standing, hands clasped behind their backs.

"I've already informed your mother of this," my father said to Miranna and me, his manner uncharacteristically tired, "but a

Cokyrian messenger came today with a request. Tomorrow at mid-morning, you must all gather in the Throne Room wearing your finest attire. The High Priestess of Cokyri desires an audience with the Royal Family, and I have granted her petition."

I heard Miranna's sharp intake of breath, as did my father.

"There is no need to be afraid," he said soothingly. "The Cokyrians come under a flag of truce, and there will be no shortage of guards in the Throne Room tomorrow."

"Do you think... are they here about Narian?" I stammered.

"If they are, Lord Nar-Kyenn will be safe. Cannan is sending for him as we speak. He will be brought to the Palace and will stay here with us for however long is necessary to learn the Cokyrians' intentions and assess the situation."

I nodded gravely, outwardly composed, but inwardly in turmoil. Then I fixated on a small detail and woodenly corrected my father.

"He chooses to be called Narian."

My father stared blankly at me for a moment, as if trying to figure out why this was important to me, but then returned to the matter at hand.

"You should return to your quarters until it is time to come to the Throne Room tomorrow."

My father then issued an order to Destari and Halias.

"You will stay at your posts through the night, as an extra precaution."

Our bodyguards nodded and bowed, and we all departed, leaving my father and mother alone in the study.

Destari and I returned to my quarters, and I sat in the parlor, feeling dazed, as he loitered by the door. After a moment, he tried to comfort me.

"The King is right, Alera. You will be in no danger."

"And Narian?" I asked, wringing my hands.

"The Captain will keep him secure," Destari assured me. "As for what the future may bring, I cannot say."

~ ~ ~

Palace Guards lined the entire Throne Room, eerily identical in their royal blue and gold tunics, with swords at their hips and silver long-spears in their hands. My parents sat regally upon their thrones, once again robed and crowned, while Miranna and I had taken our seats in the ornate chairs to my mother's left, wearing gold brocade gowns, with gold and pearl tiaras topping our softly falling tresses. Despite the glowing embers in the twin fireplaces, the room was chilled, and I buried my hands in the golden fox fur throw upon my lap. The twelve Elite Guards who protected my father formed two arcs, one on either side of the Royal Family. Destari stood directly behind my chair and Halias likewise stood behind Miranna's. Cannan was standing beside my father just as he had the week before when Steldor had made his apology, and Kade, the Sergeant at Arms, stood protectively next to my mother.

Just like the Palace Guards who lined the walls, every Elite Guard wore his uniform, a royal blue doublet, black breeches, and tall black boots, and stood with weapons at hand. The weaponry of the Elite Guards consisted of a formidable long-sword, a short-sword that strapped across the back, and a double-edged dagger that hung from the belt.

My father rose, looking majestic in his royal blue robes, as the antechamber doors were pulled opened. The Palace Guards' hands more firmly gripped their spears, and the tension in the deafeningly quiet room increased. Then the contingency from Cokyri began to walk forward, led by the woman who had at one time been our prisoner, their measured footfalls resounding in the stillness of the room.

The High Priestess' striking green eyes perused my father's face unwaveringly as she, accompanied by six guards who stood two on either side of her and two behind, neared the thrones. She was clad in black leggings and a shimmering, black, long-sleeved tunic with split sleeves that showed the scoop-necked white shirt she wore beneath. Red stitching accented the front of the tunic, as well as the black cape that was attached at the shoulders. A sword hung at her belt, and she wore a ring on her right hand and the silver pendant that I now knew concealed a dagger, but no crown graced her head.

Her guards, all women, were likewise dressed in black, but their shirts buttoned asymmetrically off to the side, just like the coat Narian had worn at the Palace celebration in his honor. All of their clothing was loose-fitting, clearly designed for ease of movement, and all had swords at their hips, bows and arrow-filled quivers across their backs, and daggers that protruded from their knee-high leather boots.

The High Priestess halted fifteen feet from the dais, watching the King of her enemy warily, her flaming chin-length hair falling around her tanned face. She extended no indication of respect or deference to my father — ruler did not bow to ruler — but waited in haughty silence.

"State your business," my father commanded as the tension in the room became almost intolerable, his words as frosty as the air.

The High Priestess did not hesitate to speak, and when she did, power seemed to pulse from her the like of which I had never before felt.

"I have come to demand the return of a Cokyrian boy who is being held in Hytanica. Do you know of whom I speak?"

"I know of a boy who was abducted as an infant and raised in Cokyri, but has now found his true home in Hytanica," my father firmly replied.

The High Priestess did not appreciate my father's disputatious response.

"You know we speak of the same boy," she said, sounding controlled yet impatient.

My father came back with a new approach.

"What reason does the High Priestess of Cokyri have to pursue the return of one runaway child?"

"I would pursue the return of any Cokyrian held within

Hytanica," she answered belligerently.

"We have not forced the boy to remain here," my father rejoined, bridling at her insinuation. "He has stayed by his own volition."

"Then you would permit his return to Cokyri if that were his choice?"

After a brief deliberation, my father declared, "I would."

The High Priestess' voice grew strong once more as she issued her second demand.

"I insist that I be allowed to speak to Narian."

My father for the first time looked to Cannan, and the imposing Captain of the Guard stepped confidently forward. I saw the High Priestess' narrowed eyes flick between Cannan and the King, as though assessing the relationship between the two prominent men.

"We will send for the boy," Cannan announced through gritted teeth, making the decision my father had silently asked of him. His dark eyes were cold and hard, and I realized how taxing it must be for those who had fought in the war to keep their tongues and their actions civil.

"Meanwhile," my father said, the need to be hospitable masking his abhorrence for the people before him, "my guards will escort you to the Meeting Hall." He then addressed the Sergeant at Arms. "Kade, arrange the necessary escort and notify the kitchens to bring bread, cheese and wine to our visitors."

Kade quickly implemented my father's orders, and Palace Guards walked in front of, and behind, the seven Cokyrians, more than doubling their numbers, as they were led from the Hall of Kings, through the antechamber, and on to the Meeting Hall. With the closing of the Throne Room doors, silence again reigned.

The Royal Family moved into the King's study while Cannan and an Elite Guard went to collect Narian from the guest room on the third floor where he had spent the night. He had been told to keep to his room until after the Cokyrians had left, so that he could be easily summoned if he were needed, and, of perhaps greater import, so that the Cokyrians would not know of his presence within the Palace.

Destari, Halias, and several of my father's personal guards stood outside the door of the study after we had entered, the rest of the Palace and Elite Guards milling about the Hall of Kings. The room felt agonizingly cold to me, despite the fire snapping in the hearth, and I sank into an armchair as close to the blaze as I dared to be. Miranna and my mother sat together on the sofa, holding hands, while my father remained on his feet. Although it was only my family in the study, no one spoke. The hush was broken a few minutes later by a sharp rap on the door, and Cannan entered with Narian. As had been the case with Steldor, Narian's face showed bruising, although his was at the temple as well as along the jaw.

Narian quickly scanned the room, and I recalled the self-defense lesson in which he had told me to always be aware of my surroundings, and to take note of every person present and of every exit. Was such conduct second nature to him? Was there ever a time when he truly relaxed his vigilance?

"I've informed Narian of the High Priestess' demands," Cannan said, closing the door.

My father nodded appreciatively, then addressed the young man standing respectfully before him.

"Do you wish to speak to her?"

Narian's eyes were steely as he answered, and he seemed to have detached himself from all emotion.

"No, Your Majesty, I do not."

"Very well. And of her other demand — do you wish to return to Cokyri?"

Narian's expression did not change, nor did his tone.

"No, I do not."

"Then it is here you shall stay," my father said kindly, clearly under the impression that Narian's detachment was an attempt to conceal the anxiety he was truly feeling. I doubted that Narian was afraid, but his real feelings were indiscernible even by me.

Cannan escorted Narian from the study, and my father gave word for the Cokyrians to be brought before us once more. The King and Queen returned to their thrones, and Miranna and I likewise took our seats, with our guards behind us. Cannan emerged from his office, where he had apparently taken Narian, and returned to my father's side just as the antechamber doors swung inward.

The High Priestess and her guards entered exactly as before, though this time they were accompanied by Kade and the many Hytanican guards who had been with them in the Meeting Hall. As the Palace Guards resumed their positions on either side of the hall, and Kade returned to stand beside my mother, the Cokyrians once again approached the dais. The High Priestess stopped before my father, warily considering him.

"Narian will not be meeting with you," the King announced, his manner tough and unyielding. "Nor will he be returning to Cokyri."

Sparks danced in the High Priestess' eyes, though the rest of her face remained composed.

"Say what you will, Hytanican King, but Narian must be surrendered into my custody," she retorted, with a clear note of animosity. "You can either release him to us voluntarily, or we will take him by force. I advise you to consider wisely, and I will know your answer in the morning."

She motioned to her six guards, and they departed in formation, their footsteps and the High Priestess' threat echoing in their wake.

After the antechamber doors had closed behind the Cokyrians, emphatic debate broke out among those assembled in the Throne Room, including the Palace and Elite Guards, as some measure of fear seized almost everyone. What had she meant by "we will take him by force?" Did the Cokyrians plan to restart the war? Would protecting Narian put the entire Kingdom at risk? And, most pressing, how should the Hytanicans reply when the High Priestess returned in the morning?

The debate grew increasingly strident as suggestions were torn apart and rejected. My father, hands moving animatedly, was conferring with both Kade, who likewise appeared to be on the verge of losing control, and Cannan, who looked quite unruffled except for the occasional twitch in his left eyebrow.

I was more distraught than ever, and Miranna shot me a fretful glance that told me she felt the same. Narian had stepped out of Cannan's office to observe the commotion, leaning with shoulder against the wall, his countenance uncharacteristically troubled.

"QUIET!!" Cannan suddenly bellowed, and everyone was struck eerily dumb. "That's better," he grumbled, sounding somewhat drained, then he pinched the bridge of his nose and shut his eyes, deep in thought.

A resolute voice resounded in the silence.

"We should send for London."

For a moment, everyone stared at Halias, who stood steadfast, his glistening blue eyes glued to Cannan's face, then all attention slowly shifted to the Captain of the Guard. Cannan glowered at Halias for several long moments, making no effort to disguise his indignation. Then he turned to Destari.

"Do you know where London is?" he gruffly asked.

Destari nodded once in confirmation.

"Find him and bring him here. Make sure he understands the situation."

Destari nodded again, and strode from the room through the antechamber doors.

I knew why Cannan had reacted so strongly to Halias' declaration. It was not because he objected strenuously to requesting London's help, but instead in response to the implication that his own knowledge of Cokyri was insufficient. Even so, he could not deny the need for someone who truly understood the enemy, someone who had been inside the enemy's realm for a significant period of time. Narian was only sixteen, too young to be depended upon or trusted in a military capacity, so London was the only choice.

The Throne Room buzzed with suffused discussion, and I tried unsuccessfully several times to catch Narian's eye. But whenever I glanced toward him, his attention was directed elsewhere, and I couldn't help but think that this was deliberate on his part.

After Destari's departure, my father turned to my mother, Miranna, and me.

"You do not need to stay any longer. It would be best if you retired to your quarters while we men discuss these developments."

My mother nodded, her face pale, and my father attempted to soothe her.

"We have dealt with the Cokyrians before, and we will deal with this situation as well. There is no need to be afraid."

My mother stood, then she and Miranna left, accompanied by several guards, although Halias remained in the Throne Room. I made no move to follow them, and my father frowned quizzically at me.

"I would like to stay," I said evenly. "I will not cause any disruption; I only want to know what decision is reached as to Narian."

He acquiesced, too distracted by the matter at hand to argue, and I sank deeper into my chair, tucking the fox throw closer about me as though to make myself both warmer and less conspicuous. Cannan approached my father to engage in a muted exchange, at the end of which he beckoned to Narian, who was still leaning with shoulder against the wall, silently observing everyone. Narian straightened, and then unperturbedly crossed the floor, giving my father a deferential bow as he came to stand before the men.

Cannan's dark eyes somberly examined Narian for several uncomfortable moments, and I began to agitatedly pick at the fur of the throw covering my lap, although Narian, calmly meeting the Captain's eyes, showed no sign of unease. Finally, Cannan spoke.

"The High Priestess would not personally pursue just any Cokyrian boy. It is time you told us the nature of your relationship to her."

My chest tightened painfully at the Captain's words, and I began to frenetically twist the golden fox fur. At my father's glance, I forced my hands to relinquish their grip and lie motionless in my lap. I did not want my nervous habit to draw Cannan's attention, lest he deduce that I knew something relevant to his inquiry. While I wasn't sure how truthful Narian would be, I knew I would never be able to conceal anything from the Captain if he turned to me for information.

Narian said nothing, his expression unfathomable.

"Perhaps you are but a run-away," Cannan continued, his commanding eyes set on Narian's face. When Narian said naught, Cannan turned to the King. "If that is the case, Sire, I see no need to go to war simply to protect a miscreant child from a parent's retribution."

I did not know if Cannan was truly suggesting we return Narian to the High Priestess, but my stomach squirmed uncomfortably at the possibility. I glanced toward the antechamber doors, hoping this conversation would end before London and Destari arrived, as they would fill their Captain in on the information he sought.

"I cannot speak to the reason I was abducted as an infant," Narian finally responded, sounding uncharacteristically cowed, and I wondered if he was just playing to his audience. "As I have told you before, I did not know I was Hytanican until last summer. Then I journeyed here only to learn of my heritage. The High Priestess is insistent upon my return because I was raised, as are others, to serve her, and she does not like to lose things she values."

He paused, hanging his head, and his bangs fell forward to hide his expression.

"I will not suffer, as you put it, a mere 'parent's retribution' should I be placed in her custody."

After a brief moment, he lifted his tortured blue eyes to my father's kindly brown ones, aware that the King was the weak link.

"I feel no loyalties to Cokyri, Your Majesty. While I will, without argument, comply with any decision you make as to my future, I beseech you to permit me to claim Hytanica as my home."

There was a pleading note in his voice, although I again questioned its authenticity.

My father, in his compassion, could not turn Narian away.

"Cannan, my decision stands. We will provide him with the same protection I would provide to any of our children."

Cannan looked one last time at Narian, taking his measure, and it seemed to me that he knew Narian was concealing something. He did not, however, pursue the subject.

"You may return to my office," he brusquely said.

"Thank you, sir," Narian said to Cannan. Then he bowed again to my father. "Thank you, Your Majesty."

This time the relief I detected seemed genuine. He did as he had been told and retreated toward Cannan's office, although he did not enter, but resumed his earlier stance against the wall.

As we continued to wait for London and Destari to arrive, I reflected upon the deliberately ambiguous nature of Narian's explanation. While he had, strictly speaking, been truthful, his precisely chosen words were capable of more than one meaning. "I cannot speak to the reason I was abducted" would be interpreted as "I don't know the reason" by my father, rather than "I know, but will not speak of it," which was their true meaning.

It was but a half hour later that Destari and London entered. They strode up the center of the Hall of Kings together, the guards in the room falling silent as they followed the progress of the man whom most of them had come to call traitor. I knew there were some who believed otherwise, and counted Cannan among them, despite the fact that he had been involved in the decision to discharge my former bodyguard. If Cannan sincerely thought London a traitor, he would not have allowed him back into the Palace at all, save to be thrown in the dungeon.

London said nothing, but watched Cannan evenly, undeniably relishing the awkward circumstances in which the Captain found himself.

After clenching and unclenching his jaw several times, Cannan finally spoke.

"London, you know the Cokyrians better than anyone. What would you suggest we do?"

"What valuable military advice could a commoner offer the Captain of the Guard?" London asked, raising a mordant eyebrow.

Cannan stared murderously at London for a moment, then cleared his throat.

"With my authority as Captain of the Guard and Commander of Hytanica's military, I officially reinstate you to your post in the King's Elite Guard and to your former military rank of Deputy Captain," he loudly pronounced.

My heart attempted to leap out of my chest. Somehow, impossibly, my horrible deed had been undone. Perhaps now London would find it within himself to forgive me. I was so elated that I could barely keep myself from running to him.

London, however, merely tilted his head toward Cannan, no change in his bearing.

"Thank you," he said, sounding a little self-satisfied.

Cannan was not willing to let London gloat for long.

"Now, what action do you propose?" he demanded.

"This is really quite simple," London replied, comfortably taking control. Turning to my father, he asked, "Do you intend to return the boy, Your Majesty?"

"No," my father staunchly replied. "He is Hytanican, and as such is granted the abiding protection of his Kingdom."

"Then this is what we must do."

London's voice had taken on an authoritative and incontestable quality.

"Inform the Cokyrians that we have prevailed upon Narian to return, but that he needs time to bid farewell to his family. Tell them that we will bring him to the bridge in five days, at which time we will transfer him to their custody.

"During these five days, Hytanica must prepare for whatever

response will be forthcoming from the Cokyrians when they learn that Narian is not actually going to be returned to them. Forces must be assembled to defend the city if indeed it comes to that."

"And of the meeting?" my father asked. "Are we to ignore it altogether?"

"I will meet the Cokyrians at the appointed time and location to try to forestall their retaliation," London said, earning a few dubious mutterings throughout the room. "I will inform them that we claim Narian as Hytanican by birth and by choice, and that he will not be turned over to them."

Though there was a fair amount of grumbling among those assembled, Cannan and my father nodded their agreement to London's proposed strategy. My father dismissed all but his personal guards, and Cannan and London moved into the Captain's office to further discuss the technicalities of the plan. As they passed Narian, I noticed that Narian's cool blue eyes never for an instant left London's face.

Chapter Twenty-Five
The Enemy Without, the Enemy Within

O nce the High Priestess had consented to meet at the bridge five days hence, the city throbbed with activity. Cannan sent patrols to the surrounding Hytanican villages to instruct the people to be ready to move into the city with little warning if such a measure became necessary.

In preparation for a potential siege, hunting parties braved the woods behind the walled city, and the villagers slaughtered whatever animals they could afford to sacrifice as part of a plan to stockpile food and other provisions. Hundreds of other supplies were gathered as well and stored within the city, to guard against a potentially long and arduous winter. Weaponry was checked, repaired, and counted, and the armories in the Palace and at the Military Complex were replenished so that not a single soldier would fall short of the required arms.

When the fifth day arrived, I awoke before dawn in order to see London and the thirty soldiers that were to accompany him on their way. Destari would be attending the meeting as well, for it would be his task to assess how great and immediate a threat the Cokyrians posed to Hytanica while London delivered the King's message.

In Destari's absence, Tadark had been reassigned as my personal bodyguard. I had not spoken to the short, young, baby-faced guard since he had betrayed me to Cannan by confessing the nature of my visits with Narian. He was, therefore, initially self-conscious around me, but I paid no heed as I had far more pressing concerns. Unfortunately, it did not take him long to conclude that all was forgotten, if not forgiven, and he soon resumed his annoying habits.

With Tadark aggravatingly close to me, I came down the Grand Staircase and went out the large doors into the central courtyard, where I saw London, Destari, Cannan, and my father standing by the gates. Destari was in uniform, as was expected of anyone who acted as a representative of Hytanica, but London, ever the rebel, was dressed in his dark leather jerkin and weathered boots. On the other side of the open gates, the troops, all in full uniform with plates of armor protecting their chests and backs, waited on horseback for the two Elite Guards to join them.

As I approached, with Tadark following just a few feet behind, the chilly morning air felt harsh and foreboding, and I shivered despite my heavy cloak. Though this was supposed to be a simple meeting, no one thought the Cokyrians would receive Hytanica's message with grace. It was probable that fewer soldiers would be returning than were departing.

I stopped a few feet away from the men, knowing I would not be welcomed, at least by my father and Cannan, but wanting London and Destari to know that I wished them well. Although London had returned to his position in the Palace, he had not yet come to see me, and I desperately hoped things were resolved between us.

London glanced at me, then strode to my side before mounting his horse.

"You should not be here," he teasingly said to me, "but then, I've never known anyone who flaunts as many rules as you do."

"I believe that can be attributed to your influence," I replied, greatly relieved by his casual manner.

"We will return without injury," he promised, "but if not, know that what happened between us is in the past, and that you never left my heart."

I nodded gratefully, my eyes unusually watery. He and Destari then mounted their horses and rode out at the head of the Hytanican troops. I retreated to the Chapel to say a prayer for the safety of our men, secure in the knowledge that my relationship with London had been mended, before returning to my quarters to await the return of our soldiers.

Time passed slowly, and with each moment, my sense of doom grew. Our men would have reached the bridge by now. How many Cokyrians would they have encountered? Had the message been delivered? How had the Cokyrians responded? And, the most terrible question of all, were my two most trusted guards alive?

As the day wore on, I would occasionally stand on my balcony to survey the city and what land I could see beyond its walls, checking for movement. It was not until the weak November sun had begun its plummet toward the horizon, however, that I saw riders approaching in the distance. I stared intently, knowing that London and Destari would be in the lead, and dread filled me as I saw that only one horse headed the group of men.

With shaking hands and a sick feeling in my stomach, I left my quarters and stumbled to the Grand Staircase, halting on the landing above the first floor. Footsteps from below drew my attention, and I leaned over the railing to see Cannan and my father emerge from the antechamber followed by several guards, obviously having been told that the troops were returning.

I stayed on the landing, knowing that my father would not approve of my presence when the soldiers entered to make their report. I swallowed several times to try to clear my obstructed throat, and for once, Tadark had the courtesy to give me some space by standing against the wall behind me.

The paradoxical tranquility was agonizing, and time slowed to a maddening crawl, although in fact it was only minutes before the doors were pulled open by the Palace Guards. As both London and Destari entered, taking rasping, exhausted breaths, I clutched the banister for support, nearly collapsing with relief.

London seemed to be relatively unharmed, albeit sweat-drenched and grimy, but as I examined Destari, I saw that his left shirt sleeve was soaked crimson. The wound on his arm, however it had been inflicted, had bled profusely for quite some time. I was somewhat nauseated by the sight of the blood, but made no sound or effort not to see.

"Report," Cannan ordered, startled by the condition of two of his finest soldiers.

"The Cokyrians were not pleased by what I had to say," London said wryly, rubbing the back of his neck as if it were sore. "They attacked us as we were leaving. My horse took an arrow in the neck, and when Destari came back for me, he took one in the shoulder."

"The arrow barely grazed my arm," Destari said, as worried eyes fell upon him. "It looks worse than it feels."

"You should have it examined straight away," my father insisted, gesturing erratically. "You have been bleeding quite heavily — perhaps the wound needs to be sewn."

"There are many who fared worse than I, Your Majesty," Destari said adamantly. "I am in need of no one's care at this moment."

"How many were injured?" Cannan probed, and I shrank from hearing the answer.

"Twenty-four soldiers returned with us," said London, after glancing at Destari and deciding it was he who would deliver the bad tidings. He sounded strangely distant as he spoke. "Of those, nine were taken to the Infirmary at the Military Base. The six who were left behind are, presumably, dead."

I clenched my jaw so fiercely that my teeth began to ache. I wanted to weep as I thought of the families of the six slain soldiers, and how they would shortly learn that their husband, or their father, or brother, or son, was dead, killed during a simple and, at first glance, low-risk mission. Perhaps their wives were waiting dinner for them, not yet knowing that they lay lifeless on the shore of the river, stuck with Cokyrian arrows. I withheld my tears with difficulty as I pictured the dignified faces of the Cokyrians who had been inside the Kingdom I called home less than a week ago, and saw not the regal figures I had initially judged them to be, but merciless killers.

"Do the Cokyrians have sufficient numbers to pose an immediate threat?" Cannan was asking as I recovered from my initial shock.

It was Destari who answered.

"No, sir, not a threat to the city. They did not pursue us, seemingly satisfied with the punishment they had managed to inflict. They also suffered injuries and, perhaps, casualties."

"Go to the Infirmary and see who lives, and Destari, have your wound treated," Cannan instructed, sounding slightly strained, as he experienced afresh the pain of war that had been absent for sixteen years. "I will send patrols out to collect the bodies, and to reinforce our protection of the bridge."

London and Destari simultaneously gave curt nods and the small group dispersed, the two guards exiting through the main doors, Cannan and my father heading in the direction of the Captain's office.

In the aftermath of the debacle at the bridge, Cannan increased the number of soldiers who patrolled Hytanica's borders by day and by night, and sent scouts into the Niñeyre Mountains to monitor the activities of the Cokyrians. Although our enemy had departed, no one expected their absence to continue, and Hytanica was on high alert for any sign of their return. But there were no incidents. Destari, who had returned to his assignment as my bodyguard less than a week after he had been injured, said it was reminiscent of the end of the war, when the Cokyrians had abandoned their attack and vacated their encampments, to remain unseen for sixteen years.

As the days plodded on, the city did not rest peacefully. An unmistakable sensation of doom hung over it, yet each new day brought another reprieve. It was when we entered the month of December, with the passage of just over two weeks since the meeting at the bridge, that the atmosphere in the city and at the

Palace became noticeably less strained. The Christmas season was rapidly approaching, and in spite of the unsettled state of affairs with Cokyri, spirits were rising. Though Cannan had not reduced the number of troops on patrol, the Hytanican people began to believe that the Cokyrians did not intend to strike, and many thought it inconceivable that they would start a war over one seemingly insignificant teenage boy.

During this stressful, but uneventful time, I saw little of Narian, though he continued to reside in our guest wing, and I had yet to speak with him. I could only assume that Cannan had forbidden him access to certain parts of the Palace, for the Captain probably still held some concern about Narian's relationship to the High Priestess. I did see much more of London, however, as he was often with Destari, and I began to feel as though I once again had two bodyguards. I was not surprised, therefore, when I left my quarters late one afternoon to visit the library and found both London and Destari outside my parlor door.

I made my way through the corridors, trailed by both guards, who were speaking to each other in hushed tones, although I was too indescribably happy to have London back to be irked by their secretiveness, whether it was conscious on their part or not. Though it was not yet time for dinner, all of the lanterns in the corridors had been lit, as the daylight hours were rapidly diminishing now that winter was upon us. Despite the fact that fires smoldered in most of the fireplaces within the Palace, the interior temperature was dropping and I pulled a shawl more tightly about my shoulders to ward off the chill.

As we entered the library, I was momentarily nonplussed to find Narian seated in one of the armchairs by the hearth, immersed in a book, light from the flames casting flickering shadows upon his serene face and adding a touch of red to his blonde hair. He raised his head, then respectfully came to his feet. For an instant he looked almost hopeful, but his cold, guarded façade emerged as he realized Destari and London were with me.

"Princess Alera," he said, giving a courteous nod as I approached.

Now that I had seen him free of his calculated aloofness on several occasions, I hated it when he employed the guise. Nevertheless, I understood the need to observe formalities whenever anyone else (especially the two guards with whom we were currently keeping company) was at hand.

"Good evening, Lord Narian," I said sociably, so conscious of acting naturally that every word and movement felt awkward. "How does living in the Palace agree with you?"

"I am well accommodated, though I feel a bit constrained," he politely responded.

Mystified, I asked, "Do you miss living with your family?"

"No," he firmly replied. "I have not lived with my family since before the Tournament. I miss being outdoors; I miss the activity."

An idea came to me, something that might give me a chance to spend some less supervised time with Narian.

"Perhaps, then, you would like to help us in preparing the Palace for Christmas," I suggested. "We will be hanging holly, mistletoe, and ivy throughout the interior of the Palace and on the exterior—"

"I don't think that's the sort of activity he is missing, Alera," London interjected, leaning casually against the wall to the left of the window, near the book-filled aisles. "I'm sure he'll tell you if you ask him — he's used to daily training and drill. You can lose your edge if you go too long without training."

Narian stared coolly at London, though a small crease between his brows had appeared. I closed my eyes briefly, hoping London had finished. Of course, he had not.

"I could continue your training," he casually offered, though he watched Narian with predator's eyes. "After all, I am well acquainted with your instructor's methods."

I took a quick, involuntary breath. Narian glanced sideways at me for an instant, then returned to impassively observing London. Destari, who had moved to the window seat, also appeared shocked by London's assertion, for his dark eyebrows had risen in disbelief.

"Oh well," London said indifferently, moving to pull a book from one of the shelves and beginning to rifle through its pages.

"Just a thought."

Though everyone in the room was gawking at him, London remained inscrutably nonchalant, and I marveled at his composure. Never before had London mentioned his ordeal in Cokyri, and now he had flippantly implied that he not only had met the Overlord, but knew a great deal about his methods and how Narian had been trained. I was the only one in whom Narian had confided; I alone knew that the Overlord had been his teacher. I should have anticipated, given what London had said to me prior to the exhibition, that he would have put the pieces together, but that he would be bold enough to tell Narian how much he had surmised was totally unexpected.

"So," I said to Narian, my throat having gone so dry that my voice sounded hoarse, "about Christmas — would you care to join us?"

Narian appeared not to have heard me. His eyes were fixated on London's hands as they turned the pages of the book.

"That ring does not belong to you," he suddenly declared.

London held his right hand up, palm turned in, displaying the ring on his forefinger. I stared at it, the only jewelry that he ever wore, and that he was never without.

The front of the wide silver band was over-lain with two pairs of stacked loops that were bound together by narrow silver links. The loops were formed from a single, continuous strip of silver that ran from the back of the band to the front where it arched up and around, then wrapped under and over itself to drop down and repeat the same shape. It then wrapped again around the back of the band to form the third and fourth loops at the front before returning to its original and unending path.

"Oh, I think it does belong to me," London disagreed, cocking an eyebrow warningly. "I more than paid for it sixteen years ago."

A thunderous silence hung in the room as Narian and London stared distrustfully at each other. Finally, Narian tore his piercing gaze away, and I repeated my question, hoping to dispel the tension that saturated the room.

"If you want my assistance," Narian politely said, sparing me a glance, "then I will be happy to oblige."

Though his reply was sincere, I could not draw his attention. I had come to believe that nothing would ever penetrate Narian's defenses, but was now forced to admit that I was wrong, for London had clearly rattled him.

"I need one thing yet for Ailith, then we will have purchased something for everyone," Miranna said, stopping to peruse the jewelry displayed on the counter in one of the shops.

She and I were visiting the Market District in search of inexpensive, yet meaningful, Christmas gifts for our personal maids and servants. Every year, we went shopping together for this purpose, though it was seen as improper for us to buy gifts for our bodyguards, who were forced to tolerate us far more extensively than our maids. While I knew London, Destari, and Halias relished working as they did, I would have liked to have been permitted to show our appreciation by giving them something for Christmas.

Winter had now descended in full force upon Hytanica, although the season was not particularly harsh. While it was rare for it to be cold enough in the river valley for the Recorah to solidly freeze, the landscape was nonetheless drab and dismal. Especially in the month of January, skies would generally be gray and a cold rain would often fall. At higher elevations, the precipitation would descend as snow, capping the mountains to our north in white.

Miranna left the shop and, weaving through the people on the street, made her way to a store where multicolored dress fabrics were sold. I continued to scan the display before me, although in truth my attention was captivated by the daggers at the end of the counter rather than by the jewelry. Ever since Narian had begun to teach me basic fighting skills, I had developed a keener awareness of the weaponry carried by Destari and the other guards who worked in the Palace. I knew little about the daggers this shop was selling, or any other form of weaponry, except that simply taking note of them would be viewed by all accounts as extremely unladylike. I pulled my eyes away from the knives and tried afresh to generate interest in the jewelry, feeling restless and bored, and was vaguely cognizant of the opening and closing of the shop door.

As I passed my eyes over the merchandise, a strong arm took hold of me from behind, wrapping tightly around my upper chest and pulling me against a well-muscled body. I clawed at the man's forearm, desperate to free myself and frantic that Destari was not coming to my aid. Then my assailant released me with a conceited chuckle, and I wheeled about to come face to face with Steldor.

"What are doing?" I demanded, cheeks aflame, temper rising. "Do you always pounce upon unsuspecting women from behind?"

Steldor raised a bemused eyebrow. "Actually, I prefer to pounce from the front," he teased, dark eyes lazily scanning my figure. Then he wickedly observed, "I thought you were learning self-defense. Perhaps you need a better teacher."

My eyes narrowed into a steady glare, both in response to his subtle criticism of Narian and the fact that he *somehow* had learned of the activities in which I had engaged during my visits to Koranis' estate. I could only assume that Tadark had once again been overly talkative.

"My teacher is the best fighter in Hytanica," I brashly countered, hoping to strike a nerve.

Steldor merely smirked, clearly enjoying my reaction, as if he had intentionally baited me.

"You know your way with words, Princess," he mocked. "But just how proficient have you become with weapons?"

I stared at him, momentarily speechless. Was he suggesting that he evaluate my skill and the effectiveness of Narian's teaching? And to what end?

"That is not your concern," I said stiffly, beginning to move away from him to find Miranna at the shop across the street.

"I don't believe your father would see Narian as an appropriate teacher," Steldor slyly commented. "Perhaps it would be enlightening to put the question before him."

I turned back to him slowly, distrustful of his motives.

His smirk broadened as he recognized that he had gained the upper hand.

"If you wish to continue to learn self-defense, you'll find that I am your only option."

"Well, since you are the person against whom I need to defend myself, I will decline your gracious offer," I replied scathingly. "If you'll excuse me, I must finish my shopping before the day is out."

I brushed past him to step out of the shop, but to my dismay, he followed right behind me, my anger, strangely enough, serving to have encouraged him.

"As I am currently off duty, I shall accompany you," he said, voice brimming with self-assurance and barely disguised humor.

"That won't be necessary," I said tersely, glowering at him in an attempt to burn a hole through his irritatingly perfect features.

"Not necessary, indeed," he agreed, moving closer as if to lay claim to me. "But it will certainly make for an interesting afternoon."

Turning my back abruptly to him, I made my way through the crowd toward my sister, doing my best to ignore the one person I would rather have seen run over by a buggy than at my side as he fell into step with me, obviously bent on ruining the rest of my day.

Chapter Twenty-Six
A History Lesson

I n the days following the encounter in the market, I saw little of
Steldor, and frustratingly less of Narian. While I glimpsed Narian
at times within the Palace, I was never able to truly speak with him.
He seemed especially reluctant to say anything as long as London
was with me, and his lack of openness was discouraging.

We were in the Grand Entry Hall when Narian joined Miranna
and me to decorate the Palace. While I had pinned my hopes on this
occasion, our conversation was fleeting at best, as there were so
many other people about that we could say nothing of consequence
to one another. I returned to my quarters in despair that evening,
then released Destari from his post as I intended to stay in my
rooms until I retired for the night. Too overwrought to try to sleep,
and needing to take my mind off my problems, I picked up a book
from the table adjacent to the sofa, moving to sink heavily into one
of the burgundy armchairs near the hearth, seeking the warmth of
the glowing embers. Opening to the first page, I began to read.

A small noise from my bedroom, scarcely louder than the slight
rattling of a shutter, briefly caught my attention. As no other
sounds were forthcoming, I did not give the incident additional
thought, but continued to read until my eyelids started to droop.

Yawning, I stood and dropped the book onto my chair, feeling
pleasantly disoriented. As I moved into my bedroom, my eyes
flitted to the window beside the balcony doors, and I caught a small

movement. I halted, my drowsiness instantly vanquished. The moon was full, shining gloriously through the glass and creating a path of light across the floor, and at the edge of it, by the window, I could make out the silhouette of a man approaching me, his silent footfalls somehow absolutely terrifying.

Before a scream could break free of my constricted throat, the man spoke, his voice gentle and familiar.

"Don't be afraid, Alera, I just wanted to see you."

I let out my breath in relief. "Narian!" I almost inaudibly exclaimed. "How did you get in here?"

"I came in by way of the balcony," he said simply.

I stared at him in amazement.

"You can't be serious..." I muttered, earning a small smile in return. "How did you get past the guards in the courtyard?"

"It wasn't that difficult." Gesturing to the balcony doors behind him, he sardonically added, "By the way, you may want to start barring those doors."

We locked eyes for an agonizing moment, both of us unsure what to say, then Narian moved forward, continuing to assess me as he approached. As he drew near, my pulse rate quickened, brought on not by fear, but merely by his proximity. While I had been desirous of spending some time alone with him, I was wholly unprepared to handle the yearning that now welled within me.

With his compelling blue eyes upon my face, Narian reached out a hand and cupped my chin, then leaned down to gently caress my lips with his own. I did not pull away, and he put his other hand upon the small of my back, drawing my body to him and pressing his mouth more ardently against mine. I closed my eyes and raised my arms to his shoulders, my fingers playing with his thick golden hair as I returned his kiss.

His lips broke from mine after a few moments and he brushed them lightly across my forehead.

"I was beginning to think I had imagined that," he murmured in my ear.

I nestled against his chest as he held me, his rich, earthy scent of leather and pine and cedar encircling me. Then reason returned and I grasped the impropriety of my circumstances. Here was a man, in my bedroom after dark, whose lips had been upon mine, and in whose embrace I now stood, with no chaperone to be found. I forced myself to step back from him, and as I did so, Narian's hands slipped down my arms and he entwined his fingers in mine.

He did not ask for an explanation as to why I had pulled away, most likely recognizing the unseemliness of my position. Instead, he led me to the balcony doors, whereupon he turned to face me with an impish smile upon his face.

"Shall we?"

"What do you mean?" I asked, hesitant, yet curious.

"I can get you out of here."

Though my common sense told me to refuse, the thought of doing something daring and impulsive was overwhelmingly appealing, especially given the person in whose company I would be. I nodded, chewing my lip nervously.

Narian retrieved a pack I had not noticed was there from the floor by the window and opened it, then tossed me a pair of black breeches and a black shirt.

"Go put these on, and bring me one of your simpler dresses so you'll have something to change into later," he instructed, once more a silhouette to me as he stood in the moonlight.

I chose a plain linen gown and brought it to him, then moved into the bath chamber to don the dark clothing. As I had become somewhat accustomed to men's trousers as a result of the lessons Narian had given me, I did not find wearing them now to be strange, though I would no doubt have felt differently if I would have had to face anyone other than him.

As I joined Narian by the doors to the balcony, he pushed his dark cloak off his shoulders, and removed the long-sleeved black leather jerkin that he wore over his black shirt, helping me into it for warmth. He then rearranged the cloak, draping it over his shoulders and covering his light hair with the hood so that he became nearly invisible against the night sky. No covering was necessary for my hair, as it was already a match to the darkness.

Narian opened one of the balcony doors, and then crouched down, motioning for me to do the same, and we slipped out into the cold night air. He shut the door behind us, then picked up the coiled rope from the floor that he had used to climb up to my room, and tied a loop in the end.

"Slide your foot in here," he said, holding it open for me.

I stood and inserted the toe of my shoe as instructed. He then encircled my body under the arms with the rope, and tied the other end to the railing.

"I'm going to lower you down," he informed me, "but first, we must wait."

He pointed to the tower in the corner of the courtyard wall, and I saw that the guard who patrolled the planked walkway that extended from the tower in two directions had just turned the corner and was walking north toward us along the wall's western side.

Narian pulled me into the shadows cast by the Palace, and we remained immobile until the sentry reversed direction and began to march south. When he reached the corner, he would pass through the tower, continuing east down the length of the front courtyard wall to the point where it intersected the central courtyard, then return.

Easily hoisting me over the railing, Narian lowered me to the ground. My hands shook and my heart thumped loudly until my feet connected with the earth, and I knew that I was safe. I melted into the stone wall as Narian had told me to do, feeling almost light-headed at the risk I was taking, then froze as he nimbly climbed down. He removed the rope from my body and tugged it off to the side of the balcony, close to the Palace, so it would be less visible.

The sentry was now retracing his path, and would soon pass through the tower and again turn north, so we lurked in the shadows. When the man had completed his tour and was once more moving away from us, Narian took my hand and led me stealthily across the courtyard to stand next to the western wall. We then crept toward the ladder leading up to the tower, a few paces behind the guard moving above us on the walkway.

After waiting a few additional moments for the guard to progress through the tower, Narian motioned for me to use the ladder. I obeyed, somewhat fearful of climbing straight skyward for fifteen feet upon a slightly rickety wooden contraption, but Narian climbed right behind, hands on the wood on either side of me, providing reassurance.

When we reached the tower, the frosty night breeze tousled my dark hair and turned the tips of my ears pink, and I shivered both from cold and excitement. Narian did not seem to notice the chill, however, as he quickly pulled a second rope from his pack, expertly fastening it around me as he had on the balcony. Moving to the western side of the tower, away from the sentry, he lowered me down, then, to my chagrin, let go of the rope so it landed at my feet. I could see nothing as I stared at the darkened top of the wall in confusion, but before my confusion could turn to fright, I heard the swish of a cloak and Narian dropped to the ground.

"Can't leave a rope hanging here," he muttered.

I marveled at our actions — Narian assisting a Princess disguised in men's garments to escape the Palace in the dead of night, then leaping off walls to join her. I was also a little embarrassed by how effortlessly Narian had evaded the Palace Guards, both when he had come for me and when we had left.

Narian again took my hand, this time to lead me down a gentle slope and into the small apple orchard that lay between the Palace and the Military Complex. We walked in silence until we came to the spot where Narian had tethered a horse.

"Care for a midnight ride?" he asked, although I knew he was not really posing a question, for he would not take "no" for an answer.

I nodded as he untied the steed, and moved closer to the large sorrel animal, preparing to mount by myself, for I knew that was what Narian would expect. Thankfully, the horse was saddled this time, allowing me to mount by the far easier method of a stirrup rather than through use of Narian's knee.

After I was situated, Narian handed the reins to me and swung onto the horse's back in the same way he had during my lesson. He wrapped his arms around my waist and I permitted him to take the leathers from my hands, then he prodded the horse with the heels of his boots so that it set off at an easy walk.

We approached the darkened city without saying a word, though the silence between us was not uncomfortable. I was happy to be with him, and to be doing something adventurous. The chill I had felt dissipated as we rode, partly from the warmth of the animal and partly from the warmth of Narian's body against mine.

The city was still as I had never before seen it, and in its tranquility seemed almost like a different place. The streets were deserted except for the occasional guard on patrol who heeded us not. I reveled in my newfound freedom, at being out in the open with no need to hide that Narian and I were together, and with no bodyguards to separate us.

We meandered through the city without speaking, the horse's hooves sometimes clacking against cobblestone, other times muffled on a dirt street, and the houses as well as their inhabitants seemed to lie in deep slumber. The moon and stars, reflected back by the rare dusting of snow upon the ground, were our primary sources of light, occasionally aided by a guard's torch or candle glow from a window. In the almost complete silence, I became much more conscious of the sound of Narian's breathing, and automatically matched it with my own. While in truth I knew little about him, I felt more at one with him than I had ever felt with anyone else; somewhat ironically, in light of London's concerns, I also felt safer with him.

Time eluded me, but all too soon we had circled around to the Royal Stables just to the east of the Palace, and I smiled as I realized from whence Narian had obtained the horse. Narian dismounted, then to my delight (as I was not used to his assistance), told me to swing my right leg over the pommel of the saddle, and I slid into his arms to land lightly beside him.

None of the grooms was working at this time of night, and I walked behind him as he led the horse into the stable, hovering by the door as he put it in one of the stalls. The barn was dimly lit by the glimmering moonlight that shone through the windows, but though there were lanterns hung at intervals on the walls, we dared not light one, lest we draw notice.

Narian came back to me after caring for our mount, and led me by the hand toward a stack of hay at the rear of the barn. We did not speak, but he motioned to me as he lowered himself upon the hay, inviting me to sit with him. I did so, and he put an arm around me, draping his cloak around us both. Feeling pleasantly tired and warm, I rested my head upon his shoulder, inexpressibly content.

Narian shifted after a moment to lean against the wall, and I could feel a change in his mood as well as his posture.

"Tell me about London," he murmured, after he had repositioned us both.

"What is it you wish to know?" I asked, perplexed by his interest.

"How long have you known him?"

"For as long as I can remember. He became my bodyguard when I was a little girl."

"Was he involved in the war?"

"Yes, he was a scout at the beginning of his military career, then sometime during the war began leading troops into battle." A now familiar pang of guilt hit me over how little I had actually bothered to find out about London over the years, as I could conjure few specifics about his life.

"Then how old is he?"

"He is similar in age to Destari and Halias, perhaps thirty-nine or forty."

Narian made a slight sound of acknowledgment, but I could tell this was not the answer he had expected, as London looked much younger than his actual age.

"How does he know so much about Cokyri?" he finally persisted.

"He was a prisoner for about ten months toward the end of the war," I answered, and his body momentarily tensed.

"Ten months?" he repeated, slowly and incredulously. "The enemy does not usually last ten *days* when the Overlord extends his hospitality."

"We don't know much about what he endured during that time," I said, my mood becoming subdued as an image of London suffering as a prisoner of Cokyri entered my mind.

Narian was clearly puzzled.

"But how did London return to Hytanica? How is it that he lived? The Overlord never releases prisoners of war."

"London escaped," I said simply. "After the Cokyrians took you from your home, there must have been great haste to withdraw from our lands, and he was perhaps less heavily guarded. I know nothing else about it, except that he was quite ill when he returned to us. When he finally recovered, he was made a member of the Elite Guard in recognition of his bravery and of his service to the Kingdom, and was assigned as my bodyguard."

Narian fell silent, satisfied for the moment with what he had learned. Then comprehension as to the reason for his interest hit me, and I sat abruptly upright to stare at him.

"Why were you so interested in London's ring?"

"It is Cokyrian," he brusquely declared. "One of a pair. Its twin sits on the hand of the High Priestess, while the one London wears belongs to the Overlord. It was thought lost in battle."

I stared incredulously at him. Had London, while a prisoner, managed to steal the Overlord's ring? As impossible as that sounded, it seemed more likely than that he had stumbled across it on a battlefield.

As I absorbed this fascinating information, I realized how meager my knowledge was of the history of the animosity between Hytanica and Cokyri.

"Narian," I timidly said, dropping my gaze, aware that he was one of the few people who might be willing to discuss such a subject with me. "Do you know how the war began? I have heard much about the war itself, but never about its beginnings."

Narian laughed quietly, probably aware himself that such an inquiry by a Hytanican woman would be viewed as improper, and I raised my head. His expression was so tender and open as he looked at me that I was certain I could see his soul in his eyes.

"I can tell you what Cokyrians believe about the beginning of the war," he responded, a hint of amusement still in his voice.

I gave a quick nod, eager for him to tell me whatever he could, and laid my head once more upon his shoulder.

"Over a century ago," he began, "the King of Hytanica sent his eldest son and heir as an ambassador to Cokyri to arrange for a trade treaty between the two Kingdoms. Hytanica intended to offer a variety of crops to our mountain Kingdom in exchange for some of the jewels and precious metals that we mined. Unfortunately, the ambassador's provincial attitude that men are superior to women was not well-received. When the ambassador was brought before the Empress of Cokyri, he insulted her appallingly by outright refusing to negotiate with a woman. The Empress had him executed for his insolence, and when Hytanica learned of his death, the King was incensed, and attacked Cokyri with all his strength. Cokyri retaliated in turn, and the fighting escalated from there."

"A hundred years of killing because one person unwittingly insulted another?" I sat up straight, gaping at him in horror. "Why was the ambassador's foolish action dealt with so ruthlessly?"

Narian bristled slightly at my accusatory tone.

"The Empress of Cokyri was a proud and dignified woman; she commanded respect and adherence, and when it was not forthcoming, no pardon was extended. The King's ambassador should have learned our protocols before approaching our ruler. It was doubly offensive that he felt no need to do so, and his arrogance was dealt with quickly and severely — with death."

"And has no one tried to negotiate a treaty since that time?" I pursued, both revolted and intrigued by the information Narian was sharing with me.

"When the Empress died, her children, the Overlord and the High Priestess, came to power, inheriting her hatred of Hytanica. The Overlord will not entertain a treaty, as he is unalterably determined to conquer this land."

I could form no reply to this, so I uneasily picked at the hay, listening to the horses snorting and shuffling in their stalls. Then Narian's eyes narrowed, and I knew he was about to pose a question of his own.

"To where does the tunnel lead?" he inexplicably inquired.

I gawked at him, utterly stupefied.

"How do you know about the tunnel?" I managed to mumble.

"Actually, I didn't know for certain it was a tunnel until just now," he said slyly. "I discovered some time ago that the floor in one of the unused stalls has greater give than the floor in the rest of the stable, and supposed it might conceal an escape tunnel. You just confirmed my hunch."

I stared at him, feeling bewildered and somewhat insulted that he would use such a ruse to get information from me, but before I could respond, he repeated his question.

"So where in the Palace does the tunnel open?"

My thoughts whirled, as this was something I should not disclose. Very few people knew there were, in fact, two tunnels that led outside the Palace, for use by the Royal Family if circumstances warranted a hasty and secretive departure. On the other hand, as Narian had already learned of this tunnel's existence, I had no doubt he would find the entry point within the Palace. As I wrestled with this decision, I became cognizant that he was patiently observing me, eyebrows raised in bemusement.

"Alera," he finally said soothingly. "You don't have to tell me anything if you feel you shouldn't. Let's just forget I asked."

He smiled reassuringly, then put his arm around me again and I nestled comfortably against his chest. As my unease evaporated, something else about which I was curious came to mind.

"I have never been in the mountains," I murmured. "Tell me what it is like there."

Narian began to describe to me the raw beauty of the land in which he had lived, a faint yearning behind his words. The steady cadence of his voice and the sweet smell of the hay were comforting, and my eyelids fell like heavy drapes. Just before I drifted off to sleep, secure in his arms, a whisper escaped my lips.

"The tunnel leads into the Chapel."

"Alera. Alera, wake up."

Narian's voice gradually penetrated my many layers of slumber, and I opened my eyes groggily. For a moment I was disoriented, but when I saw Narian gazing out one of the windows of the stable, the evening came rushing back to me, and I jolted awake, knowing we somehow needed to get back into the Palace.

Narian turned to face me, then tossed me the gown I had earlier given him to place in his pack.

"You should change now," he quietly instructed. "We need to leave before the stable hands arrive for the day."

I nodded, glancing around for a place where I would not be seen. After finding nothing more fitting, I entered an empty stall and reemerged a few minutes later wearing my simple cream-colored frock. He had not moved, and I extended the black clothing to him as I went to his side, watching as he tucked the items into his pack.

I could tell from the grayish light filtering through the window that the sun was just rising.

"How are we going to get back into the Palace?" I queried with a touch of panic.

"We'll walk through the front gates," he matter-of-factly stated.

Unable to think of a better alternative, I nodded, albeit somewhat skeptically. He reached out fondly after a moment to pluck a bit of hay from my hair and my cheeks grew hot with embarrassment.

"I'm afraid I'm not very presentable," I mumbled.

He smiled affectionately, then took my hand to draw me to him.

"I prefer you in breeches," he said teasingly, lifting my chin to give me a light kiss, "but other than that you look just fine."

I shivered, and he draped his cloak around my shoulders, donning the leather jerkin himself. He pulled open the stable door and we hastened through it, the frost-coated grass crunching beneath our feet as we approached the courtyard gates.

"Halt! State your purpose!"

One of the Palace Guards on duty was suspiciously hailing us, but before I could answer, he recognized me, and his eyes widened in astonishment.

"Princess Alera! What are you...? How did you...? Where did you...?"

"Pleasant morning for a stroll, don't you think?" Narian calmly interrupted.

"Yes, of course," the sentry muttered, eyes flicking back and forth between Narian and me, then he pounded on the gate and told the guard on the other side to grant us entry.

As the gates opened, I cast my eyes upward and saw the tower guards likewise staring at us in confusion. Struck by the incongruity of the entire situation, I quickly looked down so the soldiers would not see my grin.

We walked up the white stone path through the central courtyard to the double front doors of the Palace, where we replayed the same scene. Finally gaining admittance, we stepped into the Grand Entry Hall, and I hoped it was early enough so that we would not stumble into any of the Royal Family's personal guards, who would be far more willing to raise questions than the guards on night patrol in the corridors. We hastily climbed the

Grand Staircase, and after whispered good-byes, moved in separate directions, I toward my quarters, Narian toward the rear of the Palace and the stairway that led to the third floor guest rooms.

I felt strangely giddy as I entered my parlor, in part from tiredness, in part from the happiness I felt with Narian, and in part from how daring our actions had been. I retreated immediately to my bedroom and slipped into bed, not intending to fall asleep, but so that my personal maid and my bodyguards would not detect any change in my daily routine. As long as none of the sentries mentioned the unusual hour of our arrival to Cannan, Kade, or the King, we had gone undiscovered, and I smiled to myself, cherishing the memory and wondering if Narian felt as content as I.

Narian paid one more visit to my balcony before Christmas, although we simply talked rather than trying to steal away from the Palace. It was when we were sitting quietly together in my parlor, warmed by each other's company as well as the glowing embers in the fireplace, that he told me he had turned seventeen, although he was forced to confess that he was unclear as to which day in December was his true birthday. While his parents would know the date, Narian was estranged from his family, by Koranis' decree. Ironically, a terrible sadness clutched at me as I wished him a happy birthday, for I knew he no longer had a true family in either Hytanica or Cokyri. If he shared any of my feelings, he did not show it, but I thought his eyes as he prepared to leave were a little less bright than usual.

Chapter Twenty-Seven
Catastrophic Christmas

I t was Christmas Eve and the longest holiday of the year had just begun, as the merrymaking would continue until Twelfth Day on January sixth. The evening would commence with a sumptuous feast provided by the Lords and Ladies of the manor houses on the open land between the Palace and the first buildings of the city. At midnight, most of the celebrants would attend mass at one of Hytanica's churches, and then would resume their carousing until dawn, to disperse until Christmas Day mass in the afternoon. Following afternoon mass, the revelry would begin anew.

Miranna and I had prevailed upon Narian to accompany us into the city that night, as he had never participated in holiday rituals of the type practiced in Hytanica. Our bodyguards, as always, accompanied us, as did London, who had become extremely insistent about keeping an eye on Narian.

The darkened courtyard through which we walked was peaceful and starkly beautiful, for the trees were sugared with light snow and the white-tipped hedgerows sparkled in the moonlight. The scene as we passed through the gates into the city was definitely not. Huge bonfires burned to add light and warmth, and wild boar roasted on spits, to be served alongside stews, breads, and puddings, washed down with ale and mead. Riotously celebrating villagers, peasants, and city residents continually heaped wood upon the fires, and jostled each other as they crowded round the serving tables with their own plates and mugs to receive the food and drink.

Virtually every house and shop in the city was decorated with holly, ivy, and mistletoe in the same fashion as the Palace, and many among the throng likewise wore greenery in their hair. The exuberant crowd was not to be confined, and spilled over into the streets of the Market District and down the wide paved thoroughfare as they played games, sang carols and danced. City Guards were out in force to ensure spirits didn't run so high as to cause damage or injury.

Halias and Destari wore royal blue cloaks bearing the King's crest over their uniforms, and served as bookends on each side of the three of us, while London, in his leather jerkin layered over a thickly quilted white shirt, brought up the rear. Miranna and I were well-bundled in furs, while Narian wore the dark cloak that he had of late been sharing with me.

Miranna and I were smiling and relaxed, intent on socializing and sampling the available entertainment, but our bodyguards were unusually tense. They tried to clear some space around us, but it was impossible to avoid the occasional bump or jostle. As for Narian, he was more guarded than usual with me, although I supposed it was due to the company I was keeping, so it was difficult to know exactly what he was feeling.

Foregoing the feast for the moment, we began to watch jugglers and other performers who wended their way through the masses. Much to our bodyguards' consternation, many of the entertainers would approach us, bent on eliciting a laugh from Hytanica's Princesses. While most of this activity was welcomed by us, I was apprehensive about the mummers who would occasionally approach us. Ever since my girlhood, I had been frightened by their masked faces, and discomfited by their silence as they performed plays in pantomime. I did not like the fact that there were no clues as to the identities of the people behind the masks. Miranna, on the other hand, would clap enthusiastically to show appreciation for their efforts, while Narian, who seemed fascinated by the mummers as well, would closely scrutinize their visages and movements. I lightheartedly asked him if it were possible to mime with a Cokyrian accent and was rewarded with a small smile.

Even as I teased Narian, another group of mummers approached us, their movements eerily fluid in contrast to the constant and erratic bustle of the crowd. Though the others had slightly unnerved me, these caused me to glance uneasily in Destari's direction, as their masks were dark and grotesque. One mask was black with lines of red streaming from its eyes like tears, and its mouth was twisted into an agonizing cry of misery. Another's was gray and hideous like the face of a sickly old man. The third and final mummer wore a blank, white mask that revealed only his staring black eyes. This third mummer stepped in front of me and began to bizarrely wave his hands before my face as if casting a spell.

Suddenly fearful, I was greatly relieved when Destari stepped to my side and dealt with the man.

"Move away from the Princesses," he ordered. "You'll have to find someone else to amuse."

Destari then guided me away from the performer, and I glanced over my shoulder to see that Narian was now being entertained by him. As we began to walk onward, a strangled cry from behind reached my ears. I turned, then froze in panic as London, his eyes glazing over, stumbled forward to clutch at Destari's shoulder. Destari pivoted and caught him as he went down to his knees. My eyes darted about for Narian, and I saw several men dragging him away into the crowd, one pressing a rag over his nose and mouth.

"Guards!" Destari shouted, easing his friend to the ground, and I knew he had taken in the same scene. Halias reacted immediately, drawing Miranna protectively in front of him and likewise shouting for the City Guards. Knowing it was too late to aid Narian, who was no longer in sight, we anxiously turned our attention to London.

With Destari crouching next to him, London reached across his chest to his left shoulder and, with a jerk, extracted a small dart. I gaped at the tiny barb in London's palm, so terrifyingly identical to the ones concealed in Narian's belt — the ones soaked with enough poison to end a human life so rapidly that no antidote would be effective — and my throat constricted in anguish.

The awful truth dawned on Destari as well, and his thick eyebrows drew together in alarm as London struggled to pull himself upright.

"Cokyri... have Narian," London thickly gasped. Then his eyes rolled back in his head, and he lost consciousness, collapsing against Destari. I sank to the ground beside him, tears streaming down my cheeks, painfully aware of his shallow, ragged breathing.

As Halias, a Deputy Captain, took charge of the dozen guards who had surrounded us, Destari forced himself to focus on his obligations as a soldier rather than his commitment as a friend. With tremendous strength of will, he tore his gaze from London.

"I must return to the Palace at once and sound the signal to close the gates to the city," he staunchly said to Halias, although the slight shake in his voice gave testament to the cost to him of this decision.

Halias nodded, his face drawn taut.

"Go," he said. "The City Guards can help me get the Princesses and London back to the Palace."

Destari gently removed his arm from beneath London, then stood and strode into the crowd.

"You two," Halias commanded as Destari disappeared from view, pointing to a pair of brawny guards. "You will carry London. The rest of you will surround the Princesses, and you will *not* let anyone approach them."

Halias dropped to one knee beside me where I sat upon the cold ground. When I did not acknowledge him, he reached out to grip my arm above the elbow, and then slowly guided me to my feet. I dragged my eyes away from London's limp form to gaze uncomprehendingly at Halias, totally numb.

"We must return to the Palace," he resolutely said.

With Halias on my left and Miranna on my right, her arm entwined in mine, we began to walk slowly back to the Palace, City Guards behind us, before us, and at our sides, while the guards bearing London followed. Before we had gone more than three or four paces, a horn sounded from the Palace and I knew it was the signal to the keepers of the city gates to shut them down. My mind flew to Narian and I prayed that the city had been sealed in time to prevent his removal from Hytanica. But the cold panic that rose within me at the thought of Narian was nothing compared to the ache in every fiber of my being for London. I tried to still my mind, not wanting to consider that London might be dead before we could reach the Palace.

The noise and activity around us that only moments ago had seemed merry and inviting was now dark and threatening. I cast my eyes distrustfully at the crowd, convinced that every person I glimpsed through the barricade formed by the bodies of the City Guards was a potential enemy.

After minutes that felt like lifetimes, we reached the courtyard gates and hurried inside, feeling some sense of relief that any danger to us had now passed. Our pace increased as we walked up the hedge-lined pathway, and we soon passed through the front doors into the Palace. As we entered, Destari, Kade, and a notably careworn Cannan were deep in conversation, but all pairs of eyes were quickly directed to us.

"Alera, Miranna, are you unharmed?" Cannan asked, stepping toward us.

We nodded and he shifted his gaze to London, whose arms were around the shoulders of the two City Guards, head lolling forward.

"Follow Kade to the King's Drawing Room," he said to the soldiers. "I have already summoned the doctor."

As a servant stepped forward to take the furs Miranna and I were wearing, the Captain spoke to Halias and Destari.

"I have sent troops out to canvas the city, and I have others in my command who can coordinate that effort. You will stay with the

Princesses… and with your friend."

Cannan was uncharacteristically solicitous and I understood from his words that he knew London's death was imminent.

Kade had already led the guards carrying London down the corridor toward the King's Drawing Room, and the rest of us trailed somberly behind. We entered the room to find Bhadran, the Royal Physician, already examining London as he lay upon the sofa. As Destari stepped forward to engage in a surreptitious exchange with the gray-haired doctor, Kade departed with the City Guards.

Clearing his throat, our long-standing physician turned to address me.

"His pulse is barely detectable and his breathing is shallow. I'm sorry, but I am not familiar with this Cokyrian poison and know of nothing to counteract its effects. I could try bloodletting, on the chance we could remove some of the poison from his body, but he is already so close to death that I believe it would be pointless." Bhadran's wizened face was fraught with worry.

"Don't," I said, a bit unsteadily, although I was resolutely set upon sparing London additional discomfort.

"How much time does he have?" Destari gruffly asked, and I knew he was controlling his emotions only with great effort.

"Not long," replied Bhadran. "The best you can do for him is to try to keep him comfortable." At my stricken expression, he gently finished, "I will take my leave now, so as not to intrude upon your grief." He bowed and then left the room.

Halias discreetly moved a chair near London for my use and I sat down appreciatively, feeling so weak I would surely have fainted had I kept to my feet for but a few more minutes. Miranna came and tightly hugged me.

"I will stay, in case you need me," she whispered.

Then she moved to sit in an armchair along the side of the room. Destari and Halias remained standing, one on each end of the sofa, anguished and terribly helpless.

As I gazed at London, the memory of the afternoon when Narian had first showed us the darts surfaced.

"Destari," I exclaimed. "Cannan sent one of the darts to the alchemists. Perhaps they have been able to prepare an antidote!"

Destari shook his head sadly. "I already checked with the Captain. Our alchemists have had no success in breaking down the poison so that counteragents can be identified. I'm sorry, Alera."

I nodded feebly, my last hope extinguished, and lapsed into silence.

A chill hung over the Drawing Room, one that could not be diminished by the flames dancing in the fireplace. I reached out a hand and touched London's forehead, gently brushing his silver bangs away from his eyes.

"He is so cold," I said, to no one in particular.

Destari and Halias removed their cloaks as one and spread them over him. Their movements were so tender that tears again rolled down my cheeks. As sobs racked my body, I heard a door open and looked up in misery to see my father enter the room. His eyes were troubled as he approached me, and I stood and let him enfold me in his arms.

"Were either of my daughters endangered?" he asked the guards.

"No," Destari replied bleakly. "But the Cokyrians have Narian."

I broke from my father's embrace and sank into my chair.

"London will suffer a soldier's death," my father said, resting a soothing hand upon my shoulder, "which is the way he would have wanted it. Be at peace with that."

He then turned to Destari and Halias.

"I must go and talk with Cannan. Let me know as soon as there is a change."

Patting my shoulder one last time, he withdrew to leave us to our death watch.

As the evening gave way to the early hours of morning, London continued to cling stubbornly to life. Destari and Halias now sat upon the floor, backs against the wall, the strain evident upon their weathered countenances, while Miranna dozed in an armchair. I studied London's face in the dim lantern light, marveling at the strength within him. How could he fight so ferociously against such impossible odds? I held his right hand in my own, wanting him to know someone was with him, and that he did not wage his battle alone.

Gradually my head became heavy with stress and fatigue, and I held it in my hands as I fought to ward off sleep. Just as I was about to lose the fight, a slight moan jarred me fully awake and I saw London move the hand I had earlier been clasping.

"Destari!" I exclaimed. "London is stirring!"

Destari sprang to his feet and came to my side just as London's eyelids flickered and briefly opened.

"London," I said urgently, placing my hand upon his. "London, can you hear me?"

His eyelids flickered again as he strove unsuccessfully to draw them apart.

"Can it be? Should we summon Bhadran?" There was disbelief in Destari's weary voice as he tried to come to terms with what we were seeing.

The door swung shut and I knew that Halias had left. A few minutes later, he reentered, accompanied by the doctor, who went to London and examined him without delay.

"He has improved," Bhadran said, plainly perplexed. "I have no explanation, and it is too soon to be assured of a recovery, but he is definitely regaining some strength."

Destari shot a quizzical, and for the first time optimistic, look at me.

"Perhaps his thick clothing absorbed most of the poison from the dart before it pierced his arm," he ventured. Turning to the doctor, he urgently pressed, "Is it possible that not enough of the poison entered his body to take his life?"

"Some poisons are so powerful that even the smallest dose will kill. With others, a small amount will make you ill, while a larger dose will result in death. But," Bhadran cautioned, "a significant dose of almost any poison will cause damage to the body, so should he somehow survive, he may never be the same."

"Thank you," I choked, as Halias ushered the still bewildered physician from the room.

I did not care at that moment in what state London returned to us, simply praying that he would do so.

Miranna moved to stand behind my chair, having been awakened by the commotion, and rested her hands upon my shoulders. Halias soon rejoined us, and we four kept vigil around London, whose color was definitely improving, and whose breathing was steadier. Hope and fresh energy flowed through my veins as I began to talk to him, murmuring his name. Within a half-hour, the indigo eyes that I knew so well opened and London peered steadily at us, then tried to sit up. Destari put a hand on his chest, arresting his movement.

"Not so fast," he said. "You've been out for several hours."

London collapsed back onto the sofa, then spoke with much effort, sounding as though his throat were swollen.

"It's nice to see everyone."

I beamed happily at him, and glanced around to see exuberant expressions throughout the room. With no concern for propriety, I grasped London's hand and held it to my cheek.

"We thought we had lost you," I said, tears glistening in my eyes.

He made no attempt to withdraw from my show of affection, and a small smile fleetingly played upon his features. Then he reminded us of the seriousness of the entire situation.

"Has Narian been found?"

"Not yet," Destari answered. "Do you feel up to talking to the Captain? He will want a full report."

London nodded, and both Destari and Halias left the room, Destari to find Cannan, Halias to bring drink to sooth London's throat. Halias returned first, bringing ale, and by the time Cannan and Destari came striding through the doorway, London was swallowing and talking with greater ease. Cannan went directly to

London, his brow deeply furrowed, but then he noticeably relaxed as he confirmed London was indeed recovering.

"Good to have you back. Now, what can you tell me about the incident?" he perfunctorily asked.

"Three or four men approached Narian, and as I intervened, one of them jabbed me in the shoulder with what must have been a poisoned dart." He paused, his forehead creased in thought. "It is possible that the mummers were also Cokyrian, or at least were working for the enemy to create a diversion." He then pummeled Destari with questions. "Were the gates shut down? Have you caught them? Did you get the boy?"

"I promptly raised the alarm, and we're scouring the city. I'm confident they could not have moved fast enough to escape before the gates closed," Destari told him.

"I have deployed search parties throughout the countryside just in case," Cannan added. "But so far, neither Narian nor the Cokyrians have been located."

London again tried to sit upright, finally settling for propping himself on his elbows.

"I'm fine," he said, as Destari shot him a disapproving look. "Saddle a horse for me, so I can join the hunt."

"London, we can get along without you for a little while," Destari said in exasperation. "You need to regain your strength."

"I'm strong enough. And I'll go on foot if you won't send for a horse."

Reading the determination on London's face, Destari relented with a scowl. "Then I will saddle two horses and accompany you. I'd hate to have you fall with no one to catch you."

Their eyes locked for a moment, and I suddenly understood the depth of their friendship and how much they depended upon each other. After receiving Cannan's nod of approval, Destari departed.

"I will send Tadark to be your bodyguard in Destari's absence," Cannan informed me. "I will also inform the King of London's recovery."

After one last ponderous assessment of London, he turned on his heel to exit as well.

By the time Destari returned, London was sitting up, eating the bread and soup that Cannan had requested be brought to him.

"The horses are prepared," Destari announced, monitoring London's movements.

London set the food aside, then rose, swaying unsteadily at first, but then gaining his balance.

"I'll manage," he said brusquely to Destari. "Now, let's go."

The two men strode from the room, although London's pace was a bit less brisk than usual, leaving me dumbfounded at how quickly he had improved in the last hour. If I had not been with him, I would not have believed he had just pulled back from the brink of death.

I suddenly recalled the evening when my mother had told me of the bizarre illness from which London had suffered upon his return from Cokyri sixteen years previously. The doctors at that time had likewise predicted his death. Although I was overjoyed by London's recovery, it occurred to me that he had an odd knack for making physicians look ignorant.

Tadark bustled in, disturbing my reverie, and he and Halias escorted Miranna and me to our respective quarters. I entered my parlor and collapsed on the sofa, too tired to prepare for bed, and immediately began to doze. My maid entered to gently cover me with furs as I fell into a much deeper, and thankfully dreamless, sleep.

The next few days passed at an agonizing pace, as Narian had not yet been located. Destari had returned to duty as my bodyguard, but London had remained dedicated to the search, as he knew better than anyone the threat posed by Narian's return to Cokyri. My feelings continued to alternate between panic and despair. Panic, as London's dire warnings about the legend rattled around and around in my head; and despair, as I thought of the precariousness of Narian's position were he to be brought back to Cokyri, certain that the Overlord would hurt him if he failed to cooperate. London, however, held steadfast to his conviction that Narian was within the city, and so I dared to hope he would yet be found.

Late in the afternoon on the third day following Narian's abduction, London entered my parlor as Destari was stoking the fire.

"I need to discuss something with you," he said to Destari, and Destari stood to follow him into the corridor.

I, however, was not about to be left in the dark and forcefully objected.

"If this is about Narian, then I, too, want to hear what you have to say."

London considered me for a moment, finally acquiescing with a shrug.

"I think the Cokyrians will try to take Narian over the wall," he asserted, speaking to Destari. "They have no doubt come to appreciate the difficulty of passing through the gate, as we are continuing to check everyone who desires to leave. And to continue to hide within the city is risky. Cannan has patrols out night and day, and the citizens have been alerted to report anything out of the ordinary."

"You could be right," Destari replied broodingly, "although it would be a struggle to get an uncooperative or unconscious prisoner over the wall. Even so, they might have a stronger chance of success with the wall than with the gate." He pondered London briefly. "And what do you propose we do about it?"

"The Cokyrians are probably monitoring our patrol patterns as we speak, trying to decide where to make the attempt. Scaling the east wall would make the most sense, as they can obtain cover along the forest's edge and proceed directly toward Cokyri. We should try to dictate their choice by creating an opportunity for them to escape. If we coordinate the placement of the guards who patrol along the turrets, we can create a gap in our sentries that would provide them with ten to fifteen minutes to scale the wall. If they take the bait, we can ensnare them on the other side."

"It might work," agreed Destari, a gleam in his coal-black eyes. "Have you discussed this with the Captain?"

"No, but I will. If we don't act soon, I fear the Cokyrians will make their own opportunity." He rubbed his left shoulder where he had been pierced by the dart, and I slowly comprehended that there were more lives at stake than just Narian's.

"I will come again when I have Cannan's answer," he finished, exiting the room.

Destari returned to tending the fire, although he was noticeably more restless. An hour later, London returned with Tadark in tow, and I knew his strategy had received Cannan's approval. After stationing Tadark outside my door, he and Destari departed, leaving me to the unending task of waiting.

Chapter Twenty-Eight
A Sign of the Cokyri

It was two mornings hence when I was abruptly awakened by a loud pounding on my bedroom door.

"Alera, they have him!" Tadark sounded thrilled, and it was clear that he was pleased to be the one announcing the news.

"Who has whom?" I blearily called.

"London and Destari — they captured the Cokyrians last night and have recovered Lord Narian. He has been taken to his quarters."

I was now completely alert.

"Is he alright? Are London and Destari alright?"

"London and Destari are tired, but unscathed," Tadark jubilantly relayed, as if he personally had been involved in the successful mission. "As for Narian, I know the Royal Physician has been called, but I did not hear of any particular injuries."

"Thank you," I replied, my voice taking on some of the same exhilarated quality. "I will be out shortly and will want to visit Narian directly."

I intended to see for myself that he was unhurt.

My personal maid entered my bedroom, and assisted me as I hastily dressed. Foregoing breakfast, I left my quarters, heading toward the third floor with Tadark following closely behind. Reaching the guest room Narian was occupying, which was across the hall from the one in which he had been held prisoner, I rapped sharply upon the door, waiting to enter until London responded. Both he and Destari were in the room, but neither was surprised to see me as I crossed to Narian's bedside.

Narian's boots and cloak had been removed, and he lay upon the double bed in his shirt and trousers, lightly covered with a woolen blanket. His face was gaunter than I remembered it to be, but he otherwise looked as though he peacefully slumbered. I wanted to reach out and touch his cheek, but knew such a gesture would betray the true nature of my feelings toward him.

"He's been drugged, but the doctor says he'll sleep it off," London explained as he moved to stand beside me. "He is too important to Cokyri for them to cause him injury." He paused, then dryly asserted, "I would feel sorry for any Cokyrian who let harm befall Narian."

"Tell me about the rescue," I urged, highly interested now that I knew Narian was safe.

"It went as expected. We ambushed the Cokyrians as they came over the wall. We have three prisoners in our dungeon as a result." London frowned, then continued, "One other escaped, however, and that means the High Priestess and Overlord may already know that this attempt to recover Narian failed." He glanced at Destari, who was standing at the foot of the bed. "I worry as to what their reaction will be."

As the two men continued to talk, the door opened and Cannan entered, crossing to London.

"How is he?" the Captain asked, gazing down at Narian, and London repeated the information he had shared with me. Drawing London a few feet away, Cannan quietly inquired, "What do you think will be their next move?"

"They will retaliate swiftly and viciously," London said with a note of bitterness. "We need to bring those who live outside the city within the protection of its walls at once."

Cannan stood deep in thought for a moment, and then left the room without another word, London and Destari a step behind.

"Let us know the moment Narian awakens," London said to Tadark, who had been hanging in the background, as he departed.

Alone now with Tadark and Narian, I directed my bodyguard to draw a chair near to the bed for me. I then sat down for the second time in a week to wait for one of the men about whom I cared deeply to rouse.

Hunger finally got the best of me, and I sent Tadark to bring some bread and soup. Narian still had not stirred, but his breathing was strong and steady. With Tadark gone, I finally felt free to show my affection for Narian, and whisked a few stray strands of blonde hair from his forehead, longing to see his deep blue eyes.

Narian's face was turned to the right, away from me, and I was suddenly seized with curiosity about "the mark of the bleeding moon," as London had called it, that Narian bore. I slid out of my chair onto my knees so I could get a better line of sight, then again reached out to touch him. I brushed his thick hair back from his ear and off his neck, and gasped involuntarily when I saw the birthmark. While it was not particularly large, it was undeniably ghastly, for it was indeed in the shape of a jagged-edged crescent moon, with an irregular line of red that looked very much like blood extending from the bottom point. It was as though someone had ripped through a full moon with a saw-toothed dagger, causing an injury so horrendous that even such a heavenly body had to bleed. I pulled the hair back about his neck, for some reason wanting to hide the evidence that he was the one destined to fulfill the legend London had uncovered.

Old fears having resurfaced, I stood and dawdled about Narian's room, taking in its sparse furnishings. His bed was against the far wall, to the side of a frosty window that opened over the garden, once beautiful but now bleak and barren with winter. In addition to the four-poster bed, there were two padded gold velvet armchairs and a small oak table piled with books. The wall to the left of the door was occupied in large part by a stone fireplace in which logs snapped and smoldered, with a wooden bench on one side of the hearth and a set of shelves on the other. A door opened off the opposite wall into a bath chamber, and a wardrobe adjacent to the door stood open, revealing several articles of clothing. Narian's scabbard and sword were slung on one of the posts at the head of the bed, and his daggers lay on the shelves by the fireplace.

I idly sifted through the books on the table, marveling at the eclectic mix. There was a book on Hytanica's history, another on the use of herbs in medicine, and two on weaponry. There was also a philosophy book, a book on falconry, and, to my delight, a volume of poetry. I took up the book of poems and returned to my chair to skim through its pages. Upon Tadark's return, I ate ravenously, and then picked up the poetry again, feeling restless and bored.

Tadark cleared his throat, drawing my attention.

"We could play chess," he ventured. "I saw a game board on the bookshelf."

As Narian was sound asleep, I agreed.

Tadark cleared the small table and moved it and another chair near mine, and set up the board. An hour later, as we were immersed in the game, I was startled by Narian's parched and slightly raspy voice.

"Who is winning?"

"Narian!" I turned to him with an unrestrained smile. "How are you feeling?"

He put a hand to his head and briefly shut his eyes.

"My head is aching and I am thirsty, but other than that I'm well."

I glanced at Tadark, who had come to his feet.

"I'll bring food and drink, and inform the Captain and the others that Narian is awake."

As soon as Tadark had left, Narian's brow wrinkled in confusion. "How did I come to be here?" he slowly asked.

"Cannan will explain everything when he arrives," I said warmly, my spirits soaring.

"How long was I gone?"

"Five days."

He nodded, then winced, as if the movement had once more created pain within his head.

"Just rest," I counseled and he lay motionless with his eyes shut.

As I sat at his bedside, I suddenly felt horribly awkward. I longed to embrace him, but was acutely conscious that such a show of affection would be highly inappropriate, as we were alone and he was in bed. Much to my chagrin, I found myself hoping Tadark would make a hasty return.

Narian continued to lie still, and I wondered if he were once more sleeping. Before he roused enough to make any further attempt to speak, the door to his room swung open and Cannan entered, followed by London, Destari, and Tadark, who was bearing bread, stew, and dark ale. Narian opened his eyes and shifted as if to sit upright, then froze as he took in the men approaching him. Without any preliminaries, he gaped at London.

"I saw you stabbed with a poisoned dart! How is it that you live?" he exclaimed.

"You sound disappointed," London replied bitingly, as the group came to stand at Narian's bedside.

I impulsively answered the question, knowing of the tension that existed between the two men.

"We think most of the poison was caught on London's jerkin, and that not enough entered his body to kill him, although he was incapacitated for several hours, and gave us quite a scare." I drew a deep breath, faintly aware that I was starting to babble, but unable to stop. "London and Destari are the ones responsible for your return. They..."

"This is the military's business," Cannan said to me sternly, effectively damming the stream of words tumbling from my mouth.

He then turned to Narian.

"Now, what do you remember?" he demanded.

Narian slowly swung his legs over the side of the bed, clutching again at his head. Then he accepted the food from Tadark and began to speak.

"As you know, I was taken forcefully at the Christmas Eve celebration. I passed out shortly after I saw London stabbed, then lost track of time. My captors were using a draught in my drink to knock me out, and I tried not to consume much of it, but they had other ways to drug me as well. I was alert enough, though, to know that we were frequently changing locations, usually during the night."

He took a long swig of ale before continuing with his story.

"My captors were four in number, two men and two women. I would catch snatches of conversation between them, and knew that they were having trouble getting me out of the city. I also gathered that the Cokyrians have known of my whereabouts in Hytanica since the Tournament, but that the High Priestess wanted to give me the chance to willingly return to them."

His brow wrinkled as he tried to remember more, then he exhaled in frustration.

"That's all I can recall. Now, perhaps you can tell me how I ended up here."

"We set a trap, and when the Cokyrians tried to take you over the wall, London and Destari and others in their command rescued you," Cannan told him. "We now have three of your captors in our custody. One other escaped and has probably returned to Cokyri."

Narian froze with a piece of stew-soaked bread halfway to his mouth.

"The villagers are in danger," he ardently proclaimed. "Cokyri will not hesitate to strike now that this attempt to take me peacefully has failed."

"London thought the same," Cannan replied. "But wouldn't some attempt be made to secure the release of the prisoners? An attack could lead to their execution."

"They failed in their mission and expect that their lives are lost," Narian stated grimly.

"I see," Cannan said. "In anticipation of an attack, I have begun to move those who are ready into the city. Temporary housing is being prepared in the churches and meeting halls. Shelters will be constructed as well to handle the large influx."

London bore down on Cannan.

"They have to be brought into the city before nightfall, whether ready or not," he heatedly declared.

Cannan shot a withering look at him, but did not respond, as his orders were inviolable, regardless of London's opinion.

"I assume you had the prisoners change their clothing, and that you confiscated all personal items including boots, belts, and jewelry?" Narian's question broke the tension between London and his Captain, and once again drew Cannan's attention.

"Those were my orders, but I will check that they were fully carried out. I have also posted a twenty-four hour guard outside your door as a precautionary measure, and will assign a bodyguard to you when you are well enough to move about the Palace."

Narian nodded, but said nothing further.

"You should eat and rest now," Cannan instructed. "The King will visit later today." Settling his gaze upon me, he finished, "Destari will return to service as your bodyguard. You should depart and give Narian some time to recuperate."

He turned, then motioned to Tadark and an incensed London to accompany him, and the three men left together.

As Cannan had given me no choice, I murmured a farewell to Narian, then returned with Destari to my quarters. I entered my bedroom and immediately opened the balcony doors, stepping out into the crisp winter air. My eyes took in the activity that was underway outside our courtyard walls, as the city prepared to shelter Hytanica's entire population. Beyond the city's gates, villagers were crowding the roads, traveling toward the city in a steady stream. Shivering, I went back into my room, closing the doors behind me.

It was late afternoon when my father came to see me.

"I am on my way to visit Lord Narian and thought perhaps you would like to accompany me," he said, giving me a light kiss on the cheek in greeting.

"Yes, I would," I eagerly replied.

A shadow fell upon his face and he grew uncharacteristically grave.

"I have come to know that there are... signs... of affection between the two of you," he said, then waited for confirmation.

This was a topic I had not expected him to raise, and was sure my expression was confirmation enough.

"I am assuming this affection is based on friendship alone. He is too young... and inexperienced... to be seriously considered as a suitor for you."

He chose his words carefully, although I knew there were unexpressed reservations about Narian hidden within them.

I nodded, not trusting to my voice and at a total loss as to how to change his opinion of Narian.

"Very well, then," he said, extending his arm to me, and I knew he viewed the matter as resolved. "Shall we?"

As we left the room, he dismissed Destari, giving him leave to attend to other tasks.

My father and I visited with Narian for about a half hour, then left together, intending to share some tea. I knew, in reality, that he did not see it as proper for me to stay in Narian's room without a chaperone.

In spite of the threat from Cokyri that continued to loom over our heads, my father was in quite a good mood, most likely due to the victories that both London's recovery and Narian's return represented.

A door slammed and angry voices reached our ears, disturbing our pleasant stroll through the first floor corridors. Our attention was drawn to our left where London and Cannan stood glaring at each other in the Grand Entry, evidently having just exited Cannan's office.

"If you don't get everyone into the city tonight, you will find yourself gathering corpses in the morning!" London's stance was rigid and his fists were clenched at his sides.

I could tell my father was distressed by the scene before us, and he disentangled his arm from mine. Indicating with his hand that I was not to follow, he bustled down the hall toward the two men.

"My patrols have reported no sign of the Cokyri," Cannan said menacingly, glowering down at London. He took an additional step toward his vexatious Elite Guard so that naught but a foot was between them. "And you will *not* challenge my authority in this way."

"Then in what way shall I challenge it?" London angrily retorted.

"You will show me proper respect and address me as 'Sir' or 'Captain,' or you will find yourself confined to quarters."

It was clear that Cannan's patience with London's blatant disregard for chain of command, as well as his propensity to issue orders to his commanding officer, was growing thin.

"Then I will catch up on my reading until the next time you need me to deal with a crisis. But when that time comes, you may find me unwilling to…"

London did not finish his sentence as he had become aware of my father's approach. Tossing his Captain one final glare, he abruptly pivoted to stalk out the double front doors of the Palace.

My father and Cannan briefly spoke, but they were too far away for me to overhear their conversation. As Cannan glanced in my direction, I shifted self-consciously, wondering if I should continue to wait. I did not have long to consider the matter, however, for my father soon returned to my side.

"Forgive me, my dear, but I will have to cancel our tea," he said distractedly. "More pressing affairs, I am afraid."

"That's quite all right," I assured him, noticing that Cannan had remained in the Grand Entry.

"Would you like me to request an escort for you?"

"There is no need, as I will return directly to my quarters. Let me walk with you to the double staircase, and I will proceed from there to my rooms."

I flashed my father a pleasant smile, then took his arm to walk down the corridor. We came abreast of Cannan, whose dark and brooding visage made me uneasy. I departed from the two men at the bottom of the stairs, but fear had begun to mushroom within me at the thought of London's dark prediction.

I was sipping tea at a table in front of the bay window in the first floor tea room early the following morning, merely passing the time, for the cold drizzle that was falling on the shriveled foliage outside was limiting my options for the day. I planned to visit Narian in the afternoon, and had invited Miranna to join me, both for the company she would provide and as a chaperone. Although Destari would have been seen as satisfactory in the latter capacity, I intended to leave him in the corridor, as I knew Narian would not speak freely in his presence.

As I quietly sat, my mind revisited the argument I had witnessed between Cannan and London. I was entertaining the idea that I should ask Destari, who stood near the fireplace, about its subject, when London strode into the room.

"No one has entered the city this morning; no patrols have reported to Cannan; no villagers have sought sanctuary; no one." He sounded anguished as he spoke to his friend. "I do not believe anybody survived the night."

Destari glanced at me, then inclined his head slightly in my direction. London merely nodded.

"Do you know how many were brought into the city yesterday?" Destari inquired.

"Perhaps two thousand, but hundreds were left at risk. I intend to ride out to the countryside to judge the conditions for myself," he asserted, with an undertone of anger.

"I will ride with you," Destari automatically said.

"No. I suspect it will be dangerous, and there is no need to put both of our lives in jeopardy."

My heart leapt to my throat, but I kept my silence.

"I will see you upon my return."

London pivoted and departed, face stony. As fear once again seized me, I sought refuge in the comfort of my bedroom. Every ten to fifteen minutes, I would brave the damp chill of the balcony to watch for movement on the other side of the city's walls, but the landscape was oddly static, no signs even of smoke coming from the distant homes.

Stepping out onto my balcony for the dozenth time, I spied a rider approaching at a gallop. I rushed from my rooms, startling Destari in the process.

"London is coming," I informed him, aquiver with anxiety. As I turned to walk toward the landing of the Grand Staircase, Destari caught my arm.

"I'm not sure this is your business," he said tersely.

I rounded on him indignantly.

"Everyone in Hytanica, including me, has the right to know what is happening. It is not just the lives of soldiers that are at stake."

He reluctantly released me, and we hastened down the corridor.

"Cannan!" London bellowed angrily as he entered the Palace. Pointing to one of the guards stationed by the door, he curtly said, "Find Cannan for me. Now!" He began to pace the Entry Hall in agitation.

"I am right here." I heard Cannan's dangerously calm voice and saw him emerge from his office through the guard room as I halted on the landing, mesmerized by the confrontation taking place below.

"Are you aware that no one has entered the city this morning?" London raged, stalking toward Cannan. "Well, I can supply you with the reason! They're dead, all dead! Soldiers, villagers, men, women and children, even animals, all slaughtered sometime during the night. And the riverbanks are crawling with the enemy."

His eyes flashed angrily. "I would consider *that* to be a sign of the Cokyri," he finished scathingly.

Cannan's dark eyes locked upon London's indigo ones.

"We will not discuss this here," he said through gritted teeth, in a mighty struggle to control his temper. "You will come with me to report to the King."

"I will take men out to collect the bodies for proper burial," London retorted, "while there is still time to do so. *You* can inform the King of how well your strategy is working."

London turned his back on his Captain, but Cannan reached out and grabbed his shoulder, pulling him roughly around.

"You *will* come with me," he declared, having taken umbrage at London's accusatory tone.

He signaled with his hand to the guards by the door, who took a step forward, and his meaning became abundantly clear.

London said nothing, but his hands slowly came to rest on the grips of his long-knives. It was then that Destari rushed down the stairs, intent on ending the altercation before someone got hurt.

"London, what our Captain *requests* makes sense," Destari firmly asserted, moving to stand at his friend's side and resting a hand upon his shoulder. To Cannan, Destari respectfully said, "Sir, I request a detail of men to recover the bodies of the fallen for burial."

A long and agonizing moment passed, as London and Cannan continued to glare at each other.

"Permission granted," Cannan finally said.

Breaking eye contact with the Captain, London shifted his gaze to Destari, and I could see some of the tension leave his frame as he chose to acquiesce to his friend rather than to Cannan. He then marched passed his Captain, heading into the antechamber that led to the Throne Room. Waving off his guards, Cannan followed.

Destari returned to my side and gently pried my hands from the railing. It was only then that I realized how fiercely I had been gripping it.

"What did London mean?" I rasped, my voice sounding strange to my own ears.

"Cokyri attacked in the night, and I am afraid none of our people who were outside the city's walls survived their assault." He looked disheartened, although his voice was steady.

"Let me take you back to your quarters," he finally prompted, placing a hand on my arm to direct me down the corridor. I did not object, too horrified at the news to care about where we were going.

Chapter Twenty-Nine
Drastic Measures

A few hours later, Miranna joined me to walk to Narian's quarters. Although Halias was with her, I was, for once, without a bodyguard, as Destari had left to oversee the recovery of the bodies of the slaughtered Hytanicans.

Noticing my subdued mood, my sister asked, "Is something wrong?"

"The people who were in the villages last night were murdered," I heavily explained, then a wave of anger washed over me. "Cokyri took its revenge on the defenseless. They slaughtered not just soldiers, but men, women and *children* as well."

"I did not know," Miranna murmured, her mood having darkened as well.

"How can there be such cruelty in the world?" I demanded, my anger continuing to grow.

Miranna cast me a worried glance, as she had never before heard such venom in my voice.

By the time we arrived at Narian's room, I was almost shaking with the effort to suppress my rage. As my eyes fell upon him, the knowledge that he had been raised among the Cokyrians, the people who had committed this horrible deed, was uppermost in my mind, and I unleashed my wrath upon him.

"Do you know what your countrymen did last night?" I lashed out. "Our people have been massacred, our men, our women, our innocent children, all because we thwarted their effort to take you!"

Narian's face clouded over, and he slid off the edge of the bed where he had been sitting, a book falling from his lap to the floor with a thump and a rustle of pages.

"They are not my countrymen," he bitterly corrected. "And both London and I advised the Captain of the Guard as to their likely actions."

He scowled, letting his words hang in the air.

"This is war, Alera, and war is neither pretty nor fair."

Another pause ensued, during which he looked straight into my eyes, then he staunchly declared, "If it is your desire that I leave Hytanica, just tell me, and I will."

I glared back at him for a moment, a range of emotions churning within me, but then my anger broke, leaving me weak and trembling.

"I'm sorry," I murmured, averting my gaze. "And I do not wish for you to leave."

He keenly evaluated me, then said, somewhat stiffly, "Come sit. Both of you."

Miranna and I sat on chairs near to him as he returned to his cross-legged position upon the bed, but our conversation was stilted, and the mood in the room remained bleak.

"Maybe we should go," I finally said, after a particularly long and uncomfortable silence.

"I will be up and around the Palace tomorrow," Narian offered, almost apologetically, his eyes upon me. "Perhaps we will meet under less strained circumstances."

"Perhaps," I said morosely. Miranna and I then departed, Halias falling into step behind us.

"You cannot blame Narian for what the Cokyrians did last night," Miranna counseled me. "Although," she continued, furrowing her brow, "I do not understand why they are so insistent on his return."

She stopped and faced Halias, the fingers of her left hand

entwined in her strawberry blonde hair.

"Do you know of a reason for Cokyri to be so obsessed with recovering Narian?" she asked, sounding mystified.

"I do not," Halias answered with a small shrug, no doubt truthfully.

"I'm not sure that is our concern," I said, trying to quash Miranna's inquisitiveness.

I saw Halias raise his eyebrows skeptically, and I knew he was thinking that I was not one to leave well enough alone. I decided it was time to move on, and took Miranna's hand in mine to lead her to her quarters. As we reached her door, Miranna unexpectedly tugged me into her parlor, leaving Halias outside in the corridor.

"What is going on between you and Narian?" she queried, without any preliminaries.

"What do you mean?" I guardedly answered, though I knew my reddening cheeks would give me away.

"Come now, sister," she said teasingly, pulling me down to sit next to her on the deep blue sofa. "I know you too well not to recognize the signs." She grew more serious as she continued, "You were much too nervous while he was missing, much too eager to see him upon his return, and your outburst just now was a bit extreme. So it is time to confess."

My thoughts were scrambled, as I knew I could trust her, yet did not want to tell her some of the secrets Narian and I shared. I felt as though the clandestine time I had spent with him would be spoiled if anyone else knew about our meetings.

"I have come to enjoy his company," I said evasively.

"Have you kissed?" she audaciously demanded.

I once again knew that my rising color would give me away.

"Ye-e-es," I replied, drawing the word out as though that would prevent her from pursuing the matter.

"More than once?" she pressed.

"Yes," I said, slightly irritated that she was clinging to the topic so tenaciously. As she waited, a knowing smile upon her lips, I tentatively continued, "He is actually very warm and considerate, and he treats me differently from Steldor or any of the other young men I know."

"'Differently' in what way?" Her tone reflected true curiosity.

"With greater respect," I explained. "He actually listens to me, giving me his full and undivided attention, and he values my knowledge and seeks out my advice."

"Well, that would be a bit different from Steldor," she admitted with a laugh. "So are you going to talk to Father? After all, he believes Steldor to be the only one courting you, and does not know you have developed an interest in someone else."

"I would, but just yesterday, Father made his opinion of Narian known."

At her puzzled glance, I elaborated.

"Father came to my quarters so that I might accompany him on a visit to Narian. He said that he has come to know of signs of affection between Narian and me, but that he is assuming they are signs of friendship. He said that he would not view Narian as an appropriate suitor." I sighed heavily, then continued, "Even I admit that Narian does not meet any of Father's criteria, as he is too young, owns nothing but the shirt on his back, and has a questionable military background."

Miranna absentmindedly played with her hair for a moment as she considered what to say.

"I know you don't want to hear this, but if that is the way Father feels, then you should perhaps limit your contact with Narian. Otherwise, you may just be setting yourself up for heartache." Her manner was gentle, but her blue eyes were unusually serious.

"You are right, of course," I miserably agreed, "but I'm not sure I'll be able to keep my distance."

"Then at least stop kissing him!" she lightheartedly admonished. "Just try to keep your relationship as one of simple friendship. That shouldn't be asking too much, as I doubt you have many opportunities to be alone with him."

I couldn't help but smile, knowing how wrong she was, then adroitly changed the subject before Miranna could begin to quiz me about the *where* and *when* of the times Narian and I had kissed.

"So tell me about the romance you seem to have underway with Temerson."

It was finally my sister's turn to blush, and we spent the next half hour pleasantly discussing the young man in her life.

I left Miranna's quarters shortly thereafter, longing to take advantage of my lack of a bodyguard and the glorious freedom it provided with a brief stroll outside, but knew I could not, as rain had begun to drizzle down Miranna's windows while we had been speaking. Nonetheless, I did not want to return to my rooms, and so I chose to visit the library instead. I wandered aimlessly among the stacks, hardly glancing at the books, as I sorted through the tumultuous events of the day. Hearing a noise, I cocked my head to listen and began to amble back down the row toward the seating area. As I approached, my ears picked up London's troubled voice and I immediately froze.

"For the moment, Narian wants to remain in Hytanica, but we must contend with the possibility that he will return to Cokyri once he accepts that he cannot be with Alera."

"I take it you do not trust him." It was Destari who answered London.

"No, I don't. I think he stays only because of his interest in Alera. He has no other ties to Hytanica, as he is alienated from his family and has turned down Cannan's offer to enroll in the Military Academy."

"And if he tries to leave, what do we do?"

"If he tries to return to Cokyri..." London trailed off, and I strained to hear more, daring to creep close enough to peer at the two guards through a row of books.

An ominous silence hung in the room, then London implacably continued, "We must be prepared to take drastic measures. Even the most drastic of all. We must be prepared to end his life, if necessary, to preclude his return. Would you be willing to do that, knowing that we could be accused of murder? Knowing that we could be hanged for our actions?"

"My duty is to protect Hytanica, and I will do so even if it means I forfeit my life," Destari avowed without hesitation.

"Good. But let's pray it does not come to that."

The two men clasped arms, then Destari said, "I had better see if Alera has returned to her quarters."

I held my breath as they left the library, utterly horror-struck at what I had just witnessed. I leaned weakly back upon a row of books, my thoughts and feelings in turmoil. Knowing that Destari would soon learn that I was out and about the Palace, and not wanting him to search for me in the library, I willed my racing blood to slow and attempted to regain some semblance of composure. After several gulps of air, I stumbled to the library door and slipped across the threshold into the corridor, driving my fingernails into my palms in the hope that physical pain would momentarily hold my anger and despair at bay. As I unsteadily proceeded, feeling as though my world were askew, I saw Destari coming toward me.

"Alera," he said pleasantly. "I was just coming to find you." As he took in my ashen complexion, a peculiar look crossed his face. "Is something wrong?"

"No, I'm fine. My mother just wanted to talk to me for a minute."

I ground out the necessary lie without stopping, continuing past him with my eyes straight ahead. Although he fell into step with me, I chose to ignore him until we reached my quarters.

"I won't be in further need of you tonight," I said, turning awkwardly to face him, my voice brittle. Before he could respond, I hastened into my parlor, slamming the door in his bewildered face.

I immediately sought the sanctuary of my bedroom, tears stinging my eyes. Too disturbed to sit, I paced round and round the room, frenetic energy coursing through me as I railed against

Destari and London in my head. As my rage subsided, fear for Narian began to clutch at me, and my breathing became fast and shallow. Feeling dizzy and disoriented, and certain that my ribcage was attempting to crush my lungs, I sank onto my bed, trying to control the panic that threatened to immobilize me. Then anger again blazed white-hot, scorching my insides, as a strong sense of betrayal stole over me at how callously London and Destari had conceived of their plan. I stood and resumed my pacing, my temples thudding painfully.

For the first time in my life, I wanted to throw and break something, but what I really wanted to break was not an object, but the prejudice that kept London from seeing Narian as he truly was. As despair seized me, I sat again on my bed, twining my fingers together, the emotional battle within threatening to tear me apart. Just when I thought I could endure no more, my torment poured itself out in a rain of tears and I fell, sobbing, against my pillow.

It was sometime later, when my tears had dried and a horrible suffocating numbness had settled upon me, that my personal maid entered to assist me in preparing for bed. We spoke little, but she glanced worriedly at me several times.

"May I help you in any other way?" Sahdienne tentatively asked as she prepared to depart. "Is there anything I can bring you?"

I shook my head, murmuring, "No, thank you," then crawled, exhausted, under my covers as she snuffed out the lanterns.

I slept fitfully that night and my efforts in the morning to control my emotions were fruitless, as I obsessed over London's conversation with Destari. I had sent for my former bodyguard and by the time he entered my parlor, was madly pacing, my feet almost burning a path in the rug that lay in front of the sofa. Before London could open his mouth, I attacked him.

"I was in the library last night and heard every word you said to Destari. How can you possibly suggest taking his life?"

My hands were shaking and I tottered on the edge of hysterics as I advanced on London.

"Sit down, and calm down, Alera," he said sternly, for although I had blind-sided him, he recovered quickly.

I shook my head defiantly, then angrily continued, my whole body now atremble.

"He is innocent in all of this! He did not choose his destiny any more than I chose to be Crown Princess. Our situations are but accidents of birth."

I was almost screeching as my emotions stretched taut my vocal chords.

"And Narian will *not* return to Cokyri! You do not know him as I do, and are grievously misjudging him. He is our friend and wants only the best for me and for Hytanica."

"Perhaps you are right," London said appeasingly, obviously alarmed by my overly excited state. "Now, come and sit down," he repeated, "and we can talk about this."

I took a deep, shuddering breath, somewhat calmer in the aftermath of my outburst, and then permitted him to lead me to the sofa. I sat down gingerly, not feeling the least bit friendly toward him, and watched distrustfully as he settled beside me.

"Destari and I were discussing a last resort option if we needed to prevent Narian's return to Cokyri. If I am wrong about him, then neither you nor he has anything to dread."

London spoke soothingly, and my hysteria began to subside, but my hurt did not. We sat in silence as London continued to let my dark emotions drain away, then he unflinchingly made his position known.

"But you must understand, Alera, that I am a soldier of Hytanica and a member of the King's Elite Guard. I have sworn an oath to protect the King and the people of this Kingdom, and I will take whatever action is necessary to do so."

I gaped at him, feeling as though I no longer knew him.

"We have nothing further to discuss," I said bluntly.

London shook his head in frustration, then stood and strode from the room.

~ ~ ~

As news of Cokyri's brutal assault spread, the holiday celebrations abruptly came to an end. The victims of the slaughter had been quickly buried in several mass graves, and panic now permeated the overcrowded city. Panic then turned to terror, as it became clear over the following few weeks that Cokyri's strategy would be to contain us and starve us into submission, as no one, not even Hytanica's soldiers, could leave the city and safely return. The dreary, and often rainy, view from my balcony now included Cokyrian soldiers moving about our lands, and at night I could see numerous fires from their encampments.

In an attempt to make the city's provisions last as long as possible, the King had ordered an inventory of food supplies and had instituted rationing. Cannan, for his part, frequently met with his troop commanders, presumably belaboring strategies to retake the land between the city and the Recorah River. We would be in desperate need of supplies come spring... if we could last that long.

Security at the Palace had, of course, been tightened, and the social activities that would normally have been held at this time of year, including my mother's holiday party for the young nobles, had been cancelled.

During this tense time, Narian resumed his late night visits, eluding his guards by climbing out his window and across the roof to drop down onto my balcony. At first, he would stay but a brief time, as it permitted us a chance to talk freely. As the weeks continued to pass, he would stay for longer periods of time, and we would often sit together in front of the fireplace in my parlor, watching the flames dance while the cold January rain drummed against the windows.

There was now a persistent voice in my head telling me to put an end to these secret meetings, but I could not bring myself to do so, as I enjoyed Narian's company far more than anyone else's. I also could not deny my feelings and end my physical relationship with him, as my resolve melted every time I looked into his captivating blue eyes. I chose to live purely in the present, refusing to acknowledge the passage of time and its unrelenting march toward my birthday.

On a beautifully clear night at the end of the month, Narian helped me to escape the Palace just as he had once before, and we peacefully sat on the hill that sloped down into the military training field, gazing at brightly burning stars rather than at smoldering fireplace embers. While sneaking me out of the Palace had not posed a problem for him, returning me to my quarters represented a significant challenge. Given the increased security at the Palace, we could not expect to pass unquestioned through the front gates as morning approached. Narian, of course, had already given this problem some consideration and had fashioned a harness of sorts, which he used to assist me to both scale the courtyard wall and climb up to my balcony.

After he had returned me to my bedroom, Narian waited while I changed out of the black clothing he had brought for me. Upon reentering my room from the bath chamber, I brought the garments to him, as I dared not hide them within my quarters, lest my maid discover them and the resulting gossip reach the ears of my mother, my guards, Kade, Cannan, or the King.

"I should go," Narian said, after placing the items in his pack. "The sun will be up soon and then it will be impossible for me to climb unseen over the roof."

I nodded, going into his arms. We kissed, and as he ran his hands through my somewhat tangled hair and down my back, drawing me against him, a thrill swept through my entire body. It was becoming difficult to part from him on these nights, and I knew he felt the same. He remained a gentleman, however, and took a step back, opening the balcony doors to depart. I stepped outside with him and he gave me one last kiss before bending down to pick up the harness and rope.

"My things," he said, bewildered. "They're not here."

I, too, scanned the balcony floor, but the items were gone.

"Searching for these?" said a man from the shadows behind us.

I jumped and whirled about to see London leaning upon the Palace wall, Narian's harness and rope in his hand. My heart dropped to my feet, as I knew that we were now in serious trouble.

"Inside, both of you," London angrily commanded, and we hastily complied, neither of us daring to speak, for there was really nothing to be said that would excuse our actions.

London followed, forcefully closing the balcony doors, then brought his eyes to bear upon me.

"Tomorrow we will board shut these doors as you are plainly breathing in too much cold night air," he caustically decreed. "I wouldn't want you to catch a chill."

"London, I know what this must look like..." I fumbled for an explanation, but he cut me off.

"Don't," he said shortly. Then he spoke to Narian.

"You will come with me," he ordered. "And we will leave the *proper* way, through the parlor door. You, Alera, will stay here." He scowled darkly at me. "I will discuss your behavior with you later."

He opened my bedroom door and roughly pushed Narian through it, slamming it shut behind them. I continued to linger by the threshold, listening intently, as I knew Narian had taken offense to London's handling, and was certain he would likewise be unreceptive to London's reprimand. It was but a minute before I heard a scuffling sound and a thump as someone's back slammed against a wall.

"You will keep away from Alera or you will deal with me," London growled.

"Do you really think I would find you to be a worthy opponent?" Narian's voice was low, but steady.

"You will find me to be much more dangerous than anyone else you have met in Hytanica."

There was momentary silence, and I imagined London and Narian staring at each other, each sizing up his adversary.

"Now, we will proceed out the door, and you will return directly to your quarters, and I had better not catch further sight of you today."

London had ended their exchange, and I heard the two of them step into the corridor, leaving me alone and miserable in my quarters in the unsympathetic darkness.

London waited until late afternoon to return to discuss my early morning excursion with me. I suspected he had purposefully left me to stew over my actions all day, as a small sort of punishment. He entered my quarters with a carpenter, who he directed to my bedroom with instructions to board shut my balcony doors. As the man undertook his task, London leaned back against the wall that separated the parlor and the bedroom, arms crossed, eyeing me critically. I sat stiffly on the edge of the sofa, head pounding in rhythm with the carpenter's hammer, wishing this would all soon be over.

After the craftsman had gone, a most uncomfortable silence reigned until London, still leaning against the wall, somewhat scornfully spoke.

"Explain yourself to me, if you can."

"I don't believe I have to do so," I said, bridling at his tone.

"Then perhaps I should take you to your father," he said callously, and my bravado deflated.

"London, say what you will to me, but I beg you not to tell my father," I pleaded.

He cocked an eyebrow derisively and I felt compelled to continue.

"I have no excuses," I said miserably. "I simply wanted to spend time with Narian alone, and...these late night meetings...just developed."

Even I knew my words sounded ludicrous.

"I don't understand you," London said, shaking his head in irritation. "Both Destari and I have counseled you to stay away from him and yet you do not heed us. You place your trust where it has not been earned. You ignore your upbringing and demonstrate no sense of propriety or respect for tradition. You recklessly endanger your life without thought for those who care about you. In short, you act like a child, and at seventeen that can no longer be tolerated."

London's disapproval cut me deeply and I wretchedly examined the floor, twining my fingers together in my lap. Pushing away from the wall, he came to stand in front of me.

"Look at me, Alera," he said.

I slowly raised my brimming eyes to his face, cheeks burning with shame.

"Are you in love with him?"

"Yes," I feebly replied, tears now tumbling freely.

He crouched down before me, indigo eyes dark with concern.

"We cannot control our hearts, but we must control our minds and bodies. You cannot marry him, Alera. It is best that you keep away from him, so that these feelings will gradually lessen."

"You don't understand," I choked, feeling as if the air were being sucked from my lungs. "I *must* seek my father's permission to marry Narian. My happiness lies with him."

"Don't bring this to your father, for no good can come from his knowing," London admonished. "Now listen carefully to me. Hytanica cannot have a King with divided loyalties. We have fought far too long and sacrificed far too much in our effort to prevent Cokyri from conquering our people. We cannot let them conquer us more insidiously, through the domination of our ruler."

"It is not your opinion that counts," I irritably retorted, wiping away my tears, not wanting to concede that he was right.

London stood, wearily running a hand through his untidy silver hair.

"Then your father will need to have all the facts to make such a decision," he said, his manner resolute. "I once said that the time would present itself when your father should know Narian's true identity. It would appear that time has come."

"My father will not dwell upon his past. My father will judge him on who he is now, and who he can become in the future."

While I wanted desperately to believe these words, I did not need London to contradict me, for no one was as paranoid as my father about the dangers posed by Cokyri. I felt as though I were drowning, only this time London was not throwing me a rope.

"None of us can completely escape our pasts," London flatly asserted.

"Then perhaps I will give up my claim to the Throne so that I may be with him," I daringly put forth.

"Your father still would not permit the marriage."

I stared at London, tears again welling in my eyes, as some part of me knew he spoke the truth. He stood, but before he could move toward the door, I intercepted him with a question.

"How did you find out about us?"

He frowned, as if deciding whether I deserved to know, but then gave me a candid reply.

"I've been noticing for some time that you and he seem exhausted on the same days, and any fool could see from the way you look at each other that you are more than mere friends. I started monitoring his movements and last week discovered his remarkable talent for climbing over the roof. Then I simply waited for him to pay you another visit."

As I grasped what he was telling me, I had a new appreciation for London's shrewdness and abilities, and understood to some extent what could make him a dangerous opponent.

"If his actions hadn't been so completely inappropriate, I would have been impressed," he cynically added.

I held back my despair until after his departure, then curled up on the sofa and cried in earnest.

Chapter Thirty
An Unexpected Ally

I did not see Narian at all the next week, as London and Destari had determined to keep us apart, and had even taken to guarding my door at night. But our forced separation only made me more acutely aware that, in many ways, the young man held my life in his hands.

I had begun to try to marshal arguments in Narian's favor: he was young, yes, but mature beyond his years; he was estranged from his family, but Koranis would assuredly provide him with an inheritance were he to marry the Crown Princess; he may not have attended Hytanica's military school, but he undeniably had extensive military training. But the one objection I could not counter was the only one that truly mattered, that his loyalties might be divided. Although my heart did not want to admit it, reason told me that London's assessment of the situation was correct, for it would be foolish, and entirely unnecessary, to run any such risk when the son of the Captain of the Guard was prepared to assume the Throne. Even London, who probably disliked Steldor as much as I, would see Steldor crowned before he would put Narian in a position of power.

Just when it looked as though things could not get worse, Steldor came back into my life. My father called me to his study to inform me that our family would be dining on the morrow with Cannan's in honor of Steldor's twenty-first birthday. While I was thankful that I would not be spending the evening on my own with Cannan's despicable son, I dreaded the occasion nonetheless. I had not seen him since he had rudely interrupted my shopping trip prior to Christmas, for the siege by Cokyri had been keeping all military commanders extremely busy, and that encounter hardly constituted a warm memory.

"As it is Steldor's birthday, a small gift would be appropriate," the King was saying.

"Yes, Father," I said obediently, but glumly.

"I intend to discuss betrothal arrangements with Cannan, as I know of no other suitable candidate for your husband," he continued, and my breath caught in my throat. "This decision can no longer be delayed, for your birthday is but three months away."

My entire body tensed, causing my temples to pound. While it had become clear to me that joy lay with Narian and heartache with Steldor, I felt woefully ill-equipped to persuade my father of this, for the simple fact remained that my feelings would have no influence on my father's judgment as to whom I should marry.

"I have invited Temerson as well, as a companion for Miranna. And, of course, Galen will be in attendance."

"Yes, Father," I repeated, then curtsied as I prepared to leave. The King, however, was not through with me.

"I desire your happiness," he said unconvincingly, "as does your mother. But you must desire it as well, and within proper limits. Our hearts are not always wise, Alera, and cannot be relied upon in making certain decisions."

I nodded, wondering if he had perhaps read my thoughts, and left his study without further response, afraid my voice would betray my true feelings.

I arose early in the morning to make a hasty trip into the Market District, glad that February's sunshine was at last chasing away January's chilling rain. I had already decided what "small gift" would be appropriate for Steldor. As he had bestowed the exquisite and expensive sapphire pendant on me, I felt the need to match the lavishness of his gesture. When I came to the shop I had in mind, I surprised Destari by soliciting his advice on the purchase. Although he was uneasy about the nature of the item I had become set on procuring, he assisted me in my selection, and we returned to the Palace within an hour.

That evening, Miranna entered my quarters, already dressed for dinner, to wait for me to finish my preparations. As Sahdienne brushed my hair and swept it up off my shoulders, my sister flounced around my bedroom, more animated than usual, and I smiled broadly at her.

"Are you perhaps a little edgy about Temerson joining us for dinner?" I asked.

"Is it that obvious?" she replied, sounding vaguely mortified.

"I'm afraid so," I laughed. "But don't bother about it. I'm sure he will be equally flustered."

"It's just that we have never joined Mother and Father for such an intimate occasion before."

"I know," I soothed. "But he will pass the test."

"He will, won't he?" she agreed, and the color high in her cheeks gave away her affection for the young man.

Miranna was radiant in a deep green velvet gown that laced loosely across the bodice, permitting the skirt to split open to reveal the v-necked cream brocade dress she wore beneath. She had chosen not to put her hair up, and it tumbled about her shoulders, adorned with a gold tiara set with emeralds.

My gown was of white silk, with a bodice and tightly-fitted sleeves of deep blue, and the skirt split to reveal a deep blue underskirt. Sahdienne had just placed the silver, double-banded sapphire and diamond tiara that I had worn for Semari's birthday celebration around my up-swept dark hair, and the silver and sapphire pendant necklace that I had received from Steldor encircled my neck.

Now that I was dressed for the evening as well, I dismissed my maid, and Miranna and I chatted in my parlor until a Palace Guard arrived to inform us that our escorts had been shown to the small dining room on the first floor. Destari and Halias accompanied us down the stairs, then departed, off-duty for the night as Cannan, Steldor, and Galen together were more than capable of protecting the Royal Family.

Miranna touched my arm and we stopped briefly in the corridor outside the dining room while she moistened her lips and pinched her cheeks. I smiled as she began to fuss with the placement of her tiara.

"Your beauty already exceeds my own, and there is no need to increase the disparity," I teased.

Giggling, she stepped sprightly into the warm and inviting room, just a pace ahead of me.

As we entered, Steldor stood to the right of the dining table, one hand resting negligently on a high-backed chair, the very portrait of elegance and charm as he casually swirled the wine in the glass he held in his other hand. Temerson, rather refined in a gold doublet, stood silently next to him, looking ill at ease, his brown eyes occasionally darting to Steldor as though afraid to be in his company.

The near end of the oblong table was covered with white linen, and had been set for ten with extravagant golden plates and glass goblets. My father would sit at the head of the table, my mother on his left and Cannan on his right. I would sit on my mother's left, with Steldor beside me, then would come Galen and whomever he had invited to accompany him. Faramay would sit next to her husband, with Miranna and Temerson likewise seated on the right side of the table.

Steldor, magnificent in a black silk doublet embroidered in gold over an ivory shirt, set his goblet of wine down on the table before he came unhurriedly to greet me. As he inclined his head to kiss my hand, his dark brown eyes raked over me, and I could tell that he was quite pleased to see the sapphire pendant resting just below the hollow of my throat.

I took Steldor's proffered arm and permitted him to lead me toward the refreshment table. Miranna hung back, looking expectantly at Temerson, who nervously stumbled across the room to her side. They remained just inside the door, talking quietly, and I supposed that Temerson needed to warm up to her before braving the rest of us.

As Steldor poured me a glass of wine, Cannan and Faramay arrived. Faramay was ravishing in a deep burgundy gown, while Cannan looked as austere as ever in a black leather military jerkin, and it occurred to me that I had never seen him in any attire other than a uniform. They greeted Miranna and Temerson, but then Faramay caught sight of her son and hastily crossed to us, Cannan lagging behind. After giving me a small curtsey, Faramay began to adjust the lacing on Steldor's ivory shirt, her face radiant with joy. Cannan, inclining his head slightly, moved to my side.

Steldor indicated his dislike for his mother's pandering with a roll of his eyes. I raised a hand to my mouth to hide my amusement, and as I did so, chanced a glance at Cannan, who appeared a bit disgruntled by his wife's overly solicitous behavior toward their son.

As mother and son stood together, I was again struck by the strong resemblance between them, as her oval face shape, high cheekbones, straight and narrow nose, and perfect smile were mirrored in Steldor. Only his hair, almost black compared to her rich chocolate, and deep brown eyes came from his father.

It was but a short time later that Galen arrived with a young woman by the name of Tiersia. She was petite and feminine, but would have been rather plain were it not for her clear green eyes and long, bouncy, bronzed-brown hair. As she was two years my senior and rather reserved, I had never before spoken with her.

"Ah, Galen! Late as always I see," Steldor said as he took note of his friend's entry into the room.

"I'm never late," Galen returned good-naturedly. "You should know by now that the party doesn't begin until I'm here."

A mischievous glint flickered in Steldor's eyes as Galen guided Tiersia into our midst.

"And who is this lovely young lady who has somehow been prevailed upon to accompany you?" he disarmingly inquired

"Take it easy. I'll get to the introductions in a moment." Like Steldor, Galen was in excellent spirits. Turning to me, he bowed and kissed my hand. "Princess Alera, may I present Lady Tiersia, the eldest daughter of the Baron Rapheth and his wife, the Baroness Kalena."

I nodded politely as she curtseyed, although my eyes were appraising Galen, as I couldn't help but notice that, other than Steldor, he was the only person who greeted me with a kiss on the hand.

Galen then addressed Cannan and Faramay.

"Lady Tiersia, I would like you to meet the Baron Cannan, Captain of the Guard, and his wife, the Baroness Faramay."

Galen's manner remained formal, and he bowed his head slightly in respect.

"It is a pleasure to meet you," Cannan cordially responded, but I saw Tiersia glance apprehensively at him, and I knew his mere presence was once again having an intimidating effect.

"And this, of course, is their son, Lord Steldor, whom I sometimes claim as my best friend," Galen finished with a flourish.

Steldor clapped an arm around Galen's shoulders as he inclined his head slightly to Tiersia.

"Let's get you some wine," he said, drawing Galen to the small table that held goblets and several different types of drink.

As the younger men served themselves, Cannan took the opportunity to lead Faramay across the room toward the well-stoked fireplace, and Tiersia moved to my side.

"How have you come to be acquainted with Galen?" I inquired of her, attempting to ease her nervousness.

"We met at a holiday gala," she explained, "and he has called upon me twice since then."

She was soft spoken and genteel, and I couldn't help but think that Galen was doing well for himself.

The two friends soon returned, extending to us glasses of wine. After taking a sip from his own goblet, which he had retrieved, Steldor addressed Tiersia, continuing in his earlier vein.

"So tell me, what type of a bribe was used to entice such an enchanting woman to come as Galen's companion?" he said with a roguish smile.

Tiersia did not answer, but cast her eyes toward her escort as her cheeks turned deep pink, clearly uncertain of how to take Steldor. Lightly draping his left arm around her waist, Galen nobly intercepted Steldor's remark.

"You may have had to resort to a bribe or two to persuade young women to accompany you, but I've never had to use such measures."

"No, no, your memory is flawed, Galen," Steldor languidly rejoined. "It was *they* who bribed *me*."

"And how long was it before they demanded a return of their money?" Galen mocked, grinning widely, clearly enjoying the exchange of jibes.

Again speaking to Tiersia, Steldor said disarmingly, "I should warn you about Galen. His charm wears thin about... well, about now, after which he becomes quite a bore." Motioning to the refreshment table, he continued, a devilish glint in his eye, "So, feel free to partake of the wine throughout the evening, and when you are in need of... more stimulating companionship, come find me. I'm always willing to lend a hand to a desperate young lady."

Lifting his eyebrows, Galen gave Steldor a small shake of his head to let him know that he was overstepping his bounds with Tiersia.

"I feel the need to remind you that Princess Alera is your companion this evening," he said indulgently, "while Tiersia is mine. Do try to remember that."

"I never forgot," Steldor smirked, then he slapped Galen on the back and pulled him a few feet away, saying, "Excuse us, ladies, as we have matters of the Kingdom to discuss."

Tiersia and I now stood together in confused silence, as she clearly did not know what to make of Galen and Steldor, and I was both annoyed and amused by Steldor's scandalously flirtatious style. Thankfully, my father and mother arrived at that moment, thus saving Tiersia and me from awkward conversation about our dates.

My parents moved to greet Cannan and Faramay, who were now standing by the roaring fireplace on the near side of the room. Steldor and Galen came to reclaim Tiersia and me, and we approached our elders so that Galen could make the appropriate introductions.

"Your Majesty, My Queen," Galen said with a bow. "I would like to present to you Lady Tiersia, the eldest daughter of the Baron Rapheth and his wife, the Baroness Kalena," he said, again making a formal introduction.

"You are most welcome to join us," replied my father, smiling warmly as Tiersia respectfully curtseyed.

After a few minutes of small talk, my parents moved to the table to seat themselves for dinner, and the rest of us followed. The dinner would be served in several courses: soup first, followed by bread and thick stew, then legs of beef and mutton, as well as smoked fish. The final course would contain confections, pastries, and fruits. The feast would last two hours, as formal dinners tended to progress slowly, and often seemed like a dance, with particular movements deemed appropriate, and missteps duly noted by the older generation.

Despite the perceived pressure to display impeccable manners, the meal proceeded pleasantly enough. Steldor was, naturally, on his best behavior in the presence of my parents, and paid just the right amount of attention to me as he simultaneously charmed the rest of the room. I, on the other hand, was aloof and somewhat distant, knowing that my input was not needed in order to carry the conversation, and preferring to simply observe Steldor at his best.

As the feast concluded, my parents invited everyone into the adjacent tea room, where more intimate seating had been arranged. Steldor extended his hand to assist me to my feet as my father moved toward us, a large smile upon his face.

"I would like to steal your young man for a few moments, as I have some affairs to discuss with him. You can get along without him for a short time, can you not?" he said with a conspiratorial chuckle.

I nodded, and my father put his arm around Steldor's shoulders and drew him companionably away from me and into the tea room. I began to follow, walking with Galen and Tiersia, when I noticed Cannan standing by the doorway between the two rooms, his eyes upon me.

"Princess Alera, may I have a word?" he said as I approached.

Without waiting for an answer, he ushered me with his hand toward the dining room's bay window. I complied, feeling horribly apprehensive as it was clear he wanted no one to overhear us.

The light from the candle-lit chandeliers that cast a glow over the table where we had dined did not reach this part of the room. The moonlight filtering through the window kept the darkness somewhat at bay, but created shifting shadows on the floor.

I stood beside Cannan as he gazed out the window into the west courtyard, waiting for him to speak.

"I was once much like my son," he began, then turned to me, his face looking more lined than usual, deliberately choosing his words.

"But war forged my temper into conviction, my ego into self-confidence, and my stubbornness into fortitude. Steldor has yet to face such trials, but when he does, he will change as well."

A lengthy pause ensued, and Cannan's voice was heavy when next he spoke.

"I know that you are not in love with my son, but I am convinced that he loves you, although I doubt his pride would let him admit it. This gives you some ability to influence him and to change him as well."

He turned his back to the window, his face now lost in shadow, and I knew not how to respond. I was unsettled by his frankness, as well as his intuitive assessment of my feelings. As the silence between us lengthened, I began to frantically search for something to say, but then he continued, and his next statements were even more astounding.

"Although I believe in time that you would be able to open your heart to Steldor and permit him entry, I do not wish to force you into marriage. I will not give my permission for a betrothal until you indicate to me that such is your desire."

Gratitude broke over me in waves at the unexpected reprieve he was extending, immediately tempered by worry as to my father's reaction.

"But my father..."

"Need not know my reasons," Cannan interposed. "I can delay this decision without telling him that we have spoken." Anticipating my next concern, he continued, "I can also handle my son."

I nodded, almost inexpressibly grateful.

"It may be Steldor's birthday," I finally managed, "but you have just given me a rare gift. I thank you for your kindness, and will carefully weigh your advice."

"We had better rejoin the others," he replied, somewhat gruffly, although his change in manner did not dampen my joy, but merely confirmed that he rarely revealed this sensitive side of his nature.

As soon as we walked into the tea room, Steldor looked our way, a small furrow appearing in his brow as he contemplated his father, clearly curious as to what business his father and I had discussed. He was standing with Galen and Tiersia, his conference with the King having come to an end, and I knew from the blush in her cheeks that he and Galen must have again been tossing jibes at each other. As Cannan moved away from my side, Steldor took his place, but I was prepared for his arrival.

"I have something for you," I told him, smiling beguilingly and tugging at his arm. "Come with me."

The tactic worked, for my rare show of affection drove all thought of asking about my conversation with his father from his mind. I slipped my right hand into his left, and led him into the corridor and down the hall to the King's Drawing Room, noticing as I did so that there was a slight ridge running across his palm.

As soon as we crossed the threshold, I retrieved the package I had earlier set upon the massive oak sideboard that stood across the room from us, feeling a slight chill as no heat emanated from the barren stone fireplace. The room was appointed very similarly to the King's study, with brown leather sofas and chairs, and over-flowing bookcases. Unlike the study, however, there were also gaming tables for cards, dice and chess.

Steldor waited in the middle of the room until I returned to extend to him the narrow, tightly wrapped gift. When he reached for it, I impulsively took his left hand in mine, emboldened by my high spirits, and turned it over so I could examine it.

"I cut myself when I was a child," he said, by way of explanation.

"Badly, by the looks of it," I remarked, inspecting the pale skin of the scar that crossed from the base of his first finger to the heel of his palm.

I released his hand, Cannan's words to Koranis about having a son who "took his weapons without permission" surfacing in my memory.

Steldor studied the oddly-shaped package he now held, plainly perplexed, but then quickly removed the wrapping. He glanced between the leather sheath lying in his hands and me, and slowly extracted a dagger with a black leather grip and a ruby set into the pommel.

"I didn't know you paid so much attention to my weaponry," he remarked with admiration and approval.

He drew his sword from its scabbard and compared the two blades, then flipped the dagger over in his hand as if checking its weight and balance.

"It is a magnificent gift," he said, his expression quizzical, "but it is a bit excessive, and I can't help but wonder what led you to make such a purchase."

"I simply wanted to match the level of your gift to me," I explained with an insolent smile. "I judge we are now even."

"I see," he said, with a hint of mirth behind his words that was mildly irritating. "And is there any other way in which you would like to even the score?" He shifted his position so that he stood between me and the exit. "As you have managed to get me alone, I am quite at your mercy."

"We should return to the others," I stammered, suddenly quite flustered. "My father will be distressed to find we left without a chaperone."

"No one will begrudge us a little time alone," he countered, "especially not the King. He is… quite interested in moving our relationship along."

His eyes slowly perused my form, and the blush that burned in my cheeks seemed to spread throughout my entire body.

"As you are in a rather generous mood, and as it is my birthday," he continued, "there is one other thing I would ask of you."

I eyed him apprehensively, certain he was goading me.

"And what might that be?" I hesitantly queried.

He smirked, then said, "Come closer and I'll show you what will please me."

I scrutinized him for a moment, trying to discern his intentions, then straightened my shoulders and stepped forward so that I stood directly in front of him. His eyes flicked across my face, and I could feel the back of my neck begin to prickle, then he reached out with both hands and lightly ran his fingers over my cheekbones. My breath caught in my throat, but before I could react, he had pulled the pins from my hair so that it tumbled loosely down upon my shoulders.

"I like it better this way," he said smugly, letting it drape over the palm of his hand.

With a wicked glint in his eye, he stepped back from me and motioned with his arm toward the door.

"I believe, dear Princess, that you expressed a desire to rejoin the others," he mockingly reminded me.

I nodded, too appalled to speak, as I knew that everyone would conclude from the change in my hairstyle that we had not just been conversing. Once more my cheeks flamed, this time from both humiliation and anger, but as I could see no way out of my predicament, I moved to slip past him. Just as I was about to make my escape, he caught my arm.

"And exactly what was my father discussing with you?" His voice was a mixture of curiosity and mistrust.

"The weather," I sarcastically retorted. "He thinks we will have a good crop year."

To my relief, Steldor laughed, releasing my arm.

"Somehow I don't see my father discussing farming with the Crown Princess. But you can have your little secret, for now."

Wasting no time, I hurried back to the tea room, Steldor's footfalls telling me that he was following. I waited just over the doorsill for him, and noted that our parents were comfortably seated on the chairs and sofa clustered in front of the bay window, sipping glasses of spicy mulled wine, with Galen and Tiersia standing nearby. Temerson and Miranna were seated at a small table away from the others, their foreheads almost touching as they conversed, his cinnamon brown hair a darker version of her strawberry blonde tresses. I was glad to see that he had at least gotten over his shyness with her.

As Steldor stopped beside me, Faramay waved to him.

"Steldor, darling! Come to your mother. I didn't know where you were, and was beginning to fret!"

I could feel Steldor stiffen. With a forced smile upon his face, he began to saunter toward Faramay. I trailed a step behind, highly confused as to the reason for his mother's odd exclamation. While I knew Faramay to be overly enamored with her son, I could scarcely imagine his absence would cause her distress.

"There's no need to be upset, Mother," Steldor placated as he went to her. "I only stepped into the corridor with Alera for a moment."

"Well, you should have said something to me," Faramay pouted. "You know how I worry."

"As you can see, I am fine. I went with Alera as she had a gift she wished to give me."

Having reassured his mother, Steldor glanced, frowning, at his father.

"She thought you left without saying goodnight," Cannan bluntly explained. "As you obviously wouldn't do that, some horrible fate must have befallen you." I thought I detected a rare note of sarcasm in the Captain's words.

Moving away from his mother, Steldor extended his new dagger to his father.

"I'm sure you will appreciate this," he stated with evident pride.

As Cannan took the splendid blade, my father caught my eye, and I knew from his puzzled expression that he was trying to determine how the dagger qualified as a *small* gift. I smiled innocently at him, knowing he would forgive my extravagance in light of how well the evening was proceeding, then blushed once again as he winked at me. I could only conclude from his manner that he was delighted that Steldor and I had stolen a few unaccompanied minutes, and that he viewed my disheveled hair as an encouraging sign.

After the dagger had been passed among our parents and appropriately praised, Steldor handed it to Galen, who immediately began to flip it in his hand, and the thought that the two friends were actually one- in-the-same person flitted through my brain.

With a slight motion of his head, Steldor indicated to Galen that he wished to move away from the older adults, but before we took our leave, he turned to Faramay.

"We're going across the room to join Princess Miranna and Lord Temerson. You can keep an eye on me if you wish to do so."

Steldor's eyes flicked toward me as the four of us joined my sister and her escort, and I could tell he was somewhat embarrassed by his mother's behavior. At my inquisitive glance, he gave a small shake of his head.

"Don't ask," he grumbled.

Galen handed the dagger to Temerson, and as he and Miranna admired it as well, Steldor spoke moodily to me.

"I'm going to get a glass of wine. Would you like one as well?"

"No, thank you," I politely replied, for I still had not developed a taste for the liquid.

"I'll bring back two glasses anyway, and be happy to drink them both," he quipped, with a touch of dark humor.

A short time later, my father rose to say goodnight, signaling that the evening had come to an end. We all left the tea room together, then Galen and Tiersia bowed and parted from the group to walk toward the front entry of the Palace where Dameran, the older of Tiersia's two brothers, waited to escort her home. Before Faramay and Cannan likewise departed, Steldor made a point of saying goodnight to his mother, resurrecting my question as to why she had become so upset when she had not known his whereabouts. Steldor then strolled with me to the spiral staircase, with Temerson somewhat timidly escorting Miranna, the four of us following behind my parents. Miranna bid farewell to Temerson at the bottom of the stairs, but Steldor forestalled my attempt to do the same.

"I haven't properly expressed my gratitude for the birthday gift," he wryly asserted.

I looked pleadingly at Miranna, who grinned impishly before she sashayed up the stairs. Temerson adoringly watched her go, and then hastily made an exit as well.

As soon as we were alone, Steldor reached out a hand to caress my cheek. I eyed him warily and he softly laughed.

"It seems every kiss with you is a first kiss," he gently chided, "as too much time passes in between."

When I remained mute, he stepped closer to me, affectionately playing with a strand of my hair.

"Thank you for the generous gift, Princess," he said.

Lightly resting his hand on the back of my neck, he inclined his head and gave me a teasing and sensual kiss. As his intoxicating scent washed over me, my lips responded to his, and he placed his other hand on the small of my back, his mouth becoming more insistent. Catching myself, I abruptly pulled back from him, and he released me.

"I am willing to take things slowly, Alera," he said, brown eyes smoldering. He affectionately ran a finger along my jaw line. "I have a feeling you will be well worth the wait."

With a deep bow, he departed, and I traced my fingers over my traitorous lips, unable to comprehend how I could enjoy a kiss from someone I so greatly disliked.

Chapter Thirty-One
Ultimatum

Over the next couple of days, I obsessed about the conversation I planned to have with my father. I could no longer pretend that the King might be prevailed upon to embrace Narian as his successor to the Throne, as the primary objection to him was his trustworthiness, and I worried, given London's opinions, that my father would be unlikely to approve of him as a husband for me under any circumstances. I also knew the simple fact that I was in love with Narian would not be enough to sway him. But I had to try, as my happiness was now inextricably tied to the young man.

To add to my frustration, London and Destari had proven adept at keeping Narian away from me. I missed his company more than I would have thought possible, and worried as to what London might have told him as to the reason he could not see me. I tried to stay busy, but while I could keep my hands occupied with embroidery, gardening, and the harp, my mind and heart refused to be distracted. Then a simple solution came to me: I could have a servant deliver a note to Narian on my behalf. While I couldn't count on London or Destari to aid me, they could not prevent me from writing to him.

I was sitting in an armchair near the warm hearth, composing my note, when London exploded through my parlor door unannounced.

"Where is Narian?" he demanded.

"What?" I asked, completely baffled. "How would I know where Narian is?"

"If you know where he is, you must tell me," he demanded once again.

"London, as you well know, I have not seen him in almost two weeks."

He immediately turned around, intending to depart.

"What is it you want of him?" I called, rising from my seat to pursue him. The insistent quality of my voice averted London's exit, and he slowly turned back around, as if he did not want to explain his reasons to me.

"Cannan desires to speak with him." Seeing the question in my eyes, he added, "The Captain sent Elite Guards to retrieve him, but the boy could not be located within the Palace."

"He may just have gone into the city," I told him. "He is not a prisoner, you know."

"I checked his room. He wouldn't take all his possessions with him simply to spend an afternoon in the city." London's quiet words seemed to echo like thunder. As I absorbed their meaning, I became increasingly alarmed.

"He wouldn't just leave!" I said, the color leaving my face.

London stepped toward me, and placing a hand on my arm, guided me back to my chair. I sank into it unsteadily, then a harrowing thought hit me, and I glared accusingly at him.

"Did you tell Cannan about the legend?"

"Yes, but that cannot be the cause of his departure, as he could not have known of our meeting."

"But how did Cannan react?" I persisted.

"Not well. He is angry that Narian has not only failed to be forthcoming with him, but has failed to be honest. Cannan has little patience for those who deliberately deceive him."

"But why did Cannan send his guards? Why didn't he just go and talk to him?"

"I told you, Cannan is very angry. He takes Narian's conduct personally, and wanted to impress upon him the seriousness of the situation, as well as the seriousness with which Cannan will approach his transgressions."

I sat, still as death, trying to understand why Narian would leave so suddenly.

"Alera, I must go. Cannan has sealed the city, and I may yet be able to find him."

"You won't hurt him, will you London?" I managed to whisper, my eyes brimming with tears.

"Not unless I have to," he replied, but his words were contradicted by the steely edge in his voice. Then he left, and I shivered despite the room's crackling fire, for there had been no warmth or indecision in his indigo eyes.

It became clear by evening that Narian had indeed fled, as his bodyguard had been discovered bound and gagged in one of the other third floor guest rooms. When no trace of him was found in the city over the ensuing few days, Cannan called off the search, certain he had gone over the wall within an hour of his departure from the Palace.

In the aftermath of his disappearance, I struggled to accept that I did not know him as well as I had believed. I began to reassess my own actions and feared that I had misinterpreted his feelings for me. The painful thought that London had been right about him kept recurring. I racked my brain for some other explanation, not wanting to accept that he had left because he did not think we could be together. I didn't want to consider that he had no love for Hytanica, no feelings for anyone other than me, and no desire for my friendship, even if it could not become something more.

The only other possibility of which I could conceive was that he had somehow learned of the discussion between London and Cannan, and had fled because he judged himself to be in danger. I knew, perhaps better than anyone, that Narian had an uncanny way of acquiring information, and that he would not stay and fight if retreat seemed the wiser course of action. I also knew that it would have occurred to Narian, just as it had to London, that much danger to Hytanica would be eliminated by his death.

Although Narian was gone, the Cokyrians had not abandoned their war effort. I was baffled by this until London pointed out that it meant Narian had not returned to them, in all likelihood having fled into the mountains. This gave me cause for hope, for if Narian had not returned to Cokyri, then he certainly felt some loyalty toward Hytanica. London, too, saw this as a good omen.

As we entered the month of March and the weather began to warm beneath the spring sun, there was a definite change in mood about the Palace. The tension brought on by the siege of the city was now touched with excitement, and the gossip around the Palace was that we were preparing to attack the Cokyrians in an effort to push them back across the wide expanse of the Recorah River. The river now ran fast and wild, fed by rain and snow-melt in the mountains, and if we could force the enemy to the other side and then hold them at our boundary, we could reclaim our lands. The city's supplies were dwindling, and it would soon be imperative that we hunt and gather food, and that we be able to plant crops.

Despite this altered atmosphere, I could not seem to find solace from my grief over Narian's departure. There was sadness deep within my soul, and an ache at the core of my being that could not be vanquished no matter how I filled my day.

On a dark evening in early March we launched our attack, with London and two dozen other scouts moving out first and on foot. As Destari was not one of the soldiers to go on the mission, I nervously asked him what task this small group was to undertake, and was shaken when he told me that our men carried pouches of powdered poison. Their assignment was to add it to the food and drink of the Cokyrian soldiers at their various encampments. When I asked Destari why London was involved, he reminded me that London had begun his military career as a scout, and told me that London and Cannan had devised the scheme.

Several hours later, six large torches flamed in the dark night, and numerous Hytanican troops, some on horseback, some on foot, moved out to try to rout the Cokyrians. Destari was again my source of information as to the course of the attack.

"The torches are a good sign," he told me. "They are not only signals, but mark the locations of the primary Cokyrian encampments, so we can target them in the dark." His black eyes were cold and unfeeling as he bluntly continued, "Those who survive the poisoning should be dealt with swiftly and ruthlessly by our soldiers. It is time we clear the enemy from our lands."

I could understand his sentiment, in light of the losses we had suffered at the hands of the merciless Cokyri, but the level of hatred in his voice was unsettling.

"You may as well retire for the night," he advised, then added, his tone no longer threatening, "We aren't likely to hear anything until morning."

"I will," I promised, "but you must wake me as soon as you receive news."

"Agreed."

The sun was well overhead before our soldiers returned the next day. I was having a bite to eat in the tea room, intent on avoiding any and all social encounters while I fretfully awaited news. Destari had accompanied me, and stood just outside in the corridor.

Hearing loud and jubilant voices from the front of the Palace, I abandoned my meal, and Destari and I rushed toward the Grand Entry Hall to learn the news. Several Cokyrians, hands bound behind their backs, were kneeling on the mosaic stone floor, surrounded by Hytanican soldiers who were all speaking at the same time. Cannan emerged from his office through the guard room, and silence fell. Eyeing the captives, he gruffly directed that they be taken to the dungeon.

"Kade will see to their interrogation," he said. "Perhaps one of them will value his or her skin enough to talk." It was then I realized some of the prisoners were women.

As Cannan's order was carried out, London arrived, looking somewhat ragged, and I wondered what he and his men had suffered in the night.

"Report," Cannan ordered, eyes on London.

"The poison worked most effectively, and one-third of the Cokyrian soldiers died or fell ill as a result. There was much confusion among the rest, as they tried to determine what fate had befallen their comrades. Despite these things, they rallied to put up a ferocious fight, for they are very well-trained. Eventually, we drove them toward the river, some managing to cross the bridge, but most plunging into the Recorah. It was difficult to tell in the dark how many drowned and how many made it across to the other bank."

London sounded exhilarated, manifestly pleased that the mission had been successful.

"Our wounded have been brought to the infirmary, and I stationed the rest of our troops along the river. They are tired, however, and reinforcements should be sent."

"I will see to it," Cannan answered with a touch of anxiety, and I realized that Steldor and Galen had likely been leading some of the troops. "And how many died?"

"We did suffer casualties, although I cannot give a count at this time."

"I will send men to retrieve the bodies. Anything else?"

"There is also the issue of what to do with the Cokyrian dead," London ventured.

"We should stack and burn the corpses," Cannan replied, without a trace of sympathy.

"I think we would be well-served to bring the bodies to the bridge and let Cokyri retrieve its dead. Last night, we showed our strength; today, we can show our compassion." London spoke eloquently and persuasively.

Cannan nodded. "Very well."

"I would like to see to the undertaking," London doggedly

continued, and Cannan again agreed.

London turned to leave, but then looked back at his Captain.

"I saw Steldor directing troops at the river's edge this morning. I did not see Galen, but have heard that he is also well."

Gratitude momentarily flickered in Cannan's eyes, then he dismissed the rest of the soldiers who stood before him and retreated to his office. I knew he would soon inform my father of the details of our military maneuver.

Now that the Cokyrians had been driven across the river, the mood in the Palace and the city improved dramatically. Although the fighting was far from over, our troops were managing to hold the enemy at the Recorah's far bank, assisted by the swollen river itself, and hope was rising that Cokyri would abandon the war. Many of the men from the villages returned to the fields so crops could be planted, although they took their weapons with them and worked the soil closest to the city. Others hunted in the forest, replenishing meat supplies with venison and wild boar.

Given our recent military actions, and the flurry of activity in the aftermath of our success, my father had not yet re-visited the pressing matter of my rapidly approaching birthday. As the middle of the month neared, the matter could no longer be ignored. I was summoned rather abruptly late one afternoon to an audience with him, a Palace Guard having been sent to escort me.

I felt horribly self-conscious as I entered the Throne Room, aware of my father's eyes upon me as I walked across the wide expanse of floor to where he sat upon his throne. The hall was quiet except for my footfalls, and it was strange to have no one else in attendance. My father had instructed Destari and the Palace Guards who were posted by the doors to wait in the antechamber, and had ordered the Elite Guards who protected him to leave, desiring his words to fall on no ears but my own. Despite the logs that crackled in the fireplaces, and the thin rays of sun that filtered through the high windows above the thrones, the atmosphere was oppressive.

I came to stand in front of him, curtseying respectfully, and waited for him to speak. His countenance was troubled as he began.

"Alera, I am growing old and weary, and after almost thirty years, am ready to make way for a new King."

He scrutinized me, left hand distractedly twisting the ring he wore on his right, but when I did not react, continued with more stridency.

"I never should have ruled at all, but when my older brother died in the war, I shouldered my responsibility as next-in-line to the Throne. There were many things I had thought to do with my life, but duty came first. Perhaps this is my failing as a parent, but I am not convinced that you understand the demands of duty, or the responsibility that comes with being my heir."

He sighed, his heart obviously laden.

"It pains me to have to take this approach with you, but as you cannot seem to settle the question of a marriage partner, I will settle it for you."

There was disappointment in his usually kind eyes, and I could feel that some horrible fate was about to befall me.

"It is my decree that Lord Steldor succeed me as Hytanica's King. A wedding *will* occur on the afternoon of your next birthday, and it is up to you whether you will be the bride or a lady in waiting."

I stared at him, unable to discern his meaning.

"You can choose to marry Steldor and be crowned alongside him as his Queen. But if you cannot see your way to accept him as your husband, then you will forfeit your claim to the Throne in favor of your sister. Miranna *is* prepared to meet her obligations as a Princess of Hytanica and has agreed to marry Steldor should that be your decision."

I felt as though he were speaking in a foreign tongue and I stood frozen, unable to formulate a response to his ultimatum.

"May I talk to Mira?" I haltingly pleaded, finally regaining my voice.

"No. She has made her decision. You do not need to talk to her to make yours." His voice was firm and there was no compassion in his demeanor. "As your birthday is but seven weeks away, you will give me your answer by this time tomorrow. You have already had abundant time to ruminate over this decision, and I no longer have the patience to wait for you to bring forward a young man of your own choosing."

I knew that I was being dismissed, but could not force my body to move.

"Alera, you may go now," my father said irritably, breaking through the spell that immobilized me.

I looked wretchedly at him, then turned and hastened from his presence, tears running down my cheeks.

Destari watched me worriedly as I rushed through the antechamber, but he did not speak or try to stop me. Instead, he followed as I turned down the corridor toward the spiral staircase. With the Palace walls seeming to close in on me, I impulsively wrenched opened the doors into the garden to run down the pathway, seeking escape from my father, his decree, my thoughts, and my feelings. I was thankful that Destari did not pursue me, and I collapsed upon a bench, burying my face in my hands.

Time passed painstakingly, and in my misery, it took me a considerable while to realize that someone had approached me, and was patiently standing several feet away from where I sat. As I raised my head, my eyes fell upon London. I gratefully glanced down the path toward Destari, who I knew must have sent for him.

"London, help me," I sobbed, and he came to sit by me, taking me into his arms.

I lay my head upon his shoulder, my tears soaking into the leather of his jerkin. After a long time, my crying subsided, and I rested wearily against him, gaining some measure of comfort from the presence of his strong arm around my waist.

"Do you want to tell me what this is about?" he gently probed.

"My father has decreed that I either marry Steldor or forfeit the Throne in favor of Miranna, who *will* acquiesce to such a union. We are apparently interchangeable daughters," I bitterly explained.

London said nothing, choosing simply to listen.

"He demands my answer before sundown tomorrow, although he could just as well give me years for all the difference it would make. I know of no person but Steldor whom he would be willing to accept as King. It seems his list of criteria is designed so that only Steldor is a match."

I fell silent for a few minutes, then sat upright, brushing the tearstains off my cheeks with my hands, indignation now replacing my desperation.

"How can my father think so little of me? How can he ignore my feelings when it is I who will have to live with Steldor for the rest of my life? And what of Miranna? There is already a young man in whom she has an interest and with whom I believe she could find happiness."

With no answers to these questions, I sank into a stony silence. As my initial shock and hurt subsided, I began to shiver, for I had left the Palace with no shawl or cloak, and the temperature was falling with the setting of the sun.

"I had better return you to your quarters," London observed, "lest you become chilled to the bone."

He assisted me to my feet, and then guided me back to the door, keeping me at his side.

"Ask for some hot soup to be sent to her quarters," he muttered to Destari as we crossed the threshold. "She is quite cold."

A half-hour later, I was mechanically eating vegetable soup in my parlor, vacantly staring at London as he stoked the fire and stirred the embers into a blaze. As he became aware of my eyes upon him, he stood and came to me where I sat upon the burgundy velvet sofa.

"I'm going to leave you now, but Destari will remain outside your door for a couple more hours, and your maid will be here soon to assist you in preparing for bed."

I slowly nodded, not having the strength to form words.

"I will have Sahdienne bring something from the doctor to help you sleep," he said soothingly, lightly brushing my cheek with his fingers. "I will see you in the morning. Maybe the world won't look so bleak in the light of a new day."

As he began to turn from me, I stammered, "Where are you going? Can't you stay a little while longer?"

"I have a pressing matter to address." He sighed, then confessed in response to my distraught expression. "I'm going to have a talk with your father."

Grateful tears pooled in my eyes, and he gave me a fleeting smile as he left the room.

London was wrong. The world did not look any brighter the next morning, despite the small hope I now nursed that he had been able to affect my father's decree. But as the hours slipped by without my former bodyguard's return, my hope diminished, and the choice my father had put before me began to whirl dizzyingly through my mind. If only there were someone else I could marry, someone with whom I felt comfortable...but also someone to whom my father could not object. I reviewed every potential candidate, but still could not find a suitable alternative to Steldor. I was sitting upon my sofa, bemoaning my circumstances, when London strode through my door, Destari apparently having granted him entrance.

I eagerly met his eyes, but at the slow shake of his head, knew my father had been unyielding. He came to sit beside me, giving me the disappointing account of his conversation with my father.

"The King is unwilling to give you additional time in which to make your decision, as he has a great desire to step down from the Throne. He also feels, as do most men in Hytanica, that a father should not trust to a daughter's judgment on a decision as important as the selection of a husband. As you well know, it is his right to arrange your marriage, and he regards your resistance to Steldor as unreasonable. From his point of view, Steldor has the makings of both a good King and a fine husband."

He paused, watching me closely as tears filled my eyes. "He thinks he is being generous, as he has enabled you to walk away from the match by forfeiting the Throne if you truly cannot give yourself to Steldor."

I slowly nodded, feeling utterly miserable.

"London," I implored, "help me to see what I should do."

"I'm afraid this is one decision you alone can make," he regretfully informed me.

I dropped my gaze, examining my hands as I wrestled with the choice that had been put before me, then raised my head with a jerk as a fresh idea surfaced.

"London!" I exclaimed, feeling a bit awkward, although I knew I had hit upon the ideal solution.

"What?" he said, perplexed by my change in attitude.

"Would you consider... I mean, what if we..." My cheeks blazed as the words tumbled from my mouth. "My father would see you as having the experience and qualities necessary for a King. I'm sure he would give his permission for us to wed."

London looked shocked, then amused.

"Are you proposing to me?" he asked.

"Yes, I suppose I am," I replied, almost delirious with relief. I could not believe it had taken so long for this idea to surface. "Don't you see, this is perfect! We care for each other, and you have a strong military background, and I know my father trusts your judgment, as he and Cannan already rely upon your advice. And you are a natural leader. The troops are willing to follow your orders as much as Cannan's."

He gazed seriously into my hopeful eyes, then spoke, slowly but decisively.

"I am honored, Alera, but I cannot marry you. I do care deeply for you, and I would willingly give my life to protect you, but I cannot be King. I do not aspire to govern, and am too independent to be comfortable in such a role. I am truly sorry."

I was not ready to give up, for I was certain that London would make a far better King and husband than would Steldor.

Giving him a furtive glance, I said, only half in jest, "As Crown Princess of Hytanica and future Queen, I could simply order you to marry me."

His posture stiffened, as if he now expected the worst.

"If you order me to marry you, I will comply, but I ask you not to do so."

As much as I wanted to escape from matrimony with Steldor, I knew I could not force London into marriage against his will. I would be causing him the same pain my father was causing me, and that I was not willing to do.

"Very well," I said despondently.

London studied me for a long moment.

"While I want you to be happy, I am content with my life as it is," he said. "If you cannot see your way to marrying Steldor, then perhaps forfeiting the Throne would be the right thing to do."

I bit my lower lip woefully, twisting my hands in agitation.

"I simply cannot let my sister marry Steldor, irrespective of my circumstances. That would be terribly unfair to her, as Steldor is in love with me."

"But don't you think his feelings for you would subside over time?"

"I don't know. After all, we would both be living in the Palace and would continually come in contact with each other. I fear he would become bitter and resentful, and I don't trust that he would treat Mira well. She has such a sensitive nature that she could never withstand his anger or indifference."

"But there's more to it than that, isn't there?" London said astutely. "I suspect that you, who could never be discouraged from involvement in issues affecting the Kingdom, would have a difficult time walking away from the Throne."

"Unlike me, Mira pays no attention to the affairs of the Kingdom," I said with a sigh. "And even if she did, I doubt she would have the ability to influence Steldor's decision-making. On the other hand, I can at least get Steldor to listen to my opinions, although he may not act in accordance with them."

I rubbed my hands together, for like the rest of me, they had grown cold.

"Being the heir is my burden, and I cannot sacrifice Mira's happiness in an attempt to preserve my own. All of which means I am the one who must marry."

"It would appear that I previously misjudged you. You are quite grown up after all." There was no hint of sarcasm behind London's words; rather, there was a touch of admiration.

"Thank you for attempting to intervene on my behalf," I murmured. "But I would like to be alone now, as I have only a few hours before I must meet with my father."

After London's departure, I nibbled at the lunch that had been brought to my parlor. As the hours continued to pass, and my despair continued to deepen, I left my quarters to visit the garden, as I had always been soothed by its beauty. I strolled among the wide variety of plants, noting the buds on the trees and the first tulips of the spring, then recollected I had some other unfinished business. With a tiny surge of energy, I quickly began to walk toward my bodyguard, who stood by the back entrance into the Palace.

"Destari," I called as I approached. "Send someone to inform Cannan that I would like to see him."

Destari nodded, looking quizzical, but he asked no questions, briefly stepping into the Palace to send a guard to find the Captain. I turned away and began to pace restlessly along the garden path, eventually sitting upon one of the stone benches as I awaited Cannan's arrival. In no time at all, I saw him enter the grounds, and I rose as he approached.

"Princess Alera, I have been told you asked to speak with me," he said as he came to a halt.

Foregoing the usual niceties, I came right to the point.

"Do you know of my father's ultimatum?"

"Yes, your father and I have discussed his decision. I am truly sorry it has come to this."

"You said you would withhold your permission for Steldor to marry me if I was not ready to wed. Would you likewise withhold permission with respect to Miranna?"

I held my breath as I awaited his answer, for my last hope rested on his response. If Cannan would withhold permission for my sister as well as for me to marry Steldor, my father would have no choice but to give me additional time within which to find a husband.

"No, as she is agreeable to the marriage. You must understand. Both your father and I believe Steldor has the qualities necessary to be King. I made that offer to you so that you might find someone who not only would be a good King, but to whom you could give your love. I didn't make it because I wanted to prevent my son from taking the Throne."

I glanced away from Cannan toward the late afternoon sun, knowing my time had run out. He stood patiently by my side while I came to the only decision my heart would permit.

"Then I am ready to wed," I reluctantly declared, my desire to protect Miranna's happiness far outweighing my desire to avoid marriage to Steldor. "Will you inform my father of my decision? I cannot bear the sight of him at the moment."

"As you wish," he said steadily, not at all perturbed by the resentment I had just expressed toward the King.

Then he bowed, but spoke one last time before departing.

"I can appreciate the complexity of this decision, but believe you have made a wise choice. Your love for your sister and your devotion to duty are quite apparent. You have my utmost respect."

Chapter Thirty-Two
With This Ring

The betrothal ceremony was held the following afternoon in the Palace Chapel. My father saw the necessity of moving with haste due to the requirement that Banns be published on three consecutive Sundays preceding the wedding day. The Banns proclaimed our betrothal, and asked for anyone who knew of a reason we should not be wed to come forward and confess it.

Our parents were the only witnesses to the event. I wore the white gown that had been made for my seventeenth birthday, while Steldor wore his black leather military uniform. He and I had not talked beforehand, and I felt terribly awkward as I stood beside him in front of the somber, gray-haired Priest. The ceremony itself was short, consisting of vows of intention and an exchange of rings.

We joined our right hands, then the Priest, in an insufferably nasal tone, asked Steldor, "Do you promise that you will take this woman to wife if the Holy Church consents?"

"Yes, I will," he answered.

He then directed the same question to me.

"Do you promise that you will take this man as your husband if the Holy Church consents?"

"Yes, I will," I placidly stated, although my heart was hammering painfully against my ribcage.

"Let this be a symbol of your pledge," the Priest intoned, pressing a ring into the palm of Steldor's left hand.

Steldor removed his hand from mine and slid the golden band onto the third finger of my right hand. The Father repeated the ritual with me, and I rather clumsily slipped a golden band on the third finger of Steldor's right hand.

After blessing us, the Priest's final words were, "You may now seal your promises with a kiss."

Steldor stepped toward me, and placing a hand under my chin, pressed his lips against mine.

Our parents immediately stepped forward to congratulate us, then Cannan and my father proceeded in the direction of the Throne Room to discuss the marriage contract, and my mother and Faramay retreated to the Queen's Drawing Room to begin to plan the wedding. As the Priest moved into his prayer room, I was left alone with Steldor, who tossed me an impudent smile before sweeping me to him. He kissed me once more, but this time with greater insistence, and I found his passion almost frightening.

"A betrothal kiss should be a foretaste of things to come, don't you think?" he murmured as our lips parted, and there was hunger in his dark eyes.

I pushed against his chest, but his powerful arms held me firmly in place.

"Make no mistake, Alera, *you* are the daughter I have always favored as my wife."

He released me, but before I could respond, he took my hand and led me down the corridor to the Grand Staircase.

"I shall call on you tonight for dinner," he said, then mockingly added, "A betrothed couple needs to spend time together, to get to know each other better before they are legally wed."

He turned and strutted out of the Palace, presumably headed toward the Military Complex, and I wondered if he would be requiring me to dine with him from now on. Lamenting my loss of freedom, I climbed the stairs, fighting the impulse to disappear into the mountains as Narian had done.

~ ~ ~

Although Steldor and I did indeed dine together several times over the six remaining weeks leading up to our wedding, our meals were chaperoned by either his parents or mine, as the church had strict rules governing the activities of betrothed couples. In addition, my days became exceptionally busy. Even in times of peril such as those in which we currently lived, a Royal wedding was an affair worthy of grand celebration, and our people needed a sign of hope. Invitations were inscribed and sent to all of the Hytanican nobility, the Banns were prepared and published, a menu was established for the wedding feast, the entire Palace was thoroughly cleaned, and the Ballroom and King's Dining Hall were appropriately arranged and decorated.

As my mother was in charge of the wedding preparations, the primary decision that fell to me was the design of my wedding dress. I called on Miranna and my mother for consultation on the choices, as they had a better sense of fashion than did I. My sister and I had not talked since before my father had presented his ultimatum, and I wanted to know how she had come to agree to marry Steldor if I had refused the union.

We met the seamstresses in the Queen's Drawing Room, where numerous bolts of fabric were displayed across the sofa and chairs. My head began to spin with the myriad possibilities, both in style and fabric, with which I was being presented. After a couple of hours, I looked pleadingly at my mother.

"Can't we just keep it simple?"

My mother smiled at me and held out a beautiful piece of cream silk upon which she had laid a sheer fabric in deep gold.

"This would be lovely, and the colors are rich, but simple."

I nodded in agreement, glad that at least one decision had been made.

By the time the sun was setting, I had begun to feel like a pin cushion, as fabric had been draped in various ways across my body, but we had at last agreed on the basic design of my dress. We had also made a choice as to the fabric and style that would adorn Miranna.

As it was getting late, at least by my mother's standards, she dismissed the seamstresses and retired to her quarters. My sister and I were now alone for the first time all day, and a painful hush pervaded the room.

"I am not angry, Mira," I said softly, gesturing to the sofa. "Stay with me another minute."

Miranna looked at the door as if hoping to escape, then came to sit beside me, eyes cast upon the floor.

"Just tell me," I lightly prompted, taking her hands in mine. "How did Father prevail upon you to be my second for marrying Steldor?"

Receiving no reply, I adjusted my approach.

"I was under the impression that you fancied a different young man, one by the name of Temerson."

I was gratified to see a small smile play at the corners of her mouth, only to disappear as regret crept into her face.

"I'm not like you, Alera. I can't stand up to Father the way you can, and I have no strong opinions on most subjects. I also..." she hesitated, "don't feel the same as you about Steldor. I know he is not always a gentleman, but that is part of his charm. And I agree with Father that he would be a good King." She again cast her eyes to the floor. "As Father was insistent upon seeing Steldor take the Throne, I thought this might give you an alternative, if you really could not conceive of being his wife. I'm sorry if I made your circumstances worse."

"You are forgiven," I said in a conciliatory tone. "I don't want this to come between us. Besides, you may recall that I offered him to you at my birthday celebration almost a year ago — I can hardly blame you for taking me at my word."

She gazed at me in genuine relief. "You did, didn't you?" she said, a smile finally brightening her face.

"Now, tell me about Temerson. I believe he would have been very disappointed if you had been the one to marry Steldor."

"Yes, that was the one big drawback to Father's plan," Miranna said with a pretty blush.

We laughed together, and continued talking comfortably for quite some time before retiring for the night.

After several more fittings, my gown was finished, and the other preparations for the wedding were nearing completion as well. The final task that fell to me was the one I dreaded most. I was asked to choose a guest room on the third floor that would serve as my bridal chamber, although my mother would make it ready. After the wedding, as the coronation approached, my parents would vacate the King's and Queen's quarters so that Steldor and I could move into them, and rooms on the third floor would be renovated to suit their needs. My former quarters would be left vacant, in anticipation of an heir. As I did not really care which room was prepared for our wedding night, the only criteria I used in making my choice was that it be as far away as possible from the room in which Narian had lived.

On the last day of April, but ten short days before my birthday and the day of my wedding, my mother hosted another afternoon tea party at the Palace for the young noble women in my age group. Unlike the other gatherings she hosted of this nature, she intended this one to be purely a social event rather than an opportunity to evaluate our manners, movement, and posture, which essentially meant there would be more than ample time in which to gossip.

Miranna, Mother and I were greeted by a high level of chatter as we entered the first floor dining room, the noise level reflecting the carefree mood of the young women attending the function. As we began to greet our guests, the banter ceased and I felt as though all eyes had become riveted upon me, confirming that I had moments before been the prime topic of discussion. Indeed, my nosiest friends soon clustered around me, uncontrollably curious about the plans for my wedding, as I would be the first among us to marry. After garnering as many details as I was willing to disclose, their conversation quickly degenerated into a review of Steldor's charms, and I realized that I was the only girl in the group who did not aspire to marry him. Deciding that my infatuated friends could explore this subject without me, I glanced around for my mother. I was about to move in her direction when Reveina's voice stopped me cold.

"If it were me, I would be most excited about the wedding night," she was dreamily saying, her brown eyes slightly misty. "Lord Steldor once kissed me, and his very touch made me go weak in the knees, and now Alera will have him all to herself."

Heads began to nod, as the other girls enthusiastically agreed.

"And he no doubt has experience with other women," Reveina continued, brushing back her dark hair, "which I have been told is desirable in a husband, as he will know how to make things comfortable for his bride."

Several of the girls giggled and blushed at her rather brazen remark, but I said nothing. It had not even crossed my mind prior to this moment that Steldor might have had intimate relations with other women, and this information substantially increased my anxiety level.

"And what has become of Lord Narian?" Kalem, generally the romantic among us, abruptly asked. "He is quite handsome as well, and after what happened at the Tournament last fall, I was hoping to meet him."

The other girls joined in assent.

"The skill he showed during the exhibition was quite astounding!" announced blonde-haired Noralee, her blue eyes wide, reflecting her customary level of shock.

"Handsome, strong... and mysterious. Definitely a good second choice!" agreed Kalem. Then she looked sullenly at me, her light gray eyes shielded by her dark lashes. "Rumor has it that he showed quite an interest in *you* for a while. Really, Alera, you cannot have *both* of the most intriguing men in the Kingdom!"

"If he had not left, and you would have been permitted to choose between them, who would you have favored?" queried Reveina, as always the bold one in the group.

Everyone fell silent as they breathlessly awaited my answer. I scrambled for a response, feeling horribly self-conscious, and somewhat ambushed. I was thankfully saved from further embarrassment by Miranna, who stepped into the circle and spoke up on my behalf.

"Narian is the brother of my best friend, so naturally Alera and I have become acquainted with him, but that's all there is to it."

Glancing appreciatively at my sister, I added, "And he departed because he ardently missed the mountains and wanted to spend some time there."

Before the other girls could press further, Miranna ended the conversation.

"Come, sister," she decisively said. "Mother is preparing to take her seat and wishes us to take ours as well." With that, she took my hand and led me away, saying cheerily to our friends, "You should also find your places. This is probably your last chance to practice your manners before the wedding."

I walked by Miranna's side, my mood subdued, as my friends' comments had brought all of my fears to the forefront. Where was Narian? Why had he left? And what would Steldor expect from his bride? I knew, even if Steldor did not, that I no longer had a heart to give, for Narian had taken it with him. I sat in silence through the serving of the tea to depart as soon as I reasonably could, for the agony of Narian's flight had again surfaced. The emptiness inside was like physical pain, and I wanted to run from it, but there was no escape other than in sleep. I felt as though I lived in a nether-world, where I could neither reclaim the past nor embrace the future, but was condemned to struggle hopelessly through each day.

~ ~ ~

It rained the night before my wedding, which my mother told me was a good omen, as it washed away past hurts and insults, and permitted a fresh beginning. The morning of the wedding did indeed dawn fresh and clear, although the afternoon was likely to be warm.

My mother had sent a special wedding breakfast to my quarters, but I only picked at the food, feeling too nauseous to eat. I then bathed in scented water, and permitted Sahdienne to brush out my long hair.

Miranna, as my attendant, helped me into my wedding attire in the early afternoon. My gown was made of the fabric my mother had selected, cream silk with a sheer overlay of gold falling from just below the bust line. The rounded neckline led to ruched sleeves, and the bodice was overstitched in gold thread in a diamond pattern. A sheer gold cape swept the floor, and was attached at the shoulders so that it elegantly draped to reveal the gold lacing that ran all the way up the gown's back. Upon my head I wore a simple, one-inch-wide gold band with three jewels set evenly across its front: sapphire for purity, emerald for hope, and red jasper for love. My hair was swept up and over the back of the band into a loose bun, tied with gold ribbon, and a simple gold cross adorned my neck. I would carry in my left hand a small bouquet of flowers interspersed with herbs that would bring good fortune.

The wedding was to take place in the Ballroom, followed by a feast in the King's Dining Hall, then a return to the Ballroom for dancing and socializing. My parents would escort me to the ceremony when all was ready, and as the time for the service grew nigh, I waited for them in my quarters with ever-increasing dread.

The music of minstrels, as well as the sounds of laughter and the clapping of hands, told me that Steldor was arriving. I could see the central courtyard through my open balcony doors, and watched as he rode through the gates on his magnificent gray stallion, a footman treading off to one side. This was the only time I had ever seen a horse permitted within the Palace grounds, and my perception that nothing was as it should be grew even stronger.

Steldor rode half the distance down the path that lay between the flowering lilac hedges, then dismounted, handing his reins to the footman and turning to wave at the crowd that had followed him through the city streets. The people would continue to gather in anticipation of the ceremony, and after our vows had been exchanged, would be permitted to enter the courtyard and walk up to the front steps of the Palace, where the head of each family would receive two gold coins signifying our union from a Palace Guard.

Glancing again toward the gates, I saw Cannan and Faramay step out of a carriage, and begin to walk slowly up the white pathway. Other relatives and guests also arrived, parading sedately in their wedding finery toward the open front doors of the Palace. Unlike me, who lacked uncles, aunts, and cousins, my father's only brother having died in the war and my mother's entire family likewise perishing, Steldor had a large extended family, with nine uncles and aunts, and seventeen cousins.

I stepped away from the balcony, feeling so panicky I could scarcely breathe. Miranna crossed to me and held out a small glass of wine.

"Mother thought this might help calm you."

I took a sip and handed it back to her.

"Would you like to sit for a moment?" she worriedly asked. I shook my head and closed my eyes, willing my breathing to slow.

"You look absolutely stunning," she continued, attempting to sound reassuring.

"You are breathtaking as well," I replied, opening my eyes to examine her.

Miranna's dress was of light blue silk with a fitted waist and full skirt. Its bodice was overlaid with sheer white lace, and its sheer bell sleeves almost grazed the floor.

There was a knock on the door and my mother glided into my

bedroom, wearing a royal blue gown stitched with gold. Her beautiful blonde hair was perfectly coifed and adorned with the official crown of the Queen, a circlet set with diamonds and adorned by a single cross in front displaying five jewels, one each of sapphire, emerald, ruby, and amethyst, with a diamond in the center.

"I wanted to check on you, Alera, before your father joins us," she said, giving me an airy embrace. Her serene blue eyes assessed me as she soothingly continued. "All brides are nervous on their wedding day."

"I'm fine, Mother," I assured her, although I did not feel fine at all. I felt like the condemned facing the gallows, rather than the excited bride my mother envisioned.

"The guests have arrived, as has the groom, and all is now ready. Is there anything you need before the ceremony begins?"

"No, I'm fine" I repeated, although the cracking of my voice argued otherwise.

"Then let us move into the parlor to await your father."

It wasn't long before a rap on the door told me that the King had arrived, and he entered, regally attired in his royal blue robes, the crown of the sovereign with its four bejeweled crosses upon his gray-flecked hair. He beamed out of immense happiness as he crossed to me and kissed my cheek.

"You are a vision, my dear," he lightly complimented. "Are you ready to meet your groom?"

I nodded, cynically thinking I was going to meet my doom, and we left my parlor to walk down the corridor toward the Ballroom. When we arrived, we stopped just outside the wide doorway, and my mother stood to my left, my father to my right, their arms entwined in mine. Miranna would follow behind. A carpet of gold had been laid on the floor, creating a path upon which we would walk. We would proceed halfway into the Ballroom along the west wall, then turn left. A canopy, an altar, and a padded step for kneeling had been set up on the east side of the room. Numerous urns filled with spring flowers stood on each side of the altar, and silks in royal blue and gold hung on the wall behind. Rows of benches sat to the left and right of the carpeted aisle, and were filled to overflowing with our festively attired wedding guests.

"Shall we?" asked my father, and I took a deep breath before nodding.

We moved forward at a measured pace, then turned and stopped, preparing to process through the assembled nobility. I could see Steldor standing and facing me halfway down the aisle, incredibly handsome in an embossed black leather jacket with extended shoulders, the sleeves and peplum of which were in deep green velvet. The jacket laced closed in front and along the sleeves, providing glimpses of the white shirt he wore beneath. He wore his tall black boots over black breeches, and his ruby-studded sword hung at his left hip, the dagger I had given him for his birthday at his right.

Faramay, ravishing in a shimmering, light green gown, stood to Steldor's left, while Cannan, clad in a dress coat of deep green velvet with gold embroidery, stood to his right. Despite my frame of mind, it came to me that this was the first time I had seen the Captain in anything other than military garb. Galen, his wavy ash brown hair freshly trimmed, stood just behind the three of them, wearing a plain black dress coat over a white shirt.

As trumpets sounded, our wedding guests rose to their feet, and my parents and I walked slowly forward until my father and Faramay stood side to side. The aged Priest slowly advanced from his position in front of the altar to meet us so he could ask the necessary questions to establish that Steldor and I could lawfully join in matrimony.

"Do you know of any impediment why you may not be lawfully joined?" the Priest intoned, the nasal quality of his voice somehow befitting of my nausea.

"No," Steldor and I murmured.

"Are you of legal age to marry?"

"Yes," we both replied.

"Whose blessings accompany you?"

Our parents answered, "The blessings of their entire families."

At this point, Faramay took a step back and moved to Cannan's right. My father removed my arm from his and rested my hand upon Steldor's, and then likewise withdrew to stand beside my mother.

"Have the Banns been published?" droned the Priest.

"Yes, on three consecutive Sundays," Steldor answered.

The Priest then asked the final, and perhaps most important, question. "Do you come of your own free will and accord to be joined in marriage?

I glanced apprehensively at Steldor, who had tensed almost imperceptively.

"Yes, I come of my own free will," I stated. Steldor repeated the same, and I felt him relax, as though he had half-expected a different answer from me.

The Priest then creakily turned and arduously approached the altar. Steldor and I came next, followed by our parents, with Miranna and Galen bringing up the rear. As we reached the altar, my parents moved to the left to sit in the thrones provided for them, while Cannan and Faramay moved to the right to sit in large padded armchairs. Miranna moved to stand beside me, and I handed her my bouquet, while Galen took his place beside Steldor.

The Priest joined my right hand with Steldor's, and we turned to face one another as the exchange of vows began.

"Do you take this woman as your wife?" the Priest inquired.

"I receive you as mine, so that you become my wife and I your husband," Steldor said, gazing steadfastly into my eyes. "And I commit to you the fidelity of my body, and I will keep you in health and sickness; nor for better or worse will I change toward you until the end." His voice was strong, for he suffered from no indecision.

The Priest then addressed me. "Do you take this man as your husband?"

I looked down and took a deep breath, my heart pounding so loudly in my ears that I wasn't certain I'd be able to hear my own voice. Then I forced myself to meet Steldor's eyes.

"I receive you as mine, so that you become my husband and I your wife," I said with a slight quaver. "And I commit to you the fidelity of my body, and I will keep you in health and sickness; nor for better or worse will I change toward you until the end."

A smile flitted across Steldor's face as I finished, then we turned toward the Priest, who took the marriage ring from Galen. After blessing it, he handed it to Steldor.

Removing his right hand from mine, Steldor raised my left, palm downward, and partially slid the ring first on my thumb, then my index finger, my middle finger, and my third finger, where it finally came to rest. With each placement of the ring, he made a pledge.

"With this ring I thee wed; this gold I thee give; with my body I thee worship; and with all my worldly goods I thee endow."

We then knelt on the padded step before the Priest and shared our first communion as husband and wife. Placing a veil over us to signify our union, the priest then blessed us. We rose and Steldor removed the veil, then turned to me and untied the ribbon that held my hair in its bun, letting the dark tresses cascade loosely down my back to signify his dominion over me. His fingers lightly skimmed my shoulders, then he pulled me into his embrace and we kissed.

A cheer went up from our guests, and Steldor and I walked briskly back down the aisle, into the corridor, and over to the King's Dining Hall, where we soon began to receive congratulations from our friends and family. I was exceptionally glad to have the ceremony behind me, but fear clutched at my heart for I had no idea what marriage held in store for me.

Chapter Thirty-Three
Wishes

After the King and Queen moved to the high table that was set for our newly united families, Steldor and I followed, and the rest of the assembled guests found seating as well. We all waited for a blessing from the Priest, then the meal began. The wedding feast was served in several courses, beginning with soup, bread flavored with ale, and various types of cheeses, to be followed by torts filled with spicy veal and dates. Next came stuffed roast suckling pig, smoked fish, mutton, and a variety of roast birds, including pheasant, quail, and peacock. Stewed cabbage flavored with cinnamon and cloves, and asparagus were also served. Fruit custard in a pie followed, along with spicy mulled wine. The final course consisted of cakes made with almonds and sugar, and a variety of fresh fruits and nuts. Rose scented water was provided to the guests so that their hands could be cleansed between courses, and all was washed down with wine and ale. Throughout the meal, musicians performed, to be joined by acrobats, jugglers and singers as the tables were cleared.

At the conclusion of the feast, Steldor stood and guided me to my feet. He took my hand and led me toward a small table that held a platter upon which our guests had been stacking the small cakes they had brought as gifts. With over six hundred guests in attendance, the stack had grown several feet high. Tradition called for us to try to kiss over the top of the stack without toppling the cakes, in order to be granted luck and prosperity.

Steldor detached my gown's cape from the clips at my shoulders as he studied the task. He had an advantage, as he stood four inches taller than I, but even he could not possibly lean over the cakes. We looked quizzically at each other, then he called for benches. As Galen steadied Steldor's, and Miranna, assisted by Temerson, steadied mine, we stepped onto the seats of the benches and eyed each other over the tops of the cakes. Steldor rubbed his hands together, then held them out to me and I reached out with mine as well. We clasped hands, supporting each other, then leaned forward, trying to keep a bend in our waists so as not to nudge the stack of pastries. Our heads slowly came together and our lips briefly touched, as laughter and cheering erupted around us, but we recognized at about the same time that I was not strong enough to push myself away and back into a standing position. With a nod of his head to his right, Steldor indicated to me the direction in which he wanted us to fall. Pushing away from each other with our opposite hands, we swayed to the right, Steldor pulling me to the side and then forward as he jumped off his bench. Somehow, he managed to catch me before I hit the floor, and although the stack swayed precariously, it stayed upright. I laughed along with our jubilant guests, enjoying myself for the first time all day, as Steldor set me back upon my feet. Then a grin brightened his features, and he pulled me into a firm embrace.

"Well done!" he exclaimed, his eyes alight, and I could not help but return his smile.

Again taking me by the hand, Steldor led me through the crowd so that we could return to the Ballroom for dancing and additional entertainment. By this time, the benches had been repositioned along the perimeter of the room, the altar and other items related to the wedding ceremony had been removed, and refreshment tables had been set against the near wall.

As Steldor led me onto the dance floor, he reminded me of our last attempt at dancing.

"Remember, I'm the one who is supposed to lead," he quipped.

I tried to relax in his arms, as I knew he was an excellent dancer, and as I did so, our movements became smooth and lithe. After a few turns around the floor, he gazed down at me, an amorous glow in the depths of his eyes.

"I trust this is a sign of submission in other ways, as well," he murmured, and I was instantly wary of his meaning.

After a second dance, I desired a break, and Steldor left my side to retrieve glasses of wine. London chose to confer with me in Steldor's absence, approaching me with a melancholy smile.

"I hope you will find happiness," he wished me sincerely, "but I will also miss your company, for my duties will no longer place me within the Palace."

This had not occurred to me, and I could not help but feel upset.

"But we will remain friends, won't we?"

"Of course," he vowed, but his voice lacked confidence. "I thought you might be interested to know that I am leaving tomorrow to hunt for Narian in the mountains. If I find him, I will bring him back to Hytanica," he promised.

Steldor returned and handed me a glass of wine, looking askance at London, who immediately bowed to me and departed. I had no time to reflect on London's words as guests continued to approach my husband and me, wishing us health and good fortune.

When the group of well wishers finally began to dwindle, Lord Baelic, Steldor's uncle and Cannan's younger brother, approached. While I knew Lord Baelic's wife, Lady Lania, and his oldest daughter, Lady Dahnath, from my mother's tea parties, I had never before met him and knew little about him other than that he held the rank of Major and was the Cavalry Officer at the Military Academy.

Baelic was two inches shorter than his brother and an inch shorter than his nephew, but otherwise bore a remarkable resemblance to Cannan, with hair so dark it was almost black, intense brown eyes, a chiseled jaw line, and a well-muscled physique. It did not take me long, however, to discover a glaring difference between the brothers, as Baelic was as smiley as Cannan was grave.

After Steldor had made the introductions, Baelic gallantly kissed my hand.

"Congratulations, Lord Steldor; Princess Alera, my sympathies," he said off-handedly.

Ignoring Steldor's groan of complaint, his uncle continued, looking playfully into my eyes.

"If you're ever in need of something you can hold over his head, come talk to me. I know everything about him that he would prefer to keep from his father." He glanced merrily at Steldor, then finished, "And that's my wedding gift to you."

"Would it be impolite to refuse?" Steldor immediately retorted.

"It depends on the gift," Baelic countered, with a slightly crooked smile. "Surely you wouldn't turn down one as high in quality as this."

Before Steldor could answer, I quickly made my opinion known.

"I have no intention of turning it down," I asserted, returning Baelic's smile.

"I like her more every moment," Baelic stated approvingly. "I still can't figure out what she's doing with you."

I almost laughed out loud at Baelic's willingness to needle Steldor, and was irresistibly drawn to his light and engaging manner.

Steldor contemplated his uncle for a brief moment, the corners of his mouth pulling upward in amusement.

"She settled for a twenty-one-year-old charmer when she found that all the forty-three-year-old fools were taken," he parried.

"You cut me to the bone, dear nephew," Baelic said, in feigned offense.

"Then I shall make up for it by hiring you as my court jester, dear uncle," Steldor mockingly replied, and Baelic began to chuckle.

"It was a pleasure meeting you," Baelic said, turning to me with another deep bow. "I shall leave my incorrigible nephew in your care, and I heartily wish you the best of luck."

He then slapped Steldor good-naturedly on the shoulder and departed, leaving no doubt in my mind as to from whom Steldor had inherited his innate charm.

As soon as Baelic had left us, my father drew Steldor away from me and began to speak with him. Feeling somewhat awkward, I cast about for my sister, but instead saw Galen walking in my direction. I presumed he was coming to talk to his best friend, so was at a loss when he strode over to me instead.

"May I have the pleasure of a dance?" he inquired, bowing courteously and kissing my hand.

I examined him skeptically for a moment before tersely rebuffing him.

"I would prefer to watch the other couples."

Although I did not know him well, I assumed from my brief encounters with him, as well as his mannerisms, that he was much like Steldor, and I had therefore added him to my most-detested list.

He considered me for a moment before responding.

"'No', you don't care to dance with anyone, or 'no', you don't care to dance with me?" He sounded merely curious, no indication of offense in his tone.

Knowing that the truth would come across as rude, I began to tell a lie, but he put two fingers against my lips.

"Your hesitation speaks volumes, so I assume you would also be unwilling to keep company with me." He inclined his head to me, smiling ruefully. "I will leave you in peace, My Lady."

Stung by guilt for refusing his request, I reached out my hand and caught his arm as he turned to walk away.

"Please. A dance would be welcome after all."

"It will be my honor," he said graciously, and he escorted me onto the dance floor.

I quickly discovered that, like Steldor, Galen was an excellent dancer, and I moved elegantly in his arms as he guided me around the dance floor.

"That wasn't so bad, was it?" he remarked as he led me away from the other couples at the conclusion of the song.

"Actually, it was quite pleasant," I returned.

I glanced over toward Steldor, who was now bantering with Barid, Devant and others in the military. I sighed, having no desire to mingle with that particular group, and not trusting that I would be welcomed in any case.

"I would be happy to provide you with companionship until someone more to your liking comes along," Galen disarmingly declared, taking note of my dilemma.

I paused, unsure how to interpret his comment, but then a smile warmed my face as I noted the twinkle in his soft brown eyes and the smirk playing at the corners of his mouth.

"Your company *is* to my liking, kind sir," I told him quite truthfully.

We did not, however, have further time to converse, for a group of young women was moving toward us, clearly of a mind to speak with me.

"As I am generally not *that* popular with the ladies," Galen teased, "and as my sisters are among the throng, I will leave you in their hands."

He bowed and departed, moving toward Steldor and their mutual friends as the young women swarmed around me.

It wasn't long before I tired of my friends' conversation, as they were obsessed with comparing the marriageable potential of the remaining eligible men of noble birth. Seeing my mother, I excused myself and went to her, weariness seeping through me. As I approached, I noted that she was standing with Faramay, the Lady Hauna, who was Galen's mother, and Tiersia, who had once again come as Galen's date.

As I talked quietly with the women, I saw Steldor's eyes flit in my direction several times. The evening was growing late, as evidenced by the platters of food that servants were now bringing to the refreshment tables so that our guests could acquire the fortitude to celebrate until morning.

Breaking from his friends, Steldor advanced on me. He bowed to the Queen and kissed his mother dutifully on the cheek, then slid an arm around my waist.

"I think my wife is exhausted from the festivities, and that we should perhaps retire for the night."

A chill swept over me at the thought of what was to come, and the nausea that had dissipated in the aftermath of the ceremony returned.

With his arm encircling my waist, he drew me with him to receive permission from the King for us to leave, then also bade goodnight to his father.

I climbed the front stairway to the third floor with Steldor, trailing the Priest who had yet to bless the bridal chamber, feeling as though each slow and methodical step added a nail to my coffin. As we approached the room that I had selected, Steldor guided me away from it, further down the hallway. We then approached the room that had most recently been Narian's. The Priest and Steldor entered, but I hovered in the doorway, feeling confused and dismayed.

"This will serve us better," Steldor chastised in a low voice, returning to take my hand. "I will tolerate no ghosts in my home."

I entered the room, feeling both nervous and humiliated because Steldor had surmised that I did not want to intrude upon this space. Stopping just over the threshold, Steldor by my side, I surveyed my prison. The room had, of course, been refurbished by my mother in preparation for this night. Across from us was a large four-poster bed topped with a golden spread and numerous pillows. Rose petals had been strewn across its surface to add subtle fragrance. A small table adjacent to the bed held a lantern along with a jug of wine and two goblets. A large fireplace took up most of the wall to our left, although no fire had been kindled, as the day had been quite warm, and a sofa and several chairs were grouped about the hearth. The door to the bath chamber opened off the opposite wall, next to the large wardrobe in which I knew some of both my clothing and Steldor's had been hung. The floral-filled urns from the wedding had been brought up to the room and lined the wall immediately to our right, adding a heady scent to the air.

The Priest broke my reverie, beckoning for Steldor and me to approach him. He then blessed us and our wedding bed, in order to bring us good fortune and fertility.

After the Priest's departure, I stood in the center of the room, eyeing Steldor, painfully aware that I now belonged to him, and that no one would interfere should he choose to assert his rights as a husband. He casually perused me as he tossed his leather jacket on one of the chairs and unlaced his white shirt, and I could see his silver wolf's head talisman lying against his sturdy chest. He then came to me and unceremoniously kissed me, placing his hands on the sides of my face. As his now familiar scent washed over me, he ran his hands down my body until they rested upon my hips. I stiffened at his touch, and he stepped back from me.

"Turn around," he instructed, "and I will help you out of your wedding dress."

I silently beseeched him, but seeing no compassion in his eyes, reluctantly presented my back to him. He began to loosen the lacing of my gown, gently kissing my shoulders and neck as he did so. I shuddered, and he immediately dropped his hands. I pivoted, fearful of his intentions, and saw him standing with his arms crossed over his chest, frustration evident upon his handsome face.

"What am I to do with you?" he asked. "I would like nothing better than to lie with you tonight, but it appears you would not come freely, but solely out of duty."

I dropped my eyes to the floor, afraid to respond to his accusation. He stepped toward me once more, and with one hand upon the small of my back, the other enmeshed in my hair, pulled my body against his, kissing me with greater passion. When I again involuntarily stiffened, he abruptly released me and retreated two steps. I waited in misery as he raked a hand through his dark hair, his eyes now flashing angrily.

"It is our wedding night, Alera," he unsympathetically remarked. "You are intelligent enough to know what is expected."

"I know what is expected, but don't yet feel ready to submit, my Lord," I said faintly. I decided my best ploy would be to use his own words against him. "You told me not long ago that you were willing to take things slowly. I implore you now to be true to that promise, and permit me time to become more comfortable with you... physically."

To my surprise, he laughed.

"You really are the devil, you know," he said drolly. "Fine, I will give you some time, but, willing or not, you do have an obligation as a wife and a Queen to bear an heir."

He turned from me and moved toward the bed, pulling off his shirt, and in spite of myself, I couldn't help staring at his muscular form. Noticing my gaze, he raised a denigrating eyebrow.

"Just tell me how long you would like to look."

I quickly averted my eyes, embarrassed once more.

"As there is only one bed, it is your choice whether to join me or make use of the sofa," he callously added.

With one last disparaging glance, he snuffed out the lantern and crawled beneath the inviting covers, leaving me to stand in the dark in my wedding gown, with no creature comforts should I elect to sleep apart from him.

Disconcerted, I slowly moved toward the chair upon which he had tossed his jacket, gathering the garment into my arms and fumbling my way to the sofa. It was now too dark for me to find my nightdress, and with no maid to assist me in disrobing, it being expected that the groom would aid his wife on their wedding night, I was momentarily nonplussed. Then I pulled apart the lacing Steldor had loosened, letting the gown fall with a rustle to the floor. With Steldor's coat as a blanket, I lay down on my chosen bed in my chemise to stare sightlessly at the ceiling, knowing that I was in for a restless night.

Narian came to me in my dreams, enfolding me in his arms and whisking me away from all unhappiness. The dream was so sweet and real that I could feel his rough shirt brush across my cheek, breathe in his earthy scent, and see the love in his deep blue eyes as he bent to press his lips to mine. I abruptly awoke to lie motionless in the dark, tears trickling from the outside corners of my eyes, wondering where he was and if I would ever be with him again.

END OF BOOK ONE
THE STORY WILL
CONCLUDE
IN BOOK TWO...

Allegiance

Pronunciation Guide

Alantonya — al-anne-TONE-yuh (*al* rhymes with *shall*)

Alera — uh-LEER-uh

Baelic — BAY-lick

Cokyri — co-KYE-ree (*kye* rhymes with *high*)

Devant — dehv-AWNT

Elissia — ell-iss-EE-uh

Emotana — *ee*-mo-TAH-nuh

Faramay — FARE-uh-may

Halias — huh-LIE-uss (*lie* rhymes with *die*)

Hytanica — high-TAN-ick-uh

Kalem — KAY-luhm

Koranis — core-AWN-iss

Miranna — mer-AH-nuh

Nantilam — NAN-till-um (*nan* as in *nanny*)

Narian — NARE-ee-uhn

Niñeyre — neen-YARE

Reveina — reh-VANE-uh

Sarterad — sahr-TARE-uhd

Tanda — TAHN-duh

Tiersia — TEER-jah

About the Author:

Cayla Kluver authored her first book at the age of two and has been writing ever since. Back then, she dictated her story to her mom and drew (scribbled) pictures herself. Today, she uses a laptop and various drafting and drawing software. The tools may be different, but the need to put things on paper remains. In addition to writing, she enjoys acting, singing, horseback riding, ballroom dance, and spending time with family, friends, and her cat, Nina. She lives in Wisconsin, sandwiched between two sisters, and intends to graduate high school in spring 2008 at the age of fifteen. This is her first novel. Contact and learn more about Cayla at the Forsooth Publishing website:

www.forsoothpublishing.com

Acknowledgments

Without the following people, this novel would probably be ten pages long (with incredibly wide margins and sentences that occasionally end in prepositions).

Foremost, I would like to thank (exalt is the more fitting word) my mom, Kimberly Kluver, for being an eternal source of inspiration, a living, breathing dictionary, thesaurus, encyclopedia, and spelling-grammar checker, and for all the time and money she put into taking *Legacy* from my flash drive into the land of published works.

Recognition must be paid to my two sisters, Cara and Kendra, both of whom read more versions of the book than did I and were forced to endure endless conversation regarding plot and characters. It must also be noted that Kendra is responsible for the design of many of the gowns sported by my female characters and of the Hytanican Coat of Arms described in Chapter Two. Additional thanks to Cara, for "Tad", and to Nina (you know why).

A debt of gratitude also goes out to my English teacher, Jessica Kazeck, who put up with me for an entire semester while reading and helping to edit *Legacy* in its first complete draft (and who was the most excellent English teacher I ever had).

My most sincere appreciation is deserved by some of my greatest friends, Laura Brandt, Jocelyn Hill-Trudell, Christine Buscherfeld, and Susy Spencer, who served as test subjects in reading and critiquing *Legacy*. Josie can also be credited with sending me my first fan-mail, which was quite possibly the coolest thing anyone has ever done for me, and Susy helped a great deal with the choreography of the Tournament fight scene.

Thank you, everyone!

Cayla Kluver

Ask for *Legacy* at Your Favorite Bookstore
or
Order Additional Copies of *Legacy*
from
Forsooth Publishing
PO Box 1105
Eau Claire, WI 54702-1105

Your Name:

_____

Street Address:

_____

City: _____

State: _____ Zip: _____

Please send _____ copies of Legacy. I have enclosed payment in
the form of **check or money order** as follows:

$_____ Books ($17.95 per book)

$_____ Sales Tax (5.5% for books shipped to Wisconsin addresses)

$_____ Shipping and handling ($4.95 for the first book; $2.00 for
each additional book)

$_____ Total enclosed

If you prefer to pay with a credit card, please visit our website:
www.forsoothpublishing.com.

Forsooth Publishing™

DISCARDED